Praise for Jo

'Picoult tackles a controversial subject head on with a sense of wisdom and sensitivity. If there's only one book you read this year, make it this one.' *Daily Express*

'Brilliantly told' *Daily Mirror*

'Picoult writes with an evident understanding of the damage serious illness can do to a family.' *Daily Mail*

'This astonishing novel is beautifully and thoughtfully written, and focuses on difficult moral choices.' *Good Housekeeping*

'Engrossing . . . Picoult has a remarkable ability to make us share her characters' feelings of confusion and horror' *People*

'Very compelling' *Heat*

'Picoult has become a master – almost a clairvoyant – at targeting hot issues and writing highly readable page-turners about them' *Washington Post*

'Jodi Picoult's two UK debut titles are thought-provoking, fascinating and tense . . . Picoult's choice of subject matter is already causing a stir in the press, and she is guaranteed to become a bestseller. Watch out, she's well worth supporting' *Bookseller*

Also by Jodi Picoult

Songs of the Humpback Whale
Harvesting the Heart
Picture Perfect
Mercy
The Pact
Keeping Faith
Plain Truth
Perfect Match
Second Glance
My Sister's Keeper
Vanishing Acts

Jodi Picoult grew up in Nesconset, New York. She received an A.B. in creative writing from Princeton and a master's degree in education from Harvard. She lives in New Hampshire with her husband and three children.

JODI PICOULT

Salem Falls

First published in the United States of America in 2001 by Pocket Books
A division of Simon & Schuster Inc.

First published in Great Britain in 2005 by Hodder and Stoughton
A division of Hodder Headline

A Hodder and Stoughton paperback

17

A CIP catalogue record for this title is available from the British Library

ISBN 0 340 83553 2

Typeset in Plantin Light by
Palimpsest Book Production Limited,
Polmont, Stirlingshire

Printed and bound by
Mackays of Chatham Ltd, Chatham, Kent

Hodder Headline's policy is to use papers that are natural, renewable
and recyclable products and made from wood grown in sustainable forests.
The logging and manufacturing processes are expected to conform to the
environmental regulations of the country of origin.

Hodder and Stoughton Ltd
A division of Hodder Headline
338 Euston Road
London NW1 3BH

To Tim, with love –
so that the whole world will know
how much you mean to me

Acknowledgments

If I could cast a spell, like some of my protagonists in this novel, it would be one to acquire unlimited knowledge. After all, a novelist is only as good as her experts when it comes to learning about fields that are unknown to her. For this reason, I'd like to thank the following people: my doctors and psychiatric personnel-on-call, David Toub, MD; Jim Umlas, MD; Tia Horner, MD; Marybeth Durkin, MD; and Jan Scheiner; Betty Martin, for all toxicological information; Detective-Lieutenant Frank Moran, for police procedure following a sexual assault; Chris Farina, who took me behind the scenes at a diner; and Lisa Schiermeier, the DNA scientist who managed to teach a science-challenged gal like me genetics. Thanks to Aidan Curran for the egg pickup line; to Steve Ives for all things baseball and a keen editorial eye; to Diana and Duncan Watson for the BLT scene; to Teresa Farina for transcription under fire; and to Hal Friend for a virtual tour of the Lower East Side. I am indebted to the works of Starhawk and Scott Cunningham, from which I began to understand the Wiccan religion. Kiki Keating helped shape the beginnings of the judiciary plot here; Chris Keating provided the most incredibly prompt legal answers for the book that grew out of it; and Jennifer Sternick did such a fantastic job helping me craft the trial that I may never let her go as a legal consultant. Thanks to Laura Gross, Camille McDuffie, and Jane Picoult for their contributions in shaping and selling this novel. My sincere gratitude to JoAnn Mapson, whose private chapter-by-chapter workshop sessions made me believe in this book and turned it into something better than I even imagined.

And last, but not least, I'd like to sing the praises of Kip Hakala and Emily Bestler at Pocket Books. If every author had the unflagging support and devotion of an editorial duo like these two, publishing would be a wonderful world indeed.

March 2000
North Haverhill, New Hampshire

Several miles into his journey, Jack St. Bride decided to give up his former life.

He made this choice as he walked aimlessly along Route 10, huddling against the cold. He had dressed this morning in a pair of khaki pants, a white shirt with a nick in the collar, stiff dress shoes, a smooth-skinned belt – clothing he'd last worn 5,760 hours ago, clothing that had fit him last August. This morning, his blue blazer was oversized and the waistband of his trousers hung loose. It had taken Jack a moment to realize it wasn't weight he'd lost during these eight months but pride.

He wished he had a winter coat, but you wore out of jail the same outfit you'd worn in. What he did have was the forty-three dollars that had been in his wallet on the hot afternoon he was incarcerated, a ring of keys that opened doors to places where Jack no longer was welcome, and a piece of gum.

Other inmates who were released from jail had family to pick them up. Or they arranged for transportation. But Jack had no one waiting for him, and he hadn't thought about getting a ride. When the door closed behind him, a jaw being snapped shut, he had simply started walking.

The snow seeped into his dress shoes, and passing trucks splattered his trousers with slush and mud. A taxi pulled onto the side of the road and the driver unrolled the window, but Jack kept struggling forward, certain that the cab had stopped for someone else.

'Car trouble?' the driver called out.

Jack looked, but there was no one behind him. 'Just walking.'

'Pretty miserable weather for that,' the man replied, and Jack stared. He could count on one hand the number of casual conversations he'd had in the past year. It had been better, easier, to keep to himself. 'Where you headed?'

The truth was, he had no idea. There were countless problems he hadn't considered, most of them practical: What would he do for work? For transportation? Where would he live? He didn't want to return to Loyal, New Hampshire, not even to pick up his belongings. What good was the evidence of a career he no longer had, of a person he would never be?

The cabdriver frowned. 'Look, buddy,' he said, 'why don't you just get in?'

Jack nodded and stood there, waiting. But there was no bright buzz, no click of the latch. And then he remembered that in the outside world, no one had to unlock a door before he entered.

I

Jack and Jill went up the hill to fetch a pail of water.
Jack fell down and broke his crown,
And Jill came tumbling after.

Then up Jack got and home did trot as fast as he could caper,
To old Dame Dob, who patched his nob,
With vinegar and brown paper.

Is there no good penitence but it be public?

– The Crucible

March 2000
Salem Falls, New Hampshire

On the second worst day of Addie Peabody's life, her refrigerator and dishwasher both died, like long-term lovers who could not conceive of existing without each other. This would have been a trial for anyone, but as she was the owner of the Do-Or-Diner, it blossomed into a catas-trophe of enormous proportions. Addie stood with her hands pressed to the stainless steel door of the Sub-Zero walk-in, as if she might jump-start its heart by faith healing.

It was hard to decide what was more devastating: the health violations or the loss of potential income. Twenty pounds of dry ice, the most the medical supply store had to offer, wasn't doing the job. Within hours, Addie would have to throw away the gallon buckets of gravy, stew, and chicken soup made that morning. 'I think,' she said after a moment, 'I'm going to build a snowman.'

'Now?' asked Delilah, the cook, her crossed arms as thick as a blacksmith's. She frowned. 'You know, Addie, I never believed it when folks around here called you crazy, but –'

'I'll stick it in the fridge. Maybe it'll save the food until the repairman gets here.'

'Snowmen melt,' Delilah said, but Addie could tell that she was turning the idea over in her mind.

'Then we'll mop up and make more.'

'And I suppose you're just gonna let the customers fend for themselves?'

'No,' Addie said. 'I'm going to get them to help. Will you get Chloe's boots?'

The diner was not crowded for 10 A.M. Of the six booths,

two were occupied: one by a mother and her toddler, the other by a businessman brushing muffin crumbs off his laptop. A couple of elderly regulars, Stuart and Wallace, slouched at the counter drinking coffee while they argued over the local paper's headlines.

'Ladies and gentlemen,' Addie proclaimed. 'I'm pleased to announce the start of the Do-or-Diner's winter carnival. The first event is going to be a snow-sculpture contest, and if you'd all just come out back for a moment, we can get started –'

'It's freezing out there!' cried Wallace.

'Well, of course it is. Otherwise we'd be having a summer carnival. Winner of the contest gets . . . a month of breakfast on the house.'

Stuart and Wallace shrugged, a good sign. The toddler bounced on the banquette like popcorn in a skillet. Only the businessman seemed unconvinced. As the others shuffled through the door, Addie approached his table. 'Look,' the businessman said. 'I don't want to build a snowman, all right? All I came here for was some breakfast.'

'Well, we're not serving now. We're sculpting.' She gave him her brightest smile.

The man seemed nonplussed. He tossed a handful of change on the table, gathered his coat and computer, and stood up to leave. 'You're nuts.'

Addie watched him leave. 'Yes,' she murmured. 'That's what they say.'

Outside, Stuart and Wallace were huffing through their scarves, crafting a respectable armadillo. Delilah had fashioned a snow chicken, a leg of lamb, pole beans. The toddler, stuffed into a snowsuit the color of a storm, lay on her back making angels.

Once Chloe had asked: *Is Heaven above or below the place where snow comes from?*

'You got the Devil's own luck,' Delilah told Addie. 'What if there was no snow?'

'Since when has there been no snow here in March? And

besides, this isn't luck. Luck is finding out the repairman could come a day early.'

As if Addie had conjured it, a man's voice called out. 'Anybody home?'

'We're back here.' Addie was faintly disappointed to see a young cop, instead of an appliance repairman, rounding the corner. 'Hi, Orren. You here for a cup of coffee?'

'Uh, no, Addie. I'm here on official business.'

Her head swam. Could the accountant have reported them to the board of health so quickly? Did a law enforcement officer have the power to make her close her doors? But before she could voice her doubts, the policeman spoke again.

'It's your father,' Orren explained, blushing. 'He's been arrested.'

Addie stormed into the police department with such force that the double doors slammed back on their hinges, letting in a gust of cold wind. 'Jeez Louise,' said the dispatch sergeant. 'Hope Courtemanche found himself a good hiding place.'

'Where is he?' Addie demanded.

'My best guess? Maybe in the men's room, in a stall. Or squeezed into one of the empty lockers in the squad room.' The officer scratched his jaw. 'Come to think of it, I once hid in the trunk of a cruiser when my wife was on the warpath.'

'I'm not talking about Officer Courtemanche,' Addie said through clenched teeth. 'I meant my *father*.'

'Oh, Roy's in the lockup.' He winced, remembering something. 'But if you're here to spring him, you're gonna have to talk to Wes anyway, since it was his arrest.' He picked up the phone. 'You can take a seat, Addie. I'll let you know when Wes is free.'

Addie scowled. 'I'm sure I'll know. You always smell a skunk before you see it.'

'Why, Addie, is that any way to speak to the man who saved your father's life?'

In his blue uniform, his badge glinting like a third eye, Wes Courtemanche was handsome enough to make women in Salem

Falls dream about committing crimes. Addie, however, took one look at him and thought – not for the first time – that some men ought to come with an expiration date.

'Arresting a sixty-five-year-old man isn't my idea of saving his life,' she huffed.

Wes took her elbow and led her gently down the hall, away from the dispatch sergeant's eyes and ears. 'Your father was driving under the influence again, Addie.'

Heat rose to her cheeks. Roy Peabody's drinking wasn't any secret in Salem Falls, but he'd gone one step too far last month, wrapping his car around the town's statue of Giles Corey, the only man who'd been a casualty of the Puritan witch hunts. Roy's license had been revoked. For his own safety, Addie had junked the car. And her own Mazda was safely parked at the diner. What vehicle could he have used?

As if he could read her mind, Wes said, 'He was in the breakdown lane of Route 10, on his ride-on mower.'

'His ride-on mower,' Addie repeated. 'Wes, that thing can't go more than five miles an hour.'

'Fifteen, but that's neither here nor there. The point is, he doesn't have a license. And you need one if you're gonna operate any self-propelled vehicle on the street.'

'Maybe it was an emergency . . .'

'Guess it was, Addie. We confiscated a brand-new fifth of vodka from him, too.' Wes paused. 'He was on his way home from the liquor store in North Haverhill.' He watched Addie knead her temples. 'Is there anything I can do for you?'

'I think you've done enough, Wes. I mean, gosh, you arrested a man joyriding on a lawn mower. Surely they'll give you a Purple Heart or something for going to such extremes to ensure public safety.'

'Now, just a second. I *was* ensuring safety . . . *Roy's*. What if a truck cut the curve too tight and ran him down? What if he fell asleep at the wheel?'

'Can I just take him home now?'

Wes regarded her thoughtfully. It made Addie feel like he

was sorting through her mind, opening up certain ideas and shuffling aside others. She closed her eyes.

'Sure,' Wes said. 'Follow me.'

He led her down a hallway to a room at the back of the police department. There was a wide desk manned by another officer, a high counter with ink pads for fingerprinting, and in the shadowy distance, a trio of tiny cells. Wes touched her forearm. 'I'm not going to write him up, Addie.'

'You're a real prince.'

He laughed and walked off. She heard the barred door slide open like a sword being pulled from its scabbard. 'Guess who's waiting for you out there, Roy?'

Her father's voice now, pouring slow as honey: 'My Margaret?'

' 'Fraid not. Margaret's been gone about five years now.'

They turned the corner, Wes bearing the brunt of her father's weight. Roy Peabody was a charmer of a man, with hair as white and thick as the inner wing of a dove and blue eyes that always swam with a secret. 'Addie!' he crowed, seeing her. 'Happy birthday!'

He lunged for her, and Addie staggered. 'Come on, Dad. We'll get you home.'

Wes hooked his thumb on his belt. 'You want a hand getting him out to your car?'

'No, thanks. We can manage.' At that moment, her father felt slighter and more insubstantial than Chloe. They walked awkwardly, like contestants in a three-legged race.

Wes held open the door. 'Well, shoot, Addie. I'm sorry I had to call you down for this on your birthday.'

She did not break stride. 'It's not my birthday,' she said, and guided her father out.

At 6:30 that morning, Gillian Duncan had lit a match and waved a thermometer through it, spiking a temperature that made her father believe she truly was too sick to go to school. She spent the morning in her bedroom instead, listening to Alanis Morissette, braiding her long red hair, and painting her fingernails and toenails electric blue. In spite of the fact that she was seventeen years old and could fend for herself, her father had taken the day off from work to be with her. It raised her hackles and secretly pleased her all at once. As the owner of Duncan Pharmaceuticals, the biggest employer in Salem Falls, Amos Duncan was generally re-garded as one of its richest and busiest citizens. But then, he had always had time to take care of her; he'd been doing it since Gilly was eight and her mother had died.

She was going crazy in her room and was about to do something really drastic, like pick up a textbook, when the doorbell rang. Listening closely, Gilly heard the voices of her friends downstairs. 'Hi, Mr. D,' said Meg. 'How's Gillian?'

Before he could respond, Whitney interrupted. 'We brought her jellybeans. My mom says they soak up a fever, and if they don't, they taste so good you don't care.'

'We brought her homework, too,' Chelsea added. Painfully tall, self-conscious, and shy, she was one of Gilly's newest friends.

'Well, thank God you're all here,' her father said. 'I have a hard time recognizing Gilly unless she's glued to the three of you. Just let me see if she's awake.'

Gilly dove beneath the covers, trying desperately to look sick. Her father cracked open the door and peered inside. 'You up for company, Gilly?'

Rubbing her eyes, Gillian sat up. 'Maybe for a little while.'

He nodded, then called out to the girls. Meg led the charge up to Gillian's room, a hail of Skechers pounding up the stairs. 'I think my whole home could fit in this room,' Chelsea breathed, stepping inside.

'Oh, that's right . . .' Whitney said. 'This is the first time you've been to the manor.'

Gillian slanted a look at her father. It was a common joke in town that the reason the Duncan home sat to the east whereas all the other roads and developments sat to the west was because Amos had wanted a palace separate and apart for his kingdom.

'Yes,' Amos said, with a straight face. 'We're putting in a drawbridge this spring.'

Chelsea's eyes widened. 'For real?'

Whitney laughed. She liked Gillian's dad; they all did. He knew how to make a teenager feel perfectly welcome.

'If you guys tire her out,' Amos said, 'I'll make you dig the moat.' He winked at Chelsea, then pulled the door closed behind him.

The girls wilted onto the carpet, lilies floating on a pond. 'So?' Meg asked. 'Did you watch *Passions*?'

Meg Saxton had been Gilly's first best friend. Even as she'd grown up, she hadn't lost her baby fat, and her brown hair flew away from her face in a riot of curls.

'I didn't watch any soaps. I took a nap.'

'A nap? I thought you were faking.'

Gillian shrugged. 'I'm not faking; I'm method-acting.'

'Well, FYI, the trig test sucked,' Whitney said. The only child of one of the town selectmen, Whitney O'Neill was nothing short of a knockout. She'd opened the bag of jellybeans to help herself. 'Why can't we write a spell to get A's?'

Chelsea looked nervously at the large, lovely bedroom, then at Gillian. 'Are you sure we can do magick here, with your father right downstairs?'

Of course they could – and would – do magick. They had been students of the Craft for nearly a year now; it was why they had gathered this afternoon. 'I wouldn't have invited you if I didn't think it was okay,' Gillian said, withdrawing a black-and-white composition notebook from between the mattress and box spring. Written in bubble letters, with smiley-face O's, was its title: *Book of Shadows*. She got out of bed and padded into the large adjoining bathroom. The others could hear her turning on the faucet, and then she returned with an eight-ounce glass of water. 'Here,' she said, handing it to Whitney. 'Drink.'

Whitney took a sip, then spat on the floor. 'This is disgusting! It's salt water!'

'So?' Gillian said. As she spoke, she walked around her

friends, sprinkling more salt onto the carpet. 'Would you rather waste time taking a bath? Or maybe you've got a better way to purify yourself?'

Grimacing, Whitney drank again, and then passed it to the others. 'Let's do something quick today,' Meg suggested. 'My mom will kill me if I'm not home by four-thirty.' She scooted into position, across from Gillian on the floor, as Whitney and Chelsea made up the other corners of their square. Gillian reached for Whitney's hand, and a cold draft snaked in through a crack in the window. As Whitney's palm skimmed over Meg's, the lamp on the nightstand dimmed. The pages of the notebook fluttered as Meg reached for Chelsea. And when Chelsea clasped Gillian's hand, the air grew too thick to breathe.

'What color is your circle?' Gillian asked Chelsea.

'It's blue.'

'And yours?'

Meg's eyes drifted shut. 'Pink.'

'Mine's silver,' Whitney murmured.

'Pure gold,' Gillian said. All of their eyes were closed now, but they had learned over the course of the past year that you did not need them open to see. The girls sat, their minds winnowed to this point of power; as one snake of color after another surrounded them, plaited into a thick ring, and sealed them inside.

'Not again,' Delilah said with a sigh, as Addie hauled Roy Peabody into the kitchen.

'I don't need this from you now.' Addie gritted her teeth as her father stumbled heavily on the arch of her foot.

'Is that Delilah?' Roy crowed, craning his neck. 'Prettiest cook in New Hampshire.'

Addie managed to push her father into a narrow stairwell that led upstairs to his apartment. 'Did Chloe give you any trouble?' she called back over her shoulder.

'No, honey,' Delilah sighed. 'No trouble whatsoever.'

Through sheer will, Addie and Roy made it upstairs. 'Why don't you sit down, Daddy?' she said softly, guiding him to the frayed armchair that had stood in that spot all of Addie's life.

She could smell the stew that Delilah had prepared for the lunch rush rising through the floor and the weave of the carpet – carrots, beef base, thyme. As a child, she had believed that breathing in the diner had rooted it in her system, making it as much as part of her as her blood or her bones. Her father had been like that, too, once. But it had been seven years since he'd voluntarily set foot behind the stove. She wondered if it caused him the same phantom pain that came from losing a vital limb – if he drank to dull the ache of it.

Addie crouched down beside his chair. 'Daddy,' she whispered.

Roy blinked. 'My girl.'

Tears sprang to her eyes. 'I need you to do me a favor. The diner, it's too busy for me to take care of. I need you –'

'Oh, Addie. Don't.'

'Just the register. You won't ever have to go into the kitchen.'

'You don't need me to work the register. You just want to keep tabs on me.'

Addie flushed. 'That's not true.'

'It's all right.' He covered her hand with his own and squeezed. 'Every now and then it's nice to know that someone cares where I am.'

Addie opened her mouth to say the things she should have said years ago to her father, all those months after her mother's death when she was too busy keeping the diner afloat to notice that Roy was drowning, but the telephone interrupted her. Delilah was on the other end. 'Get down here,' the cook said. 'Your bad day? It just got worse.'

'Did you say something?' The cab driver's eyes met Jack's in the rearview mirror.

'No.'

'This look familiar yet?'

Jack had lied to the driver – what was one more lie in a long string of others? – confessing that he couldn't remember the name of the town he was headed toward but that Route 10 ran right through its middle. He would recognize it, he said, as soon as Main Street came into view.

Now, forty minutes later, he glanced out the window. They were driving through a village, small but well-heeled, with a New England steepled white church and women in riding boots darting into stores to run their errands. It reminded him too much of the prep-school town of Loyal, and he shook his head. 'Not this one,' he said.

What he needed was a place where he could disappear for a while – a place where he could figure out how to start all over again. Teaching – well, that was out of the question now. But it was also all he'd ever done. He'd worked at Westonbrook for four years . . . an awfully big hole to omit in a job interview for any related field. And even a McDonald's manager could ask him if he'd ever been convicted of a crime.

Lulled by the motion of the taxi, he dozed off. He dreamed of an inmate he'd worked with on farm duty. Aldo's girlfriend would commute to Haverhill and leave treasures in the cornfield for him: whiskey, pot, instant coffee. Once, she set herself up naked on a blanket, waiting for Aldo to come over on the tractor. 'Drive slow,' Aldo would say, when they went out to harvest. 'You never know what you're going to find.'

'Salem Falls coming up,' the cab driver announced, waking him.

A hand-lettered blue placard announced the name of the town and proclaimed it home of Duncan Pharmaceuticals. The town was built outward from a central green, crowned by a memorial statue that listed badly to the left, as if it had been rammed from the side. A bank, a general store, and a town office building were dotted along the green – all neatly painted, walks shoveled clear of snow. Standing incongruously at the corner was a junked railroad car. Jack did a double take, and as the cab turned to follow the one-way road around the green, he realized it was a diner.

In the window was a small sign.

'Stop,' Jack said. 'This is the place.'

Harlan Pettigrew sat at the counter, nursing a bowl of stew. A napkin was tucked over his bow tie, to prevent staining. His eyes darted around the diner, lighting on the clock.

Addie pushed through the swinging doors. 'Mr. Pettigrew,' she began.

The man blotted his mouth with his napkin and got to his feet. 'It's about time.'

'There's something I need to tell you first. You see, we've been having a little trouble with some of our appliances.'

Pettigrew's brows drew together. 'I see.'

Suddenly the door opened. A man in a rumpled sports jacket walked in, looking cold and lost. His shoes were completely inappropriate for the season and left small puddles of melting snow on the linoleum floor. When he spotted her pink apron, he started toward her. 'Excuse me – is the owner in?'

His voice made Addie think of coffee, deep and dark and rich, with a texture that slid between her senses. 'That would be me.'

'Oh.' He seemed surprised by this. 'Okay. Well. I, um, I'm here because –'

A wide smile spread over Addie's face. 'Because I called you!' She shook his hand, trying not to notice how the man froze in shock. 'I was just telling Mr. Pettigrew, here, from the *board of health,* that the repairman was on his way to fix our refrigerator and dishwasher. They're right through here.'

She began to tug the stranger into the kitchen, with Pettigrew in their wake. 'Just a moment,' the inspector said, frowning. 'You don't look like an appliance repairman.'

Addie tensed. The man probably thought she was insane. Well, hell. So did the rest of Salem Falls.

The woman was insane. And God, she'd *touched* him. She'd reached right out and grabbed his hand, as if that were normal for him, as if it had been eight minutes rather than eight months since a woman's skin had come in contact with his own.

If she was covering something up from the board of health, then the diner was probably violating a code. He started to back away, but then the woman bowed her head.

It was that, the giving in, that ruined him.

The part in her dark hair was crooked and pink as a newborn's skin. Jack almost reached out one finger and touched it but stuffed his hands in his pockets instead. He knew better than anyone that you could not trust a woman who said she was telling the truth.

But what if you knew, from the start, that she was lying?

Jack cleared his throat. 'I came as quickly as I could, ma'am,' he said, then glanced at Pettigrew. 'I was paged from my aunt's birthday party and didn't stop home to get my uniform. Where are the broken appliances?'

The kitchen looked remarkably similar to the one at the jail. Jack nodded to a sequoia of a woman standing behind the grill and tried desperately to remember any technical trivia he could about dishwashers. He opened the two rolled doors, slid out the tray, and peered inside. 'Could be the pump . . . or the water inlet valve.'

For the first time, he looked directly at the owner of the diner. She was small and delicate in build, no taller than his collarbone, but had muscles in her arms built, he imagined, by many a hard day's labor. Her brown hair was yanked into a knot at the back of her head and held in place by a pencil, and her eyes were the unlikely color of peridot – a stone, Jack recalled, the ancient Hawaiians believed to be the tears shed by the volcano goddess. Those eyes, now, seemed absolutely stunned. 'I didn't bring my toolbox, but I can have this fixed by . . .' He pretended to do the math, trying to catch the woman's eye. *Tomorrow,* she mouthed.

'Tomorrow,' Jack announced. 'Now what's the problem with the fridge?'

Pettigrew looked from the owner of the diner to Jack, and then back again. 'There's no point in checking out the rest of the kitchen when I have to return anyway,' he said. 'I'll come by next week to do my inspection.' With a curt nod, he let himself out.

The owner of the diner launched herself across the line, embracing the cook and whooping with delight. Radiant, she turned to Jack and extended her hand . . . but this time, he moved out of the way before she could touch him. 'I'm Addie Peabody, and this is Delilah Piggett. We're so grateful to you. You certainly sounded authentic.' Suddenly, she paused, an idea dawning. 'You don't actually know how to fix appliances, do you?'

'No. That was just some stuff I heard in the last place I worked.' He saw his opening and leaped. 'I was on my way in to ask about the HELP WANTED sign.'

The cook beamed. 'You're hired.'

'Delilah, who died and left you king?' She smiled at Jack. 'You're hired.'

'Do you mind if I ask what the job is?'

'Yes. I mean, no, I don't mind. We're in the market for a dishwasher.'

A reluctant grin tugged at Jack's mouth. 'I heard.'

'Well, even if we fix the machine, we'll still need someone to run it.'

'Is it full time?'

'Part time . . . afternoons. Minimum wage.'

Jack's face fell. He had a Ph.D. in history, and was applying for a job that paid $5.15 per hour. Misinterpreting his reaction, Delilah said, 'I've been asking Addie to hire a prep cook a while now. That would be a part-time morning job, wouldn't it?'

Addie hesitated. 'Have you ever worked in a kitchen before, Mr. . . .'

'St. Bride. Jack. And yeah, I have.' He didn't say where the kitchen was, or that he'd been a guest of the state at the time.

'That beats the last guy you hired,' Delilah said. 'Remember when we found him shooting up over the scrambled eggs?'

'It's not like he mentioned his habit at the interview.' Addie turned to Jack. 'How old are you?'

Ah, this was the moment – the one where she'd ask him why a man his age would settle for menial work like this. 'Thirty-one.'

She nodded. 'If you want the job, it's yours.'

No application, no references, no questions about his past employment. And anonymity – no one would ever expect to find him washing dishes in a diner. For a man who had determined to put his past firmly behind him, this situation seemed too good to be true. 'I'd like it very much,' Jack managed.

'Then grab an apron,' said his new boss.

Suddenly, he remembered that there was something he needed to do, if Salem Falls was going to become his new residence. 'I need about an hour to run an errand,' he said.

'No problem. It's the least I can do for the person who saved me.'

Funny, Jack thought. *I was thinking the same thing.*

Detective-Lieutenant Charlie Saxton fiddled with the radio in his squad car for a few moments, then switched it off. He listened to the squelch of slush under the Bronco's tires and wondered, again, if he should have stayed with the Miami Police Department.

It was a hard thing to be a law enforcement officer in the town where you'd once grown up. You'd walk down the street, and instead of noticing the IGA, you'd remember the storeroom where a local teen had knifed his girlfriend. You'd pass the school playground and think of the drugs confiscated from the children of the town selectmen. Where everyone else saw the picture-perfect New England town of their youth, you saw the underbelly of its existence.

His radio crackled as he turned onto Main Street. 'Saxton.'

'Lieutenant, there's some guy here insisting he'll talk only to you.'

Even with the bad reception, Wes sounded pissed. 'He got a name?'

'If he does, he isn't giving it up.'

Charlie sighed. For all he knew, this man had committed murder within town lines and wanted to confess. 'Well, I'm driving into the parking lot. Have him take a seat.'

He swung the Bronco into a spot, then walked in to find his guest cooling his heels.

Literally. Charlie's first thought, pure detective, was that the guy couldn't be from around here – no one who lived in New Hampshire was stupid enough to wear a sports jacket and dress shoes in the freezing slush of early March. Still, he didn't seem particularly distraught, like the recent victim of a crime, or nervous, like a perp. No, he just looked like a guy who'd had a lousy day. Charlie extended his hand. 'Hi there. Detective-Lieutenant Saxton.'

The man didn't identify himself. 'Could I have a few minutes of your time?'

Charlie nodded, his curiosity piqued. He led the way to his office, and gestured to a chair. 'What can I do for you, Mr. . . .'

'Jack St. Bride. I'm moving to Salem Falls.'

'Welcome.' Ah, it all was falling into place. This was probably some family man who wanted to make sure the locale was safe enough for his wife and kids and puppy. 'Great place, great town. Is there something in particular I can help you with?'

For a long moment, St. Bride was silent. His hands flexed on his knees. 'I'm here because of 651-B,' he said finally.

It took Charlie a moment to realize this well-dressed, soft-spoken man was talking about a legal statute that required certain criminals to report in to a local law enforcement agency for ten years or for life, depending on the charge for which they had been convicted. Charlie schooled his features until they were as blank as St. Bride's, until it was clear that his former words of welcome had been rescinded. Then he pulled from his desk drawer the state police's form to register a sexual offender.

March 2000
Salem Falls, New Hampshire

'What are you doing?'

Jack spun at the sound of his new employer's voice. He hid his fists behind his back. 'Nothing.'

Addie's lips tightened, and she stuffed her order pad into the waistband of her apron. 'Look,' she said, 'I don't put up with anything shady on this job. Not drugs, not drinking, and if I catch you stealing, you'll be out on your butt so quick you won't know what kicked you.' She extended a hand, palm up. 'Give it over.'

Jack glanced away from her and passed her the steel wool he'd been using.

'This is what you're hiding? A Brillo pad?'

'Yeah.'

'For God's sake . . . why?'

Jack slowly uncurled his fist. 'My hands were dirty.' He stared again at the pads of his fingers, still black with ink from when Detective Saxton had taken a set of prints for the station's records. The baby wipes at the booking room had been ineffective, and Jack could have asked to use the men's room, but the feeling of having his fingers rolled one by one, again, was so unsettling that he wanted only to put the building far behind him. By the time he'd arrived at the diner, the ink had dried, and no amount of soap had managed to remove it.

He held his breath. There was no way she'd be able to tell, was there?

'Ink,' Addie announced. 'It happens to me, too, when I read the newspaper. You'd think they could figure out a substance that stays on the page instead of your fingers.'

With relief, Jack followed her into the small pantry off the kitchen. She held out a bottle of industrial cleaner. 'I got this from a customer, once, a farmer. It's probably used to cure leather or something . . . but it also cleans just about every mess you can imagine.' Smiling, she held up her hands – chapped, red, cracked. 'You keep using Brillo, you'll wind up looking like me.'

Jack nodded and took the bottle from her. But what he really wanted to do was touch her hand, feel the tips of her fingers, see if they were the catastrophe she made them out to be or if they were simply as warm as they looked.

Roy sat up in bed with a start, cradling his head. God, it hurt. The room was spinning, but that was nothing compared to the noise that was nearly splitting his skull. Scowling, he stood. Damn Delilah Piggett, anyway. The cook thought she had a right to play alley cat with the pots and pans when people were trying to sleep just above her.

'Delilah!' he roared, stamping down the stairs that led into the kitchen.

But Delilah wasn't there. Instead, a tall blond man who looked entirely too polished to be working as a dishwasher was standing at the big sink, rinsing out cookware. He finished another cast-iron pot and set it down – with a righteous, ear-splitting clank – onto a makeshift drying rack. 'Delilah went to the bathroom,' the man said over his shoulder. 'She should be back in a second.'

Delilah had left several burgers going on the grill. *Fire hazard.* He never would have done that in his days on the line. 'Who the hell are you?' Roy barked.

'Jack St. Bride. I was just hired as a dishwasher.'

'For crying out loud, you don't do it by hand. There's a machine just over there.'

Jack smiled wryly. 'Thanks, I know. It's broken.' He stood uneasily before the old man, wondering who he was and why he'd appeared from a back staircase. The alcohol fumes coming off the guy could have pickled the cucumbers Delilah had sliced for garnish. Jack grabbed another dirty pot and set it into the soapy water. As he scrubbed, black smoke began to rise from the grill. He looked at his hands, at the pot, then at the older man. 'The burgers are burning,' Jack said. 'Do you mind flipping them?'

Roy was two feet away from the grill; the spatula lay within reach. But he sidled away from the cooking area, giving it a wide berth. 'You do it.'

With a muttered curse, Jack turned off the water again, wiped his hands dry, and physically pushed Roy out of the way to flip the hamburgers. 'Was that so hard?'

'I don't cook,' the older man said succinctly.

'It's a hamburger! I didn't ask you to make beef Wellington!'

'I can make a hell of a beef Wellington, matter of fact, if I feel like it!'

The swinging doors that led to the dining room swelled forward like an eruption, then parted to reveal Addie. 'What's going on? I can hear you yelling all the way up front . . . Dad? What are you doing down here? And where's Delilah?'

'Bathroom.' Jack turned to the sink, assuming his hired position. Let the old man explain what had happened.

But she didn't even ask. She seemed delighted, in fact, to find her father in the kitchen. 'How are you feeling?'

'Like a guy who can't get any rest because someone's downstairs banging around.'

Addie patted his hand. 'I should have warned Jack that you were upstairs napping.'

Napping? Comatose, more like.

'Jack, if you've got a minute . . . there are some booths in the front that need clearing.'

Jack nodded and picked up a plastic bucket used for busing tables. His heart started to pound as he entered the front of the restaurant, and he wondered how long it would take until he no longer felt like his every move was being watched. But the diner was empty. Relieved, he cleared one table, then headed toward the counter. Jack put a coffee cup into the bin, then reached for a full plate, the food cold and untouched. French fries and a cheeseburger with extra pickles – someone had paid for a meal and hadn't even taken a bite.

He was starving. He'd missed breakfast at the jail because he was being processed for release. Jack glanced around . . . *Who would ever know?* He grabbed a handful of fries and quickly stuffed them into his mouth.

'Don't.'

He froze. Addie stood behind him, her face white. 'Don't eat her meal.'

Jack blinked. 'Whose meal?'

But she turned away without a response and left him wondering.

At fifteen, Thomas McAfee knew he was going to be a late bloomer. Well, at least he sure as hell hoped so, because going through life five feet five inches tall, with arms like a chicken, wasn't going to make for a pleasant adolescence.

Not that ninth grade was supposed to be pleasant. After taking medieval history last semester, Thomas figured high school was the modern equivalent of running the gauntlet. The hearty survived and went off to Colby-Sawyer and Dartmouth to play lacrosse. Everyone else slunk to the sidelines, destined to spend their lives as part of the audience.

But as Thomas stood on Main Street after school that day, freezing his ass off, he was thinking that Chelsea Abrams might like to root for the underdog.

Chelsea was more than just a junior. She was smart and pretty, with hair that caught the sunlight during the keyboarding class Thomas had with her. She didn't hang with the cheerleaders, or the brains, or the heads. Instead, she was tight with three other girls – including Gillian Duncan, whose dad owned half the town. Okay, so they dressed a little weird, with a lot of black and scarves – a cross between the art freak Goths who hung out in the smoking pit and gypsy wannabes – but Thomas knew, better than most, that the package was far less important than what was on the inside.

Suddenly Chelsea turned the corner with her friends, even Gillian Duncan, who had been too sick to go to school but had made an amazing enough recovery now, to be out and about. Chelsea's breath fogged in the cold air, each huff taking the shape of a heart. Thomas squared his shoulders and came up from behind, falling into step beside her.

He could smell cinnamon in her hair, and it made him dizzy.

'Did you know the alphabet's all wrong?' he said casually, as if they'd been in the middle of a conversation.

'Sorry?' Chelsea said.

'The letters are mixed up. *U* and *I* should be together.'

The other girls snickered, and Gillian Duncan's voice fell like a hammer. 'What's it like at the moron end of the bell curve?' She looped her arm through Chelsea's. 'Let's get out of here.'

Thomas felt heat rising above his collar and willed it to go away. Chelsea was tugged forward by her friends, leaving him standing alone. Did she turn back to look at him . . . or was she only adjusting the strap of her knapsack? As they crossed, Thomas could hear Chelsea's friends laughing. But she wasn't.

Surely that was something.

Charlie Saxton ate a peanut butter sandwich every day for lunch, although he hated peanut butter. He did it because for some reason, his wife Barbara thought he liked it, and she went to the trouble of packing him a lunch each morning. Around Valentine's Day, she'd bought those little sugary hearts with messages on them, and for a month now she'd been sticking one into the soft white bread: hot stuff! crazy 4 u! With a fingernail, Charlie edged out the candy of the day and read its message aloud. 'Kiss and tell.'

'Not me, boss. My lips are sealed.' The station's receptionist hustled into his office and handed him a manila folder. 'You know, I think it's sweet when a guy over forty can still blush. This just came in on the fax.'

She closed the door behind her as Charlie slid the pages from the folder, scanning the court records of Jack St. Bride. They showed his arrest for a charge of felonious sexual assault against a minor . . . but a final disposition for simple sexual assault, a misdemeanor.

Charlie dialed the Grafton County attorney's office, asking for the name of the prosecutor listed on the fax. 'Sorry, she's out for two weeks on vacation. Can someone else help you?' the secretary said.

Charlie hesitated, making a judgment call. The list of registered sexual offenders was public record. That meant anyone could walk into the station and find out who was on it and where that person lived. As of this morning, his list stretched to all of one person. In spite of what secrets he knew as a detective, Salem Falls had the reputation of being a sleepy New England town where nothing happened, which was the way the residents liked it. As soon as word got out to the male populace that a guy who'd been charged with rape had moved in near their wives and daughters, there would be hell to pay.

He could start a snowball rolling or he could give St. Bride the benefit of the doubt and just keep an eye on the guy himself for a couple of weeks.

'Maybe you could ask her to call me when she gets back,' Charlie said.

Gillian had been the first to try Wicca, after finding a Web site for teen witches on the Internet. It wasn't Satan worship, like adults thought. And it wasn't all love spells, like kids thought, either. It was simply the belief that the world had an energy all its own. Put that way, it wasn't so mysterious. Who hadn't walked through the woods and felt the air humming? Or stepped onto the snow and felt the ground reach up for one's body heat?

She was glad to have Meg and Whitney and Chelsea as part

of her coven – but they didn't practice in quite the same way Gillian did. For them, it was a lark. For Gilly, it was a saving grace. And there was one spell she didn't share with the others, one spell she tried every single day, in the hope that one of these afternoons it would work.

Now, while her father believed she was doing homework, she knelt on the floor with a candle – red, for courage. From her pocket, she withdrew a tattered photograph of her mother. Gilly visualized the last time she'd been held by her, until the feeling was so strong that she could feel the prints of her mother's fingers on her upper arms.

'I call upon the Mother Goddess and the Father God,' Gilly whispered, rubbing patchouli oil over the candle, middle to ends. 'I call upon the forces of the Earth, Air, Fire and Water. I call upon the Sun, Moon, and Stars to bring me my mother.'

She slid the picture of her mother beneath the candleholder and then set the candle inside it. She imagined her mother's laugh, bright and full, which had always reminded Gilly of the sea. Then she sprinkled herbs in a circle around the candle: sage, for immortality, and cinnamon, for love. The room began to swim with scent. In the blue heat of the flame, she could see herself as a child. 'Mama,' Gilly whispered, 'come back.'

That moment, just like always, the candle flickered out.

Darla Hudnut twitched into the diner like a summertime mare. 'Where you keeping him, Addie?' she called, unbuttoning her coat.

Darla was the backup waitress, someone Addie asked to work when she knew she wouldn't be able to. This time, though, Addie couldn't remember calling her. 'How come you're here?'

'You asked me last week, remember?' Darla said. She adjusted her uniform, stretched tight over her bust. 'You said you were going out. But first I want to know all about the guy you hired.'

'Good lord, are there billboards on the street?'

'Oh, come on, Addie. Town like this . . . someone with a hangnail's bound to get noticed. A tall, blond, handsome mystery that comes in out of thin air . . . you don't think that might stir up some interest?'

Addie began to wipe the Naugahyde seats of a booth. 'What are people saying?'

Darla shrugged. 'So far I've heard that he's your ex-husband, Amos Duncan's brother, and the guy from the Publisher's Clearinghouse Prize Patrol.'

At that, Addie laughed out loud. 'If he's Amos Duncan's brother, he hasn't mentioned anything. As for my ex-husband, well, that's interesting, since I was never married. And I can assure you that I'm not a million dollars richer, either. He's just a guy who's down on his luck, Darla.'

'Then he's not your date for tonight, either?'

Addie sighed. 'I don't have a date tonight, period.'

'That's news to me.' Addie jumped as Wes Courtemanche breezed through the door. He was no longer wearing his police uniform but a spiffy coat and tie. 'I clearly recall you saying I could take you out to dinner on Wednesday. Darla, is it Wednesday?'

'Think so, Wes.'

'There you go.' He winked. 'Why don't you change, Addie?'

She stood rooted to the spot. 'You've got to be kidding. You couldn't possibly believe that I might want to go out with a man who arrested my father.'

'That's business, Addie. This is . . .' He leaned closer and lowered his voice to a curl of sound. 'Pleasure.'

Addie moved to another table and began to scrub it. 'I'm busy.'

'You've got Darla here to do that. And from what I hear, some new kid, too.'

'That's exactly why I have to stay. To supervise.'

Wes covered her hand where it lay on the table, stilling her motion. 'Darla, you'd take care of the new guy, wouldn't you?'

Darla lowered her lashes. 'Well . . . I could probably teach him a thing or two.'

'No doubt,' Addie said under her breath.

'Well, then. Come on. You wouldn't want me to think you've got some objection to going out with *me,* would you?'

Addie met his eye. 'Wes,' she said, 'I have an objection to going out with *you.*'

He laughed. 'God help me, Addie, but that piss-and-vinegar thing you've got going is some turn-on.'

Addie closed her eyes. It wasn't fair to have to deal with Wes Courtemanche on a day like this one. Even Job was eventually cut a break. She also knew that if she refused to go, Wes would just sit in the diner and get on her nerves all night. The easiest way to get rid of him was to simply go out, then plead sick in the middle of the appetizer course.

'You win,' Addie conceded. 'Let me just go tell Delilah where I'm off to.'

Before she could reach the kitchen, however, Jack emerged, holding her parka. Seeing the others, he blanched and ducked his head. 'Delilah said I should bring this in,' he mumbled. 'She said a night off won't kill you.'

'Oh . . . thanks. Well, I'm glad you came out. I want you to meet Darla.'

Darla held out her hand, which Jack did not take. 'Charmed,' she said.

'And this is Wes,' Addie said shortly, shrugging into her coat. 'All right. Let's get this over with. Darla, you'll tell Delilah to have Chloe in bed by eight?'

No one seemed to be listening. Darla was turning up the TV volume from behind the counter, and Wes squinted at Jack, who was trying to sink between the cracks of the linoleum. 'Have we met?' Wes asked.

Jack ducked his head, refusing to meet the man's eye. 'No,' he said, clearing a table. 'I don't think so.'

It wasn't that Wes Courtemanche was such an awful guy – he just wasn't the right one for Addie, and nothing she said or did seemed to convince him otherwise. After about twenty minutes, a date with Wes took on the feeling of slamming oneself repeatedly into a brick wall. They walked side by side through town, holding Styrofoam cups of hot chocolate. Addie glanced across the green, where the lighted windows of the diner resembled holiday candelabra. 'Wes,' she said for the sixth time, 'I really have to go – now.'

'Three questions. Just three tiny questions so I can get to know you better.'

She sighed. 'All right. And then I'm going.'

'Give me a minute. I've got to make sure they're good ones.' They had just turned the corner of the green when Wes spoke again. 'Why do you stay on at the diner?'

The question surprised Addie; she'd been expecting something far more facetious. She stopped walking, steam from her cup wreathing her face like a mystery. 'I guess,' she said slowly, 'because I have nowhere else to go.'

'How would you know, since you've been doing it all your life?'

Addie cast him a sidelong glance. 'Is this number two?'

'No. It's number one, part *b*.'

'It's hard to explain, unless you've been in the business. You get attached to creating a place where people can come in and feel like they fit. Look at Stuart and Wallace . . . or the student who reads Nietzsche in the back booth every morning. Or even you, and the other police officers who stop in for coffee. If I left, where would they all go?' She shrugged. 'In some ways, that diner's the only home my daughter's ever known.'

'But Addie –'

She cleared her throat before he could finish speaking. 'Number two?'

'If you could be anything in the world, what would you be?'

'A mother,' she said after a moment. 'I'd be a mother.'

Wes slid his free arm around her waist and grinned, his teeth as white as the claw of moon above them. 'You must be reading my mind, honey, since that brings me right to my third question.' He pressed his lips over her ear, his words vibrating against her skin. 'How do you like your eggs in the morning?'

He's too close. Addie's breath knotted at the back of her throat and every inch of her skin broke out in a cold sweat. 'Unfertilized!' she answered, managing to jam her elbow into his side. Then she ran for the buttery windows of the diner like a sailor from a capsized ship who spies a lighthouse, lashes his hope to it, and swims toward salvation.

Jack and Delilah stood side by side chopping onions, taking advantage of a slow after-dinner crowd to get a head start on tomorrow's soup. The scent of onions pricked the back of his nose and drew false tears, but anything was preferable to finding himself backed into corners by Darla. Delilah raised the tip of her knife and pointed to a spot a foot away from Jack. 'She died right there,' Delilah said. 'Came in, gave Roy hell, and collapsed on the floor.'

'But it wasn't her fault Roy had put the wrong side order on the plate.'

Delilah looked at him sidelong. 'Doesn't matter. Roy was busy as all get-out and didn't want to take any fuss from Margaret, so he just said, "You want your peas? Here're your goddamn peas." And he threw the pot of them at her.'

Delilah scraped her onions into a bucket. 'He didn't hit her or anything. It was just a temper he was in. But I guess it was too much for Margaret.' She handed Jack another onion to chop. 'Doctor said her heart was like a bomb ticking in her chest and that it would have given out even if she hadn't been fighting with Roy. I say a heart stopped that day, sure, but I'm thinking it was his. Everyone knows he blames himself for what happened.'

Jack thought of what it would be like to go through life knowing that the last conversation you had with your wife involved throwing a cast-iron pot at her. 'All it takes is a second and your whole life can get turned upside down,' he agreed.

'Mighty profound from a dishwasher.' Delilah tilted her head. 'Where'd you come from, anyway?'

Jack's hand slipped and the knife sliced across the tip of his finger. Blood welled at the seam, and he lifted his hand before he could contaminate the food.

Delilah fussed over him, handing him a clean rag to stop the bleeding and insisting he hold the wound under running water. 'It's nothing,' Jack said. He brought his fingertip to his mouth, sucking. 'Must've been hard on Addie.'

'Huh? Oh, you mean her mom dying. Actually, it gave her something to throw herself into, after Chloe.' Delilah looked up. 'You do know about Chloe?'

Jack had heard Addie speaking to Chloe in the tender, idiomatic language of a mother. 'Her daughter, right? I haven't met her yet, but I figured she was around here somewhere.'

'Chloe was Addie's little girl. She died when she was ten. Just about ruined Addie – she spent two years holed up in her house, nothing but her own upset for company. Until her mom passed and it was up to her to take care of Roy and the diner.'

Jack pressed the cloth against his cut so hard he could feel his pulse. He thought about the plate he'd stolen fries from today, heaped with food no one had touched. He thought of all the times he'd heard Addie talking to a girl who didn't exist. 'But –'

Delilah held up a hand. 'I know. Most people around here think Addie's gone off the deep end.'

'You don't?'

The cook chewed on her lower lip for a moment, staring at Jack's bandaged hand. 'I think,' she said finally, 'that all of us have got our ghosts.'

Before shutting off the grill and leaving with Darla, Delilah had made Jack a burger. He was sitting on the stool next to Chloe's now, watching Addie close up. She moved from table to table like a bumblebee, refilling the sugar containers and the ketchup bottles, keeping time to the tune of a commercial on the overhead TV.

She'd come back from her dinner engagement silent and disturbed – so much so that at first Jack was certain she knew about him. But as he watched her attack her job with a near frenzy, he realized that she was only being penitent, as if she had to work twice as hard to make up for taking a few hours off.

Jack lifted the burger to his mouth and took a bite. Addie was now hard at work on the salt shakers, mixing the contents with rice so that the salt grains wouldn't stick. On the television, the *Jeopardy!* theme music swelled through the speakers. Without intending to, Jack found himself sitting higher in his seat. Alex Trebek walked onto the stage in his natty suit and greeted the three contestants, then pointed to the board, where the computerized jingle heralded the first round's categories.

A method of working this metal was not mastered until 1500 B.C.

'What is iron?' Jack said.

A contestant on the television rang in. 'What is iron?' the woman repeated.

'That's correct!' Alex Trebek answered.

Addie looked up at Jack, then at the TV, and smiled. '*Jeopardy!* fan?'

Jack shrugged. 'I guess.'

In the 1950s, this Modesto, CA, company became the first winery with its own bottle-making plant.

'What is E. & J. Gallo?'

Addie set down the salt container she'd been holding. 'You're more than just a fan,' she said, coming to stand beside him. 'You're really good.'

Nine of the twelve chapters in this book of the Bible set in Babylon revolve around dreams and visions.

'What is Isaiah?' Addie guessed.

Jack shook his head. 'What is Daniel?'

In the original Hebrew of his Lamentations, each verse in three chapters begins with a new letter, from aleph *on.*

'Who is Jeremiah?'

'You know a lot about the Bible,' Addie said. 'Are you a priest or something?'

He had to laugh out loud at that. 'No.'

'Some kind of professor?'

Jack blotted his mouth with a napkin. 'I'm a dishwasher.'

'What were you yesterday, then?'

A prisoner, thought Jack, but he looked into his lap and said, 'Just another guy doing something he didn't really like doing.'

She smiled, content to let it go. 'Lucky for me.' Addie took the mop that Jack had brought from the kitchen and she began to swish it over the linoleum.

'I'll do it.'

'You go ahead and eat,' Addie said. 'I don't mind.'

It was these small kindnesses that would break him. Jack could feel the fissures beginning even now, the hard shell he'd promised to keep in place so that no one, ever, would get close enough to hurt him again. But here was Addie, taking him on faith, doing his work to boot – even though, according to Delilah, fate had screwed her over, too.

He wanted to tell her he understood, but after almost a year of near silence, words did not come easily for him. So very slowly, he took a handful of French fries and set them on Chloe's untouched plate. After a moment, he added his pickle. When he finished, he found Addie staring at him, her hands balanced on top of the mop, her body poised for flight.

She believed he was mocking her; it was right there in the deepest part of her eyes, bruised and tender. Her fingers wrung the wooden handle.

'I . . . I owed her, from this afternoon,' he said.

'Who?' The word was less than a whisper.

Jack's eyes never left hers. 'Chloe.'

Addie didn't respond. Instead, she picked up the mop and began to swab with a vengeance. She cleaned until the floor gleamed, until the lights of the ceiling bounced off the thin residue of Pine-Sol, until it hurt Jack to watch her acting fearless and indifferent because she reminded him so much of himself.

* * *

By the time Addie pulled the door shut and locked it behind her, it was snowing outside. Fist-size flakes, the kind that hooked together in midair like trick skydivers. Inwardly, she groaned. It meant getting up early tomorrow to shovel the walkways.

Jack stood a distance away, the lapels of his sports jacket pulled up to shield his neck from the cold. Addie was a firm believer that someone's past deserved to stay in the past – she herself was surely a poster child for keeping secrets. She didn't know what kind of man walked around in a New Hampshire winter without a coat; she'd never met someone who was bright enough to know the answers to every *Jeopardy!* question but willing to work for minimum wage in a menial job. If Jack wanted to lie low, she could offer him that.

And she wouldn't think about his unprecedented reaction to Chloe.

'Well,' she said, 'See you tomorrow morning.'

Jack didn't seem to hear. His back was turned, his arms stretched out in front of him. Addie realized, with some shock, that he was catching snowflakes on his tongue.

When was the last time she'd thought of snow as anything but a hindrance?

She opened the door of her car, turned the ignition and carefully pulled the car away. In retrospect, she did not know what made her look back into the rearview mirror. If not for the yellow eye of the streetlight in front of the diner, she might never have seen him sitting on the bare curb with his head bowed.

With a curse, she took a hard left, curving around the green to the front of the diner again.'Do you need a ride?'

'No. Thanks, though.'

Addie's fingers flexed on the steering wheel. 'You haven't got a place to stay, have you?' Before he could protest, she got out of the car. 'It so happens I know of a room for rent. The bad news is you're going to have a roommate whose disposition isn't always very sunny. The good news is if you get hungry in the middle of the night, there's a hell of a kitchen you can raid.' As Addie spoke, she unlocked the door of the diner again and stepped over the threshold. She found Jack holding back, haloed by the falling snow. 'Look. My father could use the company. You'd actually be doing me a favor.'

Jack didn't move a muscle. 'Why?'

'Why? Well, because when he spends too much time alone he gets . . . upset.'

'No. Why are you doing this for *me*?'

Addie met his suspicion head-on. She was doing this because she knew what it was like to hit rock bottom and to need someone to give you a leg up. She was doing this because she understood how a world jammed with phones and e-mail and faxes could still leave you feeling utterly alone. But she also knew if she said either of these things, Jack's pride would have him halfway down the street before she could take another breath.

So Addie didn't answer. Instead, she started across the checkerboard floor of the diner.

Tonight, one of the *Jeopardy!* categories had been Greek mythology. *This hero was given permission to bring his love Eurydice back from the underworld but lost her by turning back too quickly to see if she was following.*

Addie wouldn't be like Orpheus. She kept walking with her eyes fixed ahead until she heard the faint jingle of bells on the door, proof that Jack had come in from the cold.

September 1999
North Haverhill, New Hampshire

Aldo LeGrande had a four-by-four-inch tattoo of a skull on his forehead, which was enough to make Jack take the bunk farthest away from him. He didn't react when Jack set his things down, just continued to write in a purple composition notebook whose cover had been hand-decorated with scribbled swastikas and cobras.

Jack began to set belongings in a small tub that sat at the foot of the bed. 'Wouldn't do that if I were you,' Aldo said. 'Mountain uses that to piss in in the middle of the night.'

Jack let the warning slide off his back. He had spent a month at Grafton County. Every new inmate started out in maximum security and was then allowed to petition for a move to medium security after two weeks of good behavior. Two weeks after that, the inmate could move to minimum security. Each time Jack had moved pods, he'd had to face some kind of test from the inmates already living there. In maximum, he'd been spat at. In medium, he'd been jabbed in the kidneys and gut in corners too dark for the security cameras to see.

'Mountain will get over it,' Jack said tightly. He stacked his books from the prison library last and then shoved the plastic container under the lower bunk.

'Like to read?' Aldo asked.

'Yes.'

'How come?'

Jack glanced over his shoulder. 'I'm a teacher.'

Aldo grinned. 'Yeah, well, I work for the state paving roads, but you don't see me painting a dotted yellow line down the middle of the floor.'

'It's a little different,' Jack said. 'I like knowing things.'

'Can't learn the world from a book, Teach.'

But Jack knew the world did not make sense, anyway. He'd had four weeks to ruminate on that very topic. Why would someone like himself even bother listening to someone like Aldo LeGrande?

'You keep your ass tight and prissy like that,' Aldo said, 'and you're gonna be candy for the other boys.'

Jack tried not to feel his heart race at the other man's words. It was what every man thought about when he conjured an image of jail. Would it be irony or biblical justice to be convicted of sexual assault and then find himself the victim of a prison rape?

'What're you in for?' Aldo asked, picking his teeth with his pen.

'What are *you* in for?'

'Rape,' Aldo said.

Jack did not want to admit to Aldo that he had been charged with the same offense. He didn't want to admit it to himself, either. 'Well, I didn't do what they say.'

At that, Aldo tipped back his head and laughed. 'None of us has, Teach,' he said. 'Not a single one.'

The minimum-security pod resembled a daisy: small groups of bunks sticking out like petals from the central common room. Unlike the floors downstairs, there were no cells, just one universal locked door and a guard's booth in the middle. The bathrooms were separate from the sleeping area, and inmates had the freedom to go there as they pleased.

Jack deliberately went to the bathroom a half hour before lights out, when everyone else was still watching TV. He glanced into the common room in passing. A big black man sat closest to the television, the remote control in his fist. He was the highest in the pecking order, the one who got to choose all the programming. Other inmates sat according to their association with him, closest buddies sitting just behind him, and so on, until you got to the row of stragglers far back, who simply did their best to stay out of his way.

By the time Jack returned to his bunk, Aldo was gone. He quickly stripped down to his shorts and T-shirt and crawled into bed, facing into the wall. As he drifted off, he dreamed of autumn, with its crisp apple air and sword-edged blue sky. He pictured his team running drills through the muddy soil, cleats kicking up small tufts of earth so that by the end of the day's practice, the girls had completely changed the lay of the land. He saw their ponytails streaming out behind them, ribbons on the wind.

He woke up suddenly, sweating, as he always did when he thought of what had happened. But before he could even push the memory away, he was stunned to feel a hand at his throat, pinning him against the thin mattress. At first all Jack could see were the yellowed eggs of the man's eyes. Then he spoke, his teeth gleaming in the darkness. 'You're breathing my fucking air.'

The man was the one he'd seen earlier holding the television remote, the one Aldo had referred to as Mountain. Muscles rippled beneath the sleeves of his T-shirt, and at eye level with Jack in the upper bunk, he was easily six and a half feet tall. Jack reached for the hand pinning his windpipe. 'There's plenty of air,' he rasped.

'There was plenty before you came, asshole. Now I have to share it with you.'

'I'm sorry,' Jack choked. 'I'll stop.'

Almost immediately, the big man's hold eased. Without another word Mountain hefted himself into his own bed. Jack lay awake, trying not to breathe, trying not to recall how Mountain's thick fingers had let go of his throat and begun to caress it gently instead.

The cows surprised Jack. Chained individually to their milking stanchions, he had first thought this was some kind of cruel joke: prison animals being locked up. But a few days of the routine of the farm and he realized that they never got turned loose – not out of cruelty but because that was where they were comfortable. Jack would watch their languid, drowsy expressions and wonder if it would be like this for him, too – after so many months of being incarcerated, did you simply stop fighting it?

The twin brothers who ran the farm had assigned him feed duty, which involved mixing grains from two different silos in an automatic overhead chute and then carrying the wheelbarrow load to the small troughs in front of the cows. Jack had done it early this morning before the milking; now, at just past 4:30, he was scheduled to do it again. He maneuvered the wheelbarrow to the far end of the huge barn. It was shrouded in cobwebs and poorly lit, and this morning Jack had had the scare of a lifetime when a bat dove out of the rafters and skittered onion-skin wings along his shoulder.

The automatic mixing mechanism was powered by a toggle switch on one of the heavy upright wooden beams. Jack flipped it, then waited for the grain to fill the top of the chute. The noise made by the machine vibrating to life was deafening, sound pounding around like a hailstorm.

The first punch, square in the kidney, drove him to his knees. Jack scrambled for purchase on the cement floor, twisting to see who had attacked him from behind.

'Get up,' Mountain said. 'I ain't done.'

It cost three dollars to go to the jail's nurse. Mostly, this was because she was one of the few females on site and inmates would rather malinger and watch her breasts shifting beneath her white uniform than sit in a six-foot-by-six-foot cell, or thresh grain. Inmates who paid the fee were granted twenty minutes on one of the two padded tables and a free sample of Tylenol.

Jack was brought there by a security guard, who assured him that this visit was on the house. One of the twins who ran the farm had found Jack buried up to his neck in a heap of feed, blood spreading over his blue denim shirt in the shape of a valentine heart. Jack hadn't been asked any questions, nor had he volunteered information.

The nurse gathered her materials on a metal tray. 'Want to tell me what happened?'

Jack could barely speak past the blinding pain that came every time he moved his head. 'Nosebleed,' he choked out.

'First nosebleed I've ever seen that involved broken nasal cartilage. How about that contusion on your spine, and your ribs? Or should I guess . . . you were kicked by a cow?'

'Sounds good,' Jack said.

Shaking her head, she packed his nostrils with cotton and sent him back to the pod. There, in the common room, men sat playing board games. Jack made his way to an unoccupied table and began to play solitaire.

Suddenly, two tables away, Aldo lunged across a Scrabble board and grabbed another inmate by the lapels. 'You callin' me a liar?'

The man looked him in the eye. 'Yeah, LeGrande. That's exactly what I'm doing.'

Jack averted his gaze and turned over the queen of spades. Put it there, on the column with the five of diamonds . . .

'I'm telling you, it's a word,' Aldo insisted.

Hearing the commotion, the correctional officer on duty appeared. 'What's the matter, Aldo? Someone not want to share his toys with you?'

Aldo jammed his finger at the game board. 'Isn't this a word?'

The guard leaned closer. 'O-C-H-E-R. I've never heard it.'

'It's a word,' Jack said quietly.

Aldo turned with a smug grin. 'You tell 'em, Teach. I read it in one of your books.'

'Ocher,' Jack said. 'It's a color. Kind of orange.'

'Twenty-seven points,' Aldo added.

His opponent narrowed his eyes at Jack. 'Why the hell should I listen to you?'

'Because he studies all kinds of stuff,' Aldo said. 'He knows the answers to all kinds of questions.'

Jack wished Aldo would just shut up. 'Not the ones that matter,' he muttered.

Jack scraped the shovel along the concrete, holding his breath against the pungent stink of manure as he tossed another load into the wheelbarrow. The cows twisted their muscular necks to blink at him with great brown eyes, their udders already swollen with milk again and distending their legs like a bellows.

One of the cows lowed at him, batting eyelashes as long as his pinky. Gently, he moved his shovel to one hand and traced the marbled black-and-white pattern of her hips and side. The heat and softness of it made his throat close.

Without warning, his shovel was knocked away and he found himself sprawled facedown. He felt the scratch of hay against his temple, the fetid puddle of manure beneath his cheek, and the cold bare air on his backside as his jeans were wrenched down. The deep voice of Mountain Felcher curled at the nape of his neck. 'How much you know, Einstein? You know that I was gonna do this to you?'

Jack felt the meat of Mountain's fingers close over his neck. He heard every tooth of a zipper coming undone.

'Aw, Christ, Mountain,' came a voice, 'couldn't you pick someone else?'

Mountain ground himself against Jack. 'Shut up, LeGrande. This ain't your business.'

'Sure it is. St. Bride's got a bet going with a bunch of us. He says he can get every answer right on *Jeopardy!* before the brains who are playing do. There's a can of coffee in it for each of us if he screws up.'

Jack took small, shallow breaths through his mouth. He had made no bet with Aldo or anyone else in the pod. But he'd spend his life's savings on coffee, if that was what it took to get this monster off his back.

'We get to place our commissary order tomorrow – if he's

stuck in the infirmary tonight, thanks to you, we won't get our coffee for another week.'

Jack's arms were released. He scrambled upright to find Mountain buttoning his jeans and looking at him speculatively. 'I seen that show. Ain't no one smart enough to get them questions all right.' He crossed his arms. 'I don't want coffee if you lose.'

'Fine. I'll buy you a chocolate bar instead.'

Mountain's hands were on his shoulders in an instant, drawing him to his feet. 'You get those answers right tonight, then tomorrow I'll leave you be. But you play again next night, and the next. And the minute you fuck up, you're mine.' He touched Jack's jaw, the pads of his fingers soft. 'You lose that game, and you come to me like you want it.'

Jack froze. He watched Mountain leave the barn, then his legs gave out beneath him. Pants still down around his knees, he sat in the straw, trying to draw in air.

'You okay?'

Until he'd spoken, Jack had completely forgotten that Aldo was standing there. He wiped his nose on his sleeve and nodded. 'Thank you.'

'The only thing Mountain likes more than a piece of ass is new entertainment.' A bright flush worked its way up Jack's neck and face as he righted his clothes. 'It's no big deal,' Aldo said, shrugging. 'We've all been there.'

Jack felt himself begin to shake uncontrollably, a delayed reaction from what had nearly happened. In jail, you gave up everything – your possessions, your job, your home. The thought that any man might take even more from an inmate – something as irreplaceable as dignity – made Jack so angry his blood ran faster.

He could not let Mountain Felcher win.

Jack won. And like Scheherezade, he gained a reprieve for several nights. His days took on a frenetic quality: he'd work eight hours, then grab as many books as he could from the prison library and carry them to his bunk. He read before dinner, during dinner, after dinner . . . until the familiar strains of the television game show filled the common room. He went to sleep thinking of the ingredients in a Tom Collins; he woke imagining the history of the Sino-Russian War. But soon, he wasn't doing it alone. Prisoners who at first were angry that they hadn't gotten the coffee they'd expected had come to root for Jack, having realized that self-esteem packed just as much of a high as caffeine. Eager to help, they took books out from the library, too, and fashioned questions for him. They'd quiz Jack as he brushed his teeth, bused his cafeteria tray, made his bunk.

After a week, all of Grafton County Correctional Facility knew about Jack's bet with Mountain Felcher. The guards wagered with each other, a pool for the day that Jack would eventually stumble. The maximum- and medium-security pods followed his wins through the jail grapevine. And at 7 P.M., every TV in the prison would be tuned to *Jeopardy!*

One night, as had become the custom, Jack sat to Mountain Felcher's left, his eyes riveted on the television screen overhead. The leading contestant was a woman named Isabelle with wild curly hair. 'Quotable Quotes for six hundred,' she said.

The historian Cornelius Tacitus said these beings are 'on the side of the stronger.' The other inmates stared at Jack, waiting. Even the correctional officer on duty had given up on his crossword puzzle, and he stood nearby with his arms crossed. Jack felt the response bubbling up from his throat, easily, carelessly. 'The angels.'

In the next breath, he realized he'd given the wrong answer. 'I meant –'

'The gods,' said the contestant.

A bell rang and $600 showed up in Isabelle's account. The common room grew so quiet that Jack could hear his pulse. He'd grown so sure of his skill that he hadn't even stopped to think before he spoke. 'The gods,' Jack repeated, licking his dry lips. 'I meant the gods.'

Mountain turned to him, eyes flat and black as obsidian. 'You lose,' he said.

* * *

Out of sympathy, the others left Jack alone. When he threw up in the bathroom, when he stalked in silence to the cafeteria, they pretended not to see. They thought he was terrified past the point of speech, and it was something they could understand – by now, everyone knew that the forfeit of the bet was Jack's free will. It was one thing to be raped; it was another thing entirely to offer yourself as a sacrifice.

But Jack wasn't frightened. He was so angry that he could not utter a word, in case his fury spilled out. And he wanted to keep it inside him, glowing like a coal, hoping to burn Mountain Felcher and scar him as deeply as Jack himself was sure to be scarred.

The night that Jack lost the bet, Aldo's voice drifted to him as he lay on his bunk. 'You just do it, and then you put it behind you and never let yourself think about it,' Aldo said quietly. 'Kind of like jail.'

Jack stood in the shadows of the barn, watching Mountain's arms bunch and tighten as he lifted another bale of hay onto the stack he was making in an alcove. 'Cat got your tongue?' Mountain asked, his back still to Jack. 'Oh, no. That's right. I got your tongue. And the whole rest of you, too.'

Mountain stripped off his work gloves. Sweat gleamed on his forehead and traced a line down the middle of his T-shirt. 'I had my doubts about you paying your debt.' He sat on a bale of hay. 'Go on, drop those pants.'

'No.'

Mountain's eyes narrowed. 'You're supposed to show up wanting it.'

'I showed up,' Jack said, keeping his voice even. 'That's all you get.'

Mountain jumped him and set him in a headlock. 'For someone who thinks he's so smart, you don't know when to shut your mouth.'

It took all the courage in the world, but Jack did the one thing he knew Mountain wouldn't expect: He went still in the man's hold, unresisting, accepting. 'I *am* smart, you asshole,' Jack said softly. 'I'm smart enough to know that you're not going to break me, not even if you screw me three times a day for the next seven months. Because I'm not going to be thinking what a tough guy you are. I'm going to be thinking you're pathetic.'

Mountain's grip eased, a loose noose around Jack's neck. 'You don't know nothing about me!' In punishment and proof, he ground his hips against Jack from behind. Denim scraped against denim, but there was no ridge of arousal. 'You don't know nothing!'

Jack blocked out the feel of Mountain's body behind his, of what might happen if he pushed too hard and sent the man over the edge. 'Looks like you can't fuck me,' he said, then swallowed hard. 'Why don't you just fuck yourself instead?'

With a roar that set three sparrows in the rafters to flight, Mountain wrenched away. He had never tried to force someone who had given in yet refused to give up. And that one small distinction made Jack every bit as mighty as the bigger man.

'St. Bride.'

Jack turned, his arms folded across his chest – partly to make him look relaxed and partly because he needed to keep himself from falling apart.

'I don't need you when there's a hundred others I can have,' Mountain blustered. 'I'm letting you go.'

But Jack didn't move. 'I'm leaving,' he said slowly. 'There's a difference.'

The black man's head inclined just the slightest bit, and Jack nodded in response. They walked out of the barn into the blinding sunlight, the foot of space between them as inviolable as a stone wall.

Mountain Felcher's sentence for burglary ended three months later. That night, in the common room, there was a buzz of interest. Now that Mountain was gone, the program lineup was up for grabs. 'There's hockey on, you moron,' an inmate cried out.

'Yeah, and your mother's the goalie.'

The footsteps of the guard on duty echoed as he hurried down the hall toward the raised voices. Jack closed the book he was reading and walked to the table where the two men threw insults like javelins. He reached down and plucked the remote from one's hand, settled himself in the seat just beneath the TV, and turned on *Jeopardy!*

This Hindi word for prince is derived from Rex, latin for King.

From the back of the room, an inmate called out: 'What is Raja?'

The two countries with the highest percentage of Shiite Muslims.

'What are Iran and Saudi Arabia!' Aldo said, taking the chair beside Jack.

The man who had wanted to watch hockey sank down behind them. 'What are Iran and Iraq,' he corrected. 'What are you, stupid?'

The guard returned to his booth. And Jack, who held the remote control on his thigh like a scepter, knew every answer by heart.

Late March 2000
Salem Falls, New Hampshire

Every day for the past three weeks, Jack had awakened in Roy Peabody's guest room and looked out the window to see Stuart Hollings – a diner regular – walking his Holstein around the town green for a morning constitutional. The old man came without fail at 5:30 a.m., a collar fitted around the placid animal, who plodded along like a faithful puppy.

This morning, when Jack's alarm clock went off, he looked out to see a lone car down Main Street, and puddles of mud that lay like lakes. Scanning the green, he realized Stuart and his animal were nowhere to be seen.

Shrugging, he grabbed a fresh T-shirt and boxers – the result of a Wal-Mart shopping spree he'd gone on with his first paycheck – and stepped into the hall.

Coming out of the bathroom, Roy startled when he saw Jack. 'Aw, Christ,' he said, doing a double take. 'I dreamed you died.'

'That must have been awful.'

Roy walked off. 'Not as awful as it felt just now when I realized it wasn't true.'

Jack grinned as he went into the bathroom. When he'd moved in it was immediately clear that it had been some time since Roy had had a roommate . . . unlike Jack, who had eight months of practice living among other men. Consequently, Roy did what he could to keep Jack from thinking this was truly his home. He made Jack buy his own groceries – even ketchup and salt – and mark them with his initials before putting them into the refrigerator or the cupboard. He hid the television remote control, so that Jack couldn't just sit on the couch and flip through the channels. All this might have begun to wear on Jack, if not for the fact that every morning when he came into the kitchen to find Roy eating his cereal, the old man had also carefully set a place for Jack.

Before joining Roy for breakfast, Jack glanced out the window.

'What are you looking for?'

'Nothing.' Jack pulled out his chair and emptied some muesli into his bowl, then set up the box like a barrier. A cereal fort, that was what he'd called it as a kid. Over the cardboard wall he saw Roy take a second helping of Count Chocula. 'That stuff'll kill you.'

'Oh, good. I figured it was going to be cirrhosis.'

Jack shoveled a spoonful of cereal into his mouth. He wondered if Stuart had gone on vacation. 'So,' he said. 'How did I die?'

'In my dream, you mean?'

'Yeah.'

The old man leaned closer. 'Scabies.'

'Scabies?'

'Uh-huh. They're bugs – mites – that get right under your skin. Burrow up inside your bloodstream and lay their eggs.'

'Thanks,' Jack said dryly. 'I know what they are. But I don't think they kill you.'

'Oh, sure, wise guy. When's the last time you saw someone who had them?'

Jack shook his head, amused. 'I have to admit . . . never.'

'I did – in the navy. A sailor. Looked like someone had drawn all over him with pencil, lines running up between his fingers and toes and armpits and privates, like he was being mapped from the inside out. Itched himself raw, and the scratches got infected, and one morning we buried him at sea.'

Jack wanted to explain how following that logic, the man had died of a blood infection rather than scabies. Instead, he looked Roy right in the eye. 'You know how you get scabies,' he said casually. 'From sharing clothing and bed sheets with an infected person. Which means if I had really died of scabies, like in your dream, you wouldn't be that far behind me.'

Roy was silent for a moment. Then he stood and cleared his place. 'You know, I've been thinking. There isn't much point in both of us buying milk when we can't each get through a half-gallon in a week. Might as well do it so you buy the milk one week and the next week it's my turn.'

'Seems economically sound.'

'Exactly.' Roy rinsed his bowl. 'You still wash your own sheets, though.'

Jack stifled a grin. 'Well, of course. You never know what you're going to catch from someone else's laundry.'

Roy eyed him, trying to decide whether Jack was being sincere. Then he shuffled toward the living room. 'I knew I liked you for a reason,' he said.

Roy, who categorically refused to work in the kitchen, manned the cash register under the watchful eye of his daughter. Addie let him out of sight only briefly, and even then with warnings: 'It should only take you ten minutes to run to the bank, Dad, and I'm going to be counting.' Mostly he sat and did crossword puzzles, trying to pretend he wasn't looking when Darla, the relief waitress, bent down to tie her shoe and her skirt rode up.

It was nearly 11 a.m.; a time that was slow for the waitresses but frenetic for the kitchen staff. Roy could hear the oil in the deep fryer heating up infinitesimally, degree by degree. He would sometimes remember how he was once so good he could cut inch-long segments from a carrot with a cleaver, blindfolded, and end the last slice a half inch from the hand that held it in place.

A coin rang onto the Formica beside the cash register. 'Penny for your thoughts,' Addie said, stuffing the rest of her tip into her pockets.

'They're worth a quarter.'

'Hustler.' Addie rubbed the small of her back. 'I know what you were thinking, anyway.'

'Oh, you do?' It amazed him, sometimes, how Addie could do the most ordinary thing – blink her eyes or fold her legs beneath a chair – and suddenly Roy would swear that his wife had come back. He looked at his daughter's tired eyes, at her chapped hands, and wondered how Margaret's losing her life had led Addie to throw away her own.

'You're thinking of how easy it is for you to slide back into this routine.'

Roy laughed. 'What routine? Sitting on my butt all day?'

'Sitting in the *diner* on your butt all day.'

It was impossible to tell Addie what he really thought: that this diner meant nothing to him, not since Margaret's death. But Addie had gotten it into her head that keeping the Do-Or-Diner open would give him a purpose he wouldn't find at the bottom of a bottle of vodka. What Addie didn't understand was that what you had could never make up for what you'd lost.

He and Margaret had closed the diner for a week each summer to take Addie on a family vacation. They had driven by car, to towns with names that drew them: Cape Porpoise, Maine; Egypt, Massachusetts; Paw Paw, Michigan; Defiance, Ohio. Roy would point out a flock of Canada geese, a looming purple mountain, a sunlit field of wheat – and then he'd glance in the back to find his daughter asleep on the backseat, the whole world passing her by. 'There's an elephant in the lane next to us!' he'd call out. 'The moon is falling out of the sky!' Anything to make Addie take stock of her surroundings.

'The moon is falling out of the sky,' Roy murmured now.

'What?'

'I said, yes, there are advantages to being here.'

A customer came in, ringing the bell over the door. 'Hey,' Addie called out, her smile set firmly in place like a child's Halloween mask. As she went to seat the woman, Jack poked his head through the double doors.

'Roy,' he whispered. 'Did Stuart come in today?'

'Stuart, the old guy?' Roy said, although he himself couldn't have been much younger than Stuart. 'Nah.'

'I, uh, I'm worried about him.'

'How come?'

'He hasn't missed breakfast a single day since I've been working here. And I didn't see him out with the cow this morning, either.'

Addie walked up to the two men. 'What's the matter?'

'Stuart,' Roy explained. 'He's gone missing.'

She frowned. 'He wasn't in today – you're right. Did you try calling his house?'

Jack shook his head. 'I don't know his last name.'

'Hollings.' Addie dialed a number, her expression growing tighter with each ring. 'He lives by himself, in that old farmhouse behind the pharmaceutical plant.'

'Maybe he just went away for a while.'

'Not Stuart. The last trip he went on was to Concord, in 1982. I'll go check on him. Dad, don't let Chloe sneak any snacks before lunchtime, no matter how much she says she's starving.' She reached around her waist to untie her apron, her breasts thrusting forward in the process. Jack didn't want to notice, but he did, and he grew so flustered that it took him a moment to recognize her intentions. 'Here,' she said, tossing the apron and order pad at him. 'You've just been promoted.'

Stuart's farmhouse sat at the crest of a hill, snowy pastures draped around it like the settling skirts of a debutante. Addie parked in a hurry and got out of her car. His cow was lowing angrily from the barn – something that made the hair stand up on the back of her neck, since nothing meant more to the old man than caring for that cow.

'Stuart?' Addie let herself into the barn, empty save for the swollen cow. She raced up the path to the house, calling his name. The front door was unlocked. 'Stuart, it's Addie. From the diner. Are you here?'

She moved through the puzzle of the unfamiliar house until she reached the kitchen. 'Stuart?' Addie said, and then she screamed.

He was lying on his side in a pool of blood, his eyes open but half of his face curiously wooden. 'Oh, God. Can you speak to me, Stuart?'

Addie had to lean close and focus hard to understand the mangled word that crawled from Stuart's slack mouth. 'Sauce?' she repeated, and then she realized that the spreading red had come from a broken jar and smelled of tomatoes.

The phone was an old 1950s wall-mounted rotary. It took forever to dial 911 and get an ambulance dispatched. She returned to the pantry and got to her knees right in the puddle of spaghetti sauce. She stroked the fine silver hairs that glimmered over Stuart's scalp. To how many deaths would she have to bear witness?

Roy untied the strings of the waitress apron and handed it back to his daughter. 'How come you were waiting tables? Didn't I ask Jack to do it?'

'He was a mess. Practically broke out in hives every time he had to go over to a customer. He's shy, you know, not nearly as charming as me, so I decided to put him out of his misery.' He nodded toward the swinging doors. 'You gonna tell him about Stuart?'

Addie was already heading toward the kitchen. Delilah and Jack both looked up as she entered. 'He's okay,' Addie said without preamble. 'Wallace is with him now.'

'Thank the good Lord.' Delilah rapped the spoon twice on the edge of the pot and set it down. 'Heart attack?'

'Stroke, I think. The doctors talked alphabet soup. CVA, TIA, whatever that means.'

'Cerebrovascular accident preceded by a transient ischemic attack,' Jack translated. 'Basically, it means Stuart had a whole lot of little strokes leading up to a big one.'

Both Addie and Delilah stared at him. 'You some kind of doctor?' Delilah asked.

'No.' Embarrassed, Jack busied his hands with a rack of dry glassware. 'I've just heard of it.'

Addie crossed the kitchen until she was a few feet away from where Jack stood. 'I told Stuart that you were the one who was worried about him. You did a kind thing, Jack.' She reached out and touched Jack's hand with her own.

He froze in the motion of unloading another tray of dishes. 'Please . . . don't.' He pulled away, breaking eye contact. 'The cow,' Jack said, leaping into the silence, desperate to keep Addie from speaking. 'Who's taking care of the cow?'

She cursed under her breath. 'That's right. I need to find someone who knows how to milk by hand.'

'Don't look at me,' the cook said. 'All I know about cows is that one day I'm going to be able to braise, stew, and fry them.'

'Oh, come on, Delilah. You know everyone in Salem Falls. Isn't there someone in this town who –'

'Yes,' Jack said, looking nearly as surprised as Addie to hear his voice. 'Me.'

Starshine, the proprietress of the Wiccan Read, fixed a smile on her face as the tiny silver bells strung over the door signaled the arrival of a customer. A quartet of girls entered the occult bookstore, their laughter twining around them. The one with the greatest aura of energy about her was Gillian Duncan, the daughter of the most prosperous businessman in the county. Starshine wondered if he knew his daughter wore a small golden pentagram tucked beneath her shirt, a symbol of the pagan religion she embraced.

'Ladies,' she said in greeting, 'is there anything in particular I can help you with?'

'We're just looking,' Gillian said.

Starshine nodded and gave them their space. She watched them move from shelves crowded with grimoires – spell books, to the small vials of herbs – wax myrtle, mandrake root, boneset, joe-pye weed.

'Gilly,' Whitney said, 'should we get something to help Stuart Hollings?'

'Yeah. For a healing spell.' Chelsea smiled at Starshine. 'It looks like we do need your help, after all.'

Meg hurried over, clutching a six-pack of candles. 'Look! Last time we were here, the red candles were back-ordered!' she said breathlessly, then realized that her friends were choosing among the herbs. 'What's up?'

'For the guy who had a stroke,' Chelsea said. 'We ought to do something.'

Starshine began to empty a small quantity of something that looked like tea leaves into a tiny Ziploc bag. 'Yerba santa,' she suggested. 'And some willow. A nice piece of quartz couldn't hurt, either.'

She handed one of the girls the bag and went in search of quartz, only to realize that she had lost sight of Gillian Duncan. Frowning, she excused herself for a moment. Once, a teenage witch had shoplifted an entire vial of hound's-tongue.

She found Gillian behind the silk curtain that divided the store from the private area, where stock was kept. The girl sat cross-legged on the floor, a heavy black book cracked open on her lap. 'Interesting stuff,' Gillian said, looking up. 'How much for the book?'

Starshine grabbed the volume and shoved it back into the shelf. 'It's not for sale.'

Gillian got up, dusting off her jeans. 'I thought there were rules about those kinds of spells.'

'There are. *An it harm none, do what ye will.* Witches don't curse or make others suffer.' When Gillian's expression didn't change, Starshine sighed. 'These books are back here for a reason. You aren't supposed to read them.'

Gillian raised one brow, so confident that it was impossible to believe she was only seventeen. 'Why not?' she said. '*You* do.'

'I know,' Jack soothed. 'I'm going to make it better.' Milking by hand was not something they'd done at Grafton, but the twins who ran the barn had given him a lesson once. Now, as he curled his fingers around the teat and rippled them downward, a sweet stream of milk shot into the pail.

'Look how much better she feels,' Addie murmured. If there was such a thing as an expression of relief on a cow's face, this one wore it now. Addie could remember nursing Chloe; how sometimes she'd be delayed for a feeding and would come to her baby, full and wet, certain she would die if not for the touch of Chloe's bow mouth.

It surprised her to see Jack's obvious enjoyment in something as simple as being close to the heated hide of the cow or skimming his hand up the smooth, pink udder. She realized that Jack, who could not bear to be touched, craved physical contact.

'You grew up on a farm,' she said.

'Who told you that?'

'You did. Look at how easy this comes to you.'

Jack shook his head. 'I grew up in New York City. This is an acquired skill.'

Addie sat down in the hay. 'What did you do in New York?'

'What any kid does. Went to school. Played sports.'

'Your parents still live there?'

Jack hesitated only a second. 'Nope.'

'You know,' Addie said facetiously, 'that's what I like about you. You're so naturally talkative.'

He smiled at her, and for a moment, she could not catch her breath. 'What I like about you is how you so fiercely guard someone else's privacy.'

She blushed. 'It's not like that. I just . . . well . . .'

'You want to know where I came from before I walked into your diner.' He let go of the teat and stood up, maneuvering the stool to the cow's other side, so that Addie could no longer see him while he spoke. 'You already know a lot, actually.'

'That you grew up in New York City and could give Alex Trebek a run for his money?'

'Your dad could tell you some things.'

'Like?'

'Like I don't squeeze the toothpaste tube in the middle.'

'Well, that's good to know. I wasn't able to sleep at night because –'

Suddenly his head rose over the bulk of the cow. 'Addie,' Jack said, 'shut up and get over here. You're about to have your first milking lesson.'

The cow bellowed, and Addie shied back. 'She likes you.'

'Her brain is the size of a clam. Trust me, she couldn't care less.' He nodded toward the udder again, and Addie reached down but could not draw forth any milk.

'Watch.' Jack knelt in the hay and took two udders in his hands. He began to pump rhythmically, milk raining into the bucket. Addie marked the synchronic motion and then lay her hand over Jack's. She could feel the flex of the tendons and the muscles tightening as he froze; she looked back to find Jack's face twisted in either agony or rapture at the simple fact of a human touch. He opened his eyes and locked his gaze on hers.

The cow's tail slapped him hard across the face, damp and reeking. Addie and Jack jumped apart.

'I think I've got it now.' When she tried this time, a small squirt of milk came from the teat. She continued to focus her attention on the cow, embarrassed now that she had seen Jack with his guard down.

'Addie,' Jack said softly, 'let's trade.'

They were inches apart, close enough to breathe each other's fear. 'Trade what?'

'The truth. You give me one honest answer,' he said, 'and I'll give you one back.'

Addie nodded slowly, sealing the bargain. 'Who goes first?'

'You can.'

'All right . . . what did you do?'

'I was a teacher. At a private school for girls. Coached soccer there, too.' He rubbed the flat of his hand along the cow's bony ridge of spine, the protrusions of her hipbone. 'I loved it. I loved every minute of it.'

'Then how come you –'

'Now it's my turn.' Jack moved the pail from beneath the cow. The milk steamed, fragrant and fresh, its heat rising between them. 'What happened to Chloe?'

Addie's eyes swam. Jack's fingers grasped her upper arms. 'Addie –' He broke off, following her stare. To his hands. Which were touching her. Of their own free will.

Immediately, he let go.

'That waitress has an ass like a —'

'Thomas.' Jordan McAfee cut his son's observation off, even as he peeked around the edge of his mug to see for himself. Then he grinned. 'You're right. She does.'

Darla turned, in the middle of making rounds with the coffee. 'Refill?'

Jordan held out his cup. He bit back a smile as his son's eyes fixed directly on the waitress's cleavage.

'You know,' Jordan mused, when Darla had left them for another customer, 'you're making me feel old.'

'Aw, come on, Dad. You were fifteen . . . what? A few centennials ago?'

'Do you think of anything besides sex?'

'Of course.' Thomas looked affronted. 'Every now and then, I worry about people in Third World countries. And then I figure if they all started having sex, their lives would be considerably brighter.'

Jordan laughed. As a single father, he knew he had a very different sort of relationship with his son than most other parents had. And maybe it was his own fault. A few years ago, when they'd been living in Bainbridge, Jordan had run a little wild, had brought home his share of women whose names he could not recall the next day.

He set down his coffee cup. 'Tell me the paragon's name again?'

'Chelsea. Chelsea Abrams.'

Thomas's whole face softened, and for a moment Jordan

was actually jealous of his own son. When was the last time *he'd* been swallowed whole by love?

'She's got the most incredible pair of –'

Jordan cleared his throat.

' – eyes. Big and brown. Like Selena's.'

Just the name made Jordan's shoulders tense. Selena Damascus had been his private investigator when he'd been a defense attorney in Bainbridge. She did have beautiful eyes – a brown you could drown in. Once, Jordan nearly had. But he had not seen or heard from Selena in the fourteen months since he'd moved to Salem Falls and cut back dramatically on his caseload.

'So,' Jordan said, rerouting the topic. 'Chelsea's beautiful.'

'She's smart, too. She takes AP everything.'

'Sounds promising. And what does she think about you?'

Thomas grimaced. 'That's too big an assumption. She probably doesn't think about me at all.'

'Ah, but that's something you can overcome.'

Thomas looked at his thin arms, his concave chest. 'With my incredible physique?'

'With your perseverance. Believe me, there are plenty of times I've tried to forget about you, but you keep crawling back into my head.'

'Thanks a bunch.'

'Think nothing of it. You going to ask her to the Spring Fling?'

'Nah. I have to bone up on my perseverance first, so that when she laughs in my face I don't collapse in a heap.' Thomas pushed his French fries through an ocean of ketchup, drawing Chelsea's initials. 'Selena used to be great with girl advice.'

'That's because she's a girl,' Jordan pointed out. 'What's going on, Thomas? Why do you keep bringing her up?'

'I just wish we still knew her is all.'

Jordan stared out the window at two dogs that were chasing each other, tails scrawling trails in the snow. 'It would be nice,' he agreed softly. 'But I lost my best investigator a year ago.'

* * *

At first, when Addie was watching Jack, she told herself it was because he was a new employee – she needed to make sure he didn't put the salt back on the storage shelf where the sugar was supposed to be; she had to be certain that he loaded the dishwasher in a way that would maximize cleaning and minimize breakage. Then she admitted that she was watching Jack simply because she wanted to. There was something mesmerizing about seeing him run a mop over the checkerboard floor, his mind a million miles away. Or listening to Delilah with rapt attention, as if learning how to make bouillabaisse was one of his life's goals. He was handsome, certainly, but plenty of handsome men had come through her diner before. What was so attractive about Jack was his exoticism – the fact that he looked completely wrong there, like an orchid blooming in the desert, yet acted as if there was no place else he'd rather be. To Addie – who felt as much a part of the diner as its bricks and mortar, and equally as unable to separate from it – Jack was the most fascinating creature she'd ever seen.

She was figuring out a tab one afternoon when Jack looked up from wiping down the counter, glanced out the front window, and suddenly sprinted into the kitchen. Curious, she followed, to find him handing Delilah an order.

Addie pulled it from the cook's hand. 'There's no one at table seven,' she said.

'There will be. Didn't you see him? The kid with the long hair and the philosophy book – he's on his way in.'

Addie knew immediately to whom Jack was referring. The student was a fairly new regular but a consistent one. He came in at 2:20 every day but Sunday, slid into the booth in the back of the diner, and pulled a dog-eared paperback of Nietzsche's *Beyond Good and Evil* from his battered knapsack. Every day for the past three weeks, without any deviation, he'd ordered a BLT, hold the tomato, with extra mayonnaise. Two pickles. A side of cheese fries, and black coffee.

Delilah pushed the sandwich toward Jack, who picked it up and hurried into the front of the diner. The student was just sliding into his customary booth when Jack, smiling triumphantly, set his usual order down in front of him.

The kid paused in the act of removing his book from his knapsack. 'What the fuck is this?' he asked.

Jack nodded toward the window. 'I saw you coming. And you've ordered this almost every day for the past three weeks.'

'So?' the student said. 'Maybe today was the day I wanted a fucking burger.' He shoved the plate across the booth, so that it toppled off the edge onto the banquette. 'Fuck you and your mind games,' he said, and he stormed out of the diner.

From her vantage point by the swinging doors, Addie watched Jack begin to clean up the food. He angrily wiped mayonnaise from the plastic seat and stacked the pieces of the ruined sandwich back on the plate. When he turned around, he found Addie standing beside the table. 'I can take that for you,' she said.

But Jack shook his head tightly. 'Sorry I lost you a customer.'

'It wasn't intentional, I'm sure.' Addie smiled a little. 'Besides, he was a lousy tipper.'

There was something in the tense curve of Jack's shoulders and the flat blank of his eyes that told her he had been slapped down before when he'd only been trying to go out of his way for someone. 'Some people don't know what to do with an act of kindness,' Addie said.

Jack looked directly at her. 'Do you?'

What kindness would you show me? she thought, and shocked herself. Jack was an employee. He was as different from her as night was from day. But then she thought of how, that morning, he'd taken over the grill for Delilah and had made pancakes in the shape of snowmen, then slipped them onto Chloe's plate at the counter. She thought of how they would move around the empty diner in tandem after closing, clearing and sorting and shutting down for the night, a dance that seemed so smooth they might have been doing it forever.

Suddenly she wanted to make Jack feel what she had felt lately: that this once, there was someone on her side, someone who understood. 'Stuart's been coming here for years, and every morning I pretend I have no idea what he's going to ask for, although it's always the same – ham and cheese omelette, hash browns, and coffee. Jack, I know you were only trying to help,' Addie said, 'but on the whole, customers don't like having assumptions made about them.'

Jack stuffed the dirty wipe into the waist of his apron and took the plate back from her. 'Who does?' he said, and walked into the kitchen, leaving Addie to wonder if his response had been a wall to make her keep her distance or a clue to help her understand.

In Meg Saxton's opinion, phys ed was an inhumane form of humiliation. It was not that she was hugely fat, like the people Richard Simmons visited because they couldn't even get out of bed. Her mother said she was still growing. Her father said there was just enough of her to love. Meg bet neither of them had had to suffer through shopping at the Gap with their friends, pretending there was nothing that interested her on the sale rack so that they wouldn't see her picking from the size fourteens.

The two girls the phys-ed teacher had picked came front and center, with a confidence that said they were used to standing there. Suzanne Abernathy was a field hockey captain; Hailey McCourt had led the soccer team to a district championship last year. They stared down the group of girls, sorting the athletes from the losers in their minds.

'Sarah.'

'Brianna.'

'Leah.'

'Izzie.'

Gilly was picked – she was no athlete, but she was quick and smart. The choices narrowed, leaving only a small huddling puddle of girls who had little coordination. Meg shivered each time a name was called, as if each time one of them walked away, a piece of protective armor had been removed.

Finally, only two girls remained: Meg, and Tessie, the Down syndrome kid who'd been mainstreamed this year. Hailey turned to Suzanne. 'What do you want? The retard or the tub of lard?'

Laughter rained down on Meg. Beside her, Tessie clapped her hands with delight.

'Tessie, you're with Suzanne,' the phys-ed teacher announced.

As the ball was set into play, Meg stared at Hailey, thinking of boils and leprosy and third-degree burns, horrible things that would take away her honey hair, her Cover Girl complexion, and leave her in the same boat as the rest of the misfit world. Then the ball came directly toward her. 'Saxton!' Hailey yelled out. 'To me!'

Meg lifted her foot – how hard could it be to kick a soccer ball? – and let loose with such force she slid and landed on her butt in the mud.

The snickers of the class didn't take away from this slow-motion moment, the ball spinning skyward like a missile. Meg was a little stunned at how far it went, even if it was soaring in the complete opposite direction from Hailey. The ball continued so far out of bounds that it landed on the baseball field.

Hailey walked past Meg, deliberately splattering her with even more mud. 'If you can't shoot straight, hippo, pass the ball!'

'Hailey!' the teacher said sharply. And then sighed. 'Meg, go get it.'

Meg jogged off, painfully aware of Hailey whispering about the way she looked while she was trying to run. One day she'd be reincarnated as an anorexic. Or a supermodel. Or maybe both at the same time. Head down, Meg concentrated on the fire in the pit of her lungs and her belly, instead of the tears pricking the backs of her eyes.

'Here you go.'

A man handed her the out-of-bounds ball. He was tall, and the sun caught his hair like it did Gilly's. He had a kind smile, and she would have thought he was incredibly handsome if he wasn't as old as her father. 'Don't kick it with your toe,' he said.

'What?'

'Raise your knee, push your toes down, and hit it with your shoelaces. Swipe under the ball.' He grinned at Meg. 'You've got more power in one leg than that blond girl has in her whole body.'

Meg let her eyes slide away. 'Whatever,' she muttered. She slogged onto the field, letting the action fly around her. She was facing her own goal when the ball slammed her in the back of the knees. '*Knee up, toe down, on the shoelace!*' Meg heard his voice again, and without thinking about it, she did exactly what he said.

The ball flew low and strong, driving straight toward the opposite goal. Maybe it was the surprise that Meg Saxton had actually hit it; maybe it was – as that man had said – that she had power she didn't even realize – but for whatever reason, the ball streaked past the defense and snugged in the net.

For a moment, everything stood still, and Meg felt herself suddenly cloaked in the thick satisfaction of doing something perfectly right. 'Killer shot!' one girl said, and another patted her on the back. Gillian ran up to her side. 'Unbelievable. Did you cast a spell?'

'No,' Meg admitted, a little amazed this had happened without witchcraft.

But Gillian's attention was on the field, where the man was walking off, hands in his pockets. 'Who's your coach?' she asked.

Meg shrugged. 'Some guy. I don't know.'

'He's cute.'

'He's old!'

Gillian laughed. 'Next time,' she said, 'ask his name.'

The basement of the diner held the lion's share of the food that couldn't fit in the narrow kitchen: a stacked ladder of hamburger rolls and breads, huge tins of sweet corn, tubs of ketchup large enough to fill half a bathtub. Jack had been sent down there by Delilah for a fifty-pound bag of potatoes. Hefting the bag onto his shoulder, he yanked it out of its spot on the shelf and found himself looking right at Roy.

The old man was in back of the metal shelving, his fist closed around a bottle of cooking sherry. 'Oh, shit,' he sighed.

'Addie's going to kill you.'

'Only if she finds out about it.' Roy offered his most charming smile. 'I'll let you watch whatever you want on TV for a week if you pretend you never saw me.'

Jack considered this for a moment and nodded. Then he balanced the potatoes on his shoulder, trudged up the narrow stairs, and dumped the sack at Delilah's feet. 'Start peeling,' she ordered.

'Have you seen my father?' Addie demanded, hurrying into the kitchen. 'We've got a line a mile long at the cash register.'

Delilah shrugged. 'He's not here or I'd have tripped over him. Jack, you see Roy in the basement?'

Jack shook his head but he didn't meet Addie's eye. Then, with impeccably lousy timing, Roy sauntered through the basement door. His face was glowing, and even from across the room Jack could smell the cheap alcohol on his breath.

Addie's face went bright red. Tension filled the confines of the kitchen, and Jack tried to ignore the fact that someone was going to say something any moment that he or she would regret. Words, he knew, could scar.

So he squeezed the base of the potato he was peeling, then watched it fly in an arc over his shoulder toward the grill. Then, taking a deep breath, he grabbed for it, deliberately pressing his palm to the burning plate of metal.

'Goddamn!' he cried, geniune pain pricking behind his eyes and making him weak in the knees. Delilah pulled him away from the stove as Addie hurried to his side. With the brisk expertise of someone who'd done this before, she led him toward the hand-washing sink and ran the cold water. 'It's going to blister. How badly does it hurt?'

It hurt, but not the way she thought. It hurt to have her

fingers stroking the back of his hand, to feel her concern flowing over him like a river. Missed opportunities were never superficial wounds; they cut straight to the bone.

Addie fussed over the red streaks branded into his skin, a scarlet letter that in his imagination took the shape of an *A*. 'Really,' she scolded, now that the danger had passed, 'you're no better than Chloe.'

Jack shook his head. He pressed Addie's fingers to his chest, so that his heart beat in the palm of her hand.

Thomas glanced up to find the very girl he was daydreaming about standing less than two feet away from him. 'Uh, hi,' he managed. *Brilliant.*

'Would you mind if I sat down?' Chelsea asked, her gaze lighting on the other lunch tables. 'Pretty crowded today.'

'*Mi* table *es su* table.'

'What?'

'It's Spanish. Well, kind of. I don't know how to say *table* . . .' *Shut up, Thomas, before you hurt yourself.*

'Thanks.' Chelsea set down her lunch, then waved. And suddenly Thomas realized that the princess came with an entourage. Gillian Duncan and two others sat down, and the minute they arrived, it was as if Thomas himself didn't exist.

Still, it was better to eat his lunch with Chelsea Abrams just six inches away from him on a wooden bench than by himself. His breath caught when she mistakenly reached for Thomas's napkin and touched it to the corner of her mouth in nearly the same spot where Thomas had touched it to his own mouth. He winged a silent prayer to God for Chelsea to leave first, so that she wouldn't see his thoughts broadcast across his groin.

'Maybe he's some kind of pervert,' Meg said, and Thomas jumped a foot, wondering if they could sense his hard-on even through the barrier of the picnic table. Then he realized that Meg was talking about someone else entirely. 'You don't see other grown men lurking around outside the high school gym.'

'Lurking? God, Meg. You think you're being dramatic

enough?' Whitney tossed her hair over her shoulder. 'Perverts live in places like Detroit and L.A., not Salem Falls.'

'First off, my dad has always said that crime statistics don't mean much if you're the victim in that one percentile. Second – I talked to him, you didn't.'

'Still,' Gillian pointed out, 'I wouldn't be so quick to cast stones at someone who made you look like Mia Hamm.'

'Are you talking about the guy out by the soccer field?' Thomas asked.

Chelsea turned. 'Do you know him?'

Thomas felt the heat of their attention. 'Sure. He works at the diner in town.'

Gillian took a drink from a water bottle and glanced in the direction of the playing fields, where the man might even now be standing.

'You can work at a diner and still be a pervert,' Meg murmured. 'That's all I'm saying.'

It seemed to Jack that the kid at the counter had been there long enough to warrant concern, but then again, it wasn't his diner or his place to care. He sat stone-faced at the cash register, a job he'd won by default because he couldn't get his bandage wet.

The girl kept staring at him. She was lean and pretty, coltlike, although she wore too much makeup. She was in the process of ripping open her sixteenth sugar packet and pouring its contents on the counter.

Addie burst through the swinging doors, plates balanced on her arms like armor. 'Help me a second, will you?' Jack obligingly stood up and trailed in her wake. He lifted each dish, setting it down where Addie directed.

'Thanks,' she said. 'If I can keep Chloe from getting underfoot, I just may actually finish getting out the orders for the dinner rush.' She started back into the kitchen but stopped when Jack called her name.

'That girl . . . she's been here for three hours.'

'She can stay here for three years if she wants, as long as she's hungry and has her daddy's charge card. That's Gilly Duncan . . . daughter of the guy who owns the pharmaceutical plant.'

Jack sat back down and watched Gilly Duncan rip open sugar packets number seventeen and eighteen and pour them on the Formica. Well, hell. It was one thing if Jack himself was busing tables, but with his burn, Addie had taken on that work. The thought of her having to sweep up after this spoiled little brat fueled his courage. 'You're making a mess,' he said.

Gillian raised one delicate red brow. 'Oh, my. Did I spill?' She stuck her forefinger in her mouth, rolled it in the white grains, and started to suck on it. 'Sweet.' She coated her finger in sugar again and held it up. 'Very sweet.'

Jack jumped back, as if she'd brandished a gun.

'I didn't mean to make more work for you.' She began to scoop the spilled sugar into the cup of her hand and empty it onto the side of her saucer. 'There. I'm Gilly, by the way. And you are?'

'Going,' Jack said, and he ducked from behind the counter and walked out the diner's door.

In Whitney's garage, Gillian cupped a small heap of cinnamon in her hand and began the third casting, trailing a ring around her friends. 'Set me apart from the world of man. Set me apart from the world of spirit. Hold me between the two, so I might work my magick.' The last bit of cinnamon sparked from her fingers, and she turned to the others. 'The circle is perfect.'

She knelt in front of the altar and reached for the green candle they'd brought to the garage. Rubbing oil from the tip to the base, she began to chant: 'Heal him whole, heal him whole.' Using the quartz from the Wiccan Read, Gillian scratched into the candle a crude sketch of a caduceus, to symbolize perfect health. 'Who has the matches?'

Whitney grimaced. She pointed toward the hood of her mother's car, a silvery Volvo. 'Damn. I left them over there.'

She picked up the knife on the altar and cut through the invisible boundaries of the circle to open it, reached for the matches, and then stepped back inside. 'Here,' she said, pressing the small box into Gilly's hand.

The flame rose higher every time the girls breathed in, visualizing Stuart Holling as he rose from his hospital bed and walked away from it. Wax slid down the candle until the etched snakes were smooth again. And then, a quick draft coming from beneath the garage door blew the fire out.

'Do you think that means he's better?' Chelsea whispered.

'Either that or he's dead.'

'Maybe we should call the hospital to see.'

'They wouldn't tell us,' Gillian pointed out. 'We're not related to him. We'll just have to wait and see what happens tomorrow.'

The girls sat, lost in thought. 'It was different tonight,' Whitney said finally.

'Like I was humming inside,' Meg agreed.

'Maybe it was because we weren't just doing it for ourselves.' Whitney spoke slowly, choosing her words with care. 'When we cast a spell for money or for love . . . it was to change *us,* to help *us*. This time, we were sending all that energy to Mr. Hollings.'

Chelsea frowned. 'But if we were sending the energy away, how come it felt so powerful in the circle?'

'Because it takes more strength to change someone else's life than it takes to change your own,' Gillian replied.

'And if it works –' Whitney said.

'*When* it works.'

'*When* it works . . . it will be something he wanted all along, anyway.' Whitney stared at the altar, at the smoking candle. 'A true witch can cast spells for someone else.'

'A true witch can cast spells *on* someone else.' Gillian raised her finger, smudged brown with cinnamon, and blew so that it clouded the air in front of her. 'What if we hadn't healed Mr. Hollings? What if we made him sicker?'

Chelsea's eyes widened. 'You know that goes against the Wiccan rede, Gilly. Whatever you do comes back to you threefold.'

'Well, okay. Mr. Hollings is a stupid example. But if Wicca's all about keeping the balance of nature, then why couldn't we use magick for that?'

Whitney looked at Gillian. 'I don't get it.'

Meg leaned forward. 'She means if we help people who've helped others, it's natural to hurt people who've hurt others. Right?'

Gillian nodded. 'And to do it so that they don't know who's making it happen.' Her voice skimmed over the others' reservations, smoothing in its wake. 'Think about how powerful you felt tonight, healing someone. And then imagine how powerful you'd feel if you could ruin someone's life.'

'Hailey McCourt,' Meg whispered.

Gillian turned. 'That's a start.'

'And where have you been?' Addie demanded, as Jack entered the diner.

'Out.'

It was empty of patrons, quiet in the kitchen. Overhead, *Jeopardy!* played on the television, the sound muted. Jack pulled off his jacket, determined to help close for the night.

'Well, I hate to be the one to break this to you, but you can't just walk off a job without an explanation. Or maybe that's what got you fired from teaching?'

He fixed his eyes on the screen above her left shoulder. *The core of a quarter is made of this metal.*

What is zinc? Jack thought. 'I'm sorry,' he said aloud.

'You should be. I needed you here tonight. I may not be paying you a lot, but –'

The bells over the diner door jingled. Addie narrowed her eyes at Jack, blaming him for forgetting to lock the door behind himself. Wes Courtemanche walked in in uniform. 'Coffee, Addie?'

'Sorry, Wes. I just cleaned out the pots.'

'I have a perfectly nice Mr. Coffee in my kitchen.'

Jack stuck the mop in the bucket and inadvertently knocked it over. A small flood spread beneath Wes's feet. 'Sorry,' Jack murmured, hurrying to swab the spill.

'Even if I wasn't so tired, Wes, I couldn't. Chloe's asleep in the back, and I have to get her home.'

Wes didn't know what to say to that. 'Chloe,' he repeated.

'Yes.'

'You know, I've been blown off before, Addie . . . but never because of a ghost.'

None of your business, Jack thought to himself over and over. He pushed the mop over the black and white tiles in a smooth, easy rhythm.

The last surviving Brontë sister.

'C'mon, Addie.'

Not Emily.

'No, Wes. I can't.'

Not Jane.

From the corner of his eye, Jack saw Courtemanche reach for her, saw Addie back away.

Who is Charlotte?

He dropped the mop and wedged between Addie and Wes, pinning the policeman to the wall. 'She doesn't want to go with you.'

'Jack, don't!'

Wes shoved, sending Jack sprawling. 'I could throw your ass in jail for that.'

Jack did not move from where he'd fallen. Wes jammed his hat on his head and stormed out of the diner, furious. *Addie,* Jack thought. *I did this for Addie.*

'Are you crazy?' She leaned down so that her face was level with his, her eyes hard and cold. 'He's a policeman, Jack. He can make a small-business owner's life miserable. And if that isn't bad enough, this is only going to make him try twice as hard to come after me next time.'

Jack hauled himself to his feet, yanked on his jacket, and for the second time that day left without telling Addie where he was going, or why.

Addie's strongest memory of Chloe took place underwater. Chloe had been seven the year Addie managed to scrape together enough money to take the two of them to the Caribbean. They stayed in a tiny rental house that was sixteen giant Mother-May-I steps from the beach. Palm fronds batted against the peeling pink shutters, and every morning on the sand there would be a new coconut.

One afternoon, Addie watched Chloe streaking back and forth beneath the water, as if she were logging mileage. 'What are you doing?'

'I'm a mermaid. Come and watch.'

And so Addie had waded in with her daughter's scuba mask. Underwater, Chloe wriggled: legs tight, hips undulating, as her bright blond hair streamed out behind her. Through the ripples of the water Addie could see the sun quivering like the yolk of an egg. Suddenly Chloe turned to face her, eyes wide, hair snaking soft about her face, arms blued by the shadows of the sea.

Addie could remember being a kid in the pool at the Y, pretending that she was a mermaid, too. There were moments she was certain it had happened – that her legs had turned into a scaled tail, that her lungs could take in water, that the wide thighs of women in the water aerobics class had thickened into pillars of coral. Beneath the water, the world was a different place, and you could be anything you wanted to be. Beneath the water, you moved slowly, so slowly you might never have to grow up.

On the day that Chloe died, the nurses had let Addie sit with her body for an hour, alone in the hospital room. Addie had tucked the sheets tight around Chloe's still legs. She had witnessed those thin limbs going blue from lack of oxygen; she had seen Chloe's cheeks and temples glisten wet from the spots where her own tears had fallen – and she'd thought, *You are a mermaid, baby.*

She'd thought, *Wait for me.*

The neurologists at the hospital had never seen anything quite like it – a man with significant damage in the aftermath of a stroke suddenly get up and start the day as if nothing had happened. But the nurses had been standing right there: Stuart Hollings, who could not speak or move an entire side of his body, had awakened asking for breakfast . . . and then threatened to leave when it didn't arrive fast enough.

Three hours after finishing his bacon, eggs, wheat toast, and neurological exams, Stuart's doctors pronounced him well enough to recuperate at home.

It was standard procedure at the SFPD to alert all duty officers about potential problems . . . including felons who had recently moved to town, although in the past this had never been an issue.

There was a small piece of Charlie – the piece that would probably have gotten him tossed out of law school, had he decided to attend – that hated this part of his job. It seemed to him that if you planted the seed of doubt in people's minds, they were more likely to take a look at new growth and yank it out by its roots as a potential weed, when it could very well have turned into something as harmless as a daisy.

On the other hand, St. Bride just might drag off a local high school girl and assault her, in which case Charlie would wish he'd set up a frigging billboard.

He began to type a memo on his laptop, one that would be distributed that same day through internal mail. He'd barely gotten through the header when his secretary opened the door. 'Dispatch just got a call. You supposed to be at the district court?'

'Ah, shoot.' He'd completely forgotten an arraignment.

Hurrying to the door, he decided he'd get the St. Bride memo out when he came back; it would be there along with the other 200 things on his to-do list.

Unfortunately, his secretary didn't know that. So when she came in later to lay a fax on Charlie's desk and saw the computer still on, she shut it off. And when Charlie returned to the courthouse, he had completely forgotten about Jack St. Bride.

Hailey McCourt could not read the words in her textbook because they were tap-dancing on the page. She slid her ponytail holder out of her hair and tied it up a little less tightly. Her mom got migraines . . . maybe she was predisposed to inheriting them. But God, of all days to find that out! As long as it waited until after soccer tryouts, then Hailey didn't care if she dropped dead in the locker room.

Mr. O'Donnell asked her to put last night's homework on the board, some horrendous trigonometry proof. Hailey swallowed and stood up, trying to find her center before she walked to the front of the room. But she stumbled on a desk, collapsing on top of the kid sitting in it.

There were a few titters, and the girl she'd fallen on gave her a dirty look. Finally, Hailey reached a spot just behind Mr. O'Donnell, who was busy collecting papers. She tried to pick up the chalk, but every time she did, it slipped out of her fingers. This time, the whole class snickered.

'Ms. McCourt,' the teacher said, 'we don't have time for this today.'

She swiped for the chalk, holding it primitively, as if her hand was no better than a paw. Then she looked up.

The classroom was upside down.

She was standing, all right, and the blackboard was in front of her. But her feet rested on the ceiling, and the kids in the class, behind her, were suspended, feet first from their seats.

She must have made a sound, because Mr. O'Donnell approached. 'Hailey,' he said quietly, 'do you need to see the nurse?'

The hell with soccer. The hell with everything. Hailey felt tears spring to her eyes. 'Yes,' she whispered.

She turned and fled, forgetting about her books and her knapsack. She suddenly didn't fit into this world, and she had no idea how to move in it with grace. That was Hailey McCourt's last thought before she walked directly into the door frame and knocked herself unconscious.

Unlike many of the houses in Salem Falls, which were close together, Addie's sat all by itself in the woods up a long, winding driveway. Tiny and neat with weathered shingles and a green roof, the little cape seemed to suit her. Smoke rose from the chimney to cut a signature across the night sky. Set off in the yard, in a moonlit mud puddle, was a rusty swing set.

Jack sat on a curved rubber seat. The racket that came when he swung back and forth was painful, like old bones being brought to life. Surely, inside, Addie was listening.

When the door opened, Jack watched feelings chase across her face – hope, as she turned to the swing set; disappointment, as she realized he was not her daughter; curiosity, as she wondered what had brought him here.

As she approached, Jack saw a final emotion: relief. 'Where have you been?'

Jack shrugged. 'I'm sorry about not showing up for work today.'

Even in the dim light, Jack saw Addie blush. 'Well, I asked for it. I should never have treated you the way I did the other night. I know you were only doing what you thought was right.'

Jack sucked in a deep breath, using it to force out the explanation lodged in his chest. 'There's something I need to tell you, Addie.'

'No . . . I think I ought to talk first.' She stood in front of him, trailing the toes of her boots in the mud. 'That day at Stuart's . . . you asked me what happened to Chloe.'

Jack went very still, the way he would have if a rare butterfly suddenly landed a foot in front of him. 'I know she's dead,'

Addie confessed. 'I may say or do differently, but I know.' She set her swing rocking slightly. 'She woke up one morning and she had a sore throat. That's it – just a sore throat, the same thing a hundred other kids get. Her fever wasn't even past ninety-nine. And I . . . I had to work that day. So I stuck her upstairs at my dad's on the couch, with cartoons on TV, while I waitressed. I figured if it was a virus, it would go away. If it was strep, I'd make a doctor's appointment after the lunch crunch.' Addie lowered her face, her profile edged in silver. 'I should have taken her in right away. I just didn't think . . . she was that sick.'

'Bacterial meningitis,' Jack murmured.

'She died at 5:07. I remember, because the news was coming on TV, and I thought, *What could they possibly tell me about the world gone bad that is more awful than this?'* Finally, she met Jack's eyes. 'I go a little crazy sometimes when it comes to Chloe. I know she's never going to eat the sandwich I set out for her at the diner, not anymore. But I need to put it there. And I know she's never going to get in my way again when I'm serving plates, but I wish she would . . . so I pretend that she does.'

'Addie –'

'Even when I try my hardest, I can't remember exactly what her smile looked like. Or if the color of her hair was more gold or more yellow. It gets worse . . . harder . . . every year. I lost her once,' Addie said brokenly. 'I can't stand to lose her all over again.'

'A doctor might not have caught it in time, Addie. Not even if you'd brought Chloe in that morning.'

'I was her mother. It was my job to make it better.'

Jack repeated what she'd said to him. 'You were only doing what you thought was right.'

But she didn't answer. She stared, instead, at the ridge of burned skin on his palm that would turn into a scar. Slowly, giving him time to pull away, Addie kneeled and bent over Jack's hand. Kissed it. He couldn't help it; he flinched.

Immediately, she drew back. 'It still hurts.'

Jack nodded. 'A little.'

'Where?'

He touched his heart, unable to speak.

When Addie brushed her lips over his chest, Jack felt his body sing. He closed his eyes, terrified to let himself wrap his arms around her, even more terrified that she would pull away. In the end, he did nothing but let her lean against him while his arms remained at his sides. 'Better?' Addie murmured, the word burning into his sweater.

'Yes,' Jack answered. 'Perfect.'

April 2000
Salem Falls, New Hampshire

As Gillian watched her father schmooze on his office phone, words dripping from his lips like oil, she wondered what it would be like to shoot him in the head.

His brains would splatter the white carpet. His secretary, an older woman who always looked like she was choking on a plum, would probably have a heart attack. Well, that was all too violent, too obvious, Gilly thought. More like she'd poison him slowly, mixing one of his precious drugs into his food, until one day he simply didn't wake up.

Gilly grinned at this, and her father caught her eye and smiled back. He cupped his hand over the phone. 'One more minute,' he whispered, and winked.

It came over Gilly so quick, sometimes: the feeling that she was going to explode, that she was too big for her own skin, as if anger had swelled so far and fast inside her that it choked the back of her throat. Sometimes it made her want to put her fist through glass; other times, it made her cry a river. It was not something she could talk about with her friends, because what if she was the only freak who felt this way? Maybe she could have confided in her mother . . . but then, she had not had a mother for years and years.

'There!' her father said triumphantly, hanging up the phone. He slung an arm around her shoulders, and Gillian was enveloped by the scents she would always associate with her childhood: wood smoke and cinnamon and thin Cuban cigars. She turned in to the smell, eyes closing in comfort. 'What do you say we swing through the plant? You know how everyone likes to see you.'

What he meant was that he liked to show off his daughter. Gilly always felt self-conscious walking through the line, nodding at the gap-toothed workers who smiled politely at her but all the while were thinking, correctly, that they made less in a week than Gillian got for allowance money.

They entered the manufacturing part of the operation. Noise ricocheted around her, huge pistons calibrated meticulously, so that mixtures would be infallible. 'We're making Preventa today,' her father yelled in her ear. 'Emergency contraception.'

He led her to a man wearing protective headphones and circulating around the floor. 'Hello, Jimmy. You remember my little girl?'

'Sure. Hey, Gillian.'

'Give me a second, honey,' Amos said, and then he began to ask Jimmy questions about stockpiling and shipments.

Gillian watched the bump and grind of the machines measuring out the active ingredients: levonorgestrel and ethinyl estradiol. The device she was standing beside funneled newly formed pills through a narrow slot at its neck, counting them into batches that would be sealed dose by dose into childproof packaging.

It took only a few seconds to dart her hand into the sorting tray and grab some.

Her hand was still in her pocket, buried deep with her secret, when Amos turned. 'Have I bored you to tears?'

Gilly smiled at her father. 'No,' she assured him. 'Not yet.'

In retrospect, Addie realized that the whole event should have been much more terrifying: breaking into a cemetery near midnight, on an evening when the moon was a great bloodshot eye in the sky. But suddenly it did not matter that she was trying to gain access to a graveyard in the darkest part of the night, that she was going to see her daughter's grave for the first time in seven years. All she knew at that moment was that someone would be with her when she took this monumental step.

Heat swam from the ground, old souls snaking between

Addie's legs. 'When I was in college,' Jack said, 'I used to study in the cemetery.'

She did not know what she was more surprised by: the nature of the revelation or the fact that Jack had made it at all. 'Didn't you have a library?'

'Yeah. But in the graveyard it was quieter. I'd bring my books, and sometimes a picnic lunch, and –'

'A lunch? That's sick. That's –'

'Is this it?' Jack asked, and Addie realized that they stood in front of Chloe's grave.

The last time she had seen it, it was bare earth, covered with roses and funeral baskets from well-wishers who could not offer explanations and so instead gave flowers. There was a headstone, now, too; white marble: Chloe Peabody, 1979–1989. Addie turned her face up to Jack's. 'What do you think happens . . . you know . . . after you die?'

Jack stuffed his hands in the pockets of his coat and shrugged, silent.

'I used to hope that if we had to give up our old life, we'd get a new one.'

A huff of breath fell in the air between them, Jack's answer.

'Then . . . after . . . I didn't hope that at all. I didn't want Chloe to be anybody else's little girl.' Addie gently stepped off a rectangle around the grave. 'But she has to be somewhere, doesn't she?'

Jack cleared his throat. 'The Inuit say that the stars are holes in heaven. And every time we see the people we loved shining through, we know they're happy.'

She watched Jack pull two unlikely blossoms from his pocket to lay on the grave. The bright heads of the chives that Delilah grew on the windowsill were a brilliant splash of purple against the headstone.

This time of night, the sky was flung wide open, stars spread like a story across the horizon. 'Those Inuit,' Addie said, tears running down her cheeks. 'I hope they're right.'

* * *

Addie's hands shook as she walked Jack to the apartment he shared with her father. Did he feel it, too, every time their shoulders bumped up against each other? When he came into a room Addie was already in, did he notice the air squeezing more tightly around them? This was new to her, this sense that her bones were sized all wrong in the confines of her body. This feeling that you could be in the company of a man and not want to turn tail and run.

They reached the top of the stairs. 'Well,' Jack said, 'see you in the morning.' His hand moved to the doorknob.

'Wait,' Addie blurted out, and covered his fingers with her own. As she expected, he stilled. 'Thanks. For coming tonight.'

Jack nodded, then turned to the door again.

'Can I ask you something?'

'If it's about fixing the insulation on the receiving door, I meant to –'

'Not that,' Addie said. 'I wanted to know if you'd kiss me.'

She saw the surprise in his eyes. Apprehension rose from her skin like perfume.

'No,' Jack gently answered.

Addie could not breathe, she'd made such a fool of herself. Cheeks burning, she took a step backward, and came up against an unforgiving wall.

'I won't kiss you,' Jack added, 'but you can kiss me.'

'I – I can?' She had the odd sense that Jack was as uncertain about this as she was.

'Do you want to?'

'No,' Addie said, as she came up on her toes so that her lips could touch his.

It was all Jack could do to not embrace her. To let her trace the seam of his mouth, to open and feel her tongue press against his. He did not touch her, not when her hands lighted on his chest, not when her hair tickled his neck, not when he realized she tasted of coffee and loneliness.

This is the worst thing you could do, he told himself. *This is going to get you in trouble. Again.*

But he let Addie play the Fates, spinning out the length of the kiss and cutting it when she saw fit. Then he let himself into Roy's apartment, intent on crawling into bed and forgetting the last ten minutes of his life. He had just begun to cross the darkened living room when a light snapped on. Roy sat on the couch, in his robe and pajamas. 'You hurt my daughter,' he said, 'and I will kill you in your sleep.'

'I didn't touch your daughter.'

'Bullshit. I saw you kiss her, right through the keyhole.'

'You *watched?* What are you, some kind of peeping Tom?'

'Well, what are *you?* Some kind of gigolo? You get yourself hired and boink the business owner, so that you can steal her money in the middle of the night and run?'

'First off, *she* hired *me*. And second, even if I was stupid enough to do something like that, don't you think I would have targeted the jewelry store owner or a banker?'

'Addie's better looking than any of them.'

Jack unzipped his coat and threw it angrily on a chair. 'Not that it's any of your business, but Addie kissed *me*.'

'She . . . she did?'

'Is it so hard to believe?'

The old man stood up, a smile playing over his face as he started back toward his bedroom. 'Actually,' he mused, 'it is.'

Jordan strolled through the doors of the Carroll County Superior Court, his eyes falling into the familiar routine of scanning rooms to see which ones were involved in hearings and skimming over the sorry souls awaiting their fifteen minutes of testimonial fame. He felt naked in his Oxford cloth shirt and pullover sweater – he who used to wear Armani to try cases.

It was not that he'd ever planned on leaving the law permanently; he had just wanted to get away from it for a little while, and Salem Falls was as good a place as any to lose oneself. He had the money to rest on his laurels for a year or two, after those last few cases he'd tried down near Bainbridge, which had been particularly enervating. Each direct examination and cross-examination grew harder and harder to force from his throat, until Jordan realized that his job had become a noose, notching tighter with each client he defended.

Maybe it hadn't been his job, though. Maybe it had been his relationship with his private investigator.

If anyone had told Jordan ten years ago that he'd want to get married again, he would have chuckled. If anyone had told him that the woman he chose would turn him down, he'd have laughed himself into a hernia. Yet that was exactly what Selena had done. Turned out her best investigative work had targeted Jordan himself – revealing human weaknesses he would rather never have learned.

He made his way to Bernie Davidson's office. The clerk of the court was always a useful person to know. He was responsible for scheduling cases, and access to that came in handy when you really wanted to take a trip to Bermuda in March. But more than that, he had the ear of every district judge, which meant that things could get done much more quickly than through the normal channels – a motion slipped right into a judge's hands, an emergency bail hearing stuffed into a jammed calendar. Jordan knocked once, then let himself inside, grinning widely when Bernie nearly fell out of his chair.

'Holy Christ – if it isn't the ghost of Jordan McAfee!'

Jordan shook the other man's hand. 'How you doing, Bernie?'

'Better than you,' he said, taking in Jordan's worn clothes and ragged haircut. 'I heard a rumor you moved to Hawaii.'

Jordan slipped into a chair across from Bernie's desk. 'How come those are the ones that are never true?'

'Where are you living now?'

'Salem Falls.'

'Quiet there, huh?'

He shrugged. 'Guess that's what I was looking for.'

Bernie was too sharp to miss the hollowness of Jordan's voice. 'And now?'

Jordan concentrated on scraping a piece of lint off his sweater. After a moment, he lifted his head. 'Now?' he said. 'I think I'm starting to crave a little bit of noise.'

Addie stuck her head in through the back door of the kitchen. 'Hey, Jack, can you give me a hand?'

He looked up through a haze of steam from the open dishwasher door. 'Sure.'

It was cold outside, and the mud sucked at the soles of his sneakers. Addie disappeared behind a high fence that enclosed the garbage bins. 'I'm having a little trouble with the latch,' she said. Once Jack had followed her inside to check the mechanism, she snaked her arms around him. 'Hi,' she said into the weave of his shirt.

He smiled. 'Hi.'

'How are you?'

'Great. You?'

Addie smiled wider. 'Greater.'

'Well, see you,' Jack teased, grinning as Addie hung onto him for all she was worth. Bubbles rose inside him, the carbonation of happiness. When was the last time someone had so badly wanted him to stay put? 'Is there really a problem with the latch?'

'Absolutely,' Addie confessed. 'I'm unhinged.'

She kissed him, then, pulling his arms around her waist to hold her. They were wrapped tight as a monkey's paw, secluded from public view by the walls of the fence. The stench of refuse rose around them like a dank jungle, but all Jack could smell was the vanilla that seemed to come from the curve of Addie's neck. He closed his eyes and thought if he could hold onto one moment for the next fifty years, this might be it.

Addie burrowed closer, and the movement set her off balance. They went tumbling backward, knocking over a row of metal garbage cans. The racket scattered the few birds who were whispering like old gossips about the two of them. They swooped over Jack and Addie, picking at spilled chicken bones and vegetable peels curled into tiny tornadoes, cawing disapproval.

Jack took the brunt of the fall. 'This gives a whole new meaning to the term *trashy romance*.'

Addie was laughing, but at his words, she stopped. 'Is that what this is?' she asked, a child standing in the presence of a rainbow and afraid to blink even once, for fear that it might be gone when she opened her eyes. 'Are you my romance?'

Before Jack could answer, the door to the fence – unlatched – burst open, and he found himself staring into the single black eye of a revolver.

'Jesus, Wes, put that thing away!' Addie pushed herself off Jack and got to her feet, dusting off her uniform.

'I was walking by for a cup of coffee, and I heard the bins fall. I figured it might be a robber.'

'A *robber?* In the trash bins? Honestly, Wes. This is Salem Falls, not the set of *Law and Order*.'

Wes scowled, annoyed because Addie didn't appreciate his daring rescue attempt. 'You sure you're all right?'

'Nothing deodorant soap won't cure. I knocked over the trash can, that's all. Last time I checked, that wasn't even a misdemeanor.'

But Wes wasn't listening. He was staring at Jack, who'd been pulled upright by Addie and was still grasping her hand. Neither one seemed inclined to let go, and even more strange, neither one seemed to realize they were holding onto each other.

'Oh,' Wes said, his voice very soft. 'It's like that.'

'He works in a diner,' Whitney said, drawing on her straw until it made a slurping noise. 'What would your father think if he knew you were hot for a guy nearly his own age who washes glasses for a living?'

Gillian drew a fat *J* in the grease on her plate. 'Money isn't everything, Whit.'

'Easy to say when you've got it.'

Gilly did not hear her. She scowled, wondering why Addie had been the only employee to come into the restaurant part of the diner. If she didn't even *see* Jack, her spell would never work. Gillian lifted her elbow and deliberately knocked over a milkshake. 'We need some napkins over here!'

Addie sighed at the mess but hurried over with a packet of napkins and a Wet-Wipe. 'Let me get someone to mop the floor.'

Jack came out then, all six-foot-two inches of him. When he bent to swab beneath the table, Gilly saw the crooked part in his golden hair, a spot she had a sudden, urgent desire to kiss. 'I'm so sorry,' she said. 'I can clean it up.'

'It's my job.'

'Well, at least let me help.' Gilly reached for the napkins and this time knocked over Meg's Coke. Jack jumped backward, the crotch of his pants soaked.

'Oh my gosh.' Gilly pressed the wad of napkins high against Jack's thigh, until he stiffly removed her hand.

'I've got it,' he said, and left for the men's room.

The minute he was gone, the girls began to whisper: 'Jesus, Gilly, did you have to give him a hand job right in the middle of the diner?'

'You knocked my drink over on purpose . . . You'd better pay for a new one!'

'He does look a little like Brad Pitt . . .'

'I'm going to the bathroom,' Gilly announced. As she reached the restrooms, Jack came out of the one on the right. 'Sorry about that again,' she said cheerfully, but he didn't even answer. He sidled past her, trying hard not to touch her in any way. Well, that didn't matter. He wouldn't be able to keep his hands off her once she cast her spell.

Gilly crept into the men's room, fascinated at the site of the urinal with its smelly little cake in the bottom. The sink was still dripping water. Gilly shut the nozzle more tightly, then fished from the trash can the topmost piece of paper toweling. Surely this was the one that Jack had used; it was still damp. She tore off a square from the part she imagined had touched his skin. Then she opened up her little purse.

Inside was a scroll of paper on which she'd written JACK ST. BRIDE, a red rose, a white rose, and a piece of pink ribbon. She tucked the piece of toweling inside the scroll and rolled it up again. Then she took a Swiss army knife her father had given her the year she was ten and sliced each rose in half lengthwise. She placed together a white half and a red half, sandwiching the scroll in between, and wrapped them tightly with the ribbon.

'One to seek him,' Gilly whispered. 'One to find him. One to bring him, one to bind him. Whoever keeps these roses two, the sweetest love will come to you.'

She turned on the tap – it really should have been a stream, but this was all the running water she could find – and held the head of the combined rose beneath it, then tossed the remaining petals into the trash.

'What are you doing?'

Gilly almost jumped a foot to find Addie Peabody there. 'Washing my hands,' she said, trying to hide the posy.

'In the men's room?'

'Is it? I didn't look at the sign.' She could tell Addie wasn't buying a single word, so she decided to go on the defensive. 'What are *you* doing in the men's bathroom?'

'I *own* it. And I clean it hourly.' Addie narrowed her eyes. 'Whatever you were doing in here, just finish up and leave . . . What's that?'

Gilly quickly tucked her hand behind her back. 'Nothing.'

'If it's nothing, why are you trying to hide it from me?' Addie grabbed Gilly's arm and pried open her fingers. 'I suggest you and your friends pay your bill and leave.' Without even glancing at it, she absently slipped the posy into the wide pocket of her apron and left Gillian standing alone.

* * *

Wes had returned from the Do-Or-Diner that day on a mission. The reason Jack St. Bride looked so familiar was because Wes had seen him at the station. Now, a man could come to the police station for a hundred things – but the memory stuck in Wes's mind like a thorn. He knew better than to run a records check without reason, and he'd probably have to answer to Charlie Saxton about it when the detective checked the NCIC log – but he told himself that he was doing this for Addie's safety.

It had nothing to do with the fact that, in a heartbeat, he'd want her for himself.

In a town like Salem Falls, Wes had plenty of free time on his hands between 911 calls. He dispatched an ambulance to the old folk's home, and then typed St. Bride's name into the SPOTS terminal, which had the capability to run records throughout the country.

Wes lifted his gaze to the screen, eyes widening. 'Oh, Addie,' he murmured.

'Turn around,' Amos Duncan commanded.

Gillian pivoted in a slow circle, her black skirt flaring around her thighs, the rhinestone clips winking in her hair.

'That's a better outfit. But the skirt's too short.'

She rolled her eyes. 'Daddy, you say that even when I wear ankle length.'

'I just don't want any of those football players getting ideas.'

'As if,' Gilly said under her breath, thinking that the very last person in the world she'd ever let touch her was a Salem Falls jock. 'Meg's dad is chaperoning, anyway.'

'That's good. There's something comforting about knowing your daughter's best friend has relatives in law enforcement.'

The teakettle began to whistle in the kitchen. 'I'll get it,' Gillian said.

'I can make my own cup of tea.'

'But I want to.' She tossed a smile back over her shoulder. 'It's the least I can do, considering I'm leaving you here all alone to mope around.'

Amos laughed. 'Maybe I can find something to do to pass the time. Like count the number of tiles in the shower stall.'

'But you did that the last time I went out at night,' Gilly joked. She went into the kitchen, took a mug from a cherry cabinet, then placed a strainer filled with leaves of her father's favorite blend of Darjeeling. Before she closed the little silver hatch, she reached into her blouse and added several of the pills from her father's factory.

Ten minutes later, when she opened the strainer, there was nothing left of them. She carried the mug to the library, where her father was waiting.

'That's what you're wearing?' Jordan said, looking up from the paper.

Thomas took a swig of milk from the carton in the refrigerator, wiping his mouth with the back of his hand. 'What's wrong with it?'

'Well, nothing, I guess, given the fact that you're *acting* like a total slob, too.' Jordan frowned at his son's backward baseball hat and faded jersey, at the pants riding so low on his hips they seemed in danger of sliding down. 'When I was your age, a guy would dress up for a dance.'

'Yeah, and then you'd hook your team up to the buckboard to drive over to the little red schoolhouse.'

'Very funny. I'm talking about a nice shirt. A tie, maybe.'

'A tie? Christ, if I walked in wearing one they'd lynch me with it. They'd think I was one of those Jesus freaks who go around handing out pamphlets in the cafeteria.'

'They do?' Jordan asked. 'During school hours?'

'Careful, Dad, your civil liberties are showing.'

Jordan folded the newspaper and stood up. 'Who's driving tonight?'

'Don't worry. I've got a ride.'

'Oh, yeah?' Jordan smiled. 'Did Chelsea Abrams fall under your considerable McAfee charm and decide to take you?'

'No, I got someone else to go with me.' As soon as the words were out of his mouth, Thomas wished them back. The gleam in his father's eye was too strong.

'Details?' When Thomas shrugged, Jordan raised a brow. 'You might as well give up now. I weasel information out of people for a living.'

Thomas was saved by the doorbell. 'See you, Dad. Don't wait up.'

'Now hang on.' Jordan dogged his heels. 'I want to see her face. If I can't live vicariously through you, what's the point of having a teenage son?' He grinned at Thomas's abject humiliation. 'So? Is she hot?'

The door opened before Thomas could answer. Standing there was a six-foot black woman with a model's body and anger swimming in her eyes. 'You certainly used to think so, Jordan,' said Selena Damascus, and she pushed her way inside.

The first thing that happened: Words began to swim on the page in front of Amos Duncan. About then, he noticed that the room was warmer and that every time he lifted his eyes toward his daughter, who sat waiting for her ride to the school dance, he felt queasy. A moment later, he barely reached the bathroom before vomiting all over the floor.

'Daddy!' Gillian cried, standing in the doorway.

He was kneeling in his own puke, his eyes and nose running the way they did after a violent heave, and the only thought caught in his mind was that he was going to do it again. This time, he retched over the bowl, then rested his head against the porcelain.

He felt Gilly come up behind him; then place a cool, damp hand towel on the back of his neck. Amos vomited again, his belly a great, aching Möbius strip. In the distance, he heard the doorbell. 'You . . . go. I'll be fine,' he rasped.

'No,' Gilly answered firmly. 'There's no way I'm leaving you like this.'

Amos was vaguely aware of her moving away, of the murmur of voices. The next thing he knew, he was lying on his back in his bed, wearing a clean T-shirt and pajama bottoms. Gillian sat on a chair beside the bed, dressed in jeans and a sweater. 'How are you doing?'

'The . . . dance.'

'I told Chelsea to go without me.' She squeezed his hand. 'Who else was going to take care of you?'

'Who else?' Amos said, stroking her wrist, as he drifted back to sleep.

'You're telling me you invited *Selena* to the school dance?' Jordan was yelling by now, an ugly vein pounding in the center of his forehead. His son, and his former private investigator. His former lover.

He and Selena had always worked well together – when the situation in question was a professional one. Their minds ran on the same track; their blood heated to a boil at the thought of a challenging case. But all that had changed a year ago in Bainbridge, New Hampshire, when Jordan had defended a boy accused of murdering his teenage girlfriend. He'd done the unprecedented – had let his job get under his skin. And the moment that line had blurred, so had the one between him and Selena. That case had almost killed him; Selena had been the one who nearly struck the final blow.

'I didn't have anything to do tonight,' Selena said, grinning at Thomas. 'I always promised him I'd go to the prom, but then I heard about this Chelsea girl and realized desperate measures need to be taken. We're gonna show them, aren't we, Thomas? Can't be too many freshmen who'll show up with seventy-two inches of mouth-watering dark chocolate on their arm!'

'Can we back up? Can someone tell me how after months of no communication whatsoever, you managed to waltz back into our lives?'

'First things first,' Selena said. '*You* left *me* behind. Second, my whereabouts were never a secret. You know damn well I've never had a publicly listed residential phone number. It seems to me that if you looked half as hard as you do to find evidence for acquittal, you could have found me in less than ten minutes.'

'That's about what it took,' Thomas agreed, shrugging. 'Over the Internet.'

Sinking down on the couch, Jordan covered his face with his hands. 'You're twenty-three years older than Thomas.'

'God, Dad, this isn't a *date* date. Is that why you're losing it? You're jealous?'

'No, I am not jealous. I just can't imagine that bringing Selena to your school dance is any less jarring than, for example, wearing that tie we were talking about.'

Selena elbowed Thomas. 'Hermès silk can't move as smooth as I can on a dance floor – isn't that right?'

Thomas laughed. 'Just as long as you don't curse me if I dump you for Chelsea.'

'Honey, are you kidding? That's the whole point.'

Jordan stood. 'Okay. Okay! If you two want to act like . . . like *children,* be my guest. But I don't have to stand here and listen to the woman who ruined my life cavort with my son as if nothing ever happened in the first place!' He stormed out of the living room, and a moment later the door to his bedroom slammed shut.

'Who's acting like the child?' said Thomas.

Selena smirked. 'I didn't think we were cavorting, per se. Did you?'

'Not in the least.'

She lifted Thomas's arm and crooked it so that she could slip her hand through. 'You didn't tell him I'd be sleeping on the couch tonight, did you?'

Grinning, Thomas shook his head. 'Nope.'

'Do you think you ought to mention it? So he has time to work through his fit before we come home?'

Thomas nodded, and then on second thought, shook his head. 'A little mystery never hurts,' he said.

* * *

Wes knew that some of the officers who pulled shifts at the high school dances liked to pull low their hats and stare at the nubile girls from beneath the brims – the fluid curves and candy-glitter makeup a guilty pleasure. In his opinion, though, the ones that bore watching were the young boys. They'd push and shove at each other with their thick, sloped shoulders, take slight over whose foot fell first on a block of brick, raise their voices just to be heard – these were children's minds, trapped in the bodies of men.

'Ten bucks says that kid in the Abercrombie & Fitch hat throws a punch before the hour's out,' Wes said, leaning toward Charlie Saxton. It was strange to see him decked out like an officer; usually, as the squad's detective, he wore plain clothes beneath his shield.

'Last time I checked, Wes, betting was against the law in New Hampshire.'

'It's an *expression.*'

Charlie glanced dismissively at him. 'Thank you, Mr. Pop Culture.'

'Hey, it's the patrol officers who know what's really going on in this town.' He was bursting with his knowledge, desperate to tell. 'You ever hear of a Jack St. Bride?'

Charlie sighed. 'Aw, *goddammit.* Yeah, I have. He came in to register.'

'He did?'

'Yeah. And I fucked up. I was going to send out a memo to everyone and somehow lost track of it.'

The wind had gone out of Wes's sails. 'So you knew about him.'

'Yeah.'

'Sexual assault.'

Charlie nodded. 'It was plea-bargained down from rape.'

'And you know that he's living in Salem Falls now.'

'Ex-cons have to live somewhere. You can't round 'em up and stick 'em on a reservation.'

'We don't have to roll out a welcome mat, either,' Wes said.

Charlie turned, shielding the conversation from public view. 'I didn't just hear you say that, you understand?'

Chagrined, Wes nodded. Charlie outranked him. 'I still think people have the right to know someone's a jerk before they get involved with him.'

Charlie stifled a smile. 'Gotta admit, that policy could come in handy.'

'I'm glad you think this is so funny. Let's see how hard you're laughing the first time one of these girls is sitting across from you with her clothes torn, crying because she happened to have the bad luck to cross paths with St. Bride.'

Charlie opened his mouth to respond, but the boy in the Abercrombie & Fitch hat punched one of the other kids. 'Ten bucks,' he murmured, and followed Wes through a sea of slack-jawed teens to do his job.

Thomas could feel the weight of a hundred pairs of eyes on his shoulders as he rocked back and forth on the dance floor with Selena. She stood a full head taller than he, which made it awkward, since his face was pressed up against her breasts, and he was a *guy* after all, so of course he couldn't get that fact out of his mind, even if it *was* just Selena.

But nobody else knew that. A senior – one who'd stuffed him in a locker for the hell of it last month – had come over to ask if that was really Tyra Banks. Another wanted to know the going rate for an escort service these days. But that wasn't nearly as rewarding as knowing that Chelsea was watching. He'd seen her standing off to the side of the gym with two of the three girls she usually hung with, the look on her face almost comical.

Thomas lifted his face to Selena's. 'If you kiss me, I'll give you all the money in my college fund.'

Selena laughed out loud. 'Thomas, honey, Bill Gates couldn't pay me enough to kiss you here in the middle of a dance floor. On the one hand, see all those cops? I'm not about to be locked up for statutory rape. On the other hand, it's just plain creepy. You're like a nephew or something.'

The music ended, a faint sappy warbling. Selena patted

Thomas's cheek. 'How about you stay here and make up stories about how you met me, while I get us some punch?'

She walked off, her perfect ass twitching beneath the silk tube of her dress. And that wasn't even the most attractive part of Selena – there was her sense of humor, her sharp mind, and the way she'd yell at schoolyard bullies who killed slugs for the hell of it or kicked sand up into the faces of toddlers. Shit, Thomas thought. If he'd been his father, he would have chained her to the bed.

'Thomas.'

He wheeled around to find Chelsea standing there, and the floor dropped out from beneath him. 'Hi,' he said.

Before he could follow that up with a coherent comment, Selena returned with two dripping cups. 'Disgusting stuff,' she muttered. 'Enough sugar in it to kill a horse.' She handed one cup to Thomas, then smiled brightly at the girl beside him.

'I'm Chelsea Abrams,' she said, sticking out her hand.

'Selena Damascus. Charmed.'

'Apparently,' Chelsea whispered beneath her breath.

The DJ resumed his post at the head of the gym, and music pulsed around them again. 'So,' Thomas said, 'would you like to dance?'

'Love to,' Selena said, at the same moment that Chelsea answered, 'Sure.'

Chelsea reddened and stepped back. 'I'm sorry . . . I thought . . .'

'I did,' Thomas assured her. 'I was.'

'You two go on ahead,' Selena demurred. 'I want to finish this drink first.' Grimacing, she took a large gulp and smiled over the edge of the cup.

But Chelsea shook her head. 'My friends . . . they're waiting for me,' she said, and darted away.

Thomas's chest ached as he watched her navigate the crowd. He would have given anything to touch her hand and lead her onto the dance floor, to see her smile at something he'd said, to feel his pulse speed up at the possibility of what might happen next. And yet here he was once again, the victim of another missed opportunity. He tried to pretend that he was perfectly fine, schooling his face into nonchalance before turning to Selena.

But it was there in his eyes, this wish that things had turned out differently. Selena did a double take, as if she could not quite believe what she was seeing.

'What?' Thomas asked.

'Nothing.' Selena sipped her drink. 'For a moment there, you just looked so much like your father.'

When the door of the diner opened after hours, Jack glanced up in surprise. He'd assumed Addie had locked it, and he felt a quick flash of anger – who dared to interrupt the time he had alone with this woman?

The man who entered was a regular trying very hard not to appear as drunk as he actually was. 'Ms. Peabody,' he said, 'can you help me mainline some caffeine?'

Jack stepped forward. 'I'm sorry, but we're –'

Suddenly Addie's small hand was on his arm, and he lost the power of speech. 'I think we can manage that, Mr. McAfee.' She gestured imperceptibly toward the man, so that Jack would understand. The guy was certainly having a rough night; that much was clear from the way his hair stood on end and his eyes sank into red-rimmed sockets, from the scent of despair that buzzed around him like a cloud of midges. 'It'll just be a minute.'

Characters in this literary work include the characters Christian, Faithful, and Evangelist.

Jordan glanced up at the sound of Alec Trebek's voice. *'The Biography of Jerry Falwell.'*

Addie grinned. 'Is he right, Jack?'

'No. It's *The Pilgrim's Progress.*'

When the answer was announced, Jordan laughed. 'Impressive.' He picked up the steaming mug of coffee Addie had given him. 'Tell me then, what great oeuvre includes the characters Spurned, Screwed, and Royally Fucked?'

Jack looked at Addie and blinked.

'That,' Jordan said, belching, 'would be the story of my life.' He took a healthy swig from his mug. 'No offense, Ms. Peabody, but women . . . God, they're like broken glass lying in the middle of the road. Cut a man to shreds before he realizes what's happened.'

'Only if you're intent on running us over,' Addie said dryly.

Jordan gestured toward Jack. 'You ever have trouble with women?'

'Some.'

'You see?'

Addie refilled Jordan's coffee cup. 'Where's your son tonight, Mr. McAfee?'

'School dance. And he took that goddamn piece of glass with him.'

'Piece of . . . glass?'

'The woman!' Jordan moaned. 'The one who ruined my life!'

'I'm going to call you a cab now, Mr. M,' Addie said.

Jack leaned his elbows on the counter. It turned out people truly did cry into their coffee cups. Worse, Jordan McAfee seemed to have no idea that he was doing it. 'What did she do to you?'

Jordan shrugged. 'She said no.'

At the words, a shudder ripped through Jack.

Suddenly, the door opened as Wes blustered in, his stint as a chaperone now finished. 'Addie, you got some coffee for a guy who's been forced to listen to rap for the past four –'

'We're closed,' Jack said.

Wes's eyes passed over Jordan and landed on Jack. 'Thank God you're not alone with him,' he said to Addie.

She smiled. 'Mr. McAfee may be a little tipsy, but he's not dangerous . . .'

'I'm not talking about McAfee.' He protectively closed his hands around her upper arms. 'You okay?'

'Fine,' she said, wrenching away.

'Oh, I get it. You'll let scum like St. Bride touch you, but not me.'

'Watch what you say, Wes,' Addie warned.

The policeman whirled toward Jack. 'You gonna let her fight your battles? Maybe you want to tell your *boss* what you didn't tell her the day she hired your sorry ass.'

For a moment, the only sound was Alec Trebek's voice: *With 8,891 points, Dan O'Brien holds the world record in this track and field event.* Jack felt the floor shift beneath his feet and thought, not for the first time, that life is in the details.

He could not bear to meet Addie's eyes – Addie, who had trusted him. 'I was in jail,' Jack admitted. 'For eight months.'

It was all coming together for her now – why Jack had surfaced from nowhere, why a man moving to a town would have only a box of possessions and the clothes on his back, why he did not talk about his past. Jack waited for her to speak, his own mouth dry as a desert.

'Tell her why,' Wes prodded.

But that, Jack wouldn't do.

'I'm sure if this is true, Jack can explain,' Addie said shakily.

'He raped a woman. You think there's any explanation for that?'

The room fell away, until all that was left was the small rectangle of silence that trapped both Jack and Addie. Her nostrils flared; her eyes were bright with disbelief. 'Jack?' she said softly, urging him to set Wes straight.

Jack knew the exact moment she realized that he wasn't going to answer.

Addie grabbed for her coat, slung over a counter chair. 'I have to go,' she managed, and she stumbled out the front door.

Jack started after her, and found a hand at his throat. 'Over my dead body,' Wes said quietly.

'Don't tempt me.'

The policeman's wrist cut into Jack's windpipe. 'Want to say that on the record, St. Bride?' Then, abruptly, Wes released him. 'Do us all a favor. Lock the door behind you; keep walking until you cross the town line.'

When Wes left, Jack sank down onto a banquette and buried his face in his hands. As a kid, his favorite toy had been a snow globe, that held a small town of gingerbread buildings and peppermint streets. He'd wanted so badly to live there that one day he'd smashed the glass ball – only to find that the houses were made of plaster, the candy stripes painted on. He had known that this existence he'd carved in Salem Falls was an illusion, that one day it would crack open just like that snow globe. But he'd hoped – God, he'd hoped – that it wouldn't just yet.

'They can't do that to you, you know.'

Jack had completely forgotten that Jordan McAfee was still here. 'Do what?'

'Run you out of town. Threaten you. You paid your debt to society for eight months; you're now free to join it again.'

'I didn't belong in jail.'

Jordan shrugged, as if he'd heard this a hundred times before. 'You just spent three-quarters of a year in a place because you *had* to. Don't you think you deserve to stay somewhere because you *want* to?'

'Maybe I *don't* want to.'

A pair of headlights swept the interior of the diner, the arriving cab. 'Well, I'm a pretty good judge of character. And that sure wasn't the story I got from the look you gave me when I interrupted your evening with a certain waitress.' Jordan set his empty coffee mug in the clean-up basin behind the counter. 'Thank Addie for me.'

'Mr. McAfee,' Jack asked. 'Would you mind if I shared your taxi?'

The light from the porch fell over him, brightening an unlikely halo around Jack's head. 'I didn't do it,' he said immediately. There was still a screen door between them, and Addie pressed one hand up against it.

Jack placed his own hand on the other side of the screen. Addie thought of jail and wondered if he had received visitors, with a wall between him and them, just like this.

'Wes told me everything,' she said. 'The records are computerized down at the station. He said you even came in to register as a sexual offender.'

'I had to. It was part of the plea bargain.'

There were tears in Addie's eyes. 'Innocent people don't get sent to jail.'

'*And children don't die*. Addie, you know better than anyone that the world doesn't always work the way it ought to.' Jack hesitated. 'Did you ever wonder why I'm never the one to reach for you? Why you're the one who kisses *me*, who takes *my* hand?'

'Why?'

'Because I don't ever want to be the man they all said I was. I don't want to be some animal, out of control. And I am afraid that once I touch you, really touch you, I won't be able to stop.' Jack turned his cheek, so that his lips brushed her palm through the wire screen. 'You have to believe me, Addie. I would never rape a woman.'

'I never thought they would, either.'

'Who?'

She lifted her face. 'The boys who did it to me.'

She had been sixteen, a straight-A student at Salem Falls High School. The editor of the school newspaper, with dreams of becoming a journalist. Deadlines often kept her working late, but because her parents were busy with the diner, she wasn't missed at home.

It was cold for April, so cold that when she closed the door behind her and struck off across the playing fields she wished she'd worn jeans instead of a thin skirt. Pulling her coat tight, she skirted the football field, heading toward town.

She heard their voices first – three letter athletes, seniors, who'd led the team to a state championship this year. Shy – brains didn't mix with jocks – she gave them a wide berth, pretending that she hadn't seen their bottle of Jack Daniels.

'Addie,' one of them said, and she was so surprised they knew her name that she turned.

'Come here for a second.'

She went over the way a bird hops toward food – cautious, a little hopeful, but ready to fly at the first movement of a human nearby. 'You remember that article you wrote on the last game of the season? You did a real nice job. Didn't she, you guys?'

The other boys nodded. There was something almost beautiful about them, with their flushed faces and the bright caps of their hair, like some strange breed she had read about but never really studied firsthand. 'Problem was, you spelled my name wrong.'

'I didn't.' Addie always checked everything; she was a stickler for detail.

The boy laughed. 'I may not be as smart as you, but I know how to spell my own name!' The others elbowed each other and snuffled laughter. 'Hey, you want a sip?' Addie shook her head. 'It'll warm you up . . .'

Gingerly, she took a drink. A comet, streaking down her throat – she coughed up most of it into the grass, her eyes tearing. 'Whoa there, Addie,' he said, bracing his arm around her. 'Take it easy, now.' His hand began to slide up and down. 'You know, you aren't nearly as skinny as you look walking around the halls.'

Addie tried to draw away. 'I've got to go.'

'First I want you to learn how to spell my name.'

As a compromise, it seemed fair. Addie nodded, and the boy beckoned her closer. 'It's a secret,' he whispered.

Playing along, she bent down, her ear near his lips. And felt his tongue slide inside.

She backed away, but his arms held her tight. 'Now you repeat it,' he said, and ground his mouth into hers.

Addie did not remember much after that. Except that there were three of them. That the bleachers, underneath, were painted blaze orange. That fear, in large doses, smells of sulfur. And that there is a place in you that you don't even know exists, where you can simply stand back and watch without feeling any pain.

'Did you never wonder about Chloe's father?' Addie asked.

Standing in her living room now, Jack swallowed around the block that had settled in his throat. 'Which one was it?'

'I don't know. I never wanted to find out. I figured after that, I deserved for her to be mine and only mine.'

'Why didn't you tell anyone?'

'Because I would have been branded as a slut. And because I'm not sure . . . I've never been sure . . . that they even remembered it happened.' Her voice hitched. 'Wish I had been so lucky. For years I've wondered what I did that made them do that to me.'

'You were in the wrong place at the wrong time,' Jack murmured. *We both were.*

For eight months, he'd hated the system, which gave women the benefit of the doubt. But seeing Addie – well, a million men could be locked up wrongfully, and it still couldn't make up for what had happened to her.

'Do they . . . live in town?'

'Going to slay my dragons, Jack?' Addie smiled faintly. 'One died in a motorcycle crash. One moved to Florida. One stayed here.'

'Who?'

'Don't go there.' She shook her head. 'No one ever knew what happened except my father, and now you. People figured I was sleeping around and got in trouble. And that's okay with me, Jack.' Her features softened. 'Out of that horrible thing, something wonderful happened. I got Chloe. That's all I want to remember. That, and nothing else.'

Jack was quiet for a moment. 'Do you believe I'm innocent?'

'I don't know,' Addie admitted. Her voice dropped to a whisper. She had known Jack for such a short time that the depth of her feelings for him seemed disproportionate, as if she'd turned on a faucet and unleashed a geyser. She did not understand this, but then there was much in the world she did not understand. Raw love, like raw heartache, could blindside you. It could make you forget what you did not know to focus exclusively on those few pieces you could commit to heart. 'I *want* to believe you,' she said.

'Then that's where we'll start.' Jack closed his eyes and leaned forward. 'Kiss me.'

'I don't think this is the time or –'

His eyes opened a crack. 'I want to prove to you I'm who I say I am. I want to show you there is nothing you can do, nothing you can say, that's going to make me attack you.'

'But you said –'

'Addie,' Jack murmured, 'let's do this for both of us.'

He spread his arms wide, and after a second, Addie leaned forward to kiss him on the cheek. 'Oh, come on. That's not your best shot.' She trailed her mouth from his neck to his jaw. A filament of sensation sizzled between them, like a thin string of kerosene that, for the love of a match, could turn into a wall of fire.

This wickedness, this wanting . . . it was like seeing color for the first time and stuffing her pockets full of bright violets, rich oranges, sizzling yellows, afraid she was going to be caught for stealing something that wasn't hers, but certain that if she took no souvenir, she would never remember it as clearly.

She was ready. She wanted. Addie lifted his hands to the top button of her uniform – only to have Jack move his arms back to his sides.

He won't do it. He wants me to.

In her life, she had never undressed for a man. Her own father had not seen her naked since she was ten. Shy and fumbling, she fudged the button through its hole, then moved down to the next one. Shelled in the thin pink silk of her bra, her breasts blushed under Jack's gaze. She unclasped the catch and drew Jack's head down to map her skin.

'Are you all right?' he whispered.

In response, she kissed a trail down his chest and belly, stopping at the spot where Jack's jeans tented. Her hands unbuttoned the fly so that the plum-purple weight of him rose into her outstretched hands.

In that moment, she had never felt so safe in her life.

'Let's do this for both of us,' Addie repeated. In tandem, they reached between his legs, pulled aside her underwear, and gently fit themselves together. *He fills me,* Addie realized with wonder; at the same moment that Jack thought: *So this is what has been missing.*

July 1999
Loyal, New Hampshire

'Jack,' the police officer said, 'you need to come down to the station.'

Jack tucked the portable phone against his shoulder to finish stuffing papers into his briefcase. 'Can't. I've got a meeting this afternoon. But let's meet at the gym for a game at seven.' Since moving to Loyal and taking a job as the town's sole detective, Jay Kavanaugh had been Jack's frequent buddy and a hell of a racquetball partner – they'd whip each other's asses on alternating days and then go lament the lack of single women in the town over a beer.

'Jack, I need you here now.'

He snorted. 'Well, sweetheart, I didn't know you felt that way.'

'Shut up,' Jay said, and for the first time Jack noticed the edge in his voice. 'Look. I don't really want to go into this over the phone, all right? I'll explain when you get here.'

'But –'

A dial tone. 'Shit,' Jack muttered. 'This'd better be worth it.'

He had met Jay when the detective came to the school to talk about safety on Halloween. Immediately, Jay became the big brother that Jack had never had. On the steaming, laziest days of the summer, they went out in the Westonbrook crew launch to catch largemouth bass. Rods balanced in their hands, they'd drink beer and come up with outrageous scenarios to lure Heather Locklear to the small burg of Loyal.

'Think you'll ever settle down?' Jack had asked once.

Jay had laughed. 'I am so settled already, I'm growing roots. Nothing ever happens in Loyal.'

Jay stood up the moment Jack entered his office. He looked at the bookshelf, the carpet, Jack's coat . . . anywhere but at Jack himself. 'You want to tell me what was so damn important that it couldn't wait?'

'Why don't we take a walk?'

'What's the matter with right here?'

Jay's face twisted. 'Just humor me, will you?' He led Jack into a conference room. There was nothing inside but a table, three chairs, and a tape recorder.

Jack grinned. 'Do I get to play cop?' He folded his arms over his chest. 'You have the right to remain silent. Everything you say can and will be used against you. You have the right to an attorney . . .' His voice trailed off as Jay closed his eyes and turned away. 'Hey,' Jack said quietly. 'What the hell?'

When Jay looked at him again, his face was completely impassive. 'Catherine Marsh said the two of you have been having an affair.'

'Catherine Marsh said *what?'* Jack took a second look at the spare room, the tape recorder, and Jay's expression. 'Am I . . . you're not arresting me, are you?'

'No. We're just talking now. I want to hear your side of the story.'

'You couldn't possibly think . . . for God's sake, Jay . . . she's – she's a *student.* I swear – I've never touched her. I don't know where she'd get an idea like this.' In spite of himself, his heart was racing.

'On the basis of the evidence we have, we'll be bringing charges against you,' Jay said stiffly. Then his voice softened. 'You may want to get yourself a lawyer, Jack.'

A curtain of rage ripped across Jack's vision. 'Why did you want me to come in here to *talk* if you're going to arrest me anyway?' The accusation hung between them, and Jack suddenly realized exactly why Jay had asked for his side of the story – it had nothing to do with their friendship and everything to do with catching Jack in a confession that could be used against him in court.

* * *

Loyal was a picture-perfect town, complete with a general store, a requisite wooden bridge, and a row of white clapboard buildings that flanked the town green, mirroring the architecture of Westonbrook Academy. Jack's home was a little cape. From his front porch, he could see the house where Catherine Marsh and her father, the Right Reverend Ellidor Marsh, lived.

What Jack had liked best about the town was that he could not walk through it without saying hello to someone he knew. If not a student, then the woman who ran the general store. The postmaster. The elderly twin brothers who had never married but served as bank tellers at side-by-side windows.

Today, though, he walked with his head ducked, afraid of seeing someone familiar. He passed kids and felt their heads crane to watch him walk by. He veered around the broom of a shopkeeper, his face lighting with embarrassment as she paused in her sweeping and stared. *I am innocent,* he wanted to scream, but even that would not make a difference. It wasn't truth that held their interest; it was the fact that rotten luck might be catching.

Catherine Marsh's house was gaily laced with pink roses that grew skyward on a trellis. He rapped sharply on the door, falling back a step when Catherine answered.

She was young and pretty, with skin that seemed lit from the inside. In that first moment, Jack saw all the times he'd hugged her after a particularly fine goal on the field, all the times he'd noticed her jersey straining against her sports bra. A wide smile spread across her face. 'Coach!'

He opened up his mouth to speak, to accuse her, to ask her why, but all the questions jammed. A face appeared behind hers: Ellidor Marsh, in all his fundamentalist fury.

'Reverend,' Jack began.

It was all Ellidor needed. His face revealed an internal war for the briefest moment, and then his fist shot out and clipped Jack in the jaw.

Catherine cried out as Jack tumbled down the steps, landing in a tangle of rosebushes. Thorns cut into the summer-weight wool of his trousers. He spat out blood, then wiped his hand across his mouth.

Catherine was trying to get to him, but her father had pushed her behind his own body. Jack narrowed his eyes at the chaplain. 'Did the good Lord tell you to do that?'

'Go,' Ellidor said precisely, 'to hell.'

A few weeks before, Jack had been teaching the Peloponnesian War to the summer term fourth-formers. He stood in front of his classroom, his shirt sticking to his chest in this July heat. 'The Spartans weren't happy with the peace treaty they'd signed, and the Athenians were getting a little power hungry themselves. . . .' He'd glanced over the rows of flushed faces of students cooling themselves with hastily folded looseleaf-paper fans. 'And not a single one of you is listening right now.'

Jack winced as one girl's eyes actually drifted shut. He was not a big fan of Westonbrook's summer session, offered so students could pump up their academic credits for college applications. The hundred-year-old classrooms at Westonbrook, sweatboxes all, were not conducive to learning.

Catherine Marsh sat in the front of the class, her starched collar neat against the edge of her uniform cardigan, her legs crossed primly at the ankles. 'Dr. St. Bride,' she whined, 'what's so important about a war that happened twenty-four hundred years ago in a different country? I mean, it's not *our* history. So why do we have to learn it?'

The chorus of agreement swept like a wave. Jack glanced from one flushed young face to another. 'Okay,' he said, 'we're taking a field trip.'

He did not really have a plan in mind, beyond getting them out of those godforsaken uniforms and into something more comfortable. Swimsuits were the most obvious choice . . . each girl had one roped to her gym locker. But he also had a very good sense of the mind of sophomore girls – who would rather cut off their left arm than show off physical flaws in front of classmates who were curvier, thinner, taller . . . or in front of a male teacher. Suddenly, Jack brightened, imagining a modest way to make the kids more comfortable – a way that could even be construed as part of their daily lesson.

He led them to the cafeteria, where arthritic townies were chopping heads of iceberg lettuce into salads. 'Ladies,' he said in greeting, 'we have need of some tablecloths.'

He was directed toward the main hall, where first-formers through sixth-formers took meals together. Neatly folded linens were stacked in piles. Jack took one tablecloth and tossed it to a student. He reached for another, and another, until every girl in his class was holding one. 'When in Rome, do as the Romans do. And when in Greece . . .' He grabbed a cloth and wrapped it around his own body. '*Voilà*. The toga.'

He led them to the girls' locker room. 'I want you all to put on your swimsuits, and then drape your toga. Carry out your uniforms, just in case.'

'In case what?'

Jack grinned. 'In case we need to beat a hasty retreat from the fashion police.' *Or the headmaster,* he thought.

'Might as well paint an *L* on my forehead right now,' a student murmured. '*Loser.*'

But in spite of the grumbling, they filed inside and then emerged one by one, each holding a stack of clothes. 'You see?' Jack said. 'Don't you feel better already?'

The last girl to come out was Catherine Marsh. She was wearing her toga, too . . . but no tank suit. Her bare shoulder, smooth and tan, brushed Jack's arm as she passed by.

Jack hid a smile. Girls this age – especially girls with crushes – were about as subtle as steamrollers.

He marched them to the soccer field, had them set down their bundles, and then line up. 'Okay. At first, you're all living in harmony, thanks to a peace treaty the Spartans signed.' Then he split the girls into two groups. 'You Spartans,' he told the first bunch, 'you want to fight a land war, because that's what you're good at. And you' – he pointed to the Athenians –'you want to fight a naval war, because that's what *you're* good at.'

'But how do we know who to kill?' one girl called out. 'We all look the same.'

'Excellent question! Someone who's your friendly neighbor one day is an enemy the next, simply because of a political issue. What do you do?'

'Ask before you draw your sword?'

Jack reached behind the girl who'd spoken, and pretended to slash her throat. 'And in that second you hesitated, you're dead.'

'Stay with your own kind,' one student shouted.

'Watch your back!'

'Strike first!'

Jack grinned as his listless group grew more animated, engaging in mock combat, until they were all rolling around the field, grass stains marking the knees and bottoms of their togas. Exhausted, they lay on their backs, watching cirrus clouds stretch across the sky like the long limbs of ballerinas.

A shadow loomed over Jack, and he looked up to find Herb Thayer, the headmaster of Westonbrook Academy. 'Dr. St. Bride . . . a word?'

They walked out of earshot. 'God, Jack. You trying to get us sued?'

'For what? Teaching history?'

'Since when does the curriculum include stripping?'

Jack shook his head. 'Costuming. There's a difference. Kids this age are like puppies; they need to get their blood moving before their brains kick into gear. And the classrooms are brutal in this heat.' He offered his most engaging smile. 'This is no different from staging Shakespeare.'

Herb wiped a hand across his brow. 'For all I care, Jack, you can put them through basic training to help them remember what you're teaching. Just make sure they're fully clothed before you send them out on the obstacle course.' He started off, then turned at the last minute. 'I know what you're doing and why. But the guy who's crossing the street over there, who came in during the second act – he sees something totally different.'

Jack waited until Herb left. Then he approached his class again, curiosity playing over their faces.

'Who won?' Catherine Marsh asked.

'Well, Dr. Thayer is in favor of our mock battles but highly recommends that you do it in uniform.'

A groan rose from the group, but they began to gather the small bundles of clothing they'd carried out to the field.

'No,' Catherine said. 'I meant, who won the war?'

'The Peloponnesian War? Nobody. Both sides believed their strategy would wear down the other side and make them surrender. But after ten years, neither had.'

'You mean they just stayed at war because no one would give in?'

'Yes. By the time they signed the Peace of Nicias, it wasn't about who was right or wrong . . . just about not fighting anymore.' He clapped his hands for attention. 'Okay, now. Let's hustle.'

The girls trickled away. *Beauty is truth, and truth, beauty,* Jack thought, watching them. He took a step forward and felt something beneath his shoe. A wisp of fabric, a red satin bra accidentally dropped by one of the girls. Sewn along the inseam was a name label, de rigueur for any boarding-school student. catherine marsh, Jack read. Blushing, he stuffed it into his pocket.

Melton Sprigg's office was by no stretch of the imagination impressive. It was a walk-up above the Chinese restaurant in Loyal, and the smell of kung po chicken was thick. There was no air conditioning, and papers littered the floor and the desk and the one filing cabinet. 'Keep meaning to clean this up,' he huffed, moving a stack of journals out of the way so that Jack could sit down.

For one brief moment, Jack considered bolting. He forced himself to flatten his hands on the arms of his chair, to relax.

'So,' Melton said, 'how can I help you?'

Jack realized he had never actually said the words before. They stuck like glue to the roof of his mouth. 'I think I'm going to be charged with a crime.'

Melton grinned. 'Good thing. If you said you wanted to order moo shu pork, you'd be in the wrong place. Why do you think you're going to be charged?'

'The police said as much. They called me in to . . . *talk* . . . a few days ago. A girl . . . a student of mine . . . has implied that she and I . . . that we . . . '

Melton whistled through his teeth. 'I can guess the rest.'

'I didn't do it,' Jack insisted.

The lawyer handed him a card. 'Let's cross that bridge when we come to it.'

In spite of the heat, Jack went running. He put on his old college soccer jersey and shorts and took off dead east from the porch of his house. He ran two miles, four, six. Sweat poured into his eyes, and he gasped great drafts of air. He passed the town line and kept running. He ran the perimeter of a pond, twice. And when he realized that no matter how hard he tried he could not outrace his fear, he collapsed at the edge, buried his face in his hands, and cried.

Catherine Marsh remembered with vivid clarity the first time Jack St. Bride had touched her.

She had been playing forward, her eye on the ball, so intent on firing it into the goal of the opposing team that she'd completely missed seeing the other player hurtling toward her with the same single-mindedness. They smacked heads with an audible crunch, the last noise Catherine could remember hearing before she was unconscious. When she came to, Coach was leaning over her, his golden hair haloed by the sun, the way it always looks in the movies when the hero comes along. 'Catherine,' he asked, 'you all right?' At first she hadn't been able to answer because his hands were running up and down her body, checking for broken bones. 'I think your ankle is swelling,' he said. Then he'd taken off her cleat and peeled off her sock, examining her sweaty foot like Cinderella's prince. 'Perfect,' he pronounced. And Catherine had thought, *Yes, you are.*

She knew that there was something special between them, from the way he kept her after practice to show her a drill to the way he sometimes slung an arm over her shoulders when they were walking off the field together. When she'd confided that she was thinking of sleeping with Billy Haines, Coach had been the one to drive her to the clinic two towns over, to get birth control pills. Oh, he hadn't wanted to at first – but he'd given in because he cared about her. And when Billy had dumped her two days later, Coach had let her cry on his shoulder.

She wondered several times a day what he'd done with the bra she'd left behind after that Ancient History class. It had fallen out of her bundle of clothes completely by accident . . . or maybe it was just fate, now that she got to thinking about it. She'd realized it was missing and had gone back to the field to retrieve it . . . just in time to see Coach pick up her bra and pocket it. Something had made her turn away without asking for it back. Maybe he slept with it beneath his pillow. Maybe he just let the silk slip through his fingers and pretended it was her skin.

Yesterday, Catherine hadn't gone to school. Her father wouldn't let her. And it was probably best that way, since she did not know what she would have said to Jack. She had heard through the grapevine that he had been taken off to jail in *handcuffs,* like he was some criminal. If Catherine had been there, she would have knelt at his feet and kissed every spot on his wrists the metal touched. She would have asked to wear them in his place. She would do anything to show him how much she loved him, anything at all.

Jack leaned so close to Melton Sprigg he could see the weave of the attorney's bow tie. 'I didn't do it,' he said through his teeth. 'Doesn't that count for anything?'

'I'm just saying that in today's day and age, there are ways to make a jury understand why a man of . . . advanced years . . . might develop an interest in a younger girl.'

'Good. You can use that defense for a client who's actually guilty.' Jack sank into a chair, suddenly overwhelmed. Today, his best friend had charged him with felonious sexual assault. He'd been arraigned. His bank account was $5,000 lighter, thanks to posting bail. His wrist was bruised where the handcuff had pinched it while he was being led up to the courtroom. 'We're going to fight this. That's what the system is about, right? Giving each side the chance to speak. And who's going to listen to what a fifteen-year-old says?'

Melton nodded and smiled, for his client's sake. And did not tell him what he was thinking: that simply because Catherine Marsh *was* fifteen, everyone *would* be listening.

'I'll cut right through the bullshit,' Herb Thayer said. 'This is downright awkward.'

Finally, someone who agreed with him. 'Tell me about it,' Jack said. 'I had to walk into the station yesterday, so that Jay Kavanaugh could read me my rights! For God's sake, I played racquetball with him last Saturday, and here he was booking me.' Once he began to speak, he didn't think he'd ever be able to stop. 'It came out of left field, Herb. I have no idea what this kid is thinking.'

'You and Catherine Marsh have a close rapport,' Herb stated.

'You . . . you don't believe what she said, do you?'

'God, Jack, of course not. I'm just pointing out that I can see how . . . others . . . might have come to this conclusion.'

Jack got to his feet and began to prowl around the office. On a shelf behind him were four district championship trophies for girls' soccer, each of which he'd earned by means of the close rapport Herb was questioning now. 'I never touched her.'

Herb gazed out the window to where several students were eating lunch. 'You know,' he said softly, 'you're the best teacher in this school. You can turn kids on to learning like I've never seen before.'

Jack felt a rush in his bloodstream, the swift realization that things might not turn out to be quite as dismal as he'd believed.

The headmaster picked up a pen, drummed it on the desktop. 'Look, Jack. I believe you. But I've got parents who want to know what kind of school employs a teacher whose conduct is suspect. I've got Ellidor Marsh breathing down my neck –'

'Ellidor Marsh is a fundamentalist asshole who has no place being a private school chaplain.'

'He's also a father who thinks his fifteen-year-old daughter was having sex with a guy twice her age who should have known better!' The accusation hung between them, black as smoke, hovering over the desk.

'Nothing's been proven,' Jack said, words that tasted like dust.

Herb could not meet his eye. 'Try to see it from my point of view, Jack. For the good of the school, I can't have a teacher here who's been accused of statutory rape.' He walked around the desk. 'If there's some other way I can help . . .'

'Don't do me any favors,' Jack murmured, and left before Herb could say anything else.

Annalise St. Bride actually knew Brooke Astor. She had a tiger-skin rug in her bedroom – her husband had shot the beast on safari; she kept a home on the Upper West Side that had been featured in *Architectural Digest* more often than had Gracie Square. But these were not the amazing things about Annalise. It was far more interesting that she shared her apartment with her husband's former lover, who was now her closest friend. Or that she knew just as many prostitutes as she did debutantes. She was best known for her decade-long crusade to fight violence against women. Twenty rape crisis centers dotted the seediest parts of New York City, thanks to Annalise's checkbook and iron resolve.

So when Jack found his mother on the front doorstep of his home, he was stunned, to say the least.

That she had come to support him – without knowing all the details – cracked his heart wide. Just looking at her, Jack felt the protective wall he'd been building around himself begin to tumble down. He leaned forward to kiss her cheek, but she ducked away.

'I'm not staying, Jack. But what I came to say, I wanted to say in person.' Annalise regarded him soberly. 'Do you know how many women I've seen after a rape?'

Jack tried to draw a breath but couldn't. It was not enough that his employer, his students, his attorney, and his colleagues believed this charge. His own mother did, too.

'You . . . you can't think I'm guilty,' he whispered.

Annalise raised her brows. 'Why on earth would a woman lie about that?'

Suddenly Jack remembered when his mother had taken him to the Central Park Zoo as a child. He'd stayed too long in the dark hut of the bats, fascinated by the way they could fold themselves up like tiny umbrellas. When he'd turned around, his mother had been gone. He had not been afraid for himself, not even at seven; instead, he'd felt bad for his mother, who surely would have been frantic by now. But he found her standing outside the hut, talking to an acquaintance she'd met. Jack had pressed up against her leg, a limpet. 'Oh,' she'd said blithely, as if she'd never noticed his absence. 'Are we finished here?'

Now, Jack swallowed hard. 'You have to believe me. I'm your son.'

'Not anymore,' said Annalise.

He puts his hands under my shirt, and I feel them burning. I'm aching for him. Oh, Jack. I know it won't hurt with him, because he promises me. Even when he's sticking it in me, I don't mind, because finally we are one.

Jack pushed away the photocopied pages. 'What is this shit?'

Melton shrugged. 'Discovery. Evidence. This is the diary entry that apparently sent Catherine's father over the edge.' He shuffled through his own notes. 'Well, along with the birth control pills.'

'Did anyone ever stop to consider that maybe this is fiction?'

'Of course, Jack.' Melton pushed his half-glasses up on his nose. 'But she also says you were the one who took her to get contraception.'

'By default, Melton. She wanted to sleep with her boyfriend and no one else would take her to Planned Parenthood!'

'According to Catherine, there was no boyfriend. She says she got the Pill because you wanted to sleep with her.'

'Look. She has a crush on me. I knew that on some level, even if I didn't address it. I didn't want to embarrass her, and I figured she'd just grow out of it. Things like this happen all the time.'

'There's a difference between a minor imagining she has a crush on an older man and a minor who has sexual intercourse with that man.'

'You've got it backwards! She's imagining the sex!' Jack took a deep breath. 'Okay. So they have her testimony, and this diary. And some birth control pills. I don't see how any of that conclusively points to my carrying on an intimate relationship with her.'

'I agree,' Melton said. 'You'd be in much better shape if the police hadn't found anything when they searched your house.'

Jack frowned. The police had arrived with a warrant, and he'd let them search the premises, but he hadn't realized anything fruitful had come of it. Melton pushed a photograph across the table at him. 'What is this, a rag?'

'Apparently,' Melton said, 'it's Catherine Marsh's bra. It was in your briefcase.'

Jack stared at it for a second. Then he started laughing. 'Christ, Melton, they can't think . . . I picked it up for her after she left it in class. No, wait – that came out sounding bad. We were working on a unit on ancient Greek history in this sweltering heat, and the kids had all gotten into togas made out of tablecloths, and –'

'And the police found a bra, with Catherine Marsh's name sewn into it, in your briefcase. That's all they know, Jack. And that's plenty.'

'But I can explain it.'

'I know,' Melton said. 'Unfortunately, so can the prosecutor.'

* * *

Jack had to see her. He had read and reread the conditions of his bail, which stipulated in black and white that he stay away not only from minors but specifically from Catherine Marsh. If he was caught, there would be another hearing. He would be charged with violating his bail condition and held in contempt of court. He would most likely be put into jail until his trial came up on the docket.

If he were caught, it would contribute to the prosecution's case against him.

But if he could get away with this one small thing, he had a chance of stopping this charge from going forward.

The schedules of students at Westonbrook had been computerized two years ago, thanks to the diligence of an intern who happened to be a technical whiz. It took Jack less than ten minutes to find Catherine Marsh's whereabouts. Within an hour, he was standing behind a large oak at the edge of the campus, watching as girls passed by in small clusters, bright butterflies lighting from conversation to conversation.

Catherine was walking alone, the first stroke of luck since this whole debacle had begun. Sweat broke out on his brow as he willed her to come closer. The sun glinted off the brass clutch of her knapsack, momentarily blinding him.

He reached out to grab her upper arm. Pressing her up against the tree, his hand clapped over her mouth. Catherine's eyes went wide with fear, then suddenly softened. He let go of her. 'Coach,' she said, smiling, as if she had not overturned the whole bowl of his life.

He swallowed, reaching for reason, but it was the anger that finally pushed one sentence through, rough and rusty as a spike. 'Catherine,' Jack hissed, 'what the *hell* did you do?'

She had never seen him angry before. Well, maybe once or twice, but that usually had to do with a player whose mind was on some stupid guy instead of practice. The bite of his fingers into the bones of her shoulders scared her with one heartbeat, then thrilled her the next. *He came here for me,* she thought.

Suddenly, he got himself under control again. 'What did you tell them?'

In that moment, her feelings were a featherbed, downy and inviting. Catherine took a deep breath and jumped. 'That I love you.'

'You *love* me,' he repeated, the words sounding all wrong on the twist of his mouth. 'Catherine, you don't love me.'

'I do. And I know you love me, too.'

'Anything I've ever said to you or done with you I would have said or done with any student,' Coach said. 'Catherine, you've got to stop lying to them. Don't you see I could end up in jail?'

For a moment, Catherine's heart stopped beating. And then she realized this was a test. A way of safeguarding his heart, until her own was laid bare. She smiled tremulously. 'You don't have to hide the truth anymore.'

'The truth?'

'You know . . . how we're going to be together.'

His eyes flashed. 'Before or after I'm tried for a felony?'

'Oh, Jack,' Catherine whispered, and she reached out to him.

He recoiled, unwilling to touch her, unwilling to be touched by her. And this, finally, gave Catherine pause. Even as she called to him, he continued to back away with his palms raised, as if he was no longer seeing a pretty young girl but a poisonous snake that might strike when he least expected.

'Of course she's skittish,' the prosecutor said gently to Reverend Marsh. Loretta Winwood folded her hands on her desk, patient. 'If she wasn't reluctant to testify, I'd be concerned about her motivations. But it's common to have underage witnesses balk. In fact, a hesitant witness on the stand is a powerful piece of evidence in a statutory rape case.'

'But you heard her! She says she made the whole thing up.'

Loretta gave the man a moment to compose himself. Poor guy, to find out just a few days ago that his daughter had been carrying on an affair with a teacher and then today to have her recant in a puddle at his feet. It was at moments like this that she truly understood why attorneys were called counselors. 'Reverend Marsh, do you believe her?'

'My daughter's a good Christian girl.'

'Yes, but she's either lying about this sexual affair . . . or she's lying about lying about it.'

Marsh pressed his fingers to his temples. 'I don't know, Ms. Winwood.'

'What reason would Catherine have to make up a story about a consensual sexual relationship that doesn't exist?'

'None.'

'All right. Now, let's assume that she has been involved in a relationship with Dr. St. Bride, upsetting as that is to consider. What reason would Catherine have to suddenly retract everything she's confessed?'

Marsh closed his eyes. 'To save him.'

Loretta nodded. 'One reason it's against the law to have intercourse with people under the age of sixteen is because minors are so susceptible to manipulation. What your daughter just told me – well, I see it a lot, Reverend Marsh. Unfortunately, these girls *are* in love. And once they triumphantly tell the world and the object of their affection is carted off in cuffs, they suddenly wonder if that was such a good idea.'

'Can . . . can you force her to be a witness?'

'I can force her to sit on the stand, but if she won't testify, she won't testify. That's why so many of these cases never make it to trial.' She closed the file in front of her. 'If Catherine tells the jury this affair existed only in her imagination, I can't impeach her with her prior statements to the contrary. We have some incriminating evidence . . . but nothing as strong as Catherine's testimony. And I'm sorry to say that means Jack St. Bride will most likely be acquitted – and will most likely seduce another underage girl in the future.'

Marsh's face mottled pink. 'He'll burn in hell one day.'

This was a gray area in the law. If Catherine had been lying today about never having sex with St. Bride, it wasn't really exculpatory evidence . . . which meant her confession didn't have to be turned over to the defense . . . which meant that Melton Sprigg would not know that Catherine was unwilling to testify against his client. 'Hell would be fine,' Loretta said. 'But there might be something a little more immediate.'

'A plea bargain?' Jack said. 'Doesn't that mean they're running scared?'

The attorney shook his head. 'Most cases that go to court . . . well, ten percent are sure wins for the county attorney, and ten percent are sure losses. But the bulk of the cases – eighty percent – fall smack in the middle. Prosecutors offer pleas all the time, because they ensure a conviction.'

'So what am I, Melton? The ten percent that wins or the ten percent that loses?'

'With you, the odds are more like five percent on either side, ninety in the middle. Rape trials, Jack . . . a lot of the time, it comes down to one person's word against another's. Conviction or acquittal could hang on whether the jury had a good breakfast that day.'

'I'm not taking a plea,' Jack said. 'I won't admit to something I never did.'

'Well, just hear me out, then, all right? Because my job description says I have to read it to you.' Melton handed him the fax. 'They're willing to reduce the charge to a misdemeanor sexual assault. Eight months in jail, no probation. It's a good deal, Jack.'

'It's a good deal for someone who's goddamned guilty!' Jack cried. 'I never touched her, Melton. She's lying.'

'Do you think you can convince twelve jurors of that? Do you really want to play that kind of Russian roulette?' He lifted Jack's mug and took his napkin from underneath it, then drew a line down the middle with his pen. At the top he wrote PRO and CON. 'Let's look at what happens if you go to trial. Best-case scenario? You get acquitted. Worst-case scenario? You get convicted of a class B felony. You get sent to the state penitentiary for seven years.'

'I thought the sentence was three and a half years to seven.'

'Only if you get paroled, Jack. And to get paroled, you'd have to complete the sex offender treatment program there.'

Jack shrugged. 'How hard could that be?'

'You're not going to make it through day one unless you're very forthcoming about every aspect of your sex offense. Which means you have to walk in there and tell them you have a thing for little girls.'

'That's bullshit,' Jack said.

'Not if you're convicted. In the mind of the parole board, you've committed that offense. Period. And you don't get paroled until you're amenable to treatment.'

Jack dug his thumbnail into a scar on the table. 'The plea,' he managed to say. 'What's the pro?'

'First, you're serving eight months, period. If you spend every second screaming you're innocent, they're still going to release you after eight months. Second, you're serving time at the county jail, the Farm. You're outside, working. It's a whole different ball of wax from the State Pen. You finish your sentence and you go on with your life.'

'I'd still have a conviction on my record.'

'A misdemeanor,' Melton pointed out. 'You can get it annulled after ten years, like it never existed. A felony sexual assault charge – well, that's with you for life.'

To his horror, Jack felt tears climbing the ladder of his throat. 'Eight months. That's a hell of a long time.'

'It's a lot less than seven years.' When Jack looked away, the lawyer sighed. 'For what it's worth, I'm sorry you were the one who got his hand slapped.'

Jack turned to him. 'I didn't do anything wrong.'

'Eight months,' Melton said in response. 'You'd be out before you know it.'

The courtroom was claustrophobic. The walls were swaying in on Jack, and the air he drew in through his teeth sat like a block at the base of his stomach. He stood beside Melton Sprigg, his gaze square on Judge Ralph Greenlaw, a man whose daughter had been a goalie for Jack three years earlier. A nonpartisan trial? Not a chance. Every time the man met his eye, he could see him thinking of what might have happened if his own child instead of Catherine Marsh were sitting behind the prosecutor.

The judge scanned the plea bargain, that wisp of paper that had Jack's signature on it, just as sure as if he'd scrawled away his soul in blood. 'Did you read this form before you signed it?'

'Yes, Your Honor.'

'Has any pressure, force, or promise been made to you in an effort to get you to plead guilty to this offense?'

Jack thought of the cocktail napkin, the pro and con list, that Melton had drawn up. He had saved it after their meeting. The next day, he'd flushed it down the toilet. 'No.'

'Do you understand the rights that you are giving up by pleading guilty and not going to trial?'

Yes, Jack thought. *The right to live my life the way I always imagined it would be.* 'I do,' he said.

'Do you understand that you're entitled to a lawyer?'

'Do you understand that you're entitled to a jury trial?'

'Do you understand that the jurors' vote would have to be unanimous in order to find you guilty?'

'Has any evidence obtained illegally against you been used to secure this conviction?'

He felt Melton hold his breath as the judge asked the next question. 'Are you pleading guilty because you are guilty?'

Jack could not force a syllable from his throat.

Catherine couldn't stand any of it – the weight of her father's solid body pressed against hers, the stoic resignation of Jack sitting beside his attorney, the truth that she was the one who had set this cart in motion. And even after she'd tried to fix it, it had been too late. No matter how many times she insisted she'd made this all up, they didn't want to hear. The prosecutor and her father and the psychiatrist he'd dragged her to for counseling all told her that it was perfectly normal for her to want to keep Jack out of jail but that he deserved to be punished for what he had done.

Me, Catherine thought. *I deserve to be punished.*

She wished with all her heart that this had happened differently, but she had learned that words were like eggs dropped from great heights: You could no more call them back than ignore the mess they left when they fell.

She felt herself coming out of her seat, as if she'd swallowed helium. 'Don't do this to him!' she cried.

'Sit down, Catherine.' Her father clamped an arm around her. The prosecutor and the judge didn't stop the proceedings. It was like they'd expected her to say this.

The judge nodded at the bailiff. 'Please remove Ms. Marsh from the courtroom,' he said, and suddenly a burly man was gently leading her outside, where she wouldn't have to bear witness to her own folly.

It was as if Catherine had never spoken. 'Mr. St. Bride,' the judge repeated, 'do you admit that you knowingly had sexual contact with Catherine Marsh for the purpose of sexual arousal or gratification?'

Jack could feel the Reverend Marsh's eyes on the back of his neck. He opened his mouth in denial, only to choke on words that had been lodged in the pit of his belly, fed to him by his own attorney: *You finish your sentence, and then you go on with your life.*

Jack gagged until his eyes teared, until Melton pounded him on the back and asked for a moment so that his client could compose himself. He coughed and hemmed and hawed, but something still seemed to be caught, irritating as a bone. 'Try this,' Melton whispered, passing Jack a glass of water, but he only shook his head. He could drink an ocean and never dissolve the pride that was stuck in his throat.

'Mr. St. Bride,' the judge said, 'do you admit to committing this offense?'

'Yes, Your Honor,' Jack answered, in a voice that was still not his own. 'I do.'

Late April 2000
Salem Falls, New Hampshire

Selena Damascus kicked the tire of her Jaguar so hard that pain shot up her leg. 'Goddamn,' she yelled, so loudly that both Jordan and the mechanic jumped.

'Feel better?' Jordan asked, leaning against a tool chest.

'Shut up. Just shut up. Do you know how much money I put into that car?' Selena thundered. 'Do you?'

'Every lousy red cent I ever paid you.'

She turned on the mechanic. 'I could buy a Geo for the price you just quoted.'

The man looked distinctly uncomfortable, but Jordan understood. Selena was formidable when she was in a good mood. In a temper, she was downright terrifying. 'Um, there's something else,' the mechanic muttered.

'Let me guess,' Selena said. 'You don't have someone qualified to service Jags.'

'No, I can do that. But it's gonna take a week or so to get the part.' A telephone rang in the service station, and the mechanic excused himself. 'You make up your mind. This car ain't going nowhere anyhow.'

Selena turned to Jordan. 'This isn't happening to me. I'm just going to turn my life back twenty-four hours and when your son calls, I'm gonna let the phone keep on ringing.' She shook her head. 'You know this guy has a monopoly going on in this town.'

'Yes. The antitrust commission swung by last September to investigate.'

'Zip it, will you, Jordan?'

'You could get it towed,' he suggested. 'You could rent a car.'

Selena shrugged, considering this.

'Or you could just stay with us for a while,' Jordan said, and the moment the words were out of his mouth, he wondered where they had come from. The last thing he wanted was Selena Damascus around, reminding him of what might have worked out in a different time and place.

'You can barely stand to look at me. God, Jordan, you took your cereal bowl into your bedroom this morning to keep us from having to eat breakfast together.'

He looked away.

'Not to mention all that . . . history . . . between us.'

She was asking him, Jordan realized, not telling him. He was very quiet for a moment, remembering how he had stayed up all night waiting to hear the tumblers in the lock announcing her return with Thomas, how he'd sat on the couch after putting away her blankets this morning and realized the scent of her was now a part of it, as much as its color and weave.

'If I stayed, we'd just be asking for trouble,' Selena said.

'It would be a stupid move,' Jordan agreed.

'Stupid?' she snorted. 'It would be one of the ten biggest mistakes in the history of the world.'

He laughed along with her, both of them completely aware that they were already moving toward his car, inching in the direction of home.

If Addie was surprised to discover that she liked sex, she was absolutely stunned to realize that she was addicted to the moments afterward.

She would lie on her side, drawn into the shell of Jack's body like a precious pearl. She could feel him the whole length of her, could taste herself on his fingers, could sense the moment his breathing evened into sleep. But most of all, while they were curled together, she knew that they were equals. No one was on top, no one was pleasing someone else, no one had the upper hand. It was just Addie, listening to Jack, who was listening to Addie.

Where would you go if you could board a plane for anywhere?

What's the first thing you remember from your childhood?

Would you want to live forever?

These were the things they talked about while the night settled and bled into morning. His reticence to talk about the past had broken like a dam; now, he told her about his teaching days, about his arrest, about his time in jail. Sometimes, while Jack was asking her a question or answering one of hers, he'd slide his hand up to cover her breast. Sometimes his fingers would stroke her from the inside out, making it a challenge to listen. He did it so often, and so well, that she stopped jumping every time it happened.

'You can ask me anything,' Jack said solemnly, 'and I'll answer.'

Addie knew he was telling the truth. Which is why, sometimes, she bit down on the question she most wanted Jack to respond to: *What would it take to make you run?*

Jack stood at his window in Roy Peabody's guest room, grinning like a fool at the sight of Stuart Hollings walking his cow down Main Street once again. He felt, unbelievably, like whistling. Addie had done that to him. He opened the door and sauntered into the living room, humming under his breath. 'Roy, it's such a good morning I think I can stomach even you.'

He stopped short at the sight of Addie, arguing with her father in heated whispers.

'Jack,' she said, blushing. 'Hi.'

'Hi,' he answered. He stuffed his hands into his pockets.

Roy looked from one to the other and threw up his hands. 'For the love of God. You think I don't know what you two are up to? Christ, Jack. You've barely been sleeping here enough, Jack, for me to charge you rent. Forget the false modesty and sit down next to her. Just don't start pawing her until I've had a cup of coffee, all right? There's only so much a man my age can take without a strong jolt of caffeine.'

Addie smiled weakly at Jack. 'So,' he said, feeling like a seventh grader beneath Roy's hawkeyed regard. 'What were you two talking about?'

'Well –' Addie began, at the same minute that Roy said, 'Nothing.'

Then Jack noticed the bucket of soapy water beside Roy's armchair. A sponge floated like seaweed on the top. 'Planning on washing your car?'

Roy scowled. 'Kick a man while he's down, why don't you?'

'He doesn't have a car,' Addie said, sotto voce. 'Those DUIs.'

'Ah. Spring cleaning, then?'

Roy and Addie exchanged a look. 'Yeah,' he said, leaping on Jack's explanation. 'I've got to do these windows. It's gotten so that when I look out 'em, I can barely tell Stuart from the cow.'

'I'll do it,' Jack said, getting to his feet.

'No!' Addie and Roy said in unison.

'It's no trouble. And I promise I'll be down to work on time. Matter of fact, now that I think of it, isn't there a ladder in the storeroom downstairs I can use?' He sidestepped the bucket, strolled to the door, and opened it.

The paint was still dripping, angry and red: GO HOME.

Jack touched the words with one shaking finger. 'This isn't the first time, is it?'

'Happened yesterday, too,' Roy admitted. 'I got it off before you woke up.'

'Why didn't you *tell* me?' Jack rounded on Addie. 'Or you?'

'Jack . . . If you ignore whoever's doing this, they'll just go away.'

'No,' he said. 'If you ignore it, it steamrolls you.' Then he pushed out the door, bracing his hand on the wall, leaving behind a smudge of red paint like first blood drawn.

Gillian dreamed that the doorbell was ringing. She was in bed, so sick she could barely lift her eyelids, but whoever it was wouldn't go away. After eons she managed to swing her legs over the side of the bed. She stumbled down the stairs and yanked open the door. Standing there was her father, holding a gun. 'Gilly,' he said, and then he shot her in the heart.

She woke with a start, sweating, and pushed back the comforter on her bed. It was still early – barely 6:30 in the morning – but she could hear voices rising from downstairs.

Moments later, she inched toward the kitchen. 'All I'm saying, Tom, is that I live here for a reason,' her father said.

He was talking to Whitney's dad. Peeking in, Gilly saw Ed Abrams, too, and Jimmy from the pharmaceutical plant. 'I don't see how we can do anything about it,' Tom answered. 'Noticed you didn't invite Charlie Saxton to this tête-à-tête, either.'

'Charlie's welcome to join me anytime, so long as he checks his gold shield at the door.'

Ed shook his head. 'I don't know, Amos. It's not like he's made a move.'

'Who?' Gilly said, coming out of her hiding spot and entering the kitchen. She poured herself a cup of coffee with the aplomb of a woman twice her age, then slid beneath her father's arm. 'Morning, Daddy,' she said, kissing his cheek. 'Hi, Mr. Abrams. Mr. O'Neill. Jimmy.' The men muttered greetings, turning their eyes away from her pajamas: a baby-doll T-shirt and a pair of her dad's boxers. A thin line of powder-pink skin showed between the sagging waistband and the hem of her shirt. 'Who hasn't made a move?'

'This,' Amos said suddenly. 'This is why we have to take the first step.' He grabbed the edge of his daughter's T-shirt, wrinkling it in his hand, so that it pulled tight across the buds of her breasts. Gilly froze, caught somewhere between absolute humiliation and the strange power she had knowing her body could keep these men in thrall.

Tom O'Neill stood up. 'Count me in.'

Ed Abrams nodded, and so did Jimmy.

Amos walked the men out, talking quietly in a voice Gilly was not meant to hear. Something had happened, though, something she meant to find out. She waited for her father to return. 'Daddy, aren't you going to tell me what's going on?'

Amos stared at her for a moment before finding his voice. 'Let's get you dressed,' he said simply, and he took her hand and led her upstairs.

Charlie jumped as the door to his office burst open. Standing on the threshold, fuming, was his resident registered sexual offender, Jack St. Bride. A step behind, his secretary shrugged. 'Sorry, boss. I tried to get him to wait, but –'

'I'll take it from here. Mr. St. Bride? You want to come in for a minute?' He gestured at the chair opposite his desk as if St. Bride were any visitor, instead of a man so angry Charlie could nearly see steam rising from his skin. 'Now. What can I do for you?'

'Everyone knows,' St. Bride said tightly.

Charlie did not pretend to misunderstand him. 'The list of registered offenders is public. If a resident comes in requesting it, I have no choice but to hand it over.'

'How many?'

'How many what?' Charlie repeated.

'How many people have asked to see the list since my name's been on it?'

'I'm not at liberty to –'

'Just tell me. Please.'

Charlie pursed his lips and stared at the ceiling, at a crack that marched across it like a panoramic peak of mountains. 'None that I know of.'

'That's right. No one would know I was on that list at all if it weren't for one of your own officers.'

The detective rubbed the bridge of his nose. Goddamn Wes, anyway. 'We have protocols at the department, Mr. St. Bride, and it's always a disappointment to hear that a staff member hasn't followed them.'

'A disappointment.' Jack looked into his lap, and when he lifted his face again his eyes were shining – with fury or with tears – Charlie didn't know for sure and wasn't certain he wanted to know, either. 'This little *disappointment* of yours . . . it's going to ruin my life.'

Charlie refrained from saying what he wanted: that St. Bride had ruined his life all by himself. 'I'm sorry, but it's not within my power to keep rumors from spreading.'

'How about vandalism, Detective? Can you stop people from painting on Roy Peabody's door charming little graffiti messages about how I ought to leave?'

'You can file a complaint, but I'll tell you now that the chance of anything coming of it is awfully slim.' Charlie looked the other man directly in the eye. 'No one in this town can force you to move out of it. No matter what they say or do, it's your right to stay if you want to.'

At that, St. Bride's shoulders relaxed just the slightest bit.

'Unfortunately,' Charlie added, 'it's *their* right to say and do whatever they want to try to change your mind.'

'And if they hurt me . . . if they send me to the hospital, or worse . . . is that what it will take to get you on my side?'

'I'm on the side of the law. If it comes to assault, they'll be punished.' Charlie twisted a paper clip in his hands, until the heat that came from the motion snapped it in two. 'But that goes both ways, Mr. St. Bride. Because I'm going to be watching you, too. And if you so much as look at a teenage girl in Salem Falls, you'll find yourself moving out of town as quick as a sheriff's patrol car can take you.'

St. Bride seemed to crumble from the inside out, like a building Charlie had once seen blown up in Boston. First the eyes closed, then the shoulders dropped, then the head bowed – until it seemed to Charlie that all he was looking at was a shell of the man who had walked in on such a rush of anger. *This man is a criminal*, Charlie reminded himself, although it felt as though he were staring at something with feathers and webbed feet and a bill and insisting it was a dog. 'Is that clear?'

Jack did not open his eyes. 'Crystal.'

Gilly leaned across the aisle when Mrs. Fishman's back was turned and snatched the folded note out of Whitney's hand.

Tituba should have hexed them all, it read. She hid the paper between the folds of her dog-eared copy of *The Crucible*.

'Why did the girls accuse the goodwives of the town of seeing the Devil?' Mrs. Fishman said. 'Gillian?'

She had read the play – it was their homework assignment. Totally lame, too. A bunch of Puritan girls saying the town biddies were witches, just so that one of them could do the nasty with a married man and not have to worry about his loser of a wife finding out. 'Well, at first they didn't want to get caught for practicing voodoo. So they tried to take the heat off themselves by telling a lie. But this lie . . . it turned out to be the one thing that brought all these other truths out into the open.'

'Such as?'

'Like Proctor and Abigail hiding the salami,' the jock behind her called out, and the rest of the class laughed.

Mrs. Fishman's lips twitched. 'Thank you, Frank, for putting it so succinctly.' She began to walk through the aisles. 'Rumor has it that Abigail wound up as a prostitute in Boston. Elizabeth Proctor remarried after her husband was hung. And New Age witches, of course, are no longer accused of consorting with the Devil.'

Gilly bowed her head, so that her hair spilled forward to shield her face from view. *You'd be surprised,* she thought.

It was 8 a.m., and already Addie was so tired she could barely stand. 'More coffee?' she asked, holding the pot so it hovered like a bumblebee above the bloom of Stuart Hollings's mug.

'You know, Addie, the docs said I ought to stop drinking it because it wasn't good for my heart.' Then he grinned. 'So I said, if three cups a day got me to see the sunny side of 86, I'm just gonna keep doin' what I've been doin'!'

Smiling, Addie poured. 'Let's hope this gets you another 86 years.'

'Christamighty, no,' Wallace groaned, beside him. 'I'm hoping he'll buy the farm before me, just so's I can have a decade of peace and quiet.'

At the cash register, Roy cracked a package of pennies like an egg and let the coins shimmy into the bowl of the money drawer. 'Busy today,' he remarked as Addie passed by, seating more customers.

She sighed. 'We haven't had this kind of volume since the summer we offered free blue plate specials every time the thermometer topped a hundred degrees.'

She smiled at her father, and he smiled back, but they both knew what had caused the sudden increase in patronage. People who had never set foot inside the Do-Or-Diner had come because there was a spectacle on display in their town, a criminal who had the nerve to choose their own small hamlet as a place of residence, and they wanted to see what kind of man would be so daring, or so stupid. It seemed impossible that the news had spread so quickly from Wes to filter into this group of customers, but then Addie only had to look as far as herself to know that it had happened before. Rumor grew and morphed, until a man accused of assault might turn into a serial rapist, until a grieving mother was seen as a madwoman.

The sad truth was, nothing was better for a small-town diner than gossip.

So far, of course, they'd been denied a show. But even as Addie thought this, the door opened and Jack slipped inside, intent on making his way to the safety of the kitchen before anyone could speak to him. His appearance electrified the tiny room: Diners paused with their coffee mugs held in midair, their forks suspended with a bite of food while they stared at a man who had, overnight, transformed from 'the dishwasher at the diner' into 'the convicted rapist.' 'Sorry I'm late,' Jack muttered.

Addie planted herself directly in his path, unwilling to budge until he looked up at her. 'What happened?'

'Please, Addie. Could we just not talk about it now?'

She nodded briskly. 'Well, I need you out here to clear.'

The thought of a task was a brass ring, and Jack grabbed on with both hands. 'Just let me get my apron.' Slowly, the diner thawed into activity as Jack disappeared behind the swinging doors, the two sides snapping together in an overbite.

Jack reappeared with an empty busing bin. She watched him approach a family that had finished eating: a mother, a father, a little boy. 'Mommy,' the child said in a stage whisper, 'is that the bad man?'

Addie was at his side in a moment. 'I'll take over.' Her voice jolted Jack out of his surprise. With a nod, he crossed the room to bus the counter.

Stuart winked. 'Guess Addie sent you here because we're safe. Not a perky set of hooters between the two of us.'

Flushing deeply, Jack reached for their dirty silverware.

'Don't blame you, anyhow. You ever watch that MTV station? Heck, you'd have to be six feet under to keep from noticing that Britney Spears gal.' Stuart grinned. 'Reckon she might have given me a stroke I wouldn't have minded, if you know what I mean.'

'Them girls,' Wallace agreed. 'They're asking for it.'

Jack's hands tightened on the busboy's bin. 'They don't ask for it.'

'You're right,' Stuart said, and chuckled. 'They see a guy like you and they *beg* for it.'

It happened so quickly that later, Jack couldn't recall the exact moment he grabbed Stuart by the parchment folds of his neck, lifting him off the stool with a single hand. Or how Roy tried to wrestle Jack off the octogenarian. The collective attention of the diner was riveted on a performance beyond their wildest dreams.

'Jack!' Addie cried, her voice cutting to the quick. 'Jack, you have to stop.'

He let go immediately, and Stuart rolled to his side, coughing. The blood that had been pounding in Jack's head flowed evenly again, and he stared at his hands as if they'd grown from the ends of his wrists just moments before. 'Mr. Hollings,' he stammered. 'I'm so sorry.'

'The doc was almost right,' Stuart wheezed. 'It ain't the coffee what'll kill me, but the guy who cleans it up.' With Wallace's support, he struggled to his feet. 'Oh, you're tough, Jack. It takes a real man to beat up a guy as old as me . . . and to fuck a child.'

Jack's hands twitched at his sides. 'Stuart, Wallace,' Addie said. 'I'm so sorry.' She took a step forward, smiling as graciously as she could. 'Of course, breakfast is on the house. For everyone.'

There was a cheer, and as Stuart and Wallace became immediate heroes again, the tension dissolved like fog. Addie turned to Jack. 'Can I talk to you? In private?'

She led him into the women's bathroom, pretty and floral and smelling of potpourri. Jack didn't let himself meet her eyes; he just shuffled and waited for the storm to break.

'Thank you,' Addie said, winding her arms around his neck as delicately as ivy.

A moment later, the taste of her still on his lips, Jack spoke. 'Why aren't you angry at me?'

'I admit, I wish it hadn't been Stuart. And I wish it hadn't been in front of so many people, who came here looking for just this. But sooner or later, they're going to wonder why a rapist would have taken the victim's side.' She pulled him closer, so that his grateful face was buried against the curve of her neck, and his breath fell between the buttons of her blouse. 'Come over tonight?' she whispered. And she felt his smile against her skin.

In one corner of the Salem Falls High School cafeteria, a makeshift altar had been erected. It overflowed with carnation bouquets and teddy bears and handmade cards that wished Hailey McCourt a speedy recuperation following surgery to remove a brain tumor. 'I heard,' Whitney said, 'that it was the size of a grapefruit.'

Gillian took a sip of her iced tea. 'That's ridiculous. It would have been pushing out the side of her head.'

Meg shuddered. 'Hailey was horrible and all, but I don't wish that on anyone.'

Amused, Gilly said, 'You don't *wish* that on anyone?'

'Of course not!'

'Meg, you're the very reason it happened! Don't you find it just the slightest bit coincidental that we cast a spell on her, and the next day she started falling down?'

'Jesus, Gill, do you have to tell the whole school?' Meg glanced nervously at the altar, where two students were leaving an over-size spiral lollipop tied with ribbon. 'Besides, we didn't do . . . *that*. A person can't grow a tumor overnight.'

Gilly leaned forward. 'That's because it came from *us*.'

Now, Meg was white as a sheet. 'But we're not supposed to do any harm. Gill, if we gave her a brain tumor, what's going to happen to us?'

'Maybe we ought to heal her,' Chelsea suggested. 'Isn't that what being a witch is all about?'

Gillian dipped her spoon into her yogurt and licked it delicately. 'Being a witch,' she said, 'is whatever we need it to be.'

Amos Duncan banged a hammer on the pulpit at the front of the Congregational Church. The buzzing in the filled pews stopped instantly, and attention turned to the silver-haired man. 'Ladies and gentlemen, thanks for coming on such short notice.'

He surveyed the crowd. Most were people he'd known all his life, people born and raised in Salem Falls like himself. Many worked at his plant. All had been summoned to the town meeting with a hastily photocopied flyer, stuffed into mailboxes by enterprising young boys who had been willing to earn a few dollars.

In the rear, Charlie Saxton leaned against a wall. To keep the peace, he had said.

'It has come to my attention,' Amos began, 'that there is a

stranger among us. A stranger who slipped into our midst under false pretenses and who even now is waiting for the best moment to strike.'

'I don't want no rapist living here!' called a voice from the rear of the church, quickly seconded by a buzz of support.

Amos held up his hands for silence. 'Friends, I don't want one living here, either. You all know I have a little girl. Hell, half of you do, too. So which of us is going to have to suffer before action is taken to drive this man out?'

Tom O'Neill stood up. 'We have to listen to Amos. It's not like we don't have proof . . . this is a man who served jail time for the assault of a minor.'

Charlie sauntered down the aisle. 'So what are you guys gonna do?' he said, all innocence. 'Shoot him in front of the O.K. Corral? Challenge him to pistols at dawn? Or maybe you're planning to just burn down his place when he's conveniently in it?' He reached the podium and gave Amos a stern look. 'It's my job to remind you that no one's above the law. Not St. Bride, and not any of you.'

'We've got righteousness on our side,' someone yelled.

'We're talking about innocent children!'

A woman in a business suit popped out of her seat. 'My husband and I chose Salem Falls as a place to raise our family. We moved here from Boston precisely because there's no crime. No threats. Because we could leave our door unlocked.' She looked around the room. 'What kind of message does it send if we're not willing to preserve that ideal?'

'Beg pardon.' All eyes swiveled to the left side of the church, where Jordan McAfee lazed in a pew. 'I recently moved here, too, to get away from it all. Got a son about the same age as most of those daughters you're worried about.' Finally, he got to his feet and walked to the front of the church. 'I support Mr. Duncan's initiative. Why, I can't even count the number of crimes that might have been avoided if the trouble had been nipped in the bud before it even got started.'

Amos smiled tightly. He didn't know McAfee from Adam.

Still, if the fellow wanted to cast his support Amos's way, he wasn't fool enough to turn it down.

Jordan stepped up to the podium, so that he was standing beside Amos. 'What do I think we ought to do? Well, lynch him. Metaphorically . . . literally . . . it doesn't matter which. Do whatever it takes, right?'

There were murmurs of assent, rolling like a wave before him.

'One thing, though. If we're going to be honest, now, and we start taking care of business this way, we'd better get used to a few changes. For example, all you people out there with children, how many is that?' Hands crept up like blades of grass. 'Well, I'd recommend you go home and start spanking, or doing a time-out, or whatever it is you do for punishment. Not because those kids have done anything wrong, mind you . . . but because they just might in the future.' Jordan smiled broadly. 'For that matter, Charlie, why don't you come up here and start cuffing, oh, every fifth person. Figure sooner or later they're going to get into trouble. And maybe you could just do a computer check of license plates in the town and issue tickets at random, since someone's going to be speeding eventually.'

'Mr. McAfee,' Amos said angrily, 'I believe you've made your point.'

Jordan turned on him so quickly the bigger man fell back a step. 'I haven't even begun, buddy,' he said softly. 'You can't judge a man by actions he hasn't committed. That's the foundation of the legal system in this country. And no pissant New Hampshire village has the right to decide otherwise.'

Amos's eyes glittered. 'I will not stand by and let my town suffer.'

'This isn't *your* town.' Yet he knew, as did everyone else, that that wasn't true. He walked past Duncan and Charlie Saxton and 300-odd angry locals. At the back of the church, he paused. 'People change,' Jordan said softly. 'But only if you give them room to do it.'

* * *

Gillian sat cross-legged on her bed in her robe, her hair still damp from a shower, as she fixed her makeshift altar and considered what she had learned that day.

By this afternoon, the rumor had spread through the school: The dishwasher at the Do-Or-Diner had raped some girl back where he used to live. It was what her father had been talking about with her friends' dads; it was why she'd been told she couldn't leave the house after sundown. Gilly thought of Jack St. Bride, of his gold hair falling over his eyes, and a shiver shot down her spine. As if she would ever be afraid of him.

It made Gilly laugh to watch the townspeople scurry like field mice before a storm, hoarding bits of safety to last them through this latest crisis. They all thought Jack St. Bride had brought evil, single-handedly, to Salem Falls, but it had been here all along. Maybe Jack was the match, setting fire to the straw, but it was unfair to lay the blame at his feet.

More than ever, he needed a . . . friend.

Gillian loosened her robe, and lit the wick of the candle before her. 'Craft the spell in my name; weave it of this shining flame. None shall come to hurt or maim; hear these words and do the same.'

She was warm now, so warm, and the fire was inside her. Gilly closed her eyes, smoothing her palms up from her own waist, cupping her breasts in her hands and imagining that it was Jack St. Bride touching her, heating her.

'Gilly?' A quick knock, and then the door opened.

As Gillian's father walked into her bedroom, she pulled the edges of her robe together, holding it closed at the throat. He sat on the edge of the bed, inches behind her. Gilly forced herself to remain perfectly still, even as his hand touched the crown of her damp hair, like a benediction. 'You and those candles. You're going to burn this place down one day.' His hand slipped down to her shoulder. 'You've heard by now, haven't you?'

'Yes.'

His voice was thick with emotion. 'It would kill me if anything happened to you.'

'I know, Daddy.'

'I'm going to keep you safe.'

Gilly reached up, twining her fingers with his. They stayed that way for a moment, both of them mesmerized by the dancing flame of the candle. Then Amos got to his feet. 'Good night, then.'

Her breath came out in a rush. ' 'Night.'

The door closed behind him with a soft click. Gilly imagined the fire again, consuming her. Then she lifted one foot, inspecting the sole. The cuts she had made last week were still there, a thin spiral on the arch, like the soundhole on a violin. There was one on her other foot, too. She reached into the pocket of her robe for a penknife, then traced the seam of the skin to reopen the wound. Blood welled up, and Gilly gasped at the pain and the beauty of it.

She was clipping her own wings – making it impossible to walk away from this house, because she'd be suffering with every step. She was marking herself. But as she did, she thought of how normal it would feel to have a scar on the outside that anyone could see just by looking.

An image flashed on the screen of the Salem Falls High School auditorium: a wholesome, all-American teenage girl holding hands with an equally picture-perfect blond boy. appropriate – the word, in red letters, was stamped over their legs. The slide projector clicked, and there was the same girl. This time, though, a dark and greasy older man had his hand resting on her ass. inappropriate.

Thomas looked up from his algebra homework. He hadn't been listening to Mr. Wood, the guidance counselor, and from the looks of the 400 other students, he wasn't the only one. Kids in the front were tossing spitballs, trying to see who could land one on Wood's Stegmann clogs. In front of Thomas, a cheerleader was French-braiding her hair. A corps of Goths with their pale faces and dyed black hair sat making out with their girlfriends in the back of the room, as Mr. Wood held this forum on being touched decently.

He wouldn't have been doing his math homework, either, but fate had landed him in a seat next to Chelsea. Add this to Mr. Wood's lecture ('Breasts? Can we use that word here, please, without the snickering?') and Thomas had a boner the size of Alaska. Every time he imagined Chelsea looking over and seeing the pole growing in his pants, he turned red and got a little harder. So finally, he slapped open a book to hide the evidence – and to distract himself from the fact that if he leaned six inches to the left, he would be able to discover whether she was as soft as she looked.

'I never could do that when I was a freshman,' Chelsea said, pointing at the battered text in his lap.

All he could think was: *If the book wasn't there, she'd have her hand on me.*

'All that *x* and *y* stuff,' Chelsea whispered. 'I used to get them backward.'

'It's not that hard. You just do whatever you have to do to get *x* alone on one side of the equals sign.'

'It makes no sense. What's a negative *y*, anyway?'

Thomas laughed. 'A why not.'

Chelsea smiled at him. On the screen, the same sleazy guy was slapping a girl across the face. INAPPROPRIATE. 'Does he think we're morons?' she whispered.

'Uh . . . yes.'

'I heard he used to live on a commune in Vermont. And that he screwed sheep.'

Thomas glanced at the guidance counselor's Mexican poncho and his straggly gray ponytail. 'Well, at least he's qualified to teach us about being assaulted from behind.'

Chelsea giggled. The next slide clicked into place: the girl and the blond boy with his arm slung over her shoulder. But to Thomas, it looked like the boy's fingers were getting awfully close to copping a feel. 'A trick question,' he murmured.

'Look at her face,' Chelsea said. 'She wants it.'

'Appropriate,' Mr. Wood announced.

Thomas shook his head. 'Bad call.'

'Obviously, you need some extra help here. A little tutorial.'

'With Wood? Thanks – I don't think so.'

'With me,' Chelsea said, and just like that, Thomas couldn't breathe. She snaked her arm over the algebra book until her hand was touching his ribs. Was she thinking how skinny he was? How easy it was to string along a loser?

She pinched him, hard. 'Ow!'

Several heads turned. But by then, Chelsea's hands were folded in her lap and she was staring demurely at the screen.

'Inappropriate,' she mouthed silently.

Thomas rubbed his hand over his side. Shit, she'd probably given him a bruise. Suddenly her fingers slipped over his, weaving, until their two hands were clasped. Thomas stared, speechless at the sight of his own skin flush against an angel's.

Reluctantly, he met her gaze, certain she would be laughing at him. But she was dead serious, her cheeks bright as poppies. 'Appropriate.'

He swallowed. 'Really?'

Chelsea nodded and did not pull away.

Thomas was certain the room was going to come crashing in on him, or that his alarm clock would ring out at any moment. But he could feel the pressure of Chelsea's palm against his own, and it was as real as the blood speeding through his heart. 'I think I get it now,' he said softly.

Chelsea smiled, a dimple appearing in one cheek, an invitation. 'It's about time.'

'Do I know astral projection?' Starshine said, the silver bells of her earrings swinging. 'Yes. Will I teach you? Not a chance.'

'I can do it,' Gilly insisted. 'I know I can.'

'I never said you couldn't.' The older woman sat down on one of the rocking chairs in the Wiccan Read, stroking the cat that leaped into her lap. 'But if you're looking for a psychic vision, you can get the same effect from trance induction. On the other hand, if you're just looking to get high, try your local dealer.'

Gillian couldn't tell Starshine that what she wanted most was to fly – to leave her body behind and to live in her mind. She was destined for more than this insignificant town, she just *knew* it, and she couldn't even look forward to college providing a portal out, because her father would never let her move that far away. In Gilly's mind, that meant taking matters into her own hands. But none of the books at the Wiccan Read held the old recipe for witches' flying ointment, the herbal oil that had produced such startling psychedelic effects in the Middle Ages that witches who applied it to their foreheads believed they could soar. The newer recipes were safer, more politically correct: a mishmash of chimney soot and mugwort and benzoin. In other words, a poor substitute.

Starshine looked at the girl's stubborn face and sighed. 'No one makes astral projection ointment anymore. The recipe called for the fat of an unbaptized infant, for goodness' sake. You can't get that at the supermarket deli counter.'

Gilly thrust out her chin. 'That wasn't the active ingredient.'

'Ah, I forget who I'm talking to . . . the pharmaceuticals heiress. No, it wasn't. I believe the effect was brought on by tripping on hashish and belladonna – neither of which I sell, because the first will land you in jail and the second can land you in a coma. It just isn't safe, honey.'

At the girl's crestfallen expression, Starshine squeezed her hand. 'Why not concentrate on Beltane, instead? It's right around the corner, and it's such a wonderful sabbat to celebrate. Sensuality and sex, and the earth coming to life again.' She closed her eyes and breathed deeply. 'There is nothing like leaping naked over a bonfire.'

'I'll bet.'

'Well, except maybe for a handfasting ceremony. I did that one Beltane, you know, when I wasn't much older than you.'

'Handfasting?'

'A trial marriage. For a year and a day. A test period, if you will, before the final commitment.'

'What happened after that?'

'After a year I chose to go my separate way. But that Beltane . . . oh, we danced barefoot with my coven and wove the maypole, and then the two of us celebrated the Great Rite like the God and Goddess right there in the meadow.'

Gilly's eyes widened. 'You had sex right in front of everyone else?'

'Guess so, because I still remember it. On Beltane, the first thing to go are your inhibitions.' She began to move around the tiny shop, plucking herbs and dried flowers off the cluttered shelves. 'Here. Use primrose and St.-John's-wort, cowslip and rosemary, some bloodstone on your altar. Courage, Gillian. Beltane's all about filling your soul with the courage to do the things you might not otherwise be able to do.'

Gillian took the collection from Starshine's hands. *Courage.* If she couldn't fly, maybe this would be the next best thing.

'Figures,' Delilah said, shaking her head. 'First time I let you behind the stove and you make a mess of it.'

Jack grimaced and tried to scrape the worst of the spaghetti sauce off his clothing. Okay, so it hadn't been brilliant to leave the vat sitting on the edge of the cold table while he cleared a spot on the stove for it to heat. Now that it had fallen and splattered everywhere, he was going to have to make another pot from scratch, because Delilah had a thing about using canned sauce for her pasta dishes. 'We don't have any more tomatoes,' she said, handing Jack another clean dishrag.

'Good thing you've got me to go get some, then,' he said without missing a beat.

Addie walked into the kitchen to hand Delilah an order. 'What happened to you?' she asked, glancing at Jack.

'He got on the wrong side of a pot of sauce. I'm sending him out for fresh produce,' Delilah said.

'Better change first. People are going to think you've been gut-shot.'

Jack didn't answer, just huffed his way up the set of stairs that led from the kitchen to Roy's apartment. In his bedroom, he bent down to retrieve a clean shirt from his bottom drawer. Suddenly, above him, the window exploded.

Jack flattened himself on the carpet, aware of all the places his hands were being cut as they pressed against shards of glass. Heart pounding, he cautiously got to his feet and looked out the broken pane.

He smelled the smoke first. The brick had landed on the carpet, and the flaming newspaper it was wrapped in had already started to burn. 'Fire,' Jack whispered hoarsely. Then he lifted his head, and bellowed. 'Fire!'

Addie was the first one into the room, holding the extinguisher they kept next to the stove. She sprayed the foam all over the flames, all over Jack's feet. By the time Jack gathered his wits, Roy and Delilah had crowded into the doorway of the room, too. 'What the hell did you do?' Roy demanded.

Addie reached into the foam and pulled out the thick brick, still wrapped with a rope and some residual paper. 'Jack didn't do anything. Someone did it to him.'

'Better call Charlie Saxton,' Delilah said.

'No.' This, flat, from Jack. 'What if I hadn't been here? What if we were all working downstairs, and this happened, and the whole place burned down?'

He began to pull his clothes from the drawers: a few pairs of jeans, some underwear, his T-shirts. 'What are you doing?' Addie asked.

'Moving. I'm not staying here while all this is going on. It's too dangerous.'

'Where are you going to go?'

'I don't know yet.'

Addie stepped forward, staring at his clothes. These Hanes T-shirts and Levi's were the most beautiful things she had ever seen, simply because they were his. She thought about opening her closet and seeing Jack's things pressed up against her own. 'Come live with me,' she said, but what she really meant was: *Here is my heart; have a care.*

Their eyes met as if there was no one else in the room. 'I won't put you in danger either, Addie.'

'No one has to know. I'm the last person in the world this town would expect to have a . . . a . . .'

One corner of Jack's mouth turned up. 'A boyfriend?'

'I'll be damned,' Delilah whispered.

They turned, suddenly remembering the presence of the others. 'If you say a single word,' Addie said fiercely, 'I'll –'

Delilah pantomimed locking her lips and throwing away the key, then led Roy back downstairs. Jack stepped closer to Addie, a fistful of socks in his hands. 'It doesn't have to be . . . well, you know. Like that. I could stay on the couch.'

'I know.'

'Are you doing this to save your father?' Jack asked quietly. 'Or me?'

She cradled the empty fire extinguisher in her arms, like an infant. 'I'm doing this to save myself,' she said.

Gilly had been five the first time she had seen medicine made – an aspirin – and its unlikely source was a tree. 'Salicylic acid,' her father had explained. 'It comes from willow bark. It's why the Indians used to brew willow bark tea to bring down a fever.' Nowadays, of course, her father's R & D lab was the biggest, most impressive part of Duncan Pharmaceuticals, filled with an alphabet soup of Ph.D.s who could create synthetic compounds used to heal. Sometimes it freaked her out to walk through the lab – it always smelled of science, and there were those creepy lab rats and rabbits that had tumors pulsing out of their sides or had gone hairless from the doses of medicine sent into their bloodstreams. But Gilly knew this was where her father preferred to spend the lion's share of his day.

'Daddy?' she said, poking her head into the restricted area. She shrugged into a white coat and goggles and plastic gloves, required couture for the R & D area. It was quiet today, staffed with a few of the grunts – the guys who only had master's degrees, not doctorates. They looked up as Gilly entered but weren't surprised; most knew her by sight.

She found her father – and most of the other scientists – gathered in the rear of the lab, near those disgusting animals. Gilly's father was carrying a bowl of what looked like hairy white carrots. Like everyone else, he seemed to be holding his breath. Gilly followed his gaze to the gas chromatograph, and its capillary tube, which held the substance that was being tested. Zap – the flash of light from the mass spectrophotometer hit the gas in the tube. The technician let a computer printout feed into his hungry hands, a graph full of peaks and valleys that measured exactly what was floating around inside the thin glass thread. He handed it to Gilly's dad, who compared it for several long moments to a reference graph from a chemical library. 'Ladies and gentlemen,' Amos said, his face breaking into a smile, 'natural atropine!'

There was a volley of cheering, and Amos clapped the shoulder of his lab tech. 'Great work, Arthur. See if you can isolate one hundredth of a gram on the gelatin disc.' As the group broke up, he walked to his daughter. 'To what do I owe this surprise?'

'Just passing by,' Gilly said absently. 'Did you make a new drug?'

'No. An incredibly old one,' Amos said, leading her out of the R & D room. 'We're trying to break into the homeopathic market – going back to nature to find the sources we've been imitating in the lab. Atropine's amazingly cost effective. Did you see that tiny bit of gas? Just that much alone could provide ten thousand doses.'

Gilly tuned him out. For all that her father loved what he did, he could be talking about drawing blood from a stone and it would have made the same impression on her. As they reached his office, she sprawled across the white couch along the far wall. 'Did you hear about the fire at the Do-Or-Diner?'

'No,' he said, sitting down. 'What happened?'

'It was upstairs in Roy Peabody's apartment. Meg's mom was having lunch there when it happened.'

'Was anyone hurt?' her father asked, his hands steepled before him.

'Not that I heard.' Gilly sat up, reaching for a bowl of mints. 'But people are saying it wasn't an accident.'

'Addie couldn't get much insurance money even if she burned the place to the ground.'

'Not her. Supposedly, someone else set the fire. As a warning.' She stared hard at her father, waiting for him to confide in her.

'Gilly,' he said softly, shocked. 'You don't think I'd do anything like that?'

Something in her chest loosened. 'No. I just wondered if you knew someone who would.'

'Oh, I imagine any one of a hundred people in this town might have done it.'

'But that's awful!' Gilly burst out. 'He could have gotten hurt!'

'Better him than one of you.'

There was a knock on the door. 'Mr. Duncan,' the secretary said, 'how much more belladonna did you want ordered?'

Gilly turned. 'Belladonna?'

'Let's start with seven hundred fifty plants,' Amos said. As his secretary left, he turned to Gilly. 'What about it?'

'How come you need it?'

'It's the plant we extracted the atropine from,' Amos explained. 'Why?'

Gilly truly believed in fate. It was why, she knew, she had chosen to visit her father on the afternoon that he was working with belladonna, the same plant Starshine had mentioned a day ago when they were discussing witches' flying ointment. Hash and belladonna, Gilly remembered. Well, she could probably get hashish with a single query to one of the Goths at her school. But even if she didn't, maybe belladonna had enough strength to work by itself. Maybe she could mix her own flying ointment and no one would be the wiser. And what better time to soar than Beltane?

Courage, she thought. 'Nothing,' Gilly lied. 'It's the name of this really phat band.' She leaned over the desk to kiss her father's cheek. 'I'll see you later.'

'You're going home,' he ordered. 'I don't want you walking around town alone.'

'It's not like he's Jack the Ripper, Daddy.'

'Gilly.'

'Whatever,' she muttered, already halfway out the door. But she didn't turn left at the hallway, toward the exit. Instead, she retraced her steps back to the R & D lab. Arthur, the lab technician, was mashing those furry white carrots – *belladonna.* 'Miss Duncan,' he said without glancing up. 'What can I do for you?'

'Um, my dad asked me to bring a sample of atropine to his office.'

'What for?'

Gilly blanched. She hadn't gotten this far in her mind. 'I don't know. He just asked me to get it.'

'How much?'

She pointed to a little pool in the base of a test tube. 'He didn't say. I guess that's enough.'

The supervisor capped the tube and handed it to her. 'Wear your gloves out of the lab. You don't want to touch that stuff with your bare hands.'

'Thanks.' She slipped the vial into the pocket of her fleece jacket, keeping her hand fisted around her treasure as she walked straight home, just like her father had wanted.

'This is the bathroom,' Addie said, blushing faintly.

Jack smiled. 'You don't have to give me the grand tour. Really.' It had been some time since Addie had had to share her space. Add to that the forced intimacy in a relationship still so new Jack could still see the shine on it, and he could not help but wonder if he was making a tremendous mistake.

'And this,' Addie said, her hand on a doorknob, 'is Chloe's room.'

It was the only room in the house Jack had not seen. And as Addie slowly opened the door, he also realized it was the only room in the house that was not neat. Toys littered the floor like landmines, and clothes were draped over the back of a chair. A poster of a boys' band that hadn't made a record in nearly a decade was taped to the wall, peeling from one corner. On a shelf sat a parade of outgrown teddy bears, missing eyes and frayed at the limbs. The bed, a confection of pink ruffles, was unmade, as if Addie slept in it from time to time – a thought that tugged at Jack but seemed less heartbreaking than the alternative: that for eleven years, Addie had simply left this room as a shrine.

Still, it was only a bed, and linens could be changed. Toys could be put away. 'I could stay here,' Jack suggested. 'Give you a little more privacy.'

'No. You can't.' She stood beside the chair, smoothing her hand over the fabric of an impossibly small white shirt.

'Addie –'

'You can't,' she repeated. 'You just can't.'

'All right,' he said softly, understanding that this was a line he could not cross. He followed her out and closed the door quickly, thinking all the while of Pandora's box: of what he had let loose by breaching the seal of this room, and of hope, which might still have been trapped inside.

The scent of smoke was strong at the diner, but it didn't bother Selena. 'It's like a barbecue,' she said, watching Jordan wrinkle his nose as he slid into the booth.

'Yeah. Except it's the facility that's roasting.'

Addie came to the table carrying two mugs and a pot full of coffee. 'Cream and sugar, right?'

Selena smiled at the waitress. 'Can I get a cup of hot water, with lemon?'

Addie nodded and went off toward the counter. 'It's disgusting, you know, the way you drink that,' Jordan said. 'People use the same thing to wash their dishes.'

'Then think how clean my insides are.' She took the steaming mug from Addie.

'I had a customer who used to drink hot water,' Addie mused. 'She lived to be a hundred and six.'

'Get out,' Jordan said.

'Honestly.'

'How did she die?' asked Selena.

'Another waitress here served her coffee instead one day.' Addie winked. 'I'll be back to get your order in a minute.'

Selena watched her go. 'She seems nice enough.'

'She comes from good people, as they'd say around these parts.' Jordan shook out his copy of the paper. 'Certainly doesn't deserve all the flak she's getting now.'

'Such as?'

'Oh, the fire. And the backlash about the fellow who works in the kitchen.'

Jordan raised the paper to read the headlines. With a fork, Selena tugged down the edge. 'Hello,' she said. 'Remember me? I'm your breakfast date.'

'Give me a break.'

'Don't tempt me. What's the story with the guy who works here?'

Jordan pushed the newspaper across the table. Folded to the editorial page, there were no less than six letters addressing the 'unsavory influences' that had recently moved into town. Selena scanned the brief missives, all in favor of riding Jack St. Bride out on a rail. 'What did he do? Rob a bank?'

'Rape a girl.'

Selena looked up, whistling softly. 'Well, you can't blame a community for trying to protect itself. You ask me, that's the whole point behind Megan's Law.'

'At the same time, it's prejudicial to the person who has to report in. If an entire community identifies a guy by his past convictions, how will anybody ever get past that to accept his presence?'

Selena peeked under the table. 'What the hell are you doing?' Jordan asked.

'Making sure you've gotten off your soapbox. You know damn well that perps of sex crimes are repeat offenders. How do you think you'd feel if he targeted, oh, fifteen-year-old boys?'

'Repeat offenders,' Jordan said, snapping the newspaper open again, 'are good for business.'

Selena's jaw dropped. 'That is quite possibly the most inhuman thing I've ever heard fall out of your mouth, McAfee, and believe me, there've been plenty.'

'Ah, but defense attorneys aren't supposed to be human. It makes it easier to sink down to everyone's very low expectations.'

But Selena didn't take the bait. She was thinking that Jordan *was* human, far too human, and she should know, because she was the one who had broken his heart.

'Come on,' Gilly urged. 'What's he going to do? Attack us right on the counter?'

Beside her, Meg squinted at the neon sign overhead. The *R* had never been quite as bright as the other letters. She could remember giggling about it years ago, because back then the most hilarious thing in the world was the thought of a restaurant called the Doo Diner. 'My dad would kill me,' Meg said.

'Your dad will never know. Come on, Meggie. Do you want to be the kind of person who hides in the back when everyone else is fighting the dragon, or do you want to be holding the sword?'

'That depends. What's my chance of being burned to a crisp?'

'If he molests you, I will selflessly throw my body over yours as a substitute.'

Meg shook her head. 'I don't even want him to know what I *look* like.'

'For God's sake, Meg, this isn't even about him. I'm *thirsty* is all. He probably won't come out from the back. We'll see Crazy Addie and get our milk shakes and go.'

Slowly, Meg backed away. 'Sorry, Gill. My dad said I shouldn't.'

Gillian fisted her hands on her hips. 'Well, so did mine!' Meg was already halfway down the street. 'Fine. *Be* that way!' Smarting, Gilly pushed inside the diner. It was virtually empty, except for an old fart at the cash register who was hunched over a crossword puzzle. She sat down and rapped her nails impatiently on the table.

Within moments, Crazy Addie came over. 'What can I get for you?'

Gilly glanced at her dismissively. She couldn't even conceive of living a life so small that you'd grow up in this nothing town and work and die there. Clearly, the woman was a loser. Who looked at the bright ball of her future and thought, *Oh, one day I want to be a waitress in a totally dead-end job.*

'A black-and-white shake,' Gilly said, and then, from the corner of her eye, saw Jack come down the hallway from the bathrooms carrying a large trash bag.

He didn't notice her.

'Actually, now that I think about it, I'm not hungry,' Gillian murmured, and walked out. The sunlight was blinding; she stumbled before slipping along the edge of the building, where a fence cordoned off the green Dumpster. Jack was moving around in there; she could hear metal clanging and the rustling of plastic as trash was hauled over its wide lip.

Gilly sucked her lower lip between her teeth, to give it some color. She unbuttoned her jacket, then slid the zipper of her cropped sweatshirt low enough to show the rise of her breasts. Walking to the gate, she waited for Jack to notice her.

He did, after a minute, and looked away.

'Hey,' Gilly said, 'what are you doing?'

'Skiing the Alps. Can't you tell?'

Gillian watched his muscles flex as he lifted another bag of garbage high. She thought about him pinning her, grabbing her wrists in his hands. Hard. She wondered if the girl he had raped had liked it, even a little.

'Food's a lot better inside,' Jack said.

'I'm not hungry.'

God, his eyes were a color blue she'd never seen. Dark and smooth, like the inside of a fire. There should have been a word for it – Jackquoise, maybe, or –

'Then why did you come here?'

Gilly lowered her lashes. 'To ski, of course.'

He shook his head, as if he couldn't believe she was standing here in front of him. It only made her more determined. 'Bet you were the kind of kid who used to poke crabs on the beach to get them moving,' Jack mused, 'even if it meant they might snap.'

'What's that supposed to mean?'

'It means stick to the bunny slope, Gillian,' Jack said flatly.

Her eyes darkened, caught somewhere between tears and rage. Jack started to leave, but Gillian was blocking the exit. For an uncomfortable moment, they danced around each other, Jack unwilling to let his body brush up against hers, Gillian unwilling to let him go.

'Gillian.'

At the sound of another voice, they jumped apart. Wes Courtemanche rounded the corner, dressed in uniform. 'Something tells me your father wouldn't be delighted to find you standing back here.'

'Something tells me you're not my father,' Gillian said testily. But she stepped away so that Jack could get by.

'Going home now, aren't you?' Wes said to the girl.

'I'm not afraid of you. I'm not afraid of anyone.' As if to prove it, Gillian turned on her heel, passing close to Jack. She blew a kiss as she sailed by, a gesture meant for his eyes only that might have been a promise, or might have a threat.

7:40. Wes had twenty minutes left on duty before he could head home. Usually, this time of night, high school kids were hanging in small clots near the rear of the post office or idling in their cars in the parking lot, but these days Main Street looked like a ghost town, as if kids believed the closer they got to the Do-Or-Diner, the more likely they were to fall prey to the local criminal.

The sound of footfalls behind Wes had him turning, his hand on his gun belt. A jogger approached, reflective markings on his stocking cap and sneakers winking in the glare of the street-lights.

'Wes,' said Amos Duncan, slowing down in front of the policeman and drawing in great gulps of air. He set his hands on his knees, then straightened. 'Nice night, isn't it?'

'For what?'

'A run, of course.' Amos wiped the sweat off his face with the sleeve of his shirt. 'God, though. You'd think there was a curfew, based on what this town looks like.'

Wes nodded. 'Dead, for about seven-thirty.'

'Maybe people are eating later,' Amos suggested, although they both knew this was not the case. 'Well, I'd better get home. Gilly'll be waiting.'

'You might want to keep a close eye on her.'

Amos frowned. 'What's that supposed to mean?'

'I saw her this afternoon, down by the diner. She was talking to St. Bride.'

'Talking?'

'That's all.'

A muscle along Amos's jaw tightened. 'He started talking to her?'

'Can't say, Amos.' He chose his words carefully, knowing that alienating Duncan would put him in the doghouse with the department for months. 'Just seemed to me that Gilly . . . well, that she didn't have a real strong sense of how dangerous he is.'

'I'll speak to her,' Amos said, but his mind was elsewhere. He was wondering how a guy could come into a town where he wasn't wanted and act like he had a right to be there. He was wondering how many innocent conversations it took before a girl followed you home, a deer eating out of your hand. He envisioned St. Bride calling out his daughter's name. Imagined her turning, smiling, like she always did. He saw what he wanted to believe had happened.

Amos forced his attention back to Wes. 'You off soon?'

'Ten, fifteen minutes.'

'Good, good.' He nodded. 'Well, thanks for the tip.'

'Just trying to keep everyone safe.'

Amos held up his hand in farewell, already moving off. Wes headed back toward the green again. He never noticed that Amos had turned away from the road that led to his house and was running quickly in the opposite direction.

Tom O'Neill swung the door open, surprised to find Amos Duncan on his doorstep, panting hard.

'Amos, you all right?'

'Sorry to bother you.'

Tom glanced over his shoulder. In the dining room, his family was gathered around their dinner. 'No, no problem at all.' He stepped out onto the porch. 'What's the matter?'

Amos soberly met his gaze. 'Well,' he said. 'It's like this.'

April 30, 2000
Salem Falls, New Hampshire

Addie couldn't get Jack out of her mind. Now, she leaned forward, kissing the nape of his neck in a blatant attempt to draw his attention from the TV set in her living room. *The Formosa type of this tea is more famous than the Amoy, Foochow, and Canton varieties.*

'What is oolong,' Jack said, his elbows resting on his knees. Addie opened her mouth and licked the soft shell of his ear. 'Cut it out! I'm on a roll.'

'You could be on me.' Most hours of the day, Jack could be counted on to catch her gaze across the diner, hot enough to make her stumble, or manage to pass by her so closely their bodies brushed. But when *Jeopardy!* came on, she could have paraded in front of him completely naked without managing to capture his attention.

Jack was addicted to *Jeopardy!* In three years, he had gone only one day without seeing the show, and that was because he was driving in a sheriff's cruiser to the jail at the time. He was delighted that because he and Addie had taken the afternoon off to move his things, today he'd have the chance to watch at both 7 *and* 11 p.m. Addie, however, had a different agenda.

She began to unbutton his shirt, but Jack brushed her away. 'I'll get you back during the commercial,' he warned half-heartedly.

'Ooh . . . now I'm scared.'

Demeter brought famine upon the earth after this daughter was abducted to the underworld.

'I bet you know this one,' Jack said.

In response, she slipped her hand down the front of his jeans.

He jumped. 'Addie!' he said, even as he swelled into her palm.

'Who is Persephone?' the contestant said on the screen.

Addie squeezed gently. 'Aha. You missed.'

Beneath her, Jack's hips moved. 'I knew the answer. I was just distracted before I could give it.'

Jefferson said it 'is no excuse in any country . . . because it can always be prevented.'

Addie straddled him, blocking his view of the television set. Finally, Jack gave up fighting. He drew her face down and kissed her, slipping the answer into her mouth: 'What is ignorance of the law.'

'Ignorance,' Addie repeated. 'A very nice segue to bliss.' She arched her throat, tilting back her head, and suddenly stilled. 'Did you hear that?'

But Jack's famous concentration was now focused entirely on Addie. 'No.'

A crash, the sound of running. Addie sat up a little straighter. 'There it is again.'

'It's an animal,' Jack suggested. 'You live in the woods.'

She pulled away from him, even as he grabbed for her hand and groaned at the loss of her soft weight on his lap. Peering out the window, Addie could only see the edge of the swing set, serrated by the moonlight. 'Nothing out there.'

'Then try looking here.' Jack stood up, his erection straining against his jeans. He took Addie into his arms. 'It's probably raccoons. Why don't you go upstairs while I get rid of them?'

'You're going to miss Final Jeopardy?' Addie teased.

'Never,' he said, all seriousness, and then he winked. 'There's a rerun at eleven.'

Gilly could not get Jack out of her mind. She relived the moment outside the diner a hundred times, playing different scenarios like a slide show – things she should have said and done instead, images of Jack grabbing her and kissing her so hard her lips bled. Every time she stumbled over the part where Jack had treated her like a child, her stomach clenched, and she'd start to cry, dying a hundred deaths all over again. A moment later, she'd be spitting mad, itching for the next opportunity she might have to show him she wasn't a child after all.

Her father had kept a hawk's eye on her all afternoon and evening; then he'd gone running and made her swear she would be there when he got home. Now she was drowning her sorrows in the emotional angst of Sarah McLachlan and painting her fingernails bloodred as the phone rang. Whitney's voice came on the line. 'Gil, what time tonight?'

Gillian sighed. She didn't want to deal with her friends right now. She didn't want to do anything but figure out how to keep her father from being such a goddamned warden, so that she could make Jack see what he was missing. 'What time for what?'

'The *meeting?*'

'The meeting . . .'

'I could have sworn I put down *April thirtieth* on my calendar.'

Understanding bloomed. 'Oh, Beltane,' Gilly said.

'How could you forget?'

Gillian hadn't forgotten, exactly; she'd just been preoccupied with Jack. Her coven had made plans to meet in the woods behind the cemetery, at the base of the flowering dogwood tree. Meg was bringing Georgia fatwood to light a bonfire, Whit had been given the task of sewing herb sachets to hang on the tree as gifts to the God and Goddess, and Chelsea was going to figure out some kind of maypole. Gilly's job had been the Simple Feast, the sharing of food and drink within a circle that had been cast.

Her father would kill her if she sneaked out of the house.

Her gaze lit on a small ceramic vase that had once been her

mother's. There was a sprig of pussywillows inside, but no water. Instead, hiding at the base, was the vial of atropine she'd taken from the R & D lab.

'Eleven,' she said into the phone. 'Be there.'

They attacked him from behind. Jack had no sooner stepped out of the small halo of light cast by the lantern hanging beside the door than he was grabbed, his arms pinned behind him while fists slammed into his ribs, his belly, his face. Blood ran down his throat, tinny; he spat it back at them. He struggled to find their faces, to mark them in his mind, but they were wearing stocking caps pulled low and scarves tugged high; all Jack could see was an ocean of black, a series of hands, and wave after wave of their anger.

Addie brushed out her hair, then sprayed perfume onto her wrists and knees and navel. Jack had been gone awhile, which was strange; even stranger, she could hear an occasional crash. If it was raccoons, it was a hell of a lot of them.

She stepped to the bedroom window and pulled back the Swiss organdy curtain. It was dark for eight o'clock, and at first she could not see Jack at all. Then a foot appeared in the yellow periphery cast by the porch light. An elbow. Finally, the entire body of a man, dressed in black, his hands bright with blood.

'Jack,' she gasped, and she reached underneath the bed for the rifle she kept there. She had used it once in twenty years – to shoot a rabid coon that had wandered into the yard where Chloe was playing. She loaded it on the run, hurrying downstairs, and threw open the front door to fire once into the night sky. Five faces turned, and their owners then ran off in disparate directions into the woods behind her house, tracks spreading like the spokes of a wheel.

On the gravel, in a boneless, battered heap, lay Jack.

Addie set down the gun, ran to his side, and gently rolled him over. *Oh, God,* she thought. *What have they done to you?*

Jack coughed, his lips pulling back to show teeth shiny with blood. He tried to sit up, wincing away from Addie's hands. 'No,' he grit out, that one syllable staining the stars. *'Noooo!'*

His cry bent back the young grass lining the driveway; it shouldered aside the violet clouds and left the moon to shiver, bare-boned. 'Jack,' she soothed. But his voice rose, until it was an umbrella over Salem Falls, until people on the far side of town had to close their windows to the sweet night air just to block off the sound of his pain.

The last thing she wanted to do was poison herself. To that end, Gilly logged onto the Internet at about 8:15 p.m., hoping to find the correct dosage of atropine. Thanks to Columbine, it was common knowledge now that you could even build a bomb with the help of the World Wide Web. Surely it would be a piece of cake to find the amount of hallucinogen it took to get high.

While the Web pages loaded, she painted her fingernails – one hand at a time, so that she could zip from one search engine to another, looking up herbal journals for information about belladonna and atropine sulfate. Finally, she found a site that listed adult dosages. In pill form, 5 milligrams. To dilate pupils, 1/50,000 of a grain. And taken internally, 1/20 to 1/100 of a grain.

Gilly frowned. Seemed like quite a range. What if she could take 1/20 of a grain but Whitney, who was tiny, only needed 1/100?

The telephone rang again. 'Gilly,' her father said. 'I wanted to check in on you.'

'Check *up* on me, you mean.'

'Now, sweetheart. You know why I'm doing this.'

Her heart began to pound in triple time. 'Aren't you supposed to be jogging?'

'Just finished. I should be home soon.'

What would she do if he arrived to find her missing? 'Actually,' Gilly said, 'I'm glad you called. Meg wants to know if I can come over tonight.'

'I really don't think it's a terrific idea, Gilly, with all that's going on.'

'Please, Daddy. Her mom is going to pick us up for a ten o'clock movie, and who's going to be stupid enough to hurt me while I'm out with a detective's wife?' When he didn't respond, Gilly forged ahead. 'Mrs. Saxton says I can stay over. If it's okay with you.' She was amazed at how easily the lies came, now that she had them in her mind. She was going to celebrate Beltane tonight, come hell or high water or Amos Duncan.

She could hear her father's resolve cracking just the tiniest bit. Meg's dad was a cop; her mom, a woman they'd known their whole lives. Gilly would probably be safer in the Saxton household than in his own. 'Okay,' he said. 'But I want you to call me when you get home from the movie. No matter what time it is.'

'I will. Love you, Daddy.'

'Me, too.'

For a long moment after she hung up, Gilly just stared at the phone and smiled. Webs were the very easiest things to spin.

She logged off the computer and walked to the kitchen. Astral projection was going to be her Beltane surprise for the coven; the effects would be even more startling if they were completely unexpected. Gilly stirred the thermos of iced tea and considered the vial in her hand once again.

Courage.

She trickled a tiny bit of the liquid into the tea, then stuck her finger into the thermos for a taste . . . nope, it was still tea, if a little bit bitter – $\frac{1}{20}$ of a grain? $\frac{1}{100}$? Shrugging, Gilly emptied the entire contents of the test-tube into the thermos and screwed on the cap.

Jack woke to find Addie curled beside him, her hand clutching a washcloth that was spreading a water stain over the comforter in the shape of a bell. He came up on one elbow, wincing at the ache of his ribs, and touched the side of her face. When she didn't stir, he carefully levered himself off the bed.

What might his life have been like if he'd had someone like her standing by his side during the nightmare in Loyal? What if he'd served his time but met her every Tuesday night in the common room where inmates could face their visitors over long folding tables, under the watchful eyes of the guards? What if he'd had Addie to come home to?

He paced through the dark house, wishing he could do for her all she'd done for him. Thanks to Addie, Jack no longer spent time reviewing his mistakes. He had put them into a box and shut the lid tight. Addie, though . . . she sorted through the box daily, holding up each memory to the light like an heirloom, even though it made her bleed inside.

He found himself standing in front of Chloe's bedroom door.

Within minutes, he had stripped the bed of its sheets and covers and removed the posters from the walls. He stacked Chloe's toys in a box he'd found in her closet. If he could just clear out the constant reminder of what Addie had lost, maybe it wouldn't be so hard for her to look forward rather than back.

'What the hell are you doing?' Addie's voice throbbed, as if she'd taken a punch.

'Cleaning up. I thought that if you didn't have to look at this every day –'

'That I wouldn't see her face first thing when I wake up in the morning anyway? That I don't know her by heart? Do you think that I have to look at a . . . a hair clip to remember the person I love the most in the world?'

'Loved,' Jack said quietly.

'That doesn't stop just because she's not here anymore.' Addie sank into the tousled sheets, the fabric floating up around her like the petals of a tulip.

'Addie, I didn't do this to hurt you. If what we've got means anything . . .'

She turned her face to his. 'You will never, *ever* mean more to me than my daughter does.'

Jack reeled back, her words more painful than any blow he'd felt that night. He watched her fold herself into the pool of linens, her spine rounding. 'What did you do with it?' she said, suddenly lifting her tear-stained face.

'With what?'

'The smell of her. Of Chloe.' Addie scrabbled through the sheets and pillows. 'It was here; it was here just this morning . . . but it's gone now.'

'Sweetheart,' Jack said gently. 'Those sheets don't smell like Chloe. They haven't in a very long time.'

Her hands made fists in the fabric. 'Get out,' she sobbed, turning her face away as Jack shut the door softly behind him.

The Rooster's Spit had never, in anyone's recollection, had anything to do with either chickens or expectorating, but a few old-timers could have told you that the bar tucked at the far edge of town had been a Knights of Columbus hall in a past life, and a Baptist church in another. Now, it was a dark, close space where a man could fall into a puddle of his own troubles, or a tumbler of whiskey, which was just as good.

Roy Peabody nuzzled the lip of his drink, closing his eyes at the sweet heat that rolled down his throat to bloom in his belly. After weeks of being hounded by Addie, or kept watch over by Jack St. Bride, he was in a bar again. He was alone, with the exception of Marlon, the barkeep, who was polishing glasses until they squeaked. Unlike some bartenders Roy had known – and Roy had known many – Marlon was gifted at simply staying quiet and letting a fellow savor his alcohol. In fact, Roy felt more at home in this bar, where no one expected a goddamn thing of him, than in his apartment.

When the door to the Rooster's Spit swung open, both Roy and Marlon looked up in surprise. It was rare for people in Salem Falls to be out drinking at 10 p.m. on a weeknight, and Roy felt a small needle of resentment at the thought that now he would have to share this wonderful moment with someone else.

It was hard to say who was more stunned when each first saw the other: Jack or Roy.

'What are you doing here?'

'What does it look like?' Roy grimaced. 'Run along now; go tell my daughter.'

But Jack just sat heavily down on the barstool beside him. 'I'll have whatever he's having,' he said to Marlon.

The whiskey was stamped before him like a seal of approval. Jack could feel Roy's eyes on him as he took his first long swallow. 'You going to watch me the whole time?'

'I didn't figure you for a drinking man,' Roy admitted.

Jack laughed softly. 'People aren't always what they seem.'

Roy accepted this, and nodded. 'You look like shit.'

'Thanks so very much.'

The old man reached out and gingerly touched the cut over Jack's eye. 'You walk into a wall?'

Jack glanced at him sidelong. 'You drinking lemonade?'

At that, Roy hesitated. 'I take it Addie knows you're here.'

' 'Bout as much as she knows *you* are.'

'I told you, St. Bride, if you break her heart –'

'How about when she breaks mine, Roy?' Jack interrupted bitterly. 'What are you going to do for me in that case?'

Roy took one look at the deep grooves carved beside Jack's mouth and saw in his face something too, too familiar. 'I'll buy you a drink,' he said.

Once, on a Girl Scout campout, Gillian had built a fire. While the other kids were busy making their s'mores and singing 'Kum ba Yah,' Gilly had fed things to the flame: sticks and pine needles and shoelaces, bits of bread and pennies and even a hapless toad. She had been mesmerized by its greed, by the way it devoured everything in its path. She'd stared at the bonfire and thought: *I don't have a heart. I have one of these inside of me.*

Tonight's bonfire was smaller . . . or maybe she was bigger. She stood holding hands with the others around it. But they were no longer Gillian, Chelsea, Whitney, and Meg. Goddesses all, they were a coven. And she was their high priestess.

The wind, ripe with spring, slipped between Gillian's thighs like a lover. It was her only covering; her clothes lay in a pile by the dogwood. When she'd said that she wanted to be as pure as possible, the others had been surprised. But Whitney had whipped off her shirt. Chelsea shivered in her bra and panties. Only Meg, self-conscious, was fully dressed.

Gilly met the eyes of each of the others. Did they feel it? Never had her body buzzed like this. She tilted her head back, casting her voice into the night sky. 'Guardians of the watch-towers of the east, where sun, moon, and stars are born, I do summon, stir, and call you up!'

The words wrote themselves, drawn from her heart like a ribbon, and for the first time Gilly understood what Starshine had meant about the power of writing your own spells. 'Travel over our skin like a whisper, caress us. Bring us imagination; teach us to dance. Blessed be.'

The others swayed slightly. 'Blessed be,' they repeated.

Whitney turned, her face glowing. 'Guardians of the watch-towers of the south, passionate and hot, I do summon, stir, and call you up. Share your heat with us; make us burn inside. Blessed be!'

'Blessed be!'

'Guardians of the watchtowers of the west,' Chelsea contin-ued, 'the blood of the earth, I do summon, stir, and call you up. Let your mystery flow over us. Blessed be!'

'Blessed be!'

Finally, Meg spoke. 'Guardians of the watchtowers of the north, night of cool magick, I do summon, stir, and call you up. Bury us deep in your soil; give us the power of earth and stone. Blessed be!'

'Blessed be!'

'Spirit,' Gilly cried, 'come play with us as we weave our

ribbons; sing with us as we light the fire. Take us to a world without words. Make this night magick . . . blessed be!'

'Blessed be!'

She knelt before the altar, her breasts swaying, and touched the incense burner, the water, the earth, and then sliced her hand through the flames of the bonfire. 'I do cast out any and all impurities both of the spirit and the world. As I will it, so mote it be.' Gillian cast the circle three times – with water and earth, with incense, and finally with energy. Then she smiled. 'The circle is perfect.'

Gillian brushed a branch of the dogwood tree, and a festival of delicate white petals rained over her shoulders. She raised her hands, her body slender and blued by the moon. 'Mother Goddess, Queen of the night, Father God, King of the day, we celebrate your union. Accept these gifts.' Digging into the L.L. Bean canvas bag, she pulled out a sachet filled with the herbs she'd bought at the Wiccan Read. There were twenty in there, all crafted by Whitney. 'You do it,' Gilly suggested, and she handed the sachet to her friend.

Whitney strung it on a branch, a poppy red ornament. She reached into the bag and handed out the rest of the sachets to the others, who began to trim the tree. Their gifts winked out from the thick profusion of blooms, a rainbow of offerings.

'Ouch!' Whit said, jumping. 'I got nailed by a twig.'

'See, there's a reason we wear clothes,' Meg said.

Chelsea sank down on the ground. 'Well, nudity aside, it seems to me that the God and Goddess have all the fun.'

'What do you mean?'

'Beltane's all about sex, right? But I don't see Freddie Prinze Jr. hanging with our coven. No offense, Gill, but you don't have the right equipment.'

Gillian turned. 'But that little geek Thomas McAfee does?'

Chelsea's cheeks flamed. 'He's not like that –'

'No? Then tell us what he *is* like. You've been hanging out with him so much I thought you might bring him along. You have to do that when you're training a puppy, right? Keep a close eye on them?'

'Gilly –' Meg said, trying to keep the peace.

'Let's conjure a man,' Whitney suggested. 'We're all just jealous. Right, Gill?'

But Gillian didn't answer. The other girls exchanged glances, unsure of what to do, what to say. 'We'd never agree on what to call up,' Whitney hastily continued. 'You know, like I have a thing for redheaded guys, but Meg likes those squat, stubby bull types.'

'Italian,' Meg corrected. 'And they're not stubby.'

Finally, Gillian smiled. The others were careful not to show it, but inwardly, they all relaxed. This was the Gilly they knew, the Gilly they loved. 'Maybe if we're really good little pagans, the God and Goddess will give us a gift, too.'

She walked to the tree beside the dogwood, a pillar of a pine. God knew how, but Chelsea had managed to affix long streamers of ribbon from a branch nine feet off the ground. Gilly picked up a silver ribbon and smoothed it between her breasts, over her belly and thigh. She arched her back, and the other girls were transfixed – channeling a spirit was one thing, but here Gilly was shifting shape, turning into a siren as if she had done this a hundred times before. 'Now,' she said softly, 'we celebrate.'

Addie woke up, her cheek flush against Chloe's pillow. It was so easy to see her daughter's little face, her flyaway hair. She touched her hand to the worn cotton, pretending that it was Chloe's soft skin beneath her fingers.

It isn't.

She heard the words as clearly as if Jack had spoken them, a thought that dropped like a grenade, and was just as devastating. Even more upsetting was the intrusion of Jack into her mind when she was stubbornly trying to think about Chloe. She tried to force her memories to the surface but kept seeing more recent ones: Jack sliding his arms around her waist; Jack looking up at her as he chopped peppers in the kitchen, Jack's slow smile. The truth was that although she found it hard to believe and had no idea how it had happened, she could no more picture her life without Jack than she could without Chloe.

Frustrated, she threw back the covers of the bed and began to pace through the house. At the bottom of the stairs, she automatically touched the small picture of Chloe that hung there, the same way she did every time she came up and down, as if it were a mezuzah. And that was the moment she realized she'd lied.

Jack might never mean more to her than Chloe. But God, he meant just as much.

Addie sank down onto the bottom step and rested her forehead on her knees. The last person she'd loved had been taken away. This time around, her second chance, she should have been holding onto him tightly, with both hands.

'I love him,' she murmured out loud, the words bright as a handful of new coins. 'I *love* him. *I* love him.'

Addie stood suddenly, giddy and dazed, like a cancer patient who'd just been told that the disease had disappeared. And in a way, it was not all that different – to find out a heart she'd believed irrevocably broken had somewhere along the way been fixed. She took a deep breath and felt it: every space in her soul that had been left empty when she lost Chloe was now swelling with the very thought of Jack.

She had to find him. She had to apologize. Addie slipped on her clogs and shrugged into a coat. She was halfway to the door when she hesitated. With the resignation of a man walking to the execution chamber, she started back up the stairs.

In Chloe's room, she stripped the bed. She carried the linens downstairs in a bundle, remembering what it had been like to hold her newborn just like this in her arms and walk her through her colic at night. She threw the sheets and pillowcases into the washing machine, added soap, and turned the dial.

The fresh scent of Tide rose from the bowl of the machine. 'Good-bye,' Addie whispered.

Amos Duncan couldn't sleep.

He sat up in bed and turned on the light, finally giving in to his insomnia. He was being ridiculous, he knew. As a parent, he was overprotective; more than a few times he'd heard town matrons talking about the tragedy it was that he'd not married again, for Gilly's sake. But Amos had never found anyone who meant more to him than his daughter. Where was the tragedy in that?

It was 11 p.m.; the movie she'd gone to see would probably let out in half an hour. It made sense to have Gilly stay over at the Saxtons' because the movie theater and, well, just about everything else was on the other side of town. Plus, Charlie probably slept with a gun next to his bed. For all Amos knew, so did his wife. And not even Jack St. Bride would be stupid enough to tangle with the detective's family.

Gilly would be in good hands.

Which didn't explain why, at 11:30 P.M., Amos got dressed and drove to the Saxtons' house to take his daughter home.

Jack tried to wipe the back of his mouth with his hand, but it took him three tries before he could connect. That made him laugh – great guffaws that gave him the hiccups, so that he had to take another long swallow of whiskey to get rid of the spasms – and by the time he did, he couldn't remember what he had been laughing about. He canted back in his seat, only to realize his stool didn't *have* a back. The next thing he knew, he was staring at the pitted ceiling, flat on the floor. 'Roy,' he yelled, although the man was sitting ten inches away. 'Roy, I think I may be getting a little drunk.'

Marlon snorted. 'Fucking Einstein,' he muttered.

Jack staggered to his feet – something truly commendable, because he couldn't sense anything past his knees – and hauled himself up by yanking on the rungs of Roy's stool. He peered into the empty insides of his whiskey tumbler. 'Jus' one more,' he said, pushing it toward Marlon . . . but Marlon was no longer beside the bar. Craning his neck, he found the bartender standing beside Roy, who had passed out cold.

Jack would have been horrified . . . if he'd been in a condition to feel anything at all. Roy was slumped over the bar, snoring. 'Lemme help,' Jack insisted, but the moment he stood up, the entire room became a tornado around him.

Marlon shook his head as Jack wilted back onto the stool. 'You should have stopped after the fifth one.'

Jack nodded, his head as heavy as a bowling ball. 'Absholutely.'

Rolling his eyes, Marlon heaved Roy into a fireman's carry.

'Where're you taking him?' Jack yelled.

'Relax, buddy. Roy's slept off plenty of late nights in the back room here.' He disappeared into an adjoining nook not much bigger than a closet. Jack could hear him banging around, dumping Roy's unconscious body on a cot.

'I gotta go home,' Jack said, when Marlon reappeared. 'But I don't have a home.'

'Well, Roy here just took the only accommodations. Sorry, pal.' Marlon scrutinized Jack, assessing just how bad off he was, and apparently decided he was just about as bad as they come. 'Hand over your car keys.'

'Don't have any.'

The bartender nodded, satisfied. 'Good thing. How much trouble can you get into walking?'

Jack staggered up from his stool. *'Trouble,'* he said, 'is my middle name.'

Charlie opened the door in his bathrobe. 'You may be the richest fucking guy in this town, Duncan, but that doesn't mean you own the civil servants. Whatever it is can wait until tomorrow.'

He started to close the door but was stopped by Amos. 'For Christ's sake, Charlie. I just came to pick up my daughter. She isn't back yet, I take it?'

'What the hell are you talking about?'

It was the absolute calm in Charlie's voice that frightened Amos to the core. Charlie functioned under pressure by turning down his internal emotional thermometer.

'Meg invited her to a movie. Your wife . . . she went with them.'

'My wife is upstairs, asleep,' Charlie said. 'Meg told me she was staying over at *your* house.'

'Charlie –'

But the detective had moved away from the door to grab his radio. Amos stepped inside the foyer, and Charlie met his sober gaze. 'It's Saxton,' he said, when dispatch picked up. 'We've got a problem.'

Wes was in his cruiser, wishing for a cup of coffee, when the APB came through. Two – possibly up to four – teenage girls missing. They could be anywhere at all. Christ, that was a recipe for all hell breaking loose, especially with a rapist in town.

He turned on his cruiser's silent blue lights and began to prowl slowly, ten miles an hour, through the back streets of Salem Falls. Dispatch would have called in the reserve officers, but as of right now there were only three cops on patrol in the town. If Wes found the girls before anyone else, he stood a very good chance of being awarded a promotion.

He had just turned the corner by the Rooster's Spit when he saw something moving jerkily along the edge of the road. Something rabid? Every now and then the department had to shoot a coon. But no, it was too big for that. A deer?

Wes angled the car so that the beam of blue light caught the moving creature in its crosshairs. 'I'll be damned,' he said softly, and parked his car.

Jack found it amazing that almost of their own accord, his feet managed to alternate one after the other, instead of just hopping left-left-left or right-right-right the whole time. Add to that the uncanny fact that the moon was the exact shape of a cat's slitted eye, and the world was a wondrous place. He shuffled down along the road that led into Salem Falls, stumbling and managing to catch himself before he pitched face first onto the ground.

It was a few moments before he realized there was a car following him. Its headlights looked like the eyes of a wolf, yellow and tilted up at the edges. The motor purred behind him, dogging his every step.

Jack tried to walk faster, glancing over his shoulder every now and then.

Had the men who had beaten him up come to finish it? If they killed him, who would care enough to notice?

Breathing hard, he turned just enough to see that a man sat behind the wheel. He was too far away and dizzy to make out the features, but it looked like a man who had dark hair . . . or a man who was wearing a black knit stocking cap.

Christ, the car was speeding up. Jack could hear the rev of the motor beating in his brain, the knot of panic clotting the back of his throat. *I'm going to be run over.* Terrified, wild, he ran diagonally across the road to throw off the driver, stumbling once and slamming his hand against the hood of the car as he righted himself and scrambled down an alley between two buildings.

He emerged on a different block and was trying to control the violent shaking of his body when the town began to glow, as if some huge UFO were beaming down rays in preparation for landing. Jack's gaze lit on the neon edges of the storefronts and curbs. Awestruck – it was fucking *beautiful,* in his mind – he stood in the middle of the street, so mesmerized that he completely forgot about his brush with death.

Suddenly, there was a police car not three feet away from him, and he had to hold his hand up to the glare. 'Hey,' Wes Courtemanche called out. 'You all right?'

It was that simple kindness that made Jack realize something was wrong. If Wes were the last guy on earth, he'd go out of his way to make sure Jack knew he was disliked. The whole town wanted him out; it would be easy for a cop to shoot someone and say it had been self-defense. Had Wes beaten him up earlier? Had it been his cruiser that had almost hit Jack? Without thinking beyond the fact that he wanted to be as far away from Wes as humanly possible, Jack started to run through the field behind the street, up paths that could not be followed by car.

Jack heard Wes swear, heard his boots hitting the pavement as he strained to catch up. He ducked into the woods behind the town cemetery, hoping to lose the policeman in the dark, and ended up hurting himself – he fell over an exposed root and scraped the palm of his hand, the cut over his eye reopened, and a branch snapped back and scratched his face, drawing blood. But even with these stumbling blocks, Jack, who'd been an athlete, easily outstripped Wes. He ran for five minutes, until he was certain he was safe, and then wandered through the woods, not sure of where he was or how he would get back to town.

When he paused to catch his breath and his bearings, he heard it: laughter. All the Greek myths he'd taught at Westonbrook came back in a flood, of Apollo chasing Daphne and Artemis running with her bow. And then, as if he'd dreamed her, he saw the Goddess herself – a flash of white skin silvering through the trees, her heels tripping on the air, her hair flying out like a banner behind her. Jack was momentarily confused: She was naked, like a nymph, but she seemed to be singing to him like a Siren.

Suddenly he realized that there were four of them, some in clothes and some without, and that the girl he'd been staring at was calling his name.

He heard the sound of sobbing first.

Charlie had caught plenty of that sound during his career on the force – what you hoped to be an animal with its leg trapped in a forked branch always wound up to be something far more human and heartbreaking. He forced himself to stop and listen more carefully, and then took off at a dead run toward the south.

Meg's orange anorak was a flag, and with energy he didn't know he possessed Charlie sprinted closer. Four girls were huddled together at the gate to the town cemetery. Their hair was straggling free of their combs and clips, and any one of them would be horrified to be seen in public looking the way they did, but Charlie counted them all in one piece and breathed an internal sigh of relief.

Meg, Whitney, and Chelsea were gathered around Gillian, who was crying. They hugged and soothed her, but she was inconsolable. In fact, Charlie had seen grief like that only once that he could remember – when he'd had to break the news to the survivor of a car crash that her two-year-old had not been as fortunate as she.

His daughter spotted him. 'Daddy,' she said, and threw herself into his arms.

'Shh. Meggie, honey, it's going to be all right.' With his girl tucked close, he approached Gillian. 'What happened?' But none of the four spoke.

Charlie squatted down at Gillian's side. 'Honey,' he said, his careful eye noticing, now, the blood streaked over her shirt, the hastily mismatched buttons. 'Are you all right?'

Her face came up, white and stained with tears, like a web of scars. Gillian's throat knotted visibly, her mouth twisted as she forced her voice free. 'It . . . was . . . *him.*'

Every muscle in Charlie's body tensed. 'Who, honey?'

'He raped me,' Gillian sobbed, the words shredded raw. 'Jack St. Bride.'

II

When Jill came in, how she did grin to
see Jack's paper plaster;
His mother, vexed, did whip her next
For laughing at Jack's disaster.

Let either of you breathe a word, or the edge of a word about the other things, and I will come to you in the black of some night and I will bring a pointy reckoning that will shudder you.

– The Crucible

May 1, 2000
Salem Falls, New Hampshire

They made her stand on a piece of paper and brush off her clothing, so that bits of dirt and leaves from the forest floated down. Gillian stared at the pristine white sheet, transfixed by the way it grew dirtier and dirtier.

The doctor, thank God, was a woman. She had asked Gilly's age, height, weight, the date of her last period and Pap smear. She wanted to know if Gilly had ever had any surgeries or hospitalizations, if she'd been under psychiatric care, if she was on any medications, if she'd been sexually assaulted before. Then she asked where penetration had occurred, so she'd know where to collect evidence. Gillian had stared at her blankly. 'Vaginally,' the doctor explained. 'Orally. Anally.'

Gillian had no recollection of giving answers. She felt as if a steel shell had formed around the core of her, making it impossible to hear clearly or move swiftly. She pictured the shell growing thicker, until one day it cracked and inside there was nothing but dust. 'Is my father here?' she whispered.

'Any minute. Okay?' The doctor smiled gently and put down the file she had been writing on. Gilly saw words scrawled across the top: *Patient reports a sexual assault.* It made her shiver.

Gillian unbuttoned her shirt. 'My socks,' she begged in a whisper. 'Can't I leave them on?'

The doctor nodded. She glanced at the bloodstain on the blouse and carefully placed it into a paper bag marked for forensic testing. Gillian's underwear – a yellow bikini marked friday, although it wasn't – went into a separate paper bag.

Finally, she folded the piece of paper beneath Gilly's feet and put it in an evidence bag.

While Gilly stood like a horse on the auction block, the doctor walked in a slow circle around her. 'I'm just looking for cuts and bruises,' she explained, bending down to get a closer look at a mark on Gillian's thigh. 'Where'd this come from?'

'Shaving,' Gilly murmured.

'And this?' the doctor pointed to a bruise on the bottom of her wrist.

'I don't know.'

A camera was removed from a drawer; a photo was taken. Gilly thought of the carvings on the bottoms of her feet, the scars they could not see. Then the doctor asked Gilly to climb onto the examination table. She swallowed hard and clamped her thighs together as the doctor came closer. 'Are you going to . . .'

'Not yet.' After the doctor turned off the lights in the room, a bright purple bulb flared to life. 'This is just a Wood's lamp.' She held it an inch above Gilly's arms and breasts as she moved it over the surface of her skin.

It was pretty, the violet glow over her shoulders and belly and hips. With prompting, she relaxed the muscles in her legs so that they parted. The lamp swooped over and up. 'Bingo.'

On her inner thigh, a small paisley-shaped spot gleamed alien green beneath the lamp. 'What is it?' Gilly said.

The doctor looked up. 'Dried semen, most likely.'

Amos Duncan roared into the hospital, wild-eyed and terrified. He stalked right to the nurse's station in the ER. 'My daughter. Where's my daughter?'

Before the nurse could answer, Charlie Saxton slid an arm around his old friend's shoulders. 'Amos, it's all right. She's here, and she's being taken care of.'

At that, the big man blanched, his face contorting. 'I need to see her,' he said, heading in the direction of the swinging ER doors.

'Not now, Amos. God, think of what she's been through.

The last thing she needs is you barging in while the doctor is doing the physical exam.'

'A physical exam? You mean someone else is in there poking and prodding her?'

'DNA evidence. If you want me to catch the son of a bitch, I need to have something to work with.'

Slowly, Amos turned. 'You're right,' he said hoarsely, although he didn't like the idea at all. 'You're right.'

He let Charlie lead him to a bank of chairs that faced the door Gilly would exit. Clasping his hands between his knees, he rocked back and forth. 'I'm going to castrate him,' Amos said softly, his tone completely at odds with his expression.

Then Gillian walked out beside a young female doctor carrying a stack of evidence bags. Amos looked at his daughter and felt his insides constrict. Anxiety rose inside him, until it fairly pushed him off his chair. 'Daddy,' Gillian whispered.

For a long moment they simply stared at each other, exchanging an entire conversation in silence. Gillian flew into his arms, burying her sobs against his shirt. 'I'm here now,' Amos said soothingly. 'I'm here, Gilly.'

She lifted a tear-stained face. 'D-Daddy, I – I –'

Amos touched his fingers to her lips and smiled tenderly. 'Don't you say anything, sweetheart. Don't say a word.'

Ed Abrams and Tom O'Neill had driven their own hysterical daughters home and had returned to the hospital to keep a support vigil for Amos Duncan. Now that Gillian had been treated, Charlie would begin an investigation. There was nothing left for them to do now but return to their families.

They walked through the lobby of the ER. 'God, it's a shame,' Ed said gruffly.

'Amos'll make sure the motherfucker hangs. He's got the resources to make it happen.'

The men stepped into a night as warm and rich as silk. As if by unspoken agreement, they stopped at the curb. 'You don't think . . .' Tom began, then shook his head.

'That he saw us?' Ed finished. 'Jesus, Tom, I've been thinking that from the moment Charlie told us what had happened.'

'It was dark, though. And we all were wearing black.'

Ed shrugged. 'Who knows what he focused on when we were beating him to a pulp? Maybe this . . . this was his way of getting back at us.'

'It worked.' Tom rocked back on his heels. 'Think we ought to tell Charlie?'

'It's not going to change anything now.' Ed let his gaze slide away. 'I think . . . I think it's best kept between us. That's what Amos would say.'

'If I knew that something I'd done had hurt my own daughter, I'd want to shoot myself,' Tom murmured. 'This must be killing him.'

Ed nodded. 'That's why he'll kill Jack St. Bride instead.'

Charlie knocked on the door of the hospital lounge before entering. Amos had requested a moment alone with his daughter, and he wasn't about to refuse the man. They sat huddled in plastic seats, their fingers knit together tightly. 'Gillian. How are you doing?'

Her eyes, when they met Charlie's, were absolutely blank. 'Okay,' she whispered.

Charlie sat down. 'I need you to tell me everything,' he said gently. Glancing quickly at Amos, he added, 'It can wait until tomorrow morning, if you feel that's better.'

'She wants to get it over with,' Amos answered.

'I'm going to have to ask you to leave us alone for a minute.'

'No!' Gillian cried, clutching at her father's arm. 'Can't he stay with me?'

Charlie stared at her, seeing not the bedraggled teenager sitting across from him but a ten-year-old playing Capture the Flag in his backyard. 'Of course,' he said, although he knew this would not be pleasant for Amos. Hell, if he'd been in the man's position, he wouldn't want to hear in graphic detail what had transpired.

He removed a tape recorder from his pocket and set it on the table between them. 'Gillian,' Charlie said. 'Tell me what happened tonight.'

Jack let himself into the diner with the key that Addie had given him weeks before, wondering how he could have been so stupid. To deliberately head toward those girls, instead of running in the other direction . . . well, maybe he could lay the blame on the fact that in his thirty-one years he could not remember ever feeling this awful. He reeked of alcohol. His head pounded; the scrape on his cheek throbbed. His eye, the one that had been punched, had nearly swollen shut. His mouth felt as if fur were growing on its roof; add to that the unwelcome realization that he was currently homeless, and Jack wanted nothing more than to turn the clock back twenty-four hours and rethink all his choices.

Jack was drawn toward the seating area of the diner, instead of the old man's empty apartment. He moved cautiously in the darkness past the sleeping iron giant of an oven, past the warming table and the rows of canned goods. As soon as he pushed through the swinging saloon doors, he saw Addie, asleep in one of the booths.

He knelt before her with reverence. Her eyelashes cast a spider shadow, her mouth tugged down in a frown. She was so beautiful, although she never would have believed him if he'd said so. At his touch, she startled and cracked her skull against the edge of the Formica table. 'God, I'm sorry. I'm so sorry, Addie.'

As the sharp smack of pain dulled, she realized that Jack was there with her. 'No,' she said slowly, her voice husky with sleep. 'I am.' She kissed her fingers, then skimmed them over the purple knot of his eye. 'You were right, Jack. You're not my daughter.'

'No.'

'But you remind me so much of her.'

'I – I do?'

'Yes.' Addie gifted him with a smile. 'Because I love you both.'

In that moment, Jack felt something inside him crack at its seams. He swallowed hard; he breathed deeply. And Jack, who knew when the first weather map had been created and where the sardine got its name and the only country in the world that began with the letter Q, did not know what to say.

He pulled Addie close and kissed her, hoping that his touch could communicate what his words could not. That he loved her, too. That she'd given him back his life. That when he was with her, he could remember the man he used to be.

She rested her face against his neck. 'I think we deserve a happily-ever-after.'

'If anyone ever did, it's us.'

Addie wrinkled her nose. 'I also think you need to take a shower. It's hard to tell over the whiskey, but it smells like you've been rolling in decaying leaves.'

'It's been . . . a pretty bad night.'

'My thoughts exactly. Why don't we just go home?'

'Home,' Jack said. He could not keep the grin off his face. 'I'd like that.'

Meg inched past her parents' room, pausing when her mother rolled over in her sleep. Downstairs, silent as a whisper . . . and then out the kitchen door, because the click of the lock in that room was less likely to register.

It took her fifteen minutes to jog to the woods at the edge of the cemetery, the small canvas ballet bag she'd last used when she was six tucked under her armpit. By then, she was gasping for air, sweating.

You could not grow up as the daughter of a detective without absorbing, through osmosis, a rudimentary understanding of police procedure. There would be officers crawling through the woods within a matter of hours, searching for any evidence they could unearth that would give credence to what Gillian had said. And the first thing they would find was the fire, the maypole, the sachets – all the remnants of their Beltane celebration.

It couldn't happen.

Part of the reason she had wanted to try being a witch was because of the mystery and the secrecy, the feeling that she knew something about herself no one else would ever guess. She shuddered, imagining what her parents would say if they found out; what the other kids at school would think of her. It was hard enough fitting in when you were thirty pounds heavier than every other seventeen-year-old; she could only guess at the sneers that would be directed her way when *this* became common knowledge.

Her head still hurt from last night's celebration; it throbbed with every footfall. It was only because of the flowering dogwood that she managed to find her way back to the spot where they'd all been, and for a moment she had a vision of Gillian's swollen, wet face as she sobbed onto Meg's father's shoulder.

It fortified her.

Spilled across the ground were the paper cups left over from last night's feast, and Gillian's thermos. Meg shoved these into the ballet bag, then plucked the sachets from the dogwood tree and stuffed them in as well.

The maypole ribbons had unwound themselves and now danced like ghosts. Chelsea was taller than Meg; she felt like a troll staring up at the high branches where the ribbons had been tied. Biting her lower lip, she tugged at one, and to her delight it unwrapped itself easily. She bunched it up and tugged on the next, and the next, rolling the ribbons like volunteers had once rolled bandages during wartime. Finally, she tugged on the last ribbon, a silver one. It had been tied slightly higher than the other three. Meg yanked, but this one was more stubborn.

Frustrated, she glared up at the tree. With determination, she wrapped the free end of the ribbon around her wrist and jerked hard. It snapped so suddenly that Meg fell backward, sprawling on the forest floor. In the tree, Meg could still see a tiny flag of silver. Well, who would think to look up there, anyway? Resolved, she stuffed the last ribbon into the ballet bag.

She glanced around at the small clearing the same way she'd seen her mother look through hotel rooms at the end of a vacation, to make sure no one had left a teddy bear or bathing suit behind. And with their secret tucked firmly beneath her arm, Meg hurried home.

Chief Homer Rudlow was a figurehead in Salem Falls, a former high school football coach for whom Charlie had once played. Their everyday dealings were not much different from high school, actually: Charlie would bust his butt on a regular basis while Homer stood on the sidelines and occasionally offered a different page from the playbook.

Charlie sat in Homer's living room. The chief wore a tartan robe over his pajamas, and his long-suffering wife had made fresh coffee and set out a plate of doughnuts. 'The rape kit is all bagged,' Charlie said. 'I'm going to take it down to the lab in Concord tomorrow.'

'Any chance of DNA evidence?'

'The bastard used a condom,' Charlie said. 'But there was blood on the victim's shirt, hopefully his.'

'Oh, that would be delightful,' Homer said wistfully. He took a long sip of his coffee and cradled the mug between his big hands. 'I don't have to tell you, Charlie, what kind of heat there's gonna be on this. Amos Duncan's not going to let us fuck up.'

'I wasn't planning to.'

'Didn't mean it that way,' the chief said.

'I know, I know. I've heard for years how Amos saved the town with his goddamned factory.' Charlie's brows drew together. 'I'm gonna catch this asshole, Homer, but not because Amos is breathing down my neck. I'm gonna do it because it could just as well have been Meg.'

Homer regarded him for a long moment. 'Try Judge Idlinger. She's less likely to jump down your throat when you wake her up to get an arrest warrant.' The detective nodded but remained seated, his head bowed. 'What now?'

'It's just . . . when I was in Miami . . .' Charlie lifted his gaze to the chief's. 'Things like this don't happen in Salem Falls.'

Homer's mouth flattened. 'They just did.'

The police car pulled up to the curb of Addie Peabody's home. In the passenger seat, Wes Courtemanche began to open the door and get out. He was champing at the bit, but Charlie shook his head, rested his wrist on the steering wheel. 'Just wait a sec,' he said.

'I don't want to wait a sec. I want to cuff the son of a bitch.'

'Cool down, Wes.'

The officer turned, his heart in his eyes. 'He's in there with her, Charlie. With Addie.'

Charlie knew Addie Peabody, of course – anyone who lived in town did. He'd known her before that, too, when they were both kids growing up in Salem Falls. But since he'd moved back, he'd had little contact with her.

Wes had told Charlie about Addie and Jack's relationship . . . and he didn't fault Addie one bit. People misjudged other people all the time – Charlie ought to know. And now he was going to have to walk in there and arrest Jack St. Bride in front of her.

He thought of the way her face would crumble the moment she opened the door and saw him holding his badge. It made him remember the way she had looked in high school, too: all pinched and quiet and curled up into herself.

Charlie sighed. 'Let's go,' he said, and turned off the ignition.

Over a bowl of cereal, Addie realized she could quite comfortably spend her life with Jack St. Bride. His hair still damp from a shower, he was bent slightly over his Lucky Charms – a brand that had made his face light up *('When did they start doing blue stars?')*. As Addie poured him a glass of juice, he slipped his arm around her hips, as if it were the most natural thing in the world. And when she sat down across from him to eat, too, the space between them was stuffed with the easy quiet of people who are sure of each other and will be for years.

Suddenly, he looked up, his mouth stretching into a lazy grin. 'What?'

'Nothing.'

'Nothing, with a blush?' Jack laughed. 'You look like I'm the next course.'

Addie raised one brow. 'Not the worst idea you've ever had.'

'We have to get to the diner. There are hungry people out there.' But as he spoke, Jack tugged Addie into his arms. 'Then again, there are hungry people in here.'

He began to nibble at her neck and kiss the freckle behind her ear, and Addie heard music. Tiny, tinkling silver chimes, the kind tied to the wings of angels. It took her a moment to realize that the noise was real and was coming from the doorbell.

On the threshold of the front door stood Charlie Saxton, with Wes slightly behind him. Addie stared at the policemen and felt all the life draining out of her, an island town evacuated before a storm. 'Charlie,' she said stiffly. 'What can I do for you?'

His face was red, and he couldn't make eye contact with her. 'Actually, I'm looking for Jack St. Bride.'

Addie felt a soft touch on her upper arm as Jack came to stand beside her. 'Yes?'

Charlie waved a piece of paper, then stuffed it into his coat pocket. 'Mr. St. Bride, I have a warrant for your arrest. You've been charged with committing the offense of aggravated felonious sexual assault against Gillian Duncan last night.'

Addie felt her entire body start to shiver from the inside out.

'*What?*' Jack cried. 'I was nowhere near Gillian Duncan last night! This is crazy!' He gazed wildly around, his eyes seizing on Addie. 'Tell them,' he said. 'Tell them I didn't do it.'

He didn't do it, Addie thought. And on the heels of that: *He was not with me last night. He was drunk. We'd had a fight.*

He might have done to Gillian Duncan what once was done to me.

Jack must have seen it, the what-if that flickered over her face before she managed to get her mouth to move. 'He didn't do it,' she whispered, but by then Jack had already turned away.

'We're just gonna take a little trip to the station,' Charlie said. He stood back as Wes slid handcuffs over Jack's wrists, then tugged him none-too-gently out the front door and into the waiting police car.

Addie wanted to throw up, to crawl into bed and die. She did not want to see Jack St. Bride, never again. She wanted to hold him close and tell him she believed in him.

She was so upset, in fact, that it took her a moment to realize Charlie remained on the steps outside the front door. 'You all right?' he asked softly.

Her face came up, eyes hard and dark. 'How *dare* you ask me that?'

Chagrined, Charlie reached forward to close the door, then hesitated. 'It would be a big help if we could get the clothes he was wearing last night.'

'Do whatever you want,' she answered, crying. She remained in this small shell during the five minutes she could hear Charlie moving through her home. And she did not bother to glance up when he left with Jack's muddy boots, his dirty clothing, and a handful of condoms from the nightstand beside her bed.

When Charlie led Jack to the booking room to take his mug shot and his prints, St. Bride moved through the routine easily, as if it were a complicated dance to which he had long ago learned the steps. Charlie photographed the cuts on his brow, his swollen eye, all without St. Bride saying a single word or giving him any trouble. He paid careful attention to a long scratch on the man's cheek – a scratch Gillian Duncan had said she'd given him while trying to fight the guy off.

Charlie had gotten a warrant for Jack's person, too, which meant securing blood and hair samples. Now, as he drove to the hospital, he glanced at St. Bride in the backseat. The man was staring out the window, deep in thought. 'You got something on your mind, Jack?' Charlie said conversationally. 'Or maybe on your conscience?'

St. Bride's eyes met his in the rearview mirror. 'Go to hell,' he murmured.

Charlie laughed. 'Maybe later. First we're going to the ER.'

In the parking lot, Charlie got out of the car and opened the back door for Jack to do the same. 'I'm not coming,' he said. 'You can't force me to.'

This surprised Charlie; St. Bride had been so complacent up till now. 'Actually, I can. I have a warrant that says I'm getting your blood and your hair whether you like it or not.' He squatted down, so that he was at eye level with his suspect. 'And I'm thinking that when your trial comes up and I testify that you refused to give us samples, that jury is going to believe you have something to hide.' Charlie shrugged. 'If you didn't do it, then you've got nothing to worry about, right?'

'Right,' Jack said tightly, and unfolded himself from the car.

He was led into the ER in his handcuffs and almost immediately shuffled into a tiny cubicle. A nurse came in and efficiently drew blood from the veined valley of Jack's arm. Charlie initialed the vial, so that he could verify the chain of custody of the blood. Jack hopped off the examination table, but Charlie stopped him with a shake of his head. 'I'm not done with you.' Slipping his hand into a rubber glove, he yanked a swatch of hair from St. Bride's head.

'That hurts!'

'Like I care,' Charlie muttered, sealing it into an envelope.

Jack's gaze was murderous. 'Are we finished yet?'

'Nope. Drop your pants.'

'I don't think so.'

Charlie regarded him evenly. 'Either I can pull your pubic hairs or you can have the honor.' Slowly, Jack extended his wrists, shaking the cuffs. 'You don't need a lot of range of movement for this,' Charlie said. 'Nice try.'

Exhaling through his nose, Jack unbuttoned the fly of his jeans and reached into his boxer shorts. The handcuffs caught on the buttons, but Charlie pretended not to notice. If the asshole sliced his dick off by accident, the world would be a safer place. Jack flinched as he pulled out the first hair and set it on a sheet of white paper Charlie had placed on the exam table. 'How many?'

For DNA analysis, the lab needed only a few hairs – five to ten, at most. Charlie met Jack's gaze without flinching. 'Thirty,' he said, and settled back to watch.

May 1, 2000
Salem Falls, New Hampshire

Matt Houlihan had the instincts of a pit bull and the face of Opie Taylor, a combination that led to a stunning number of convictions in his job as assistant county attorney and that made most local defense lawyers want to strangle him in his sleep. As he stood outside a conference room at 7 a.m. at the Grafton County Courthouse, listening to a particularly loud and obnoxious defense attorney argue with his equally loud and obnoxious client, he closed his eyes and thought of Molly.

He could conjure the exact cornflower blue of her eyes, and the softness of her skin, and even the sweet smell that he breathed in when he buried his face in her neck. She kept him up all night, but he didn't mind at all. He was head over heels in love with her.

Had been, in fact, since the moment she was born six months ago.

He had always enjoyed getting convictions, but now that he had a baby, he was a man driven. He wanted to get every single bad guy behind bars, so that by the time his daughter was walking free in this world, it was a safe place to be. Sydney, his wife, told him he was headed right for hypertension medication and that he couldn't play Superman all by himself. 'Watch me,' Matt had answered.

Matt crossed his arms, wishing he could just be done with this case. The perp had been found with drugs in his hand, so the very fact that Matt had offered him a plea seemed a remarkable act of graciousness on his part, at least in his opinion. His lawyer had argued anyway, trying to get the state to reduce the charges. Matt had refused but offered to step out into the hall to let the attorney talk things over with his client.

'No,' the client said, for the fourth time. 'I ain't gonna take it.'

Rolling his eyes, Matt walked back into the conference room. He plucked the form out of the defendant's hand and ripped it up, raining the pieces down over the man's upturned, stunned face. 'The plea's no longer on the table.'

'Jesus!' the defense attorney shouted. 'He was on the verge of accepting!'

Matt had the smaller man backed up against the table within seconds. 'I don't want him to plead,' he said, his voice soft. 'I'm going to body-slam your client at trial until he wishes he had been more cooperative and you wish you had been more persuasive.' He stepped away suddenly, straightening his jacket. 'Good-bye,' he said, and exited.

Matt checked his watch and smiled. He had two hours before he was expected at the office. With any luck, he could feed Molly her breakfast.

The room was airless and bare, with the exception of a card table, two folding chairs, and a tape recorder. A fluorescent bulb overhead spit and blinked at random intervals.

It was difficult to believe that this was really happening, that the steel circles linking his wrists were not playthings and that history had, in fact, repeated itself. Jack wasn't frightened – instead, he was almost resigned, as if he'd been expecting this shoe to drop for a while. The painted messages on the diner and the beating should have been warning enough. But nothing so far – not the arrest nor Wes's comments nor even the samples taken in the hospital – had left as deep a scar as the moment he realized Addie had her doubts.

The door opened and Charlie Saxton walked in. He slid a pack of cigarettes toward Jack. 'Want one?' Jack shook his head. 'Oh, that's right. Big-time athlete, weren't you?'

When Jack didn't answer, Charlie sighed. He pushed the Record button, so that it glowed red and the tape began to turn.

'You have the right to remain silent,' he said. 'Anything you say can and will be used against you in a court of law. You have the right to speak to an attorney and to have an attorney present during any questioning. If you can't afford a lawyer, one will be provided for you at government expense.' Charlie folded his hands on the table. 'You want to tell me your story, Jack?'

Jack turned his head away, silent.

Charlie nodded; this wasn't a shock. 'Got a lawyer you want phoned?'

The last lawyer Jack had trusted with his life had landed him in jail for eight months. His jaw tightened at the thought of putting himself at the mercy of another leech who couldn't care less about winning the case, as long as there was a retainer.

'Okay,' Charlie said on a sigh. He beckoned to another officer, who came into the interrogation room to lead Jack back to the holding cell. They were nearly out the door when Charlie's voice made Jack stop. 'Is there anyone you want me to call?'

Addie.

Jack stared straight ahead, and kept walking.

'Did you know,' Matt said, watching his wife sprinkle nutmeg onto cottage cheese for her own breakfast, 'that if you inject that stuff intravenously it can kill you?'

'Cottage cheese? I would think so.'

'No, nutmeg.' Matt dipped the rubber-coated spoon into the jar of peaches again and held it to their daughter's lips. Predictably, Molly spit it back at him.

Sydney slid into the seat beside Matt's. 'Do I want to know where you picked up such an esoteric knowledge of spices?'

He shrugged. 'I put away a woman who killed her diabetic husband by mixing some in his insulin.'

'I'll have to file that one away,' Sydney said, smiling. 'Just in case you start getting on my nerves.'

Matt passed a washcloth over Molly's face, and for good measure, rubbed it over his cheek as well. 'I feel like I ought to invest in a haz mat suit.'

'Oh, I have great faith that by the time she marches down the aisle, she'll be able to use a spoon with finesse.'

Molly, on cue, burst into a peal of giggles. 'You're not gonna walk down any aisle, are you, muffin?' Matt cooed. 'Not until Daddy's done background checks –'

They were interrupted by the telephone. Molly's head swiveled toward the sound, her eyes wide and curious. 'It's for you,' Sydney said a moment later. 'Charlie Saxton.'

He had last worked with Charlie over a year ago, on a grand theft auto charge that was pleaded down. Truth was, not too many cases came out of Salem Falls. 'Charlie,' Matt said, taking the receiver. 'What can I do for you?'

'We've got a rape case. A guy who just got out on an eight-month sentence for misdemeanor sexual assault attacked a teenage girl here last night.'

Matt immediately sobered. 'The victim wants us to prosecute?' Too often, women who had been raped would suffer through the collection of evidence . . . and then decide they couldn't go through with it.

'Yeah. Her dad is Amos Duncan.'

'Duncan, as in the drug company?' Matt whistled. 'Holy cow.'

'Exactly.'

'So,' Matt repeated, 'what can I do for you?'

'Meet me at the crime scene?' Charlie asked. 'Nine o'clock?'

He took down directions. For a long moment after Charlie hung up, Matt absently listened to the dial tone while stroking the soft, vulnerable crown of his daughter's head.

Meg, Whitney and Chelsea arrived at Gillian's house shortly after 8 A.M. 'Girls,' Amos said soberly, greeting them at the door. 'Shouldn't you be in school?'

They were too polite to comment on his bloodshot eyes, his rumpled clothing. 'Our parents said we should stay home.' Whitney spoke for the three of them.

'We wanted to make sure that Gilly was doing okay,' Chelsea

added, her voice nearly a whisper, as if speaking of what had happened would only make it worse.

'I don't know if she's up to seeing . . .' Amos's words trailed off as the girls shifted their attention to something over his shoulder. Gilly stood behind him, looking as fragile as a milkweed pod, a big quilt wrapped around her shoulders. Her feet were bare like a child's, and this made Amos's stomach knot.

'No, Daddy,' Gilly said. 'I want to talk to them.'

The girls surrounded her, a princess's court. They moved as a single unit up to Gillian's bedroom and closed the door. As soon as they did, Whitney flew toward Gilly with a small cry, hugging her close. 'Are you okay?'

Gillian nodded against her shoulder. Now that it was morning, it seemed impossible that last night had really happened.

'What did they make you do?' Chelsea asked, wide-eyed.

'A lot of tests at the hospital. And I had to talk to Mr. Saxton.' She looked from one girl to the other. 'If *I'm* the one who went through it, why do you all look so awful?'

No one answered at first, embarrassed to have been caught thinking selfishly when Gillian had suffered the most. Whitney began toying with a stray fiber on the braided rug. 'They're going to find out about us now, aren't they?'

'None of our fathers found out last night, did they?' Gilly said.

'But they'll go back today. They'll have to, after what you said.'

Meg, who had been uncharacteristically quiet, shook her head. 'I took care of it.'

Gilly turned. 'Took care of it?'

'I got rid of . . . everything. I went early this morning.'

At that, Gillian kissed Meg on the forehead. 'You,' she pronounced, 'are amazing.'

Meg blushed. Being the object of Gillian's direct praise was a little like being a cat stretching itself in front of a sunny window – it felt so good, to the marrow of the bones, that it was impossible to turn away.

Gillian reached beneath her mattress and pulled out their *Book of Shadows*. 'Keep this at your house,' she told Chelsea. 'It's too risky for me to have it here right now.'

Chelsea skimmed the pages – including the last entry, where Gillian had written a detailed account of the Beltane ceremony. For the first time since she'd been practicing Wicca, she felt empty inside. 'Gilly,' she said quietly, 'last night . . .'

'Who do you think everyone is going to believe?' Gillian's gaze turned inward, until it seemed that she was very far away from the rest of them. 'After what he did to me,' she said so quietly that the others had to strain to hear, 'he deserves this.'

An entourage of men – Amos, Charlie, Matt, and a team of cops skilled at securing crime scenes and collecting evidence – followed Gillian up the path that led from the cemetery into the woods. She was pale and withdrawn, although they had done their best to handle her with kid gloves. Suddenly, she stopped. 'This is where it happened.'

The marker was a huge flowering dogwood, its petals carpeting the floor of the forest like an artificial snow. Under Charlie's direction, an officer roped off the area with yellow crime scene tape, using the trunks of the trees as stakes. Others knelt to take soil samples and to scour for anything else that might help in the prosecution of Jack St. Bride.

Charlie headed toward Amos and his daughter. Gillian's eyes looked as big as dinner plates, and she was shaking uncontrollably. 'Honey,' Charlie said. 'do you remember where he held you down?'

Her gaze swept the small clearing. 'There,' she pointed. It was a spot free of leaves, a spot that looked no different from any other spot nearby, but Charlie knew that experts could turn up treasures that weren't visible to the naked eye.

He sent two of his men to check it. 'Why don't you take her home?' Charlie suggested to Amos. 'She looks like she's about to fall apart.'

'Gillian's strong. She –'

'– doesn't need to be here. I know you want to help us. And right now, the best way to do that is to give her a little TLC, so that when we need her to step up to the plate, she's ready.'

'TLC,' Amos repeated woodenly. 'I can do that.'

'Good. The minute I know anything . . .' he promised, and went to rejoin his colleagues.

Two men were working at the site of the rape. 'Anything?' Charlie asked.

'No smoking gun. Or spurting, as the case may be.'

'Spare me,' Charlie muttered. 'You find the condom yet? Or a wrapper?'

'Nope. But we got footprints. Looks like a struggle, too. Then again, a lot of people might just have walked over the same spot. We're taking pictures.'

Matt Houlihan tapped Charlie on the shoulder. 'Check this out.' He led the way across the clearing and pointed to the dark soil. 'See that? Ashes.'

'So?'

'There was a fire here.'

Charlie shrugged. 'Gillian said that, in her statement. I told you that already.'

'Yes, but it's nice to have some corroboration.'

'Did you doubt her?'

'You know how hard sexual assault cases are to win . . . even when the perp has a prior. I need everything I can get that corroborates what the girl said.'

'She said she scratched the guy,' Charlie pointed out. 'And I've got the proof of it on Kodak paper.'

'Mug shots alone aren't going to get him convicted. She needs to be more precise.' Matt glanced up. 'You couldn't get her to pin down the length of the assault?'

'She said it was between five and ten minutes.'

'That's the difference between a world record run and a high school track meet, Charlie.'

'Well, shit, Houlihan. I think she was a little too preoccupied at the time to take out her stopwatch.'

Sighing, Matt looked down. 'She seeing a rape crisis counselor?'

'She's seeing someone. A Dr. Horowitz, a shrink her dad knows.'

Matt nodded, then picked up a charred stick and began to toy with it, until a cop took it out of his hands with a scowl and stuck it into an evidence bag. 'What did you get from the perp, besides his pictures?'

'Oh, well,' Charlie said. 'Naturally, he wasn't here.'

'He told you this after you mirandized him?'

Charlie shook his head. 'He wouldn't even *look* at me after I mirandized him. He said this about two seconds after I told him he was under arrest. A total knee-jerk response.'

Matt mulled this over. There would be a fight to get that statement admitted. Then again, he'd done it before.

'Lieutenant Saxton,' a cop called. 'Come see this.'

Matt and Charlie ambled over to a spot beneath the dogwood tree. Almost perfectly delineated in the damp soil was a boot-print – one considerably larger than the foot of a teenage girl. The policeman who'd beckoned turned over the man's boot he was holding, the same one Charlie had taken from Addie's house. 'I'm not saying it's a match till the expert looks at the plaster cast,' the cop said, 'but this looks pretty damn close to me.'

It was, right down to the crags in the pattern of the sole. Held up alongside, it was exactly the same size as St. Bride's boot. And St. Bride had insisted he was nowhere near Gillian Duncan last night.

Matt smiled his wide, gap-toothed grin. 'Now this,' he said, 'is an excellent start.'

The judge was a man. In some corner of his mind, Jack breathed a sigh of relief. A man would surely know when another guy was being railroaded. He fixed his gaze on the Honorable Lucius Freeley, as if it were possible to sear his story right into the judge's mind.

But the judge didn't seem to notice him much at all. He glanced dispassionately at the cameras in the rear of the courtroom, and then at the prosecution's table, where a tall redheaded guy who looked like the kid on *Happy Days* was leafing through some notes. Then he turned his attention to Jack and frowned. 'We're here today in connection with the State of New Hampshire versus Jack St. Bride. Mr. St. Bride, you've been charged with aggravated felonious sexual assault. That's a class A felony, and you have the right to an attorney in connection with this offense. If you can't afford one, one will be appointed.' The judge glanced meaningfully at the empty seat beside Jack, managing to convey in a single look that he thought Jack was a moron for not taking advantage of this quirk of the law.

Jack thought of Melton Sprigg and set his jaw. 'Your Honor, I would prefer not –'

He broke off, feeling the cold green eyes of the prosecutor on him. 'I can't afford one,' he said, sealing his fate.

Bernie Davidson, the clerk of court, phoned the public defender's office thirty minutes later, when Judge Freeley – who needed prostate surgery, and badly – called for his fourth bathroom break of the morning. 'I need one of your guys,' he said, after faxing over the complaint.

'I got your stuff . . . but we can't help you,' the coordinator said. 'One of our attorneys defended the victim three years ago in a misdemeanor shoplifting charge, back before he joined the PD's office. And you know we're too tiny, Bernie, to build a Chinese wall around whoever takes St. Bride on.'

Bernie sighed. For a Friday, it was feeling a hell of a lot like a Monday morning. 'Okay. I'll go to my backup list. Thanks.'

He hung up and shuffled through a rubber-banded sheaf of cards he kept in the front compartment of his desk, a group of attorneys in private practice whom he called on, now and then, when the public defender's office had a conflict. Finally, his eye caught on one name. 'Here we go,' Bernie said, smiling slowly, and he picked up the phone.

* * *

The third time he heard a crash, Jordan put down his cup of coffee and went to investigate. He moved through the hallway like a bloodhound on a scent, until he found the source of the noise – behind Thomas's closed bedroom door. Which was exceptionally strange, since Thomas had left for school nearly two hours earlier.

Another crash. Then: 'God*damn!*' Jordan pushed open the door to find Selena sprawled on the carpet, which had been covered with newspaper. She wore a tank top and a pair of his own boxer shorts. Her mahogany skin was dotted with blue freckles, and a paint roller lay several feet away, in a puddle of its own pigment.

'Whatever kind of look you were going for . . . you missed,' Jordan said.

Selena narrowed her eyes, 'If I throw a stick, will you leave?'

He stepped into the room. 'Not until I figure out why you're painting Thomas's ceiling . . .' He paused to read the label on the can a few feet away. 'Woodsmoke blue.'

'Because you haven't done it?' She waved a hand about. 'For God's sake, Jordan. The kid's fifteen. You think Easter egg purple and bunny wallpaper work for him?'

Jordan glanced around, seeing Thomas's room through new eyes. It had belonged to a little girl when they'd bought the house. For a year now, Jordan had been promising Thomas it was something they'd tackle together. He glanced down at his sweatpants and river driver's shirt. Nothing that couldn't get ruined, he supposed. Stepping closer, he picked up the paint roller. 'At least I know how to climb a ladder. Christ – from the racket, it sounded like you were holding a WWF tournament.'

'For your information, I could stay on the ladder just fine.' Selena frowned. 'It was the roller that kept losing its balance, every time I let go of the handle.'

Jordan rolled a smooth rectangle of blue paint onto the ceiling. 'Didn't think you'd even need a ladder, Amazon that you are.'

By now, Selena was standing. She automatically lifted the

paint tray so that Jordan wouldn't have to dismount to refresh the roller. 'Very funny.'

'Sarcasm is just one more service we offer.' He squinted. 'Why blue?'

'It's calming. And you're missing that whole section. See?'

Jordan scowled. 'It looks perfectly fine to me.'

'That's because you're as good as blind.' Selena slapped her hands on the rungs of the ladder, encircling Jordan, and began to climb up behind him. He twisted to allow her access to duck beneath his arm, as she reached up and pointed to a spot that had not been covered thoroughly. 'There,' she said.

But Jordan wasn't listening. He was inhaling the scent of Selena's skin, feeling the heat of her pressed behind and beside him. He closed his eyes and, moving just the slightest bit, inclined his head closer to hers. 'I'm not blind, Selena,' he murmured.

They remained tangled in a knot of possibility. And just as Jordan tipped forward to kiss Selena, she turned so that he grazed the nape of her neck, instead. 'Jordan,' she whispered. 'We know better.'

'This time, it could be different. *I'm* different.'

She smiled softly. 'An erection doesn't count as personal growth.'

He opened his mouth to contest that, but before he could, the telephone rang. Trying to extricate himself from his position on the ladder, he wound up knocking down both Selena and the paint roller once again. He leaped over her, ran down the hall, and grabbed the portable from the living room.

A moment later, he appeared at the threshold to Thomas's bedroom. Selena stood on the ladder again, the muscles in her arms flexing as she stretched overhead to paint. When she turned, her gaze was positively blank, as if what had just passed between them had never happened. 'Please tell me it's that idiot mechanic telling me my car's ready.'

'It was Bernie Davidson, at the courthouse,' Jordan said, still a little dazed. 'Apparently, I'm back in practice.' He turned to

Selena, a question in his eyes.

'Count me in,' she said, and stepped down beside him.

Like every other human over the age of eight in Salem Falls, Jordan knew that Jack St. Bride had been convicted once for sexual assault. That he was now on the receiving end of a rape charge didn't bode particularly well, either. One thing was for certain: with a prior under his belt, St. Bride wouldn't be getting bail. Which actually suited Jordan just fine, because a guy who was locked up couldn't get himself into any more trouble.

His hair was still wet from his shower when he arrived at the county attorney's office in Ossipee. As far as he was concerned, he had one job, and that was to get as much information as he could early in the game. Rape trials were always a bitch; the more Jordan knew, the better chance he'd have of landing on his feet.

He waited for the secretary to buzz Matt Houlihan, an assistant county attorney Jordan disliked just on general principles. The fucker was too cocky, and if *Jordan* felt that, it was really saying something. Jordan wasn't sure what pissed him off more – the young county attorney's persistence or the fact that his hairline wasn't receding even the tiniest bit.

Matt appeared around the corner of a cubicle, grinning. 'He has risen!'

Smiling just as widely, Jordan held out his hand to shake. 'Reports of my demise have been greatly exaggerated.'

Matt gestured down the hall, toward his office. 'Where *have* you been, Jordan? After the Harte case, you dropped off the face of the earth.'

'No . . . just into Salem Falls.' Jordan's mouth twitched. 'So you may have been right in the first place.' He took a seat across from Matt. 'I've been appointed as counsel for Jack St. Bride,' he said without preamble.

'Thought he was getting someone from the PD's office.'

'Apparently, there was a conflict. What you see is what you get.'

Matt's eyes sparked. 'I like a good challenge.'

There wasn't much Jordan could say to that without the words getting stuck in his throat. Defending a guy who seemed to be a two-time loser against Matt Houlihan ranked just about at the bottom of things Jordan enjoyed doing. 'I don't see any reason to contest your bail request,' Jordan said confidently, although no attorney in his right mind would think there was any chance in hell St. Bride might be released. 'Assuming you can give me the police reports you have up to this point.'

Matt tossed him a file. 'There's the charge, and the victim's statement.'

It was a gift, Jordan knew. Without it, the victim would be a complete cipher and it would be nearly impossible to prepare a case. He opened the file, and the name of the victim leaped out. Jordan kept his face poker straight. 'Well,' he said, getting to his feet. 'We'll talk again.'

'About what?' Matt steepled his fingers, his casual pose completely at odds with the grim determination in his eyes. 'I've got a young girl saying some jerk raped her, a jerk who was just in jail for doing the same thing. There's nothing to talk about, Jordan. I'm gonna lock your client up for twenty long years.'

The moment Jordan McAfee walked into the celled corridor of the sheriff's department beneath the county court building, Jack got to his feet. Jordan met his gaze immediately, something the deputies tried not to do. 'Hi, Jack,' he said smoothly. 'I know we've met, but I'm not sure you realize why I'm here. I've been practicing law for nearly twenty years, and occasionally I help out when the court needs someone because the public defender's office has a conflict. I've been asked to stand up in your case.'

Jack opened his mouth to say something, but Jordan held up his hand. 'There's not much we can accomplish this morning, so we're just going to keep our powder dry. We're not going to say anything about the case, and we're not going to ask the judge for anything.'

'You have to get me released on bail.'

'Jack, you have a prior conviction. You have about as much chance of walking out of here today as a groom at a shotgun wedding. You're going to have to trust me on –'

'*Trust* you? Trust *you?*' Jack's eyes were wild. 'I don't even know you.'

Jordan was quiet for a moment. 'You know I take my coffee light and that I read the *New York Times* and not the *Globe*. You know I leave a twenty percent tip, every time. That's more than most defendants know about their attorneys. Now, I wasn't the one who landed you in this cell. . . . Apparently, you were able to do that all by yourself.'

'I don't want to go back to jail,' Jack said desperately. 'I didn't do what they said.'

Jordan looked at Jack's disheveled clothing, his wild eyes, the long scrape on his cheek, and let the words roll right off his back. If he'd had a nickel for every time he'd heard that, he'd have been living the high life in Belize. 'I understand you're upset right now. Let's just get through the arraignment, and then we'll start to look at our options.'

'The last time a lawyer told me we'd look at my options,' Jack said, 'I spent eight months in jail.'

Jordan shrugged, silent. But he was thinking: *This time, it's going to be much worse.*

'If this isn't déjà vu,' said Judge Freeley, opening the file on his desk again. 'Mr. St. Bride, I see you're now being represented by Mr. McAfee.'

Jordan stood and neatly buttoned his suit jacket. Immediately, he could feel the eyes of the cameras in the back of the courtroom blinking to life. 'Yes, Your Honor. I've explained the complaint to my client, and he's read it and he understands it. If I could ask the court to enter a not-guilty plea on the defendant's behalf?'

'Fine,' the judge said. 'Is there an issue about bail?'

Matt Houlihan unfolded his lanky body and glanced at Jack. 'This was an extremely violent crime, Judge. Moreover, the defendant already has a prior conviction and has virtually no ties to the community – he just moved here, has no family nearby, owns no property – all these facts indicate that he's a flight risk. Finally, Your Honor, this community would not be safe if he were to be released. This man has been charged with violently sexually assaulting a young girl, and he has already been convicted once of doing the exact same thing. The court could expect that on release, he'd only go out and find yet another victim. For these reasons, Your Honor, the state requests that bail be denied.'

The judge turned toward the defense table. 'Mr. McAfee?'

'I don't have a problem with that at this point, Your Honor.'

Judge Freeley nodded. 'All right then –'

'The reason,' Jordan interrupted, 'that I don't feel a need to contest the state's request for denying bail is because frankly, it's the safest place for my client. You see before you a man whose first amendment rights have been stripped away by the force of rumor and conjecture – a man who has committed no crime but in reality has been victimized. Your Honor, the town of Salem Falls has been out for Jack St. Bride's blood since the moment he arrived.'

The judge gestured at the cameras. 'I'm sure the academy is enjoying your Oscar-worthy performance, Mr. McAfee,' he said dryly. 'Let's pity the justice who draws your trial. Next?'

As the clerk called the following case, Jordan turned to his client, who was speechless. 'What?' he demanded.

'I . . . I didn't expect you to stick up for me,' Jack admitted.

Jordan stuffed the manila file from the county attorney's office in with his other papers. 'Well, if I can give you the benefit of the doubt, maybe you can find it in yourself to do the same.' He watched the bailiff approach to take his client away to the jail next door.

'Wait,' Jack called over his shoulder. 'When am I going to talk to you again?'

'Not today. I've got a really busy schedule.' Jordan tucked his briefcase beneath his arm and walked out of the courtroom, wondering what Jack St. Bride would think if he knew that for the rest of the day, Jordan had absolutely nothing else to do.

November 1998
Loyal, New Hampshire

Sometimes, when Jack watched his girls fly down the field, time stopped. He would hear only the beat of his own heart and see the small dark stitches sewn by their cleats as they ran from goal to goal, and he would think: *It does not get any better than this.*

'Let's go, let's go,' he called out, clapping. 'Arielle's open!'

He watched his strikers scuffle against the opposing team, a hurricane of feet and mud obliterating the play for a moment. Then his right wing sent the ball spinning toward Arielle, his center. The senior captain of the team, Arielle was the best striker he had. She was on the field continuously, with the second- and third-string centers coming in only briefly to give her a chance to catch her breath . . . and even then, only when Jack felt that they were winning by a decent margin. Jack watched with pride as she sped toward the net with her eye on the ball, intent on heading it in. But just as the crown of her head connected, she slammed her left shoulder into the post. The ball skimmed off the top of the net, rolling offside, as Arielle crumpled to the ground at the goalie's feet.

A hush fell over the field. Players from both teams stood restless as colts, pawing at the ground in an effort to stay loose while they waited for Arielle to get up.

But she didn't. Jack's breath caught as the ref blew his whistle. He ran out across the field to where Arielle lay flat on her back, staring at the sky.

'I misjudged the goal,' she moaned, cradling her arm against her belly. Jack watched her hold the limb tight against her, rounding her shoulders against the pain. He'd bet anything it was her collarbone. Christ, he'd smashed his own three times when he was playing in college.

Sliding an arm around her waist, Jack helped Arielle off the field. There were cheers from the fans of both teams. 'Maybe if I rest a minute, I can go back in,' Arielle suggested.

He loved her for that. 'I think we'd better play it by ear,' Jack said. The ref held up his hands, looking to Jack for a replacement so that play could be resumed.

The second- and third-string centers on the bench stared up at him like wallflowers at a dance, praying with all their hearts that this time, they might be chosen. Jack's eyes flickered from one to the next, settling on Catherine Marsh, the daughter of the school chaplain. Her teammates seemed to like her; Jack had never really paid enough attention to form an opinion. Now, she stared up at him, full of hope. It seemed to light her from the inside.

'All right,' Jack said. 'You're in.'

Ohmygod, Catherine thought. *Ohmygod ohmygod ohmygod.*

She stood in the spot usually handled by Arielle, who had been taken to the hospital. Catherine's eye was so focused on the ball that any minute she expected it to burst into flames. Coming in at the goal kick, the very play where the ball had gone out of bounds, gave her no time to ease into this.

Shaking out her arms and legs, she loosened her body and instructed herself to relax. Not that it did any good.

Settle down, she ordered, but it only made her heart beat harder. She imagined her blood raging like a river. Her eyes followed the trajectory of the ball as the wing attempted a shot. The goalie, a bulk of a girl if Catherine had ever seen one, deflected it with one massive hand . . . but the ball spiraled up and over the metal rim of the net, thudding down beyond the boundaries of the field.

'Corner kick,' the ref yelled from somewhere behind her. Catherine knew her position. As the wing stood at the squared edge of the field behind the goal, Catherine moved closer to the net. Her right fingertips brushed the goal, a sensory print of where she was standing. A hundred thoughts raced through her mind: *If she arcs it, I can head it in. The rim of the goal is warm to the touch. The sun's in my eyes. God, what if I miss?* Fingertips grazing again, she fought to see around the goalie, who was a full head taller than she was. *Eye on the ball. Wait. Head it square in. Don't look like an idiot.*

The wing's foot shot out, but she whiffed the ball – Catherine craned her neck to see it arch, heading away from the goal. *Oh, God, I'll never get to it,* thought Catherine, and an enormous pressure lifted from her chest, because she was no longer obligated to perform. Catherine watched the ball hang like a second sun in the air . . . and then it outpaced her, a spinning sphere angling over her right shoulder in a sweet, true arc.

Without conscious thought, Catherine leaped. As her shoulders dropped down, her legs came up, and she scissored her legs in a bicycle kick, so that her right foot rocketed the ball back in the direction from which it had come.

Catherine didn't see the ball speed over her shoulder, to stretch the upper left corner of the net. She didn't know at first why all her teammates were screaming and piling on top of her, so that she couldn't have gotten up even if she'd wanted to. Instead, she lay flat on her back with the wind knocked out of her.

A teammate offered her a hand up. Catherine searched the sea of faces on the sidelines, all cheering for her . . . for *her!* She finally stopped when she found the one she was looking for. Coach St. Bride stood on the sidelines with his arms crossed. 'Thank you,' he mouthed silently.

Catherine smiled so wide she was sure all her happiness would simply spill out at her feet. 'My pleasure,' she whispered back, and turned to the field to play.

Muddy and spent, but buzzing with the euphoria that comes on a victory, the girls gathered their water bottles and jackets and headed into the locker room. Fans drifted from the sidelines like milkweed blowing from a pod, wandering to the white buildings of Westonbrook or the parking lot, where they could wait for the players they had come to cheer on.

The school nurse had passed along the news that Arielle's collarbone had snapped; she'd be out of commission for six weeks. But where this news would have sent Jack into a tailspin just that morning, he was now remarkably calm. And all because of Catherine Marsh, a little wren he'd never even noticed simply because he'd been too busy admiring the peacock.

She was straggling behind. Her blond hair had managed to untangle itself from a ponytail and swung in front of her face like a veil as she bent to pick up her belongings. 'Hey, Pelé,' Jack called out.

She glanced up blankly.

'God, you're making me feel old. Forget Pelé. Mia, then. Or Brandi.'

'Not quite.' Ruefully, Catherine tugged at her jersey. 'See, I still have my shirt on.' After a moment, she added, 'Thanks for giving me a chance today.'

'A smarter move,' Jack said soberly, 'would have been to let the wing trap the ball and bring it back into play. I could just as easily be standing here asking you what the hell you were doing, instead of holding you up as MVP.'

'I know.'

'If you're going to do such a low percentage kick, I'd better teach you how to do it without hurting yourself in the process.'

Catherine's head snapped up. 'For real?'

'Yeah. Come here.' He tossed her a ball and ushered her toward the flag so that she could do a corner kick. In the meantime, he assumed the position she'd been in, by the goal. 'Go on.'

She tried, but the first shot landed in the goal. 'Sorry.'

Jack laughed. 'Don't ever apologize to your coach when you score.'

Smiling, Catherine tried again. The ball curved toward the midfield, and Jack started running. His blond hair caught on the wind, and he could feel every cell of his body straining with the pure joy of play as he kicked his feet up and pedaled them to change position, catching the ball and firing it back over his dropped right shoulder. As he fell, he braced his palms, landing on the flat of his upper back and rocking forward.

'Wow,' Catherine said. 'You make it look so easy.'

'I make it look less *painful.*' Jack got up, then put his hands on Catherine's shoulders. She smelled of powder, and there was mud caked on the tip of her ponytail. 'You land here,' he said, skimming his palm over her upper back. He slid his arms down over hers, flexing the palms out. 'You're going to roll down your spine, so that you hit your shoulders and your elbows and your forearms and *then* your butt makes contact.'

They switched places, so that Jack could lob the ball over her shoulder from behind. With each try, Jack offered a new piece of advice; with each try, the sun sank a little deeper in the sky. On the seventh attempt, Catherine landed perfectly. 'I did it. I *did* it!' She leaped to her feet and threw her arms around Jack's neck. 'This is so *cool!*'

Laughing, Jack set her away from him. If he could bottle the enthusiasm of the average fifteen-year-old, he'd be a very rich man. He tossed Catherine her water bottle and jacket. 'Go on home, Pelé.'

'That's Brandi, if you don't mind.'

He grinned as she bounced her way across the darkening playing fields. And he wondered how, in the three months she'd been on his team, he ever could have underestimated Catherine Marsh.

'You're shitting me.' Jay Kavanaugh stared at the television set over the bar, his bottle of Bud arrested halfway to his lips. 'She's not sixteen.'

'She is,' Jack insisted. 'I kid you not.'

They both watched the teen pop princess jiggle her way

through an MTV music video. 'But . . . but . . . Jesus, look at her face.'

'It's all makeup.'

'Guess she keeps the cotton balls to apply it stuffed in her bra, then?'

Jack took a pull of his drink. 'Early bloomer.'

'That's no bloom,' Jay muttered. 'That's a whole fucking tropical rainforest.' He grabbed the remote control off the bar counter and turned the channel to a movie in which Arnold Schwarzenegger was pummeling a man bloody. 'There. Something less inflammatory.' Jay slid his empty bottle across the counter and gestured for another one. 'I don't know how you do it.'

'Do what?'

'Stick yourself smack in the middle of sin every day.'

'What the hell are you talking about?'

'Jeez, you're surrounded by . . . by sixteen-year-old pop princesses all day long.'

'Jessica Simpson is not enrolled at Westonbrook.'

Jay shrugged. 'You know what I mean. I know DAs who won't drive home their teenage baby-sitters. How can you look at them day in and day out and not . . . notice?'

'Because I'm their teacher and that would make me as moral as a slug.' Jack grinned. 'You don't interview felons and suddenly decide to turn over a new leaf of crime, do you?'

Jay twisted the top off the bottle that the bartender set in front of him. 'No . . . but sometimes I look at a drug dealer all decked out in Armani and before I can stop myself, I think: "It's got to be a nice life, long as you don't get caught." '

Jack lifted the beer to his lips. 'Well,' he admitted, laughing, 'sometimes I think that, too.'

Dinner at the Marsh household was a stiff affair, with Catherine and her father sitting across from each other at a long, polished table and eating whatever she'd managed to cook for them. 'Pasta again?' Reverend Marsh asked, picking up the bowl and bringing it closer to heap on his plate.

'Sorry. We're out of meat and chicken.'

'The Lord turned water into wine. All I'm suggesting is a trip to the grocery store.'

Catherine reached for her glass of milk. 'I haven't had a chance, Daddy.'

'Ah, but that's where you're wrong. You've had the chance. You just chose to use that time for a different purpose.'

'You have no idea how amazing an opportunity it is for me to be able to play first string. I can't just throw that away.'

Ellidor twirled his fork in the spaghetti. 'Barbaric, if you ask me. All those half-dressed young girls being put through their paces by some drill sergeant.'

'Daddy, we're not half dressed. And Coach St. Bride isn't the Devil.'

The minister pinned his daughter with a stare. 'They are still not the sorts of girls you ought to be spending time with,' he said. He stood up, walked to the sideboard, and tossed a *Glamour* magazine onto the table. 'Which one of them gave you this smut? It was right in your gym bag.'

'It's not smut –'

Ellidor lifted the magazine and read from its cover. ' "*How to look like a siren for less than $25" "Can you keep your man happy?*" ' He glanced at Catherine. ' *"Ten sex secrets to drive him wild.*" '

Catherine stared at her plate. 'Well, that one's worse than normal. It was last year's Valentine's issue. Cynthia gave it to me because there was this really cool haircut in it.'

'I brought you here to Westonbrook so that you'd be less tempted by the things that lead young women into trouble. Magazines like this are just the first step. From here, it's an easy slide to boys, to drugs, to drinking.' Ellidor sighed. 'Catherine, what would people think if they knew that the chaplain's daughter was a slut?'

'I am *not* a slut,' she said, her voice pitched low. 'And if they saw me reading *Glamour,* they'd think I was like any other fifteen-year-old girl.'

'That's the problem,' Ellidor said, touching his daughter's cheek. 'You're better than all of them.'

Catherine leaned into his palm. And thought, *But what if I don't want to be?*

'Well,' Jack said, looking up from his seat as Catherine emerged from the locker room. 'You look nice.'

It was an understatement. Dressed in a short black skirt and a tight sweater, she appeared nothing like the ragged scrapper who'd run up and down the field under his explicit orders until he was certain she'd collapse if asked to take another step. He *hadn't* asked, for just that reason: If he'd wanted it, Catherine would have driven herself into the ground.

Jack closed the salt-and-pepper composition book he used to record notes on the team's practice. 'Your dad taking you out to dinner?'

Catherine smiled wryly. 'On a weeknight? That's got to be a sin.'

Jack had wondered more and more often how a prig like the Right Reverend Ellidor Marsh had managed to create a girl as vibrant as Catherine. He knew Catherine's mother, a free spirit who didn't fit the mold of church wife, had walked out on the family when Catherine was still a toddler. Maybe that was where her personality came from.

'I am going out to dinner,' Catherine admitted shyly. 'But on a date.'

'Ah. Your father knows, of course.'

'Oh, absolutely.' Catherine glanced at Jack's book. 'You write about me in there?'

'You bet.'

'What do you write?'

'All my wicked little thoughts,' he joked. 'And a few decent plays we might try every now and then.'

The door opened, and Catherine's date entered. His eyes lit on Catherine as if she were a feast. 'You ready?'

'Yeah.' Catherine slipped her arms into her coat. ' 'Night,

Coach.' At the door, the boy very properly put his hand on the small of her back.

'Catherine,' Jack said, 'can you come here for a moment?'

She came so close that he could smell the conditioner she'd used in the locker room, and the harsh pink soap from the showers. 'How well do you really know this guy?' Jack asked softly.

'I'm a big girl. I can take care of myself.' Catherine walked toward her date again. 'But Coach,' she added, 'thanks for wanting to do it for me.'

'For Christ's sake!' Jack bellowed.

For the sixth time that day, the ball had sailed right past Catherine Marsh. His intersquad scrimmage was going to hell because his center couldn't keep her mind on the game.

Jack blew his whistle and strode angrily to the middle of the field. 'I'm sorry,' she said immediately.

'Sorry isn't going to do you a hell of a lot of good when you get slammed in the head by a ball going twenty miles an hour! Or when we lose Districts because this team never gets itself together!' With every word she seemed to fold in on herself.

'Catherine,' he sighed. 'What's the matter?'

'Coach,' another player called. 'It's five-thirty. Can we go shower?'

He looked at his watch. Technically, it was 5:20. But this entire afternoon had been a waste of a practice, because whatever fog Catherine had contracted seemed to be catching. 'Go,' he barked. Catherine started to slink away, but he grabbed her upper arm. 'Not you.'

She took one look at him and started to cry. 'I need to get to Woodhaven.'

There was no public transit to Woodhaven, which was thirty miles away, and a cab ride's cost would seem astronomical to a fifteen-year-old without an income. But as far as Jack knew, there was nothing in particular in Woodhaven that merited a visit. 'What's there that you can't find in Loyal?'

'Planned Parenthood.'

The words fell between them like a wall. 'Catherine, are you pregnant?'

She turned the color of the sunset. 'I want to keep from getting that way.'

With a fundamentalist father, asking for birth control wasn't going to go over very well. But there were other options that didn't involve visiting a women's clinic.

'He won't wear them,' Catherine admitted softly, reading Jack's mind. 'He says they're not a hundred percent and he doesn't want to take that chance.'

Jack jammed his hands in his coat pockets, distinctly uncomfortable. Although he had taught teenagers long enough to know that sexual intercourse occurred shockingly young, there was something about Catherine doing it that made him feel a little sick. She had been his Atalanta, swift and unspoiled, running faster than anyone could catch her.

'Please, Coach,' she begged, just as embarrassed to be pleading as he was to be hearing her.

'Catherine,' he said, 'we never had this conversation.' And he walked off, determined to believe that this was not – and never would be – his problem.

Catherine, a straight-A student, failed a test. And the next day's pop quiz. 'I want to talk to you,' Jack said to her as the other students filed out. 'Wait for a minute.'

She remained at her desk. The exam, with its unprecedented scarlet letter, glared up at her. Jack slid into the seat beside hers. 'You know this stuff cold,' he said quietly, and she shrugged. 'I could give you a makeup test.'

She didn't answer, and Jack felt temper swell like a wave inside him. 'You're too smart to throw your academic career away for some guy,' he argued.

Catherine turned slowly. 'If I'm going to fuck up my life,' she said, 'does it really matter which way I do it?'

Her eyes, which had always seemed to take in the whole

world at once, were absolutely flat and expressionless. It was this that tugged the words from Jack he truly did not want to say. 'Have you . . . has it . . .'

'No. We're waiting, to be safe.'

Jack forced himself to look at her. 'Are you sure? Because if you pick this moment, with this guy, you're stuck with it for the rest of your life.'

Her brows drew together. 'How do you know if you're sure?'

God, how to answer that? His first time had been in the back of a limousine owned by the father of the rich girl he'd been seducing. Years afterward, he never could look their chauffeur in the eye.

'There's one person,' Jack said, stumbling. 'When you find him, you'll know.'

Catherine nodded. 'He's the one.'

'Then I'll drive you to Woodhaven.'

She had come out of the squat brown building holding a little compact full of birth control pills, which, when opened, looked like the toothed jaws of a gator. 'I have to take them for a month before they start to work,' Catherine said, although by then Jack did not want to hear any more.

One month and four days after Jack had driven her to Woodhaven, Catherine showed up late to practice. She played hard that day, doggedly running up and down the field and firing the ball so hard at the practice goalie that twice, she knocked her down. She played, Jack realized, like she was punishing herself.

And that was how he knew it had happened.

Although he could not really articulate why, Jack didn't speak to Catherine after that, unless it was to instruct her in a certain play. Catherine didn't seek him out to ask questions on her technique. They won four games. And still Jack and Catherine moved quietly around each other, like two magnets of the same pole who are forced into close contact and cannot help but shy to the side.

* * *

It took all the courage in the world to knock on the door of his classroom.

'Come in.'

Catherine took a deep breath and wiped away the mascara underneath her eyes. Coach St. Bride stood in front of the chalkboard in the empty classroom. Posters dotted the walls: Charlemagne, Copernicus, Descartes. She walked up to one, mostly so that she wouldn't have to look at Coach. 'What made Alexander so great anyway?' she murmured.

'Take my class next year and you'll find out.' He frowned and took off the wire-rimmed glasses he sometimes wore. 'You okay?' he asked quietly.

She had always thought his voice was as lovely as wood smoke – a strange thing to compare it to, but in her childhood nothing had quite made her feel as much at home as walking through a brisk afternoon and seeing the curl of gray snailing out of the chimney. He started walking toward her, and oh, God, she was going to absolutely lose it. She had to tell him, she had to tell someone, and she thought that if she did, she would die of humiliation. It would be like . . . what was it, from biology . . . *sublimation.* Like being here one moment, and then *poof,* evaporating into thin air without a trace, so that no one would ever know you had even been there.

'Catherine?' he asked, just her name, and she turned away.

She found herself facing a map larger than any she'd ever seen. It covered nearly one entire wall of the classroom, an uneven patchwork quilt of countries and oceans. Lakes were the size of diamond chips, cities no bigger than a pinprick. You could step inside and lose yourself.

With a sob, she whirled and threw herself into Coach's arms. He staggered back at the unexpected embrace, and when he realized she was crying, lightly patted her back. He did it awkwardly, not used to giving comfort to his students, and somehow that made it even sweeter.

'He broke up with me. He . . . he *did* it . . . and then . . . and then . . .' She couldn't finish, and it didn't matter, because Coach St. Bride understood.

His hand fell onto the crown of her head. 'Oh, Catherine. I'm sorry.'

'No, I am. I am, because I was so *stupid.*' She wrapped her arms tighter around him. And she gradually noticed how the fine hairs on his nape were the color of Spanish gold; how his hands were large enough to hold her together. With great care, she opened her mouth and pressed it against his neck, so that he would think it was only her breath. But she could taste his skin, the salt and spice of it, and her eyes drifted shut. *You were so, so right*, she thought. *When you find the one, you know.*

May 2000
Salem Falls, New Hampshire

Different jails smell the same.

Stale. A little bit like piss and a little bit like biscuits rising. Sweat; swabbed disinfectant. And over all this, the heady scent of anxiety. Jack shuffled beside the correctional officer, his handcuffs swinging between his wrists. *I am not here,* he thought dizzily. *I am lying on my back on a wide, green lawn, sleeping in the sun, and this is just a nightmare.* Knowing that he was about to be locked up again when he was wrongfully accused was enough to make him tremble. Who would believe the man who pleaded his *second* case from the confines of a cell?

'Name,' barked the recording officer. He was overweight, stuffed into his little glass booth like a dumpling in a Pyrex dish. 'St. Bride,' Jack said, his voice rusty. 'Dr. Jack St. Bride.'

'Height?'

'Six-two.'

'Weight?'

'One-ninety,' Jack answered.

The officer did not glance up. 'Eyes?'

'Blue.'

Jack watched his answers being scrawled across the booking card. *Allergies. Medications. Regular physician. Distinguishing characteristics.*

Person to call in the event of an emergency.

But, Jack thought, *isn't this one?*

* * *

The guard led Jack to a room the size of a large closet. It was empty, except for a desk and a row of shelves stacked with prison-issue clothing. 'Strip,' he said.

At that moment, it all came back: the feeling of being a number, not a name. The absolute lack of privacy. The mindlessness that came when every decision was made for you, from when you ate to when the lights were turned off to when you were allowed to see the sky. It had taken almost no time at all to strip him of his humanity at the Farm – and it had all started the moment Jack had put on the uniform of a convict.

'I'd rather not.'

The guard looked up at him. 'What?'

'I'm here in custody. I'm not a prisoner. So I shouldn't have to dress like one.'

The correctional officer rolled his eyes. 'Just get changed.'

Jack looked at the stack of orange clothing. Faded and soft, from years of others wearing it. 'I can't,' he said politely. 'Please don't ask me to do this.'

'I'm not asking you to do anything. I'm *telling* you, quite clearly, to take off your goddamned clothes.'

Jack glanced down at his Hanes T-shirt, his striped boxers, and a pair of sweatpants he'd bought with Addie at Kmart. He had no great attachment to this wardrobe beyond the fact that he had been wearing it the moment before Charlie Saxton arrested him.

Jack set his jaw. 'The only way you're going to get those things on me is to do it yourself.'

For a second, the guard seemed to consider this. He was larger than Jack by half a head. But something in Jack's eyes – some bright angry nugget of resolve – made him take a step back. 'Shit,' he muttered, handcuffing Jack to the desk. 'Why does this happen on my shift?'

He walked out, leaving Jack alone to wonder what avalanche he'd set in motion.

Roy's eyes were so bloodshot that he was literally seeing red. He watched with astonishment as the orange juice poured crimson into his glass, then frowned at the label and squinted. It said Tropicana. He sniffed at the insides – and realized it was tomato juice, which he'd poured into the empty juice carton last week when the glass container of V8 didn't fit in his fridge. Relieved, he took a sip, then cracked a raw egg inside and added a dollop of whiskey.

Best hangover remedy he'd ever found, and he should know.

Behind him the door opened. Roy tried to turn fast, and nearly heaved up his insides. Addie was on the rampage, not that he would have expected any less. 'I know, I know,' Roy began. 'It's completely irresponsible of me to . . . *Addie?*' Now that she was closer, he could see tears on her face. 'Honey? What's the matter?'

'It's Jack. Charlie Saxton arrested him.'

'*What*?'

'He said . . . oh, Daddy. Charlie said Jack raped Gillian Duncan last night.'

Roy sank onto a chair. 'Gillian Duncan,' he murmured. 'Holy mother of God.' There was something tickling the back of his mind, but he couldn't seem to quite reach it. Then it came to him, and he looked up. 'Addie, Jack was with me last night.'

Hope broke over her face. 'He was?'

'You're not gonna want to hear it, but we were at the Rooster. Drinking.' Roy grimaced. 'Still, I guess it's a sight better to be pegged a drunk than a rapist.'

'Jack was with you last night? All last night? And you can tell the police this?'

'He showed up about ten. I can vouch for him until about eleven-thirty, I guess.'

'What happened then?'

Roy ducked his head. 'I, uh, passed out. Marlon – he's the bartender – he let me sleep it off in the back room. I guess Jack left when the bar closed.'

'Which is when?'

'Midnight.'

Addie sat down beside him on the couch, thinking. 'I didn't see him until one-thirty in the morning. Where *was* he?'

Roy turned away so that he would not have to see the ache in his daughter's eyes. 'Maybe they made a mistake,' he said uncomfortably, when he was really thinking, *Maybe we* all *did.*

You had to pay your dues in jail. If you wanted a candy bar, it meant behaving well enough to be granted the commissary form. If you wanted the freedom of medium security, where you could wander through the common room during any hours except lockdown, you had to prove that you could conduct yourself well in maximum security. If you wanted to run in the courtyard, you had to earn the privilege. Everything was a step, a reckoning, an inch given in the hopes of receiving one in return.

Conversely, if you made trouble, you were punished.

And so Jack, who had been in the custody of the Carroll County Jail for less than an hour, found himself being escorted between two cor-rectional officers to the office of the superintendent for a disciplinary review.

He was a big man with no neck, a silver buzz cut, and glasses from the 1950s. In fact, Jack realized, it was entirely possible the superintendent had been sitting here, pushing papers, for half a century. 'Mr. St. Bride,' the superintendent said, in a voice so feathery Jack had to strain to hear, 'you've been charged with failing to follow the instructions of a correctional officer. Not an auspicious beginning.'

Jack looked at a spot over the man's shoulder. There was a calendar hanging behind the desk, the kind you get free from the bank. It was turned to March 1998, as if time had stopped. 'From your past history, Mr. St. Bride, I'm sure you're aware that transgressions that occur in a correctional facility . . . even minor ones . . . can have a significant effect on the sentence you receive if convicted. For example – this little tantrum of yours could add three to seven years to the time you'll have to serve.' The superintendent folded his arms. 'Do you have anything to say in your own defense?'

'I'm not guilty of any crime. I don't want to look like someone who is.'

The superintendent's mouth flattened. 'Son,' he said quietly, 'you don't want to do this, believe me. This freedom-fighter angle doesn't play well here. If you just keep your nose to the wheel and follow the rules, your stay will be a lot more pleasant.'

Jack stared straight ahead.

The older man sighed. 'Mr. St. Bride, I find that you're guilty of violating the rules of this facility by refusing to wear the required clothing, and you're sentenced to spend three days in solitary.' He nodded to the two correctional officers. 'Take him away.'

The worst part about being a prosecutor, in Matt Houlihan's opinion, was that even when you won, you didn't. The world was too black and white for that. Even if he got Jack St. Bride locked up for twenty years, it didn't take away the fact that this asshole, who'd been convicted before, had committed a crime again. It didn't change the truth that Gillian Duncan would have to live with this memory for the rest of her life. It was like securing the bull after he'd careened through the china shop – yes, you could pen him for a little while, but you still incurred the cost of the mess he'd left in his wake.

Matt had chosen to meet Amos Duncan and his daughter at their home. Normally, he didn't make house calls, but he was willing to bend the rules. Inviting the girl into his office would only bring to the forefront the legal battle that lay ahead of her. Right now, it was in everyone's best interests to keep Gillian calm, so that when Matt finally needed to call in his chip, she would respond the way he needed her to in front of the jury.

He reached for a cup of coffee that Gillian handed him, and he took a sip as she sat down beside her father on the couch. 'Excellent stuff. Kona?'

Amos nodded. 'Hi-test.'

'The Jamaican blend is just as good. Of course, back at the office, we're lucky to get watered-down Maxwell House.'

'I will personally buy the county attorney's office an espresso machine,' Amos vowed, 'if you lock up this bastard.'

Latching onto the segue, Matt nodded. 'Mr. Duncan, I understand completely. And that's why I'm here today. St. Bride has been charged with aggravated felonious sexual assault, which carries up to twenty years in the state penitentiary. I fully intend to ask for the maximum sentence. That means this case isn't going to go away with a plea.'

'Is he going to get out?'

Matt did not pretend to misunderstand Amos. 'St. Bride is being held without bail, so he'll stay in jail until the trial. After his conviction, he'll serve twenty years and then be on lifetime supervision. A third sexual assault offense will land him in prison for life.' He smiled mirthlessly. 'So, no, Mr. Duncan. He's not going to get out anytime soon.'

Matt turned to Gillian. 'Our office can get you in touch with rape crisis counselors, if you need that kind of support.'

'We've taken care of that already,' Amos answered.

'All right. We're currently in the process of interviewing witnesses. Gillian, are there people that you can think of who would know something about last night?'

Gillian looked at her father, who'd gotten up to pace. 'The others, I guess. Whitney and Chelsea and Meg.'

Matt nodded. 'Detective Saxton will be speaking to them.'

'What about the stuff from the hospital?' Amos asked. 'Did you find anything?'

'We won't know for a couple of weeks, Mr. Duncan.'

'Two weeks? That long?'

'As long as we have lab results before we go to trial, we're in good shape. I'm confident that we'll find physical evidence to support Gillian's testimony.'

'My testimony?'

Matt nodded. 'I'm going to have to put you on the stand.'

She immediately started to shake her head. 'I don't think I can do that.'

'You can. We'll go over your testimony; there won't be any surprises.'

Gillian's hands twisted the bottom of her sweater. 'But what about the other lawyer? You don't know what he's going to ask.' A bright thought swelled in her mind. 'If something from the lab proves he was there, do I still have to testify?'

This was a very common reaction for a rape victim, and even more common for a teenager. Smoothly, Matt said, 'Don't worry about it now. I don't have all the evidence yet. I don't have all the police reports. I don't have all the witness statements. Just let me do my job, let Detective Saxton do his . . . and then we'll put together the best possible case we can.' Matt hesitated. 'There *is* one thing I need to know,' he said. 'Gillian, I have to ask you if you were a virgin before this happened.'

Gillian's gaze flew to her father, who had stopped in his tracks. 'Mr. Houlihan . . .'

'I'm sorry. But the answer's important.'

Her eyes were fixed on her father as she murmured, 'No.'

Amos stood and walked away, gathering his composure. 'I want to help with the investigation,' he announced suddenly, changing the topic.

The statement seemed to take his daughter by as much surprise as it did Matt. 'Thank you for the offer. But it's best to let the professionals take care of the details, Mr. Duncan. The last thing you want is to have St. Bride freed on a technicality.'

'Do I get to see it?' Amos demanded.

'See what?'

'The reports. The police statements. The DNA evidence.'

'During the course of this trial,' Matt said, 'I'll make sure you know everything I know after I know it, as soon as possible. I'll show you anything you want to see.'

That appeased Amos. He nodded stiffly.

But Matt was more concerned with Gillian, who still seemed

tangled in the unexpected realization that she would have to get on the stand. 'Gillian,' he said softly. 'I'll take care of you. Promise.'

The lines in her forehead smoothed, and she smiled tentatively. 'Thanks.'

Amos sat down again and slid his arm around his daughter, as if to remind her that he was there to help her, too. Matt looked away, to give them a moment of privacy. And he made a fierce vow to himself to put his entire self on the line for the Duncans, if only so that they could have back a fraction of the life they'd had before Jack St. Bride entered it.

The last time Gilly had been in Dr. Horowitz's office, she'd been nine years old. She remembered playing with dolls while Dr. Horowitz wrote in a notebook. And that the psychiatrist had always given her mint Milano cookies when the sessions were over. One day, her father decided that Gillian had put to rest her mother's death, and she stopped going for her weekly sessions.

'Gillian,' Dr. Horowitz said. 'It's been a while.'

Dr. Horowitz was now two inches shorter than Gillian. Her hair had gone gray at the temples, and she wore bifocals on a beaded chain. She looked old, and this shocked Gilly – if all this time had passed for Dr. Horowitz, it meant that it had passed for *her* as well. 'I don't need to be here,' Gillian blurted out. 'I can take care of this by myself.'

Dr. Horowitz only nodded. 'Your father thinks differently.'

Gillian remained silent. She was terrified of talking. It was bad enough speaking to the county attorney and Detective Saxton, but they at least came expecting to learn. Dr. Horowitz – well, her job was to pick through Gillian's head, to see exactly what was there.

'Why don't we decide together if I can help you?' the psychiatrist suggested. 'How are you feeling today?' Gillian shrugged, silent. 'Have you been able to eat? Sleep?'

'I haven't wanted to.'

'Have you been able to concentrate?'

'Concentrate!' Gillian burst out. 'It's the only thing that's on my mind!'

'What is?'

'Him.'

'Do you keep remembering what happened?'

'God, yes, over and over,' Gillian said. 'But it's like I'm not there.'

'What do you mean?'

Her voice became tiny. 'Like I'm sitting . . . way up high and seeing this girl in the woods . . . how he grabs her . . . and when he runs away, it's like all of a sudden I'm gone too.'

'That must be very upsetting.'

She nodded, and to her horror, tears came to her eyes. 'I'm sorry. I'm okay, really. I just . . . I just . . .'

Dr. Horowitz handed her a tissue. 'Gillian, it wasn't your fault. You have no reason to be ashamed or embarrassed about what happened.'

She brought her knees to her chest and wrapped her arms around them. 'If that's true,' Gilly said, 'then of all the people in the world, why did he pick me?'

The solitary cell had a river of urine in its upper right corner and shiny, dried splotches on the cement block wall, the legacy of the last inmate to be confined. As the door was slammed shut, Jack sank down onto the metal bunk. The silver lining: He was wearing his clothes. His own clothes. He thought of all the Super Bowl winners who'd edged out the first goal, of countries that had won the first battle of an ultimately victorious war.

If the Carroll County Jail had custody of his body, then Jack would damn well keep custody of his own free will.

He felt along the metal links of the bunk and beneath the mattress, over the upper rim of the shower and in the drain, even around the base of the toilet. *A pen,* he prayed. *Just a single pen.* But whoever had neglected to disinfect the solitary cell had managed to strip it clean of anything that might be used for diversion.

Jack sat back down and inspected his fingernails. He scratched at a loose thread in his jeans. He unlaced his sneaker, and then retied it.

He closed his eyes, and immediately pictured Addie. He could still smell her on his skin, just the faintest perfume. Suddenly he felt his chest burn, his arm creep and tingle. A heart attack – Jesus, he was having a heart attack. 'Guard!' he yelled at the top of his lungs. He shook the bunk, rattling it against the clamps that moored it to the wall. 'Help me!'

But no one heard him – or if anyone did, no one came.

He forced himself to concentrate on something other than this pain. *If you have pogonophobia, you'll probably be avoiding these.*

Focus, Jack. *What are beards.*

The unique food you'd give a butterwort plant.

Inhale. Exhale. *What are insects.*

An archtophilist would have a pile of these.

What are teddy bears.

He spread his hand over his chest as the pain ebbed, eased, stopped. And was not really surprised to find that he could no longer feel the beat of his heart.

Gillian watched the last of the candle flame sputter and sink into a pool of wax. A piece of paper with her mother's name on it sat smoking down to ash in a silver dish. Gillian stared at the candle, at the make-shift altar. *Maybe the reason she doesn't come is because she hates the person I've grown up to be.*

It wasn't a new thought for Gillian, but today, it nearly brought her to her knees. She stood up slowly, drawn to the mirror. Picking up a pair of scissors, she stood in front of the glass and lifted a thick strand of her red hair. She chopped it off at the crown, so that a small tuft stood up, and the rest cascaded to the floor like a silk scarf.

She lifted another section, cutting it. And another. Until her skull was covered with uneven spikes, short as a boy's. Until her bare feet were covered with hanks of her hair, a pit of auburn snakes. Until her head felt so light and free that Gilly thought it might lift from her neck like a helium balloon and soar as far away as possible.

Now, she thought, *he wouldn't look twice at me.*

The conference rooms at the jail were narrow and ugly, with battered legal books stacked on a scarred table, windows that had been sealed shut, and a thermostat cranked up to eighty degrees. Jordan sat on one of the two chairs, strumming his fingers on the table, waiting for Jack St. Bride to be brought through the door.

St. Bride was clearly a loser – getting himself caught in a similar situation twice. But to learn that Jack had also managed to get thrown into solitary within an hour of his arrival . . . well, defending him was like being given a sow's ear and told to make a silk purse.

The correctional officer who opened the door pushed Jack in. He stumbled once, glancing over his shoulder. 'Nice to know the Geneva Convention doesn't apply here,' he muttered.

'Why would it? This isn't a war, Jack. Although, rumor has it you've been ready for combat from the moment you stepped in here.' Jordan came to his feet in one smooth motion. 'Frankly, it doesn't do me any good to find you in solitary after just one day. I had to offer my balls on a silver platter to the guards to get to meet with you in private in a conference room instead of through the slit in the steel door down there. You want to play the rebel here, fine – just be aware that everything you say and do here is going to wind up getting back to the prosecutor, and that you might feel the ripples all the way through your case.'

The speech had been intended to put the fear of God into Jack; to scare him into good behavior. But Jack only set his jaw. 'I'm not a prisoner.'

Jordan had been a defense attorney long enough to ignore

him. Denial was something his clients excelled at. Christ, he'd once stood up for a guy who was arrested in the act of plunging a knife into his girlfriend's heart, and who maintained all the way to the State Pen that the cops had mistaken him for someone else. 'Like I said yesterday, you've been charged with aggravated felonious sexual assault. Do you want to plead guilty?'

Jack's jaw dropped. 'Are you kidding?'

'You did the last time you were charged.'

'But that was . . . that was . . .' Jack couldn't even get the words out. 'I was wrongly accused. And my *attorney* said it was the safest course of action.'

Jordan nodded. 'He was right.'

'Don't you want to know if I committed this crime?'

'Not particularly. It isn't important to my job as your defense attorney.'

'It's *crucial.*' Jack leaned over the table, right in Jordan's face. 'The last thing I need is another lawyer who doesn't even *listen* to me when I tell him the truth.'

'*You* listen to *me,* Jack. I didn't put you in jail last year, and I didn't get you arrested this time around, either. Whether you get acquitted or convicted, *I* get to leave that courtroom free and clear. My role here is simply to be your advocate, and to translate that into the simplest terms possible, it means I'm your best goddamned hope. While you're sitting in solitary, I get to go out and fight on your behalf. And if you cooperate with me rather than jump down my throat every other fucking minute, I'm bound to fight considerably harder.'

Jack shook his head. '*You* listen. I didn't rape her. I was nowhere even close to her that night. That's the God's honest truth. I'm innocent. That's why I don't want to wear their clothes and sit in their cell. I don't belong here.'

Jordan returned his gaze evenly. 'You were willing enough to do it before when you accepted a plea, in spite of your . . . innocence.'

'And that's why,' Jack said, his voice breaking, 'there's no way I'm going to do it again. I will kill myself before I sit in jail again for a crime I didn't commit.'

Jordan looked at Jack's rumpled clothing, his wild eyes. He'd had clients before who seemed to feel that an impassioned cry for justice was the only way to muster an attorney's enthusiasm for a case; they never seemed to realize that a good lawyer could identify bullshit by its stink. 'All right. You weren't there that night.'

'No.'

'Where were you?'

Jack picked at his thumbnail. 'Drinking,' he admitted.

'Of course,' Jordan muttered, amazed that this case could get any worse. 'With whom?'

'Roy Peabody. I was at the Rooster's Spit until they closed up.'

'How much did you drink?'

Jack glanced away. 'More than I should have.'

'Fabulous,' Jordan sighed.

'Then I went out for a walk.'

'A midnight walk. Did anyone see you?'

Jack hesitated, for only an instant. 'No.'

'Where did you go?'

'Just . . . around. Behind town.'

'But not near the woods behind the cemetery. Not anywhere near Gillian Duncan.'

'I told you, I never saw her that night, let alone touched her.'

'That's funny, Jack. Because I'm looking at that scratch on your cheek, the one that Gillian Duncan said she gave you in her victim's statement.'

'It was a branch,' Jack said through clenched teeth.

'Ah. From the forest you weren't in?' Jordan's gaze skimmed over Jack's bruised face. 'Did she beat you up, too?'

'No. It was a bunch of guys in ski masks.'

'Ski masks,' Jordan repeated, not buying a word of it. 'Why were people in ski masks beating you up?'

'I don't know.'

Jordan sighed. 'What else can you remember about that night?'

Jack hesitated. 'I remember leaving Addie's . . . and then finding her again at the diner.'

'How much time elapsed in between?'

'Four hours.'

'And what were you doing during those four hours?'

At Jack's silence, Jordan rolled his eyes. 'You don't want to plead. You say you weren't in the woods that night, but you can't provide an alibi. You tell me, then – what have we got?'

'A liar,' Jack said succinctly. 'I don't know why she's doing it, or what she's got against me. But I didn't do this, I swear it. *I didn't rape Gillian Duncan.*'

'Fine,' Jordan said, although he didn't believe him in the least. 'We'll go to trial.'

'No,' Charlie said.

On the other end of the phone, Matt paused in the notes he was writing to himself on a yellow pad. 'What do you mean, no?'

'I mean I can't, Matt. I don't have the time for this.'

Matt set down his pen. 'Maybe you've forgotten the way this works, Charlie. We have a case; I tell you what I need; you get it. And if that means putting down your doughnut and getting your ass out of your swivel chair to interview Addie Peabody, then do it.'

'I've got to drive the rape kit down to the lab in Concord. Then I've got three teenage girls to interview. And somewhere in there I have to figure out who the hell stole the VCR from the high school audiovisual lab. Did I mention that I happen to be the only detective on staff here at the SFPD?'

'I'm sorry your town budget doesn't include the salary for a sidekick. But be that as it may, you're the only one who can take Addie's statement.'

'You can do it,' Charlie suggested. 'Besides, you aren't the one whose face she remembers every time she thinks back to the moment her boyfriend was arrested. She'll probably be more forthcoming with you.'

Matt knew Addie Peabody would talk to him. Hell, everyone talked to him. Even after they said they didn't want to, he'd ask a question, and they'd start spilling their guts. The issue here was what would happen if she told Matt one thing and then said another thing on the stand. 'She's not a sure thing, Charlie. If she changes her story between now and the trial, I can't call myself as a witness to impeach her.'

'She won't lie.'

'You don't know that,' Matt said. 'So what if she was shocked at the arrest? Who *wouldn't* be? By now, she may have decided that she'll stay on St. Bride's ship until it sinks. Or that she can play Mata Hari with the prosecution and somehow secure his acquittal. She's exactly the kind of witness who'll keep me up nights before the trial.'

'Look, I know Addie. I've known her my whole life.' Charlie sounded as if the words were being tugged out of him, all angles and cramps. 'She's the kind of person who takes a shitty situation and deals with it, instead of pretending it never happened. If it makes you feel better, take Wes Courtemanche along during the interview; he can take the stand for you if it comes to impeaching Addie. Now, are you finished? Or do I have to let your physical evidence sit in the fridge during another lecture?'

'I hope you hit traffic,' Matt growled, and slammed down the receiver.

She'd been all thumbs since the moment she set foot in the diner that morning – breaking three glasses, letting a platter of pancakes tumble over the front of her apron, spilling coffee on a customer's paper. 'Addie,' her father said, putting his hand on her shoulder, and that was enough to nearly make her topple the entire tray of table six's food. 'I think maybe you ought to call in Darla.'

Ignoring him, she swung into the kitchen, Roy following.

'Thank the holy Lord,' Delilah said. 'I hope you're here to wash.' She nodded toward the stack of filthy china piled high.

Addie tucked an order into Delilah's rotating file. 'Sorry. Too swamped.'

The cook lifted the slip of paper and frowned. 'Well, honey, I'll make you your frittata, but I'm gonna have to serve it up on a dirty plate.'

'Frankly, Delilah, I don't care if you bring it out in one of your shoes.'

Addie held tight to the last thread of her self-control. She had gone to work in the hopes that staying busy would keep her from dwelling on what had happened. After all, it had helped after Chloe. But it seemed that everywhere she went in the diner, all she could concentrate on was the fact that Jack wasn't there, too.

'Addie,' her father said, 'you're a mess. No one's going to think any less of you if you go up and lie down for a little while.'

'Some of us might even think a little more of you if you found us a new dishwasher,' Delilah muttered.

It was the last straw. Tears sprang to Addie's eyes as she ripped off her apron and flung it onto the kitchen floor. 'Do you think I don't know that I haven't slept in three nights? Or that we don't have enough kitchen staff? A man that I . . . that I thought I could love was arrested right in front of me for rape. And I can't tell you if he did it or not. That's what I'm thinking about, not whether the goddamned dishes get washed or if I've dropped an order all over the floor. I am *trying* to make everyone happy. For God's sake, what do all you people *want* from me?!'

The voice that answered was unexpected, quiet, and cool. 'Well,' said Matt Houlihan, standing behind her with Wes. 'For starters, how about a little talk?'

Houlihan seemed like a perfectly nice man, even if he was aiming to lock Jack away for twenty years. When he smiled, there was a gap between his front teeth, and to Addie's surprise, his eyes seemed to reflect an understanding she never would have expected to find. 'This must be very difficult for you, Ms. Peabody,' Matt said. In the corner of Roy's living room, Wes snorted, then covered it with a cough.

'Do I have to talk to you?'

'No, of course not. But I'd *like* to talk to you, so that you'll know what I'm going to be asking you in court, instead of just subpoenaing you cold turkey.' He smiled sympathetically. 'I understand you were intimately involved with Mr. St. Bride.'

Addie nodded, certain that she wouldn't be able to force a single word of explanation out of her narrow throat.

'Can you tell me about him?'

She picked up her father's television remote control in her hands and thought of Jack watching *Jeopardy!* 'He's very smart,' Addie said softly. 'A trivia buff.'

'How long have you been involved with him?'

'I hired him two months ago, in March. He started working as a dishwasher.'

'Did you know at the time that he had a criminal record?'

Addie's cheeks burned. 'I thought . . . he was down on his luck.'

She could feel Wes's eyes on her, and studiously ignored them. 'Did St. Bride ever say anything to you about Gillian Duncan?' Matt asked.

'No.'

'Did you ever see them together?'

'Only when she and her friends came to the diner and Jack had to clean their table.' As she spoke, her mind fishtailed back, trying to remember if she'd ever seen Jack smiling at the girls, flirting, staying a moment too long after clearing their plates. What had she missed? What had she *wanted* to miss?

'Did he ever read pornography?'

Addie's head snapped up. 'What?'

'Pornography,' the county attorney repeated. '*Playboy* magazines, maybe a video . . . Internet sites of nude children?'

'No!'

'Was your own relationship with him sexually deviant?'

'Excuse me?'

That wide, gap-toothed smile again. 'Ms. Peabody, I realize these questions are rude and personal. But I'm sure you see why it's information we need to have.'

'No,' she said.

'No, you don't see . . . ?'

'No,' Addie interrupted, 'he was not sexually deviant.' In the background, there was a snap as Wes broke the arm off a little clay figurine of a fisherman that sat on her father's bookshelves. He hastily balanced it and turned away, muttering an apology.

'Was St. Bride ever violent toward you?'

Addie raised her chin. 'He was the gentlest man I've ever met.'

'Did he drink?'

Her lips formed a thin line. She knew what the prosecutor was getting at; and God help her, even if Jack was guilty, she didn't want to contribute to his downfall any more than she already had.

'Ms. Peabody?'

Then again, a girl was out there. A girl who had been raped.

'He was drinking that night,' Addie admitted. 'With my father.'

'I see,' Matt said. 'Were you together that night?'

'He left my house about nine-thirty P.M. My father was with him until eleven-thirty P.M. I didn't see him again until one-thirty in the morning.'

'Did he tell you where he'd been?'

Addie closed her eyes. 'No. And I . . . I never asked.'

The dimpled ball sailed over the wide, green sea of the driving range, landing somewhere in the vicinity of a sand trap. Without missing a beat, Jordan bent down and took another one out of the bucket to balance on the tee. He lifted his club, readying for the swing . . . and jerked at Selena's voice.

'Whose face are you seeing on that little thing? Houlihan's . . . or St. Bride's?'

Jordan swung and carried through, shading his eyes against the sun to see the ball fall way off the mark. 'Didn't anyone ever tell you not to interrupt a golfer?'

Selena set down the peel of the orange she was dissecting and popped the first section into her mouth. 'You're not a golfer, Jordan; you're a dilettante.'

Ignoring her, Jordan hit three more balls. 'Got a question for you.'

'Shoot.'

'If you were charged with murder, who would you get to defend you?'

Selena frowned, considering for a moment. 'I think I'd try for Mark D'Amato. Or Ralph Concannon, if Mark wasn't available.'

Jordan glanced at her over his shoulder. 'Mark's good,' he conceded.

She burst out laughing. 'God, Jordan, you've got to work on your poker face. Go on, ask me why I didn't pick you.'

He set down his club. 'Well . . . why not?'

'Because you're the only person I'd ever get angry enough with to actually kill, so you wouldn't be around to defend me. Happy now?'

'I'm not sure,' Jordan frowned. 'Let me think on it.'

Selena glanced at the half bucket of balls. 'You get enough stress out of your system to tell me about your meeting this morning?'

'That might take six buckets.' He rubbed the back of his neck. 'Why do I feel that this one's gonna be a huge pain in the ass?'

'Because St. Bride is dragging you out of a cushy retirement. An open-and-shut acquittal would still make you grumpy. Is he gonna plead?'

'Nope. Our marching orders are to go to trial.'

'No kidding?'

'You heard me.'

She shrugged. 'Okay. Do we have a game plan?'

'We've got nothing from our esteemed client, who's conveniently amnesiac. Which means you get to prove the girl is a liar.'

Selena was so quiet that Jordan went through six more shots before he realized she hadn't responded. 'I know,' he commiserated. 'It'll be next to impossible. Everything I've seen in her statement checks out so far.'

'No, that's not what I was thinking.' She looked up. 'Who's Dr. Horowitz?'

'You've got me. Someone from *ER*?'

'He . . . or she . . . is the doctor mentioned in the victim's statement. My guess is a psychiatrist Gillian Duncan met with in the past.'

For the first time that day, Jordan's ball landed within spitting distance of the flag. He turned slowly from the green and stared at Selena, who raised her brows and handed him the last slice of the orange. As he took it, their fingers brushed. 'Good guess,' he said.

It was all Jack could do to look at the pile of clothes folded neatly on the chair beside him and not start scratching.

In the three days he'd been in solitary confinement, he'd been fastidious about showering. At first, he'd dried off with his T-shirt. Then, as it began to mildew, he let himself air dry, bare-chested. But to be brought to the superintendent's office, the guard made him put on his shirt again. It stuck to his skin and smelled like the bottom of a sewage tank.

Jack looked longingly at the clothes. 'Attractive, aren't they?' the superintendent said. 'They're yours for the taking.'

'No, thank you.'

'Mr. St. Bride, you've made your point.'

Jack smiled. 'Tell me that when you're standing in my shoes.'

'The clothing is for your own safety.'

'No, it's for *yours*. You want me to put on that jumpsuit so that every other man in here knows I follow your rules. But the minute I do, you've got control of me.'

The superintendent's eyes gleamed; Jack knew he was treading on very thin ice. 'We don't use our solitary cells as penthouse suites. You can't stay there forever.'

'Then let me wear my clothes into a regular cell.'

'I can't do that.'

Jack let his gaze slide to the fresh clothing on the seat beside him. 'Neither can I,' he answered softly.

The guard behind him stepped forward at a nod from the superintendent. 'Put Mr. St. Bride back in solitary for six days. And this time, turn off the water line to his shower.'

Jack felt himself being hauled to his feet. He smoothed the front of his shirt as if it were the tunic of a king.

'Mr. St. Bride,' the superintendent said. 'You're not going to win.'

Jack paused, but did not turn around. 'On the other hand, I have nothing to lose.'

Francesca Martine had the body of a *Playboy* centerfold and the brain of a nuclear physicist, something that didn't usually sit well with the men who got up the nerve to ask her out. Then again, she had learned her lesson: Instead of telling dates that she was a DNA scientist, she simply said that she worked in a lab, leaving them to assume she spent her days getting lunch for the *real* scientists, and cleaning out the cages of mice and rats.

She set a sample beneath a microscope. 'So, Frankie,' Matt said, grinning. 'That come from one of your boyfriends?'

'Oh, yeah. I have so little to do here I've taken to swabbing myself to see what's swimming around, just in case the fact that I haven't had a relationship in six months isn't enough to tip me off.' She squinted into the lens. 'How's that cute kid of yours?'

'Molly . . . God. I can't even describe how incredible she is. So I guess you'll have to have one yourself.'

'How come perfectly normal people become matchmakers the minute they get married themselves?'

'It's Darwinian, I think. Trying to keep the species going.' Restless, Matt got to his feet. 'Besides, you brainy types need to be reminded that it's nice to replicate DNA in something other than a thermocycler.'

'Thanks, Mom,' Frankie said dryly. 'Did you specifically come here to talk about my pathetic love life, or is there something else?'

'That rape kit Charlie Saxton brought in –'

'I haven't gotten to it yet, Matt. I was in court yesterday, and this morning I –'

'I'm not rushing you.' He smiled sheepishly. 'Well, not any more than I usually do, anyway. I just wanted to let you know what I'm looking for.'

'Let me guess,' Frankie said deadpan. 'Semen?'

'Yeah. I'd like to know about the blood on the shirt, too. And the soil from the boots.' He swung away from the counter. 'So, you'll get me my results in two weeks?'

'Three,' Frankie murmured, peering into a microscope.

'Gosh, yeah – ten days would be great.' Matt backed away before she could complain. 'Thanks.'

Frankie turned to the scope again. Sperm frozen in time, tailless and immobile. 'That's what they all say,' she sighed.

Addie didn't know where she got the courage necessary to knock on the heavy door of the Carroll County Jail. *If they don't come, I'll just turn away,* Addie thought. *I'll go home and try some other day, when I feel more the thing.*

A guard opened the door. 'Can I help you?'

'I . . . I . . .'

A kindly smile spread across the man's face. 'First visit? Come on in.'

He led Addie into a vestibule, where a small line of people snaked like a tapeworm from a glass-enclosed booth. 'Wait here,' the guard said. 'They'll tell you what to do.'

Addie nodded, more to herself than to the guard, who had already moved away. Visiting hours were Wednesday nights, from 6 to 9. She'd called the switchboard for that information, which had been easy enough. Getting in her car and driving there had been slightly more challenging. Downright impossible would be the moment she saw Jack again and struggled for something to say.

It was after speaking to Matt Houlihan that she realized she needed to do the one thing she hadn't: hear Jack's side of the story, before she believed anyone else's.

She was terrified that he would lie to her, and that their whole time together would just have been an extension of that lie. She was equally terrified that he would tell her the truth, and then she would have to understand how God could be cruel enough to let her give her heart to a man who'd committed rape.

'Next!'

Addie advanced as the man before her was buzzed through a barred door. She found herself facing a correctional officer with a face as misshapen as a potato. 'Name?'

Her heart leaped beneath her light jacket. 'Addie Peabody.'

'Name of the inmate you're here to visit.'

'Oh. Jack St. Bride.'

The officer scanned a list. 'St. Bride's not allowed visitors.'

'Not allowed –'

'He's in solitary.' The guard glanced over her shoulder. 'Next!'

But Addie didn't move. 'How am I supposed to get in touch with him?'

'ESP,' the officer suggested, as Addie was shoved out of the way.

The human scalp has 100,000 hairs.

In an average lifetime, a person will grow 590 miles of hair.

Jack scratched at his thickening beard again, this time drawing blood. There was a rational part of him that knew he was all right, that going without a shower for a week wouldn't kill him. And in spite of what it felt like, a colony of insects had not taken up root on his scalp. But sometimes, when he sat very still, he could feel the threads of their legs digging into his skin, could hear the buzz of their bodies.

Insects outnumber humans 100,000,000 to one.

He thought of these things, these useless facts, because they were so much easier to consider than other things: Would Addie come to see him? Would he remember what had happened that night? Would he, once again, be convicted?

Suddenly, from a distance, there were footsteps. Usually, no one came down here after the janitor's soft-soled shoes paced the length of the hall, rasping a mop in their wake. These shoes were definitive, a sure stride that stopped just outside his door.

'I take it you're still mulling over your decisions,' the superintendent said. 'I wanted to pass along a bit of information to you. You had a visitor today, who of course was turned away, since you're in a disciplinary lockdown.'

A visitor? *Addie?*

Just the thought of her walking into a place like this, the knowledge that she wouldn't have had to if not for Jack, was enough to make him cry a river. Tears sluiced down his face, washing away the grime, and maybe a little bit of his pride.

Reaching up, he scratched vigorously at his temple.

The average person, Jack thought, *accidentally eats 430 bugs in a year.*

As a defense attorney, Jordan had dealt with his share of society's losers – all of whom were convinced they'd been given the fuzzy end of the lollipop. It wasn't his job to judge them on the things they'd done, or even on their own misconceptions of entitlement. Never, though, had Jordan been treated to a client who was so single-mindedly hell-bent on his own destruction – and all in the alleged pursuit of justice. He pulled in his folding chair as another cavalcade of prisoners returned from the exercise yard, disrupting the meeting he was holding on the other side of the solitary cell's metal door. 'They're clothes, Jack,' Jordan said wearily, for the tenth time in as many minutes. 'Just clothes.'

'You ever hear of the human botfly?' Jack answered, his voice thin.

'No.'

'It's a bug. And what it does, see, is grab another insect – like a mosquito, for instance – and lay its eggs on the mosquito's abdomen. Then, when the mosquito lands on you, your body heat makes those eggs fall off and burrow under your skin. As they grow, you can see them. Feel them.' He laughed humorlessly. 'And the whole time, you're thinking that the worst that's happened is a mosquito bite.'

A psych exam, Jordan thought, *would not be out of order here.* 'What are you trying to tell me, Jack? You're infested?'

'If I put on their uniform, I become one of them. It's not *just* clothing. The minute it touches me, the system's gotten underneath my skin.'

'The system,' Jordan repeated. 'You want me to tell you about the system, Jack? The system says that as soon as Superintendent Warcroft decides he needs your little cell for someone else, he's gonna ship you over to the State Pen's secure housing unit. And if you think being stuck here is no picnic, believe me, you ain't seen nothing yet. Down in Concord, in the SHU, the COs wear full body armor – shields and helmets with face masks and steel-toed boots. They escort you everywhere, anytime you have to leave your little pod, which is next to never. And oh, yeah, the pods are arranged around a bulletproof control booth, where the COs sit and watch every move you make. They watch you eat, they watch you sleep, they watch you shit. They watch you breathe, Jack. You and the other three assholes who share your cell, and who probably got sent there for doing something far more violent than refusing to wear a jumpsuit.'

'I won't go to the State Pen.'

'They don't *fucking* ask your permission!' Jordan yelled. 'Don't you understand that? *You are here.* Deal with it. Because every minute I spend worrying whether you're behaving yourself is time taken away from your case, Jack.'

For a while, there was no noise from inside the cell. Jordan placed his palm against the door. Then a voice came back, quiet, broken. 'They're trying to make me into someone I'm not. This shirt . . . these pants . . . they're the only things I have left of the person I know I am. And I need to keep seeing them, Jordan, so I don't start to believe what they're saying.'

'What *should* they be saying, Jack?' Jordan pressed. 'What really happened?'

'I can't remember!'

'Then how the hell do you know for sure you *didn't* rape her?' Jordan argued. He fought for control, shaking his head at the door separating him from his client. He wasn't going to fall for a sob story. If his client was intent on getting shipped off to Concord . . . well, the court would pay Jordan for mileage incurred. 'I filed a motion for a speedy trial, and the prosecutor already signed off on a *subpoena ducef tecum,'* he said briskly, changing the subject. 'We should be receiving Gillian Duncan's psychiatric records shortly.'

'She's crazy. I knew it.'

'These come from when she was a child and might have no bearing on this case.'

'What else have you got?' Jack asked.

'You.'

'That's all?'

'That's got to be enough.' Jordan leaned his forehead against the metal. 'Now do you see why I need you to shape up?'

'Okay.'

The consent came so softly, Jordan frowned, certain he'd misheard. 'What?'

'I said I'll do it. I'll put on the jumpsuit. But you have to do me a favor.'

Jordan felt anger bubbling inside him once more. 'I don't have to do you any favors. You, on the other hand –'

'A pen, for Christ's sake. That's all I want.'

A pen. Jordan stared at the Rollerball in his hand. Jack's change of heart had been too hasty. He imagined his client taking the pen and jamming it into his jugular.

'I don't think so . . .'

'Please,' Jack said quietly. 'A pen.'

Slowly, Jordan slipped the pen through the slot in the metal door. A few seconds later it came back, wrapped tight with a pale blue scroll. T-shirt, Jordan realized. Jack had ripped off a piece of his goddamn precious T-shirt to write something.

'Can you get that to Addie Peabody?' Jack asked.

Jordan unrolled it. A single word was written on the cloth, a word that might have been meant as praise or accusation. 'Why should I help you?' he asked. 'You aren't doing anything to help me.'

'I will,' Jack swore, and for just a moment – the time it took the attorney to remember to whom he was talking – Jordan actually believed him.

'Jesus, Thomas.' Jordan winced as the door slammed shut. 'Do you have to be so damn loud?'

Thomas stopped at the sight of his father, sprawled on the couch with a washcloth covering his forehead. Selena touched him on the shoulder. 'Poor baby had to work today,' she clucked. 'He's cranky.'

'He can hear you talking about him, and he has a headache the size of Montana,' Jordan scowled.

'More accurately, the size of Jack St. Bride,' Selena murmured.

Thomas walked into the kitchen and took a carton of milk from the refrigerator. After swilling a long gulp, he wiped his mouth on his sleeve. 'Lovely,' Selena said.

'I learned it all from my role model of a dad.' Thomas set the milk on the counter. 'What's the problem with the guy, anyway? He seemed nice enough at the diner.'

'So did Ted Bundy,' Jordan muttered.

'Ted Bundy used to work there?' Thomas said. 'No shit!'

Jordan sat up. 'What are they saying in school?'

'Everything. By fourth period there was a rumor that he'd escaped and raped some seventh grader.'

'He hasn't escaped, and it's only an *alleged* rape.'

'Amazing, isn't it,' Selena mused, 'how he can stick to doing his job even when the client is driving him up a tree?'

'Not so amazing, but then again, he insists he loves me, and still, I've been grounded by him before.' Thomas sat down on the floor and reached for the remote control of the TV, but Jordan grabbed it first.

'Hang on,' he said. 'Tell me more.'

Thomas sighed. 'I guess some people feel bad for Gillian.'

'And the others?'

'They think what they've always thought . . . that she's a bitch.'

'A bitch? Gillian Duncan isn't the homecoming queen?' Selena asked.

Thomas burst out laughing. 'She'd probably kill herself if she got elected. She thinks she's better than all that, and she lets everyone know it. Just goes around with her little circle of friends and tries to keep them from mingling with the peons. When I first tried to talk to Chelsea –'

'Who's Chelsea?'

Thomas gave him a long look. 'Dad. *You know.*'

'Ah, right.'

'Well, anyway, Gillian was all over that, trying to tell Chelsea I wasn't worth her time. I mean, you ask me, Gillian had this coming – acting better than everyone else, you're gonna piss someone off sooner or later. But when I said that to Chelsea, she told me it wasn't like that at all.'

'No?'

'She was there, when Gillian came out crying . . . afterward. And she told me Gillian could barely talk. That she's still pretty messed up.'

Jordan balled the damp washcloth into a knot. He exchanged

a glance with Selena, then looked at his son. 'Thomas,' he suggested, 'find out what else Chelsea has to say.'

The envelope was tucked between an electric bill and a flyer advertising the candidacy of George W. Bush for president. addie peabody, it said, scrawled in block lettering she did not recognize. There was no stamp; someone had dropped this off while she was at work.

She slit open the envelope with her finger.

Inside was a small roll of fabric, the same blue as the T-shirt Jack had been wearing the morning of his arrest. Addie unraveled it and found, in his handwriting, one word.

Loyal.

She sank onto the ground at the base of the mailbox, turning the fabric over and over in her hands and trying to understand the cryptic message. Was he accusing her of not sticking up for him during the arrest? Was he begging for her support?

The corners of her memory began to curl, like paper set on fire.

Then again, maybe this was not an adjective at all.

The phone startled Jordan out of a sound, deep sleep. He knocked over his clock-radio reaching for it, and dragged the base halfway across the bed. 'Hello,' he said gruffly.

'You are about to receive a collect call from Carroll County Jail,' a computerized voice said. 'Are you willing to accept the charges?'

'Oh, fuck,' Jordan muttered.

'I'm sorry, I did not understand your –'

'Yes,' Jordan yelled. 'Yes, yes!'

'Thank you.' The next moment, St. Bride was on the other end. 'Jordan? Jordan, you there?' Jack was frantic, breathless.

'Calm down. What's the matter?'

'I gotta see you.'

'Okay. I'll come by tomorrow.'

'No, I've got to see you now.' Jack's voice cracked on a sob. 'Please. I remember. I *remember* now.'

'I'm on my way,' Jordan said.

An hour later, Jack stood before him, sweating and wired from the story he'd just told. The clock on the wall of the tiny conference room ticked like a bomb. 'Let me get this straight,' Jordan said finally. 'You keep seeing things hanging from the trees.'

Jack nodded. 'Tied to them.'

'Like tinsel?'

'No,' Jack said. 'Ribbons, and little sachets. Weird shit. Like that movie . . . *The Blair Witch Project*.'

Jordan folded his arms across his stomach. 'So creepy twig crucifixes were hanging from the trees when you were walking past them, in the dark, in the forest where you did *not* encounter Gillian Duncan. This is what you woke me up for?'

'There was something strange going on. I thought that was patently important to my case, but pardon the hell out of me for disturbing your beauty sleep.'

'Well, it's not important, Jack. Important would be if you remembered someone who saw you between midnight and one-thirty. Important would be just admitting you slept with the girl.'

'I didn't have sex with Gillian Duncan,' Jack yelled. 'Why don't you believe me?'

'You were *drunk!* What would you find easier to believe – that some guy who's six sheets to the wind got a little too aggressive with a girl he happened across . . . or this *Halloween/Scream* decor in the middle of the forest you're telling me about? Stuff, I might add, that neither the cops nor my investigator found traces of?'

Jack flung himself into a chair. 'I want a polygraph,' he said.

Jordan closed his eyes. *God save me from defendants*. 'Even if you took a polygraph and passed, it's not admissable in court. You'd be doing it only for yourself, Jack.'

'And for you. So that you know I'm telling you the truth.'

'I already told you, I don't care whether you committed the crime. I'm still going to defend you.'

Jack bowed his head over his knotted hands. 'If you were sitting in my seat,' he said quietly, 'would that be enough?'

Roy blinked at his daughter again, certain that what he'd heard her say had been a misunderstanding.

It was Delilah who asked outright. 'You're telling me that you're up and leaving Salem Falls? That this ol' washed-up drunk is in charge?'

'This old washed-up drunk was in charge before you were hired,' Roy scowled.

Addie jumped into the fray. 'Not in charge, Delilah. More like a foster parent.'

'Then this little diner of yours is gonna grow up crooked, honey.'

'I just don't understand why you have to go off on this . . . this *quest,*' Roy said.

Addie tried to ignore the small voice inside her that was asking the same thing. Ironically, it was Jack who had taught her, through Chloe, that she needed to put things to rest. Finding out that he had lied to her could not possibly be any more painful than not knowing for sure if he had done this horrible thing. 'I'm not asking you to understand. I'm just asking you to help me.' Addie turned to her father. 'It'll only be for a little while.'

Roy glanced around at the gleaming countertops, the sizzling spit of the grill. 'And if I don't want all this back?'

Addie hadn't thought of that. 'I don't know,' she said slowly. 'I guess we'll close.'

'Close!' Delilah cried.

Roy frowned. 'Close? We haven't closed for years. We haven't closed since . . .'

'Since Mom died,' Addie finished quietly. She took a deep breath. 'Darla's agreed to work my shifts. Delilah, it's going to be the same old routine for you, except a new face is going to be handing you tickets. And Daddy, all you have to do is to take general responsibility.'

Roy looked into his lap. 'That's not my strong point, Addie.'

'Do you think I don't know that? Do you think I wouldn't be asking if this didn't mean so much to me? All these years I've watched you sneak out to drink, and I pretended I didn't see. All the times I've understood that sometimes a person needs to do something, and the hell with the consequences . . . why can't you grant me the same privilege?'

Her father leaned forward, covering Addie's hand with his own. 'Why are you doing this to yourself? When something bad happens, why do you have to pick at it until it bleeds all over again?'

'Because!' Addie cried. 'What if he didn't do it?'

'And what if Chloe hadn't really died? And what if your mom walked right through those swinging doors?' Roy sighed. 'You're not going because you want to prove to yourself he's guilty; a court is gonna do that soon enough. You're going because you don't want to believe the truth that's right in front of you.'

'You don't even know where to start looking,' Delilah added.

'I'll figure it out.'

'And if you don't find what you're looking for?'

At Roy's question, Addie looked up. 'Then all I've lost is time.'

It wasn't true, and all of them knew it. But neither Roy nor Delilah, nor even Addie, wanted to admit that after a certain point, a heart with so many stress fractures would never be anything but broken.

Jordan stood in front of the bathroom mirror with a towel wrapped around his waist and scraped the razor over his beard stubble. Each stroke cleared a line through the shaving foam, like a snowplow. It made him think of Jack, who had been showered and shaved – thank the good Lord – when he'd summoned Jordan in the middle of the night to talk about twig crucifixes or whatever the hell was hanging from the trees.

He tapped the razor against the edge of the sink and rinsed the blade before lifting it to his jaw again. He could always go with a variation of the infamous Twinkie defense, which had acquitted a murderer by suggesting he was on a sugar high. Or he could imply that physical impairment wasn't the only side effect of liquor . . . that psychologically, one's thoughts were disabled, too. Maybe he could even find a crackpot shrink to say that drinking caused dissociation, or some other nifty catchword that excused Jack of being aware of his actions at the time he committed them. It was a cousin to the insanity defense . . . not guilty by reason of inebriation.

'Dad?'

As Thomas opened the door, Jordan jumped a foot, lost in his own thoughts. The razor nicked his cheek, and blood began to run freely down his jaw and neck. 'Goddamn, Thomas! Can't you knock?'

'Jeez. I only wanted to borrow the shaving cream,' he said. He squinted in the mirror at his father's face. 'Better do something about that,' he advised, and closed the door behind him.

Jordan swore and splashed water onto his cheeks and jaw. The shaving cream burned where it seeped into the cut. He patted his face dry with a towel and looked up.

It was one long, straight, thin cut, carved down the center of his right cheek.

'Jesus,' he mused aloud. 'I look like St. Bride.'

He blotted toilet paper against it, until it stopped bleeding, then wiped up around the sink and started out of the bathroom to get dressed. A moment later, he found himself in front of the mirror again, staring more carefully at his cheek.

Gillian Duncan stated that she'd scratched Jack in an effort to get him away from her. Charlie Saxton had photographed the corresponding scrape on Jack's cheek when he was being booked; it was in the file. But a man who had been scratched by a girl fighting off a rape would have four or five parallel marks – the scars of several fingernails, where they'd connected with his skin.

And Jack didn't.

May 2000
Salem Falls, New Hampshire

Jack and Gill went up the hill
To fetch a pail of water.
Jack poked Gill just for the thrill
Of nailing Duncan's daughter.

Charlie crumpled the handwritten ode that had been left taped to his computer terminal. 'Not funny,' he yelled in the general vicinity of the rest of the precinct, then plastered a smile to his face as the first of his three interviewees entered the building, clutching her father's arm.

'Ed,' Charlie said, nodding. 'And Chelsea. Good to see you again.'

He led them to the small conference room at the station, which in his opinion was a slight cut above the interrogation room. These girls were nervous enough already to be party to an investigation; he didn't need to make them any more jittery. Holding the door open, Charlie let Ed and his daughter pass inside.

'You understand why it's important for me to take your statement?' Charlie asked, as soon as they all were seated.

Chelsea nodded, her blue eyes wide as pools. 'I'll do anything to help Gilly.'

'That's good. Now, I'm just going to tape our talk here today, so that the prosecutor gets a chance to hear what a loyal friend you are, too.'

'Is that really necessary?' Ed Abrams asked.

'Yeah, Ed, I'm afraid it is.' Charlie turned to Chelsea again, then started the microcassette recorder. 'Can you tell me where you went that night, Chelsea?'

She glanced sideways at her father. 'We were just getting cabin fever, you know?'

'Where did you go?' Charlie asked.

'We met at the old cemetery on the edge of town, at eleven P.M. Meg and Gilly came together; Whit and me were waiting when they got there. Then we all went up that little path that goes into the woods behind it.'

'What were you going to do?'

'Just talk, girl stuff. And build a fire, so we'd have, like, some light.' Her head snapped up. 'Just a tiny fire, not the kind you need a permit for or anything.'

'I understand. How long were you there?'

'I guess about two hours. We were getting ready to go when . . . Jack St. Bride showed up.'

'You knew who he was?'

'Yeah.' Chelsea brushed her hair away from her face. 'He worked at the diner.'

'Had he talked to you before that night?'

She nodded. 'It was . . . kind of creepy. I mean, he was a grown man, and he was always trying to make jokes with us and stuff. Like he wanted us to think he was cool.'

'What did he look like?'

Chelsea sat up straighter in her chair. 'He was wearing a yellow shirt and jeans, and he looked like he'd been in a fight. His eye, it was all bruised and swollen.' She wrinkled her nose. 'And he smelled like he had been swimming in whiskey.'

'Were there any cuts on his face?'

'Not that I remember.'

'How did you feel?'

'God,' Chelsea breathed, 'I was so scared. I mean, he was the reason we were all supposed to be at home that night.'

'Did he seem angry? Upset?'

'No.' Chelsea blushed. 'When I was little, my mom used to make me watch this commercial about not taking candy from strangers. And that's what he reminded me of . . . someone who looked all normal on the outside but who would turn to the camera when we weren't looking and smile like a monster.'

'What happened?'

'We said we were getting ready to leave, and he said goodbye. A few minutes later, we left, too.'

'Together?'

Chelsea shook her head. 'Gilly went in a different direction, toward her house.'

'Did you hear anything, after you left?'

Chelsea bowed her head. 'No.'

'No screaming, scuffling, hitting, shouting?'

'Nothing.'

'Then what happened?' Charlie asked.

'We were walking for a while, just out of the woods on the edge of the cemetery, when we heard something crashing through the trees. Like a deer, that's what I thought. But it turned out to be Gilly. She came running at us, crying.' Chelsea closed her eyes and swallowed hard. 'Her . . . her hair, it was all full of leaves. There was dirt all over her clothes. And she was hysterical. I tried to touch her, just to calm her down, and she started to hit me. It was like she didn't even know who we were.' Chelsea pulled the sleeve of her shirt down over her wrist and used it to wipe her eyes. 'She said that he raped her.'

'Why did you let Gilly leave by herself?'

Chelsea looked into her lap. 'I didn't want to. I even offered to walk her home.'

'But you didn't.'

'No,' Chelsea said. 'Gilly told me I was being just as bad as our parents. That nothing was going to happen.' She twisted the hem of her shirt into a knot. 'But it did.'

Whitney O'Neill frowned at a spot on the conference table. 'None of your friends suggested it might not be a bright idea to let your friend go off into the woods alone?' Charlie asked.

'Is my daughter a witness or a suspect?' Tom O'Neill blustered.

'Daddy,' Whitney said. 'It's okay. It's a good question. I guess we were all just tired, or maybe even a little shaky after having him show up . . . Chels and Meg and I hadn't gone ten feet before we realized that we probably ought to go with her. That's when I yelled for Gilly.'

'*You* yelled,' Charlie clarified. 'Not Chelsea or Meg.'

'Yeah,' Whitney said defensively. 'Is that so hard to believe?'

Charlie ignored the heated stares of the girl and her father. 'Did Gillian answer?'

'No.'

'And you didn't go back to check? To make sure Gillian was all right?'

'No,' Whitney whispered, her lower lip trembling. 'And you have no idea how I wish I had.'

When Meg had been a little kid, she used to hide under the sofa every time her father dressed in uniform. It wasn't that she was afraid of police officers, exactly . . . but when her dad wore his shiny shoes and brimmed hat and sparkling badge, he was not the same man who fixed her Mickey Mouse–shaped pancakes on Sundays and who tickled her feet to get them underneath the covers at night. When he was working, he seemed harder, somehow, as if he could bend only so far before snapping in half.

Now, it was totally weird to be sitting on her bed with all her stuffed animals . . . and to have her dad interviewing her with his tape recorder. Even weirder, he looked just as freaked out as she was.

Meg's heart beat as fast as a hummingbird's, so fast she was certain it would just explode out of her chest any minute. That whole night was a blur, one that faded in and out like the colors on a kaleidoscope. Not for the first time, she wished she'd been able to give her statement with Chelsea and Whitney in attendance. *You can do this,* she told herself.

She closed her eyes and thought of herself sneaking back to the woods, to clear the branches of the dogwood and the ribbons from the maypole. She'd done that, and no one had found out.

'Honey?' her father asked. 'You all right?'

Meg nodded. 'Just thinking of Gillian.'

He leaned forward, brushing her hair back from her face and catching it behind her ear. 'You're doing great. We don't have much more to go over.'

'Good, because it's hard to talk about,' Meg admitted.

Her father turned on the recorder again. 'Did you hear anything after you left?'

'No.'

'No screams from Gillian? Fighting? Trees rustling?'

'Nothing.'

Charlie looked up. 'Why did you let her go off alone?'

'It . . . it's hard to remember exactly . . .'

'Try.'

'It was Gilly's idea,' Meg said faintly. 'You know how she is when she gets something in her head. After talking with him for a while, I guess she figured she was brave enough to handle anything.'

'Did someone try to get her to rethink this?'

Meg nodded quickly. 'Chelsea . . . or maybe Whitney, I can't really remember. Someone told her she shouldn't go.'

'And?'

'And she just . . . didn't listen. She said she wanted to walk through the lion's den and live to tell about it. She's like that sometimes.'

He stared at her, every inch a detective, so that it was impossible to tell what he was thinking. 'Daddy,' Meg whispered. 'Can I say something . . . off the record?'

He nodded, and turned off the tape recorder.

'That night . . . when I sneaked out of the house . . .' Meg lowered her eyes. 'I shouldn't have.'

'Meg, I –'

'I know you didn't say anything when I told you on tape,' she continued in a rush. 'And I know it's your job to be the detective, not the dad. But I just wanted you to know that I should have stayed home, like you wanted. I knew better.'

'Can I say something, too? Off the record?' Her father looked away, at a small watermark on the ceiling, blinking hard as if he were crying, although that impression must have been a mistake, because in her whole life Meg had never seen him do that. 'The whole time I was taking Gillian's statement, I kept hearing your voice. And every piece of evidence I drove to the lab I pictured coming from you. I hate that this happened to your friend, Meg . . . but I'm so goddamned grateful that it didn't happen to you.'

He leaned down to embrace her. Meg buried her face against her father's neck, as much for comfort as to keep herself from confessing something he was not allowed to know.

Molly's pink feet churned like pistons as Matt slapped the front of the diaper over her and secured the tapes at the sides. 'Get her on a changing table,' he mused, 'and suddenly she wants out as bad as Sirhan Sirhan.'

Charlie reached into his pocket and pulled out his gold shield. He dangled it over the baby's reaching hands, distracting her long enough for Matt to get her jumpsuit snapped at the crotch again. 'I don't think Meg was ever that tiny.'

'Yeah, well I don't think Molly is ever gonna get that big.'

Matt lifted his daughter off the table and carried her into the living room of his house, Charlie following.

'You'd be surprised,' Charlie said. 'You go to bed one night singing her a lullaby, and she wakes up listening to Limp Bizkit.'

'What the hell is Limp Bizkit?'

'You don't want to know.' Charlie sat on the couch as Matt slid the baby beneath a brightly colored activity gym.

'I've been thinking of marketing these in prisons,' Matt joked. 'You know, you hang them from the ceiling . . . little mirrors and jingly shit and squeaky buttons to keep the inmates busy. Figure they've got about the same brainpower as a five-month-old, although Molly may actually have an edge there.' He sank down into a chair opposite Charlie. 'Maybe it'll make me the million I'm *not* going to get as a prosecutor.' Reaching across the coffee table, he picked up a stack of statements.

Immediately, Charlie shifted gears into his work mode. 'Looks like a pretty straightforward case, doesn't it?'

Matt shrugged.

'Victim can ID her attacker, attacker has a history, and there's an excellent chance of physical evidence. And now you've got three corroborating eyewitness reports.'

'Corroborating,' Matt repeated. 'Interesting word choice.' He lifted the first transcript and flipped it open to a page where part of the dialogue had been highlighted with a marker. 'You see this?'

Charlie took it from him and scanned it. 'Yeah. After she left, Whitney O'Neill got a conscience and yelled for her friend, who was too busy being attacked to answer.'

Matt handed him a second transcript, Chelsea's. 'This girl says she offered to walk Gillian home *before* leaving. Which Whitney O'Neill doesn't mention in her statement.'

Charlie snorted. 'That's not exactly a salient point. So what if they can't recall every single instant of that night? For Christ's sake, they all say the same thing about what time the guy showed up, what he said to them, what he looked like. They all admit they heard nothing after walking off. That's the stuff that's going to snag your jury.'

'Your own daughter,' Matt continued, ignoring the detective, 'says Gillian insisted on walking home alone, as a dare. Gotta tell you . . . if I had been there that night, *that* would have stuck in my head.' He slapped the three transcripts down on the table. 'So which is the right story?'

Charlie glanced at the cooing baby on the floor. 'You get back to me when she's sixteen. You talk to a girl who's scared shitless after her friend gets raped in the woods in the middle of the night, and see how much she can recall detail for detail. Jesus, Matt, they're *kids*. They were an arm's length away from the Devil and lived to tell about it . . . but they're still shaking. And even if they can't remember this one thing exactly right, they weren't the ones who were assaulted. Their statements aren't as substantive as Gillian's – they're only supposed to be used to verify what she said.'

When Matt didn't answer, Charlie exploded. 'You're telling me you made me put those girls through hell for nothing? They're upset. A jury is going to weigh that against some pissy little discrepancy that doesn't even signify.'

'Doesn't signify?' Matt's voice rose. 'Everything signifies, Charlie. Every damn thing. The job *you* do impacts the job *I* do. This isn't some petty theft. This is a predator, and the only person who's got a gun to shoot him down is me. If every *t* isn't crossed and every *i* isn't dotted, it's that much easier for this asshole to walk out of the courtroom and do it all over again.'

'Hey, look, it isn't my fault –'

'Then whose is it? Whose fault is it going to be when Gillian Duncan wakes up with nightmares and has trouble trusting men for the rest of her life and can't have a normal sexual relationship? Even if St. Bride spends forever locked up, the victim never gets to walk away from this. And that means neither do you, Charlie, and neither do I.'

The fury in his voice startled Molly. She rolled away from her baby gym and started to cry. Matt swept her into his arms, holding her close against his chest. 'Shh,' he whispered, bouncing her, his back to Charlie. 'Daddy's here.'

Loyal, New Hampshire was the kind of town that looked just right when the leaves were falling like jewels or when the snow settled in a down blanket to even the hills and valleys. Even now, in mud season, the whitewashed buildings and uniformed schoolgirls made the sloppy central green feel like a movie set instead of a place where people went about their lives.

Addie parallel-parked in front of a general store, where a woman wearing hiking boots and a handkerchief skirt was painting a sale sign on the front window. Shading her eyes from the sun, Addie approached her. 'Boots for $5.99? That's a good deal.'

The shopkeeper turned, assessing her with a single glance. 'We still get girls who come to board at Westonbrook who haven't figured out the land's a swamp from April till June. We sell Wellies like they're going out of style.'

'I imagine you get a lot of business from the school.'

'Sure, since it's the only show in Loyal. Put our town on the map back in 1888, when it was founded.'

'Really?' Addie was surprised it had been around for that long.

The woman laughed. 'You'll get the grand tour and fancy brochures at the admissions office. Come to check it out for your daughter, have you?'

Addie turned slowly. This woman had just given her the means to an end. She couldn't very well barrel into the headmaster's office and ask him about Jack. On the other hand, if she was a concerned parent who'd heard rumors . . . well, she might find more people who were willing to explain what had happened.

'Yes,' Addie said, smiling. 'How did you guess?'

'Mrs. Duncan, is it?' Herb Thayer, headmaster of Westonbrook, walked into the office. Addie was waiting on a Hepplewhite couch, drinking tea from a Limoges cup, doing everything she possibly could to try to hide her battered old boots beneath the furniture.

'Oh, please, don't stand on ceremony.' He gestured to his own feet, encased in thick rubber boots. 'Unfortunately, when William Weston founded this school on the banks of his brook, he forgot about how the mud would be exacerbated by a New Hampshire spring.'

Addie simpered, pretending that he'd said something remotely amusing. 'It's a pleasure to meet with you, Dr. Thayer.'

'Mine, completely.' He sat down across from her, taking his own cup of tea from the tray. 'I'm sure you were told in admissions that the application deadline has unfortunately passed for next term –'

'Yes, I have. Gillian's been at Exeter . . . but Amos and I would much prefer it if she were at a school a little closer to Salem Falls.'

'Amos,' the headmaster repeated, feigning surprise. 'As in Amos Duncan of Duncan Pharmaceuticals?'

'Yes, that's right.'

Thayer smiled more broadly. 'I'm certain that we'd be able to squeeze her in, with a little ingenuity. After all, we wouldn't want to turn away a girl who would be a real asset to Westonbrook.'

More like you're considering all her daddy's assets and what they could endow. 'We're very interested in your school, Dr. Thayer, but we've heard some disturbing . . . information. I was hoping you might be able to clear things up for me.'

'Anything I can do,' Thayer said solemnly.

Addie looked him straight in the eye. 'Is it true that one of the faculty here was convicted for sexual assault?'

She watched heat creep up the headmaster's cheeks like mercury in a thermometer. 'I assure you, Mrs. Duncan, our faculty is an elite corps of the finest teachers.'

'You didn't answer my question,' Addie said coolly.

'It was a very unfortunate situation,' Thayer explained. 'A consensual relationship between an underage student and a faculty member. Neither one of them is affiliated with Westonbrook anymore.'

Addie's heart fell. She had been hoping Thayer would say that it had never happened at all. And here, close enough to touch, were the words that proved Jack had lived here, done something, been convicted.

Then again, statutory rape was different from forcible rape. Falling for a girl half his age wasn't the same crime as assaulting one by force. Addie could understand neither . . . but this one, she could possibly forgive.

'What happened, exactly?'

'I'm not at liberty to say – protecting a minor and all that. I assure you that the school has taken measures to ensure that this will never happen again,' the headmaster continued.

'Oh? Are all your teachers now younger than sixteen? Or are your students older?'

The minute she said the words, she wished them back. She gathered her coat and her dignity and stood quickly. 'I think, Dr. Thayer, that Amos and I will have to discuss this further,' she said stiffly, and left before she could make any more mistakes.

'So when you move the variable to this side, dividing it,' Thomas explained, 'it's like you're pulling a rug out from under its feet . . . and it disappears on this side of the equals sign.'

Chelsea was so close to him that he was amazed he could even explain basic algebra to her. The scent of her shampoo – apples, and a little bit of mint – was enough to make his head swim. And God, the way she leaned down over his notebook to see what he'd written . . . her hair brushed back and forth over the metal rings, and all Thomas could think about was what it would feel like to have those curls sweeping over his skin.

Thomas took a deep breath and put an extra few inches between them. It didn't help that they were sitting on Chelsea's bed – her *bed*, for Christ's sake! – where every night she slept in something pink and flimsy that he'd seen peeking out from beneath one of her pillows.

When he shifted away, Chelsea smiled up at him. 'I'm starting to get the hang of this.' She moved in the direction he had, erasing the buffer zone he'd so carefully put between them. Then, scrawling a few more lines with a pencil, she grinned triumphantly. 'A=5B + ¼C. Right?'

Thomas nodded, and when Chelsea whooped with delight, he scooted backward again. She'd invited him here to teach her math, not to attack her. Swallowing hard, he forced himself to ignore how amazingly gorgeous she was when she smiled, and he put another foot between them for good measure. His hand slid beneath her blankets and bumped into something hard, dislodging it from beneath the comforter.

'What's that?' he asked, at the same time Chelsea jumped on the black-and-white composition notebook.

'Nothing.' She tucked it under her leg.

'If it was nothing, you wouldn't be so freaked out.'

Chelsea chewed on her lower lip. 'It's a diary, all right?'

Thomas wouldn't have read it if it was private, but that didn't keep him from wondering whether the reason Chelsea didn't want him to see it was because, holy God, there might even be an entry in there about him. He looked at the salt-and-pepper cover, peeking out from under her thigh. '*Book of . . .*' he read.

Suddenly Chelsea was in his arms, pressing him back on pillows that released her scent and surrounded him, the most wonderful web. 'What's the going rate for a math tutor these days?' she whispered.

Pinch me, Thomas thought, *because I have to be dreaming.* 'A kiss,' he heard himself say, 'and we can call it even.'

And then her mouth moved over his. She drew back for a moment, surprise in her eyes, as if she never expected to quite find herself here, either . . . and was astonished to realize it was this good a fit. More slowly this time, their heads dipped together. And Thomas was so stunned by the soft weight of the goddess on top of him, by the sugar taste of her breath, that he never noticed Chelsea slipping the diary between the bed and the wall.

Jordan was engrossed in reading about Gillian at age nine, which explained why he didn't even look up when Selena opened the passenger door and slid into the seat beside him with a look that could have stopped a Gorgon in its tracks.

'You're not gonna believe this,' she said.

Jordan grunted.

'The factory is on strike. The part's not coming in for ages. Shit, I ought to just rent a car and go.'

'Maybe not quite yet.'

Selena turned to him. 'Care to elaborate on that?'

But Jordan's nose was buried in a folder. Selena grabbed it from him. 'What's got you so entranced?' She turned the envelope, reading the name on the side. 'Gillian Duncan's psychiatric records? Houlihan gave these to you without a fight?'

Jordan shrugged. 'Don't look a gift horse in the mouth. And listen to this stuff, it's beautiful. "No evidence of psychosis . . . information from collateral sources contradict her account . . . manipulative . . . history of mendacity regarding interpersonal relationships." ' He grinned. 'And she stole shit from stores, too.'

'Give me that.' Selena snatched the folder again and scanned the pages. 'Why was she seeing a shrink when she was nine?'

'Her mother died.'

Selena clucked softly. 'Makes you feel sorry for her.'

'Feel sorrier for Jack St. Bride,' Jordan suggested.

'So what are you going to do with this?'

He shrugged. 'Use it to impeach her, if I need to.'

'But presumably, she's better now.'

He arched a brow. 'Who's to say this isn't the way Gillian Duncan reacts under stress? Here's a girl who historically says whatever she needs to, to get attention.'

Selena winced. 'I hate it when you use me for test runs of your defense theories.'

'Yeah, but how is it?'

'The jury isn't going to let you go there. You're being too hard on a victim. You'll lose your credibility.'

'You think?' Jordan sighed. 'Maybe you're right.'

'Plus, there's every bit as much of a chance that St. Bride's the one who's lying.'

'Yeah,' he admitted. 'There is that.' He drummed his fingers on the steering wheel, looking straight ahead. 'So . . . should we look for a Hertz dealership?'

Selena busied herself with securing her seat belt. 'I'm in no rush,' she said.

His hand was on her, melting the skin where it touched. It slid from her hip to her waist, then fumbled over her breast. Hot, like a stone in the sun. She froze, hoping he'd pull away, praying he wouldn't.

'Are you prepared in the event of an accident?' said the announcer on the radio spot, waking Meg instantly. She rolled over and hit the alarm's button to shut it off.

A knock on the door. 'You up?' her mother called.

'Yes,' Meg murmured. But instead of rising, she stared at the ceiling; wondering why she was soaked in sweat, breathing so hard she might have run a mile in her dreams.

Charlie tried very hard not to stare at the hatchet job that was now Gillian Duncan's hairstyle. He'd seen enough victims in Miami to know that she'd done this to herself, and it was probably better than cutting up her arms or worse, trying to commit suicide. 'What you need to remember,' he said, as he walked Gillian through the police station, 'is to keep a cool head. You have all the time in the world when it comes to a lineup.'

She nodded, but Charlie could tell that she was still nervous. He glanced at Matt, who shrugged. This was the first time they'd insisted the girl be separated from her father during the investigation, and with her anchor missing, she was completely adrift. But Matt had been adamant – today, he didn't want anyone around who could influence Gillian. Not even Amos Duncan.

Matt stepped around them to open the door. A uniformed officer stood guard over the proceedings. 'All right.' Charlie let Gillian step up to a table, while he and Matt stood a few feet behind. 'Do you remember which one you saw that night?'

The table was covered with six different kinds of condoms in an array of colors and variations. Charlie knew this for a fact, since Matt had made the detective go out and buy them himself at the drugstore. There were ribbed ones and natural-skin ones and even glow-in-the-dark . . . and mixed up among them was the brand Charlie had seized from the nightstand beside Addie Peabody's bed.

Voice shaking, she asked, 'Can I . . . can I touch them?'

'Of course.'

She reached out, going straight for the purple-packaged Trojan. But her hand veered to the left, and her fingers skimmed over a Contempo, two LifeStyles, and a Durex.

She picked up the Durex, then the Prime sitting beside it.

Suddenly, she flung the condom back onto the table and buried her face in her hands. 'I don't know,' she cried. 'It was dark . . . and I was . . . I was so scared . . . and . . .'

Matt jerked his head toward Gillian, and Charlie quickly slid his arm around her shoulders. 'It's okay, honey. You just relax.'

'But you wanted me to be able to pick it. For evidence.'

'We have other evidence,' Matt said.

Gilly sniffed loudly. 'Really?'

'Yeah,' Charlie said. 'This is just icing on the cake. Okay?'

She nodded. 'Okay.'

'You want to stop?'

'No.' Gilly turned back to the counter, her hands clenched at her sides as if she could will herself to remember. 'It was purple,' she said a minute later. 'The package was purple.' When she smiled, it transformed her entire face. 'I'm right, aren't I?'

'You bet,' Matt said, collecting the condom from her hand.

Charlie walked her to the door and opened it. 'Joe,' he said to the officer standing outside. 'Would you be kind enough to walk Miss Duncan back to her father?'

'Sure, Lieutenant.'

Charlie watched Gillian walk away with the big patrolman, then went back inside to the county attorney. He stuffed his hands in his pockets. 'She picked the Trojan.'

Matt nodded. 'Unfortunately,' he said, 'that wasn't the brand you took from the house.'

* * *

It made Jack look good.

The unexpected thought hit Jordan like a punch to the belly, driving all the air from his lungs. To his absolute shock, there were things in the discovery he'd received from Matt Houlihan that evening that actually worked in his favor.

Jordan blew a ring of cigar smoke in the direction of his bare feet, levered onto the railing of the porch. The police statement from Charlie Saxton lay open on his lap. Beside him on the wooden floor were the testimonies of the girls who had been eyewitnesses, and the surprising result of the condom lineup. The only missing piece of the discovery was the forensic scientist's workup, which had been delayed for a week owing to lab overload.

The past two weeks had not convinced Jordan of Jack St. Bride's innocence – he was certain his client's one-note performance of the I-wasn't-there refrain was grounded in nothing more than wishful thinking. The Nelson Mandela tactics in jail were not a measure of a clear conscience as much as they were a nuisance. And the crazy story about decorations in the forest said less about the man's credibility than the brand of whiskey he'd been drinking.

But right now, staring over the county attorney's discovery, Jordan wondered whether Jack St. Bride might not be the real thing.

He slid open the door and padded down the hallway to his own bedroom, which he'd chivalrously given up to Selena. A pie slice of moonlight illuminated her, and for a moment the sight of this woman in his bed again took his breath away. He was not surprised when Selena sensed his presence and immediately woke, sliding her hand under the pillow.

'You don't sleep with a gun at my house,' Jordan murmured. 'Which is a good thing for me, I imagine.'

Selena rolled away. 'Get out of my bedroom, Jordan,' she muffled into the covers.

'It's my bedroom.'

'I still don't want you in it. And that's a clear invite to leave, unless you've been taking lessons from your client on social interaction with females.'

'It's about Jack. I need to talk to you.'

Resigned, Selena flopped onto her back. 'At three in the morning.'

'Four, but who's counting?' Jordan eased down onto the bed beside her. 'Did you read the discovery?'

'Some of it.'

'Well . . . there are holes.'

Selena shrugged. 'There are always holes. Or so you tell me.'

'But half the time I'm lying. In this case, it's true.'

'Such as?'

'The scratch. Remember I told you about that? And the psych records. And the girls' stories don't match a hundred percent.'

'What about the physical evidence?'

'Hasn't come back from the lab yet,' Jordan admitted.

Selena read over the transcript, then looked at him. 'But you're thinking . . . ?'

'Yeah,' Jordan said with surprise. 'That it just might tell us what Jack's been telling us all along.'

In his nightmare, Matt was in court.

He stared at the jury as if he had the power to mesmerize, because a rape case really came down to whom they believed the most. The judge called his name. 'Mr. Houlihan!'

'Yes, Your Honor. Excuse me.' He pulled at his collar, trying to keep from being strangled by his tie. 'The state calls Gillian Duncan to the stand.'

There were camera flashes and rustles of movement as the entire gallery strained to see the prosecution's star witness make her way toward the front of the courtroom. But the doors did not open; the girl didn't appear. Matt tried to ask the bailiff where his witness was but was stopped once again by the judge's voice. 'Counsel, now what's the problem?'

'My witness,' Matt said. 'I can't find her.'

'She's right here.' The judge pointed down at the stand.

But Matt couldn't see anything past the lip of the box. He walked toward the bench quickly, although his legs felt like pudding beneath him, and put his hand on the carved railing. 'Please state your name for the record,' he said. When no answer came, he peered into the witness box.

And saw his own baby lying at its base, smiling up at him as if she knew he'd be able to save her.

There was some guilty pleasure that came from watching Jack appear with a correctional officer at the door of the small conference room, still rubbing the sleep from his eyes. 'Jordan,' he said, 'it's the middle of the night.'

'Didn't bother you before.' Jordan sat back, studying his client.

'What?' Jack asked, looking down at his jumpsuit as if there might be bloodstains or some other incriminating evidence on it. 'Did I get convicted?'

At that, Jordan almost smiled. 'You would have been in the courtroom with me if you had.'

'Then why are you here?'

Jordan rested his elbows on the table. 'Because,' he said slowly, 'I am having a spiritual moment of sorts.'

Jack looked at him warily. 'Good for you.'

'And for you, actually.' Jordan pushed a manila envelope across the table to Jack. 'I got the discovery from the county attorney today. Everything but the lab results, anyway.' As he watched Jack open the packet and scan the pages, Jordan cleared his throat uncomfortably. 'This isn't something I've said very often, and never directly to a client, so it's a little hard for me. Christ.' He shook his head, a crimson flush rising up his neck. 'Three little words, and I can't even choke them out.'

Jack glanced up, eyes guarded. 'You're not going to tell me you love me, are you?'

'Hell, no,' Jordan said. 'I *believe* you.'

Then Jack managed to draw a breath into his burning lungs. 'You *what*?'

'I think the girl's lying. And I don't know where you were that night, but it wasn't with her.'

He watched Jack's eyes darken with surprise. 'I would have gotten you off no matter what,' Jordan said brazenly. 'But now I actually *want* to.' He felt drunk, dizzy. As if something bound tight inside him had broken free, making him able to move mountains, to bring down giants.

Stunned, Jack turned away. 'I don't believe this.'

Jordan laughed. 'Jack,' he said. 'You're not the only one.'

1989
New York City

The girl had to be drunk, that was the first rule.

If she wasn't on the verge of passing out, she usually freaked and spoiled it right in the middle of the fun. Every now and then one had gotten her bearings and gone all skittish, but it hadn't taken much more than another beer to convince her to stay. After all, this was why she'd come in the first place.

The idea had come indirectly from Coach, when some of the guys were getting pissed about the minutes of playing time they were getting on the field. Factions began to fight; players cut each other down the second Coach's back was turned. *A soccer team,* he said, *has no room for a superstar.* He was trying to make the players understand that how well they played together was a direct reflection of how well they interacted off the field. *Visit the Empire State Building together,* he'd suggested. *Go bowling. Split a pizza in Little Italy.* But the Columbia University varsity soccer team had found something else to share.

There were always a number of girls hanging around their team bashes, soccer groupies who cared less about the sport than they did about being seen with and by winners. By unspoken agreement, the high scorer got to pick one from the crowd. He'd ply her with alcohol, even though she'd usually arrived ready, willing, and able. And after they screwed, he'd ask her if she wanted to meet one of his friends.

Once a girl had passed out cold and all eleven players had gotten to fuck her.

Jack pushed through the press of bodies in his apartment, trying to reach the Holy Grail of the keg. He was not a particular fan of this tradition, never having been one who liked sharing what he considered his. But as the lead scorer all season, he was first . . . so it was easy to pretend he was the only, too.

He filled up two plastic cups and wove back toward the girl he'd been talking to. She had green eyes and tits that looked like they'd fill up his hands. He couldn't remember her name. 'Here you go,' he said, offering his most charming smile.

'Thanks.' She took the cup, and then stumbled against him as someone pushed her from behind. 'Sorry. It's just so crowded in here.'

She did this thing with her eyes, making them go all slanty and looking up from underneath her lashes, all of which was getting Jack as hard as a railroad spike. 'You want to go somewhere quieter?'

'Okay.'

He tugged her by the hand toward his bedroom. Chad, his roommate, was standing near the threshold. 'Save me some,' he said.

Jack closed the door. The girl walked around his room, touching the trophies on his shelves, his team jacket, the battered soccer ball his dad had given him as a kid. He set his hands on her shoulders. 'See anything you like?'

She turned in his arms. 'Yeah,' she said, and kissed him.

They needed to turn down the music. Jack pulled a pillow over his head, wishing he could drown out the sound. The bass alone was killing him.

Beside him, the girl lay sprawled on her stomach. He must have dozed off too, after. Wouldn't have minded just crawling under the covers right now, either, except for the fact that his teammates were out there waiting.

Rap rap rap.

'Jack!' Chad's voice came muffled through the door. 'Jack, c'mere!'

Naked, Jack stumbled off the bed and cracked the door open. 'I'm almost done.'

'It's not that. Your mother's here.'

'My *mother?'*

Granted, his parents lived on the Upper West Side, just a stone's throw away. But they rarely saw each other, in spite of their proximity. The elder St. Brides did not move in the same circles as a college senior. Plus, it was nearly midnight, on a Saturday. Jack glanced over his roommate's shoulder and saw the impeccably dressed Annalise sticking out like a hothouse flower in a tangle of weeds. He hiked on his jeans and pulled a shirt over his head. As he started out of his bedroom, he looked back to see Chad unbuttoning his fly, and easing down beside the girl.

Something stabbed at Jack's conscience. *Cynthia.* Her name was Cynthia, and she'd told him a story about how her father – a farmer – would cut fields of hay in a spiral and make all the rabbits run out of the center. 'Chad,' he said quietly, and his roommate looked up.

'What?'

Maybe she doesn't want to. Maybe she ought to be asked, at the very least, instead of waking up with some guy on top of her. 'Jack?' Cynthia said, her voice slurred, and she reached out to tug Chad down.

It's not my problem, Jack thought, shrugging. *It's someone else's, now.*

Pushing it out of his mind, he shoved through the thick snarl of people. It had gotten more crowded, if possible, these past twenty minutes. 'Mom. Are you all right?'

Annalise St. Bride looked at him. She tried to speak, then covered her mouth with her hands.

'Mom, I can explain –'

His mother glanced up, tears in her eyes. 'Jack,' she said, 'your father's dead.'

The funeral was attended by a multitude of men in the finance industry, society women, and Mayor Ed Koch. Jack moved around his childhood home in his charcoal gray interview suit, shaking hands and accepting condolences. Everyone wanted to talk to him, to offer sympathy, to let him know that his dad had been a great man.

It had been a heart attack, his mother said. She was still shaky, and Jack assumed it was because she hadn't been at her husband's side when it had happened. Out on one of her crusades, she had come home to a message saying that Joseph St. Bride had been taken to Columbia-Presbyterian.

Slinking away from the well-wishers, Jack escaped to his old bedroom. It was much like his apartment, filled with paraphernalia from soccer. Jack sat on the narrow bed and fingered a blue ribbon that hung from one of the bedposts. For league play. He'd been ten.

His father had been the one to teach him. Every Sunday, in Central Park, they'd kick a ball around. Closing his eyes, he pictured the little boy he had been, and the young man who was his dad, weaving around each other's defense. With a start, he realized that right now, he looked exactly like his father had back then.

Footsteps approached down the hallway – his mother, probably, telling him to put on a good face and suffer in public along with her. But the sound stopped short of his bedroom door, and then Jack could hear two of his father's colleagues talking.

'He was so young,' one said.

'Yeah.' The second man laughed. 'But what a way to die!'

A muffled chuckle. 'Well, you know. You come . . . and go.'

Jack's head rose slowly. He walked out of the bedroom, pushing past the two surprised men. In the living room, he located his mother. 'Can I speak to you?'

'Just a second, sweetheart,' Annalise said.

'No. *Now.*'

Jack didn't hear what excuse she made, but she followed him to his father's library, a rich russet room with wall-to-wall bookshelves. 'What is so important that it can't wait until after your father's funeral?' Annalise demanded.

'How did he die?'

'I told you. He had a heart attack. The doctors said it came on suddenly.'

Jack took a step forward. 'Mom,' he said quietly. 'How did he die?'

She looked at him for a long minute. 'Your father had a heart attack. On top of a prostitute.'

'He *what?*'

'I would rather assume that the people here do not know. I may be fooling myself, but in the unlikely event that they haven't yet heard, I'd like to keep this information private.'

'Dad wouldn't do that.' Jack shook his head, rooted in denial. 'He *loved* you.'

Annalise touched his cheek. 'Not enough.'

As a kid in New York City, Jack had been repeatedly warned by his mother to stay out of this part of the town, because you were likely to leave it knifed, mugged, or in a body bag. The taxi pulled up in front of an apartment building that might have been dumped into a run-down section of any city. Annalise paid the cab driver and swept up the pitted sidewalk as if she were entering a castle.

He did not understand his mother. Jack couldn't even forgive his father yet, much less visit the prostitute he'd been fucking when he died. He wondered with a mild curiosity how his mother planned to get past the first hurdle: a locked front door. But she only rang the buzzer beneath the apartment number she'd been given and said clearly into the speaker, 'I'm here about Joseph.' Immediately, the door buzzed open.

The woman was waiting for them when they climbed to the third floor – thin, worn, with red hair that came out of a bottle. Her hands twisted in front of her, as if she were pulling invisible taffy. The moment she saw Jack, her mouth rounded into a silent O. 'You . . . you look like him.'

Jack turned away, pretending to study the peeling paint on the hallway walls.

His mother stepped forward. 'Hello,' she said, holding out her hand. Even after years of working with underprivileged women, Jack couldn't understand how she was managing to make this look easy. 'I'm Annalise St. Bride.'

The woman blinked rapidly. 'You're *A,*' she said.

'I beg your pardon?'

Remembering herself, the woman blushed and stepped back. 'Please come in.'

The entire apartment could have fit inside the living room of the penthouse in which Jack had grown up. They stood uncomfortably in the living room – a nook, really, with a battered floral couch and a television. *Is this where they did it?* Jack wondered, his throat burning to shout that he hated this woman, hated her place, hated that she had stolen his father away. With someone like his mother at home, *this* was what his father had run to?

'I thought about calling you,' the woman confessed. 'But I couldn't get up the nerve. He left something here . . . Joseph.'

She reached into a drawer and pulled out his father's gold Rolex. Annalise took it and smoothed the engraved words on the back: *To J, forever. Love, A.*

Jack read over her shoulder. He snorted. 'Forever.'

'It's kind of you to return this to me,' Annalise said, lifting her chin.

'More like she was going to steal it until you showed up,' Jack muttered.

'Jack,' his mother warned sharply. 'Miss . . .'

'Rose. Just Rose.'

'Rose, then. I came here to thank you.'

'You . . . you wanted to thank *me?*'

'The paramedics said you wouldn't leave his side. If I . . . couldn't be with him when this happened, then I'm glad someone else was.' Annalise nodded, as if assuring herself that she'd said the right thing. 'Did he come . . . often?'

'Once a week. But I wouldn't take his money. I'd slip it back in his wallet when he slept.'

That was the last straw for Jack. He stepped in front of his mother, the veins in his neck and forehead pulsing. 'You cheap fucking whore! Do you think she wants to hear this? Do you think you could possibly make it any worse?'

'Jack, that's *enough,*' his mother said firmly. 'I haven't laid a hand on you since you were ten, but God help me, I will. Whatever your father did was not this woman's fault. And if she made him happy, when I obviously didn't, then the last thing you should be doing is yelling at her.'

Tears ran down his mother's face, and Jack was certain if he stayed there another second, his heart was going to simply explode. He gently touched his mother's cheek, felt her sorrow slip over his fingertips. 'Ma,' he whispered brokenly. 'Let's just go.'

'*You made him happy.*'

They turned at the sound of Rose's voice, quiet as a memory. 'He talked about you all the time. He said he didn't deserve someone as fine as you.'

Annalise closed her eyes. 'Thank you for that,' she said softly.

When she blinked and looked at Rose, hard, Jack's jaw dropped. He had seen this expression before on his mother's face – the specter of a crusade. 'Mom – don't.'

But Annalise grasped Rose's hand. 'You don't have to live like this.'

'Not much call for my skills in the professional world.'

'There are things you could do. Places you can start over.'

'I'm not going to a shelter,' Rose answered firmly.

'Then come home with me.' Annalise bridged the shocked silence with words. 'I need a housekeeper,' she explained, although Jack knew for a fact she currently had one. 'I'll pay a fair wage and offer room and board.'

'I can't . . . I can't live with you. Joseph –'

' – is smiling,' Annalise finished.

There was a poetic justice, Jack supposed, in this prostitute coming to literally clean up a mess she'd made. And this generosity of spirit was certainly nothing new for Annalise, who had a heart so wide that people tripped into it and landed square on her good faith before they realized they had been falling. Maybe it was even a selfish act of his mother's, because between herself and Rose, they couldn't help but keep Joseph's presence strong.

Then again, maybe his mother just wanted to kill Rose in her sleep.

Annalise strapped his father's watch onto her wrist, although it was too large. 'Rose,' she said warmly. 'Meet my son.'

'I am going to have to remember her every day for the rest of my life,' Annalise said that evening, before Jack left to go back to school. 'So I might as well get to like her.'

'There's nothing to like,' Jack said.

'That's not what your father thought. And I certainly approved of his *first* choice.'

'She's not your responsibility. Mother Teresa wouldn't even have done this.'

'Mother Teresa didn't have a cheating husband.' Annalise's lips twitched. 'When it's all over, Jack, you're remembered for what you did, not what you said you were going to do. Your father found that out too late.'

Jack kissed his mother's cheek. 'I want to grow up to be just like you.' They were silent, both reading the subtext of what he had *not* said.

'You will,' Annalise answered. 'I'm counting on it.'

The cab dropped him off at his apartment shortly after eight o'clock. Even from the street, Jack could see the silhouettes in the windows, could hear the heavy drumbeat of the music. It was as if he'd never left, as if this party had been going on all weekend, in spite of the fact that his own personal world had stopped spinning.

He let himself in with the key and found Chad sitting on the couch with a few of the other guys on the team. A girl he didn't recognize was draped across Chad's lap like a knitted throw. 'Hey,' he said, immediately pushing her aside, getting to his feet, and approaching Jack. 'Sorry about your dad, man.'

Jack shrugged. 'Thanks. I'm just going to go hang out in my room.'

Chad pressed a cold beer into his hand. 'Maybe you just need to take your mind off things,' he suggested pointedly.

Jack handed back the bottle. 'I'm not in the mood, Chad.'

'You sure?'

He started to nod, then looked at the girl, who smiled at him. 'Maybe you're right.'

A knowing grin spread across Chad's mouth. But he turned toward the others with a somber face. 'Jack's father just passed away.'

On cue, Mandy sighed. 'You poor thing.'

'He could use someone to talk to,' Chad hinted.

Jack felt himself go into his room, felt this girl sit down beside him and hold his hand, felt his arms go around her – all without making any of it happen. It was as if his body knew how to go through the motions and his mind didn't have to be there at all. When the tears came – hot, huge sobs that wracked his big frame – Mandy held him tight and stroked his hair. 'I'm sorry,' he said thickly. 'I'm really sorry.'

In that instant, Jack thought of Rose. He thought of the girl he'd slept with the night his father had died, and he wondered where she was and what she would remember about that experience, long after all of the team had forgotten. He imagined his mother's shelters overflowing, stuffed with women who no longer understood how to help themselves.

If he died with his next breath, what would he leave behind?

Jack lightly tugged Mandy to her feet. 'Come,' he said softly. He steered her into the living room, where the others looked up in surprise.

At the front door, Jack raised her hand to his lips and kissed her knuckles. 'You need to go home and pretend that you never came here tonight.'

Chad began to curse, loudly and fluently. Jack forced himself to concentrate on the sound of this girl's retreating footsteps. They were light as snow, nearly as silent, but they crashed and swelled within him like an opera.

'Jesus!' Chad yelled the minute Jack turned around. 'How the hell could you do that?'

How couldn't I, Jack thought.

June 2000
Salem Falls, New Hampshire

The blood on the victim's shirt was definitely the suspect's.

Matt felt a smile fight its way out from inside. 'I *knew* it,' he murmured. He'd met Frankie, at her request, at a 1950s-style restaurant. They sat at an outside table beneath a big green umbrella while waitresses with change counters on their belts roller-skated by to take the orders of other patrons.

She looked up at Matt. 'I know you're dying to ask . . . so yeah, there was semen on the swab from the thigh.'

'Yes!' Matt smacked his fist onto the table, delighted. Rape cases without DNA evidence were the hardest kinds to win.

'Let me finish.' Frankie cocked her head. 'What do you remember about DNA?'

'It couldn't nail O. J.'

'Other than that?'

'Well . . . it's why I have ten toes,' Matt answered.

'And, no doubt, that razor-sharp mind,' Frankie said dryly. 'Did you even pass biology in high school?'

'I was a wordsmith, not a scientist.'

'Okay. Basic genetics: everything about you came from your mom and your dad. She gives you one allele, he gives you another . . . and that's why you wind up with blue eyes or good teeth or dangling earlobes.'

'Or excessive charm,' Matt added.

'Well, sometimes you get the short end of the straw,' Frankie sympathized. 'Anyway, all those traits are on the DNA molecule, which is microscopically over six feet long. But for forensic purposes, you don't care if someone has dangling earlobes. So

I test eight areas that the general public has no idea about – like TPOX or CSF1P0. Every person is going to have a "type" at those areas – two alleles . . . one from Mom and one from Dad.'

Matt nodded, and glanced at Frankie's results.

Item	CSF 1P0	TPOX	TH01	VWA	D16 S539	D7 S820	D13 S317	D5 S818
100	12, 12	8,11	6, 7	17, 17	12, 14	9, 12	9, 13	12, 12
200	12, 12	11,11	6, 7	15, 15	13, 13	8, 8	11, 11	10, 12
Shirt	12, 12	11,11	6, 7	15, 15	13, 13	8, 8	11, 11	10, 12
Nails	12, 12	11, (8)	6, 7	17, (15)	12, 14, (13)	9, 12, (8)	9, 13, (11)	12, (10)
Thigh	N/A	8, (11)	6, (7)	17, (15)	N/A	12, (8), (9)	13, (9), (11)	12, (10)

'The one hundred line is the sample of blood that came from the victim. The two hundred line is the sample that came from the suspect. These are the standards . . . the known samples that we use to compare everything else we get. The numbers in each of those boxes are alleles, found at different places on the DNA molecule. The DNA we extracted from the blood on the shirt, as you can see, is an identical match to the suspect's standard.'

'So far,' Matt said, 'I'm a happy camper.'

'Good. Because the fingernail residue is a slightly different story. The victim's own skin cells are naturally there, as well as some skin cells that are not hers.'

'Like a mixture?' Matt asked.

'Exactly. You'll see numbers that correspond to the victim and the other party.'

'Is that what the parentheses are for?'

'Yup. Different intensities, based on the combination of alleles from each person. Say, for example, that the suspect and the victim both have an eleven at the TPOX location . . . but only the victim has an eight. In a combination of their DNA, I'd expect to find a thicker band at the eleven than I would at the 8. The parentheses suggest just that.'

The waitress sailed over and slapped two chocolate milk shakes down on the table. 'Thanks,' Frankie and Matt said simultaneously.

They left the glasses sweating rings, their attention absorbed by Frankie's chart. 'For the semen, unfortunately, the results were inconclusive.'

Matt's face fell. 'Why?'

'There's no result in the CSF system and the D16 system. That's because sometimes, when there's not much DNA, we can't get readings at those loci.'

Staring at the numbers, Matt frowned. 'Can you tell me anything about it?'

'Yes. Since we're talking about semen, I know it's going to be a mixture of the victim's inner thigh skin and some male's sperm.'

'Like the fingernail residue?'

Frankie nodded. 'Compare those two lines.'

Matt studied the chart for a moment, then shrugged. 'The numbers are all the same . . . they're just mixed up in a few spots. That means you can't eliminate the suspect, doesn't it?'

'Technically, that's right,' Frankie admitted. 'But there's something there making me a little hesitant to finger him, too.'

Matt tossed the papers down and leaned back in his chair. 'Talk.'

'Think of all the people in the world, and all the different alleles they've inherited. I've never seen a mixture of two unrelated individuals where I didn't have four distinct numbers at *some* location. You'd think, just by probability statistics, that there'd be some place where the suspect would be – let's say – a twelve, thirteen and the victim would be an eleven, fourteen . . . but not according to this.' She pointed to the thigh analysis. 'Look at the overlap. In fact, at only a handful of locations is there any number foreign to the victim's own DNA.'

'Are you telling me there's a lab error?'

'Thanks *so* much for the vote of confidence.'

'Maybe you didn't have enough DNA. Isn't it possible that if the sample was better, you might have gotten four alleles?'

'It's remotely possible,' Frankie conceded. 'But that's not all that's bugging me. Look at the TH01 system, for example. The victim and a suspect are both six, seven there, so a mixture of their DNA should *always* be six, seven there.'

'It is.'

'Not in the semen sample. There's a lighter seven, along with the six. That doesn't make sense.' She shook her head. 'I'm not trying to ruin your case. But while I can't eliminate your suspect . . . he's not the most perfect fit, either.'

Matt was silent for a moment, tracing his finger through the wet stain the milk shake had left on the table. 'C'mon, Frank. You could combine the DNA of every guy in Salem Falls with my victim's and still not come up with a precise textbook mixture.'

Frankie considered this. 'Maybe they're related.'

'Suspect and victim? Not a chance.'

'Well, then, the suspect you gave me to test . . . and another guy who actually did contribute to the sperm sample. Relatives have DNA profiles that overlap . . . which can sometimes account for bizarre results.'

Matt exhaled slowly. 'You're telling me my victim scratched the hell out of the suspect, who bled all over her shirt . . . and then brought his brother in to rape her?'

Frankie raised an eyebrow. 'It's a possibility.'

'It would be if the suspect *had* a brother!'

'Don't shoot the messenger.' Frankie gathered up her reports. 'A private lab could test more systems to see if there's an elimination further down.'

'And if we don't have the funding for that?'

'I'd go check your suspect's family tree.'

Matt drained his milk shake and took out his wallet. 'Is it his blood?' he asked.

'Yes.'

'And is there a good chance that he got scratched by the victim?'

Frankie nodded.

'And you can't say that sperm sample *isn't* his.'

'No.'

Matt tossed a ten-dollar bill on the table. 'That's all I needed to hear.'

The girls arrived, flushed and sweaty in their silky shorts and bouncing ponytails, like a flock of sparrows that had swept into the locker room through an open door. Chattering in twos and threes, they made their way toward the showers, ignoring the woman who stood in the entry staring at last year's varsity photo.

Jack was pictured with his team, his hair as bright as the gold that glinted off the trophy one of the girls held. His head was turned in profile, admiring these young women.

'Are you lost?'

The voice jolted Addie out of her reverie. 'Sorry,' a teenage girl said, smiling. 'I didn't mean to scare you to death.'

'No . . . no, that's all right.'

'Are you somebody's mother?' the girl asked.

Addie was stunned by the personal question, until she realized that she was taking it the wrong way. This girl was not talking about Chloe at all; in fact, Addie was only being mistaken, once again, for someone she was not. Why wouldn't a student invite her mother to join her after practice, maybe for a cup of tea?

'I'm a prospective mother,' Addie said.

The girl grinned, a dimple showing in her cheek. It was so guileless that Addie felt her stomach cramp; she was wishing that hard that this child might have been hers. 'Oh. One of those,' the student teased.

'What does that mean?'

'That your daughter plays all-state and that you want to talk to the coach.'

Addie laughed. 'Where is he, then?'

The girl's eyes darted to the photo. 'She should be here any minute now.'

'She?'

'We got a new coach this year. After our old one . . . had to leave.'

Addie cleared her throat. 'Oh?'

The girl nodded and touched her hand to the glass. 'It was some big horrible scandal, or it was supposed to be, anyway. But if you ask me, it was like *Romeo and Juliet,* a little. You know, falling in love with the person you're not supposed to.' She frowned slightly. 'Except they didn't die at the end.'

'Romeo and Juliet?'

'No . . . Coach and Catherine.'

'Ladies! Why don't I hear water running?' A strident voice boomed through the locker room as the new coach clapped her hands and scattered her team toward the showers.

'That's her,' the girl said. 'In case you didn't figure it out.' With a tiny wave, she jogged toward the bathroom section of the locker room.

The coach approached with a smile. 'Can I help you?' she asked.

'I was just looking around. If that's all right.' Addie pointed toward the gleaming trophy. 'That's quite a Cracker Jack prize.'

'Yeah, they worked hard for it. Good group of kids.'

Addie leaned closer to the photo. But instead of looking at the girls, she scanned the calligraphy of the caption. *L to R: Suzanne Wellander, Margery Cabot, Coach St. Bride, Catherine Marsh.*

The girl next to Jack, holding the trophy. The girl who, Addie now realized, he was staring at.

'This is a copy of your statement,' Matt said, handing it across his desk to Gillian. 'I want you to take it home and read it, so that you remember everything you said.'

Beside her, Amos glanced at the thin leaflet. 'I damn well hope you've got more for your case than just that.'

'We do,' Matt answered smoothly. 'But your daughter's allegations are the foundation of our case.' He opened up another folder and gave Duncan a copy of Frankie's forensic report. 'These results all corroborate what Gillian said. His blood on her shirt, the skin beneath the fingernails, the semen.'

'Semen?' Gilly whispered.

'Yes.' Matt grinned. 'I was delighted to hear that, too. I had my doubts, since you said he used a condom. Apparently, a swab of seminal fluid was taken from your thigh for DNA analysis. And that will go some distance toward establishing the burden of proof.'

'From your thigh,' Amos repeated, and squeezed his daughter's hand.

The county attorney completely understood their astonishment. He'd told the Duncans, going into the process, that a rape conviction could be a long shot – and this dramatically altered the odds. Matt smiled broadly at Gillian and her father. 'Sometimes,' he said, 'we just get lucky.'

Thomas tossed the Airborne Express envelope onto his father's lap. 'For you.'

Jordan put down the joystick he was using to cream his son at Nintendo and slit open the package. 'Must be the DNA,' he said, and quickly skimmed the brief note Matt Houlihan had written as a cover sheet – not saying much of anything, really, which was exactly what Jordan would have done if faced with the sort of results the forensic scientist must have turned up . . . namely, that Jack was nowhere near Gillian Duncan that night.

He leafed through the first page, then the second, and with a curse slapped the entire package down on the floor before getting to his feet. 'I've got to go out,' he muttered.

On the screen, Thomas killed off one of his father's players. 'But you're winning.'

'No,' Jordan said. 'I'm not.'

* * *

Clients lie. It was the first thing you learned as a defense attorney, a rule Jordan had cut his teeth on. After all, a guy who shoots his mother in cold blood or robs a convenience store is going to be not a paragon of honor but rather someone who will do or say just about anything to save his own ass. Jordan was not surprised to find out Jack had been bullshitting him for weeks now. What did stun him was the fact that he'd been so gullible.

His mood was markedly different from the last time he'd been sitting in this conference room, filled with the righteous belief that he was saving a truly maligned soul from the channels of the court system. Jack noticed the change, too, the moment he came in. The smile fell off his face and fluttered to the floor like the old skin of a snake.

'You know,' Jordan began pleasantly, 'it doesn't particularly surprise me to find out that you lied.'

'But you . . . you said the other day –'

'In fact, I couldn't care less. What does upset me is that you have completely fucked yourself over by telling Saxton you weren't anywhere near Gillian Duncan that night.'

'I wasn't.'

Jordan slammed his palms on the table. 'Then what the hell is that soil doing in your boots, Jack? What the hell is your blood doing on her shirt, your skin under her nails? And your goddamned semen on her thigh? You want to explain that to me? Or perhaps you'd like to wait and explain it to the jury when you get up on the stand and Houlihan impeaches you with an inconsistent statement.'

Jack sank down into a chair, silent.

'First thing the prosecutor is going to do is ruin your credibility by dragging that up. If I were sitting on that jury and heard that a guy lied to the police . . . a guy whose DNA was found all over the place, I'd vote in an instant to hang you. Why lie . . . unless you had something to hide?'

Frustrated, Jordan tossed the forensic lab report toward his client and let Jack skim the results. 'So,' he said briskly. 'I assume we're going with consent.'

'What?' Jack's head swung up, slow as a bull's.

'You were obviously in the woods that night with the girl.'

'I was,' Jack said evenly, 'but we didn't have sex.'

'Could we just stop with the Boy Scout act, Jack? Because frankly, I'm losing my patience.' Jordan frowned. 'Or are you going to pull a Clinton and come up with a creative definition of *intercourse*?'

'I didn't have intercourse with her, Jordan, not any kind. I was drunk, and I saw them all in the woods. And . . . she was naked. *She* came on to *me*.' Jack looked up, miserable. 'Can you see why I didn't want to tell this to you? Or to Saxton? Who'd believe me?'

'Seems to me it didn't make much of a difference,' Jordan muttered.

'All I wanted to do was get away, and she kept trying to get me to stay.'

'How? What did she do? Say?' Jordan demanded.

'I can't remember! Jesus, Jordan, I try. I try so hard I think my head is going to explode. So I was there – so what? It doesn't mean I had sex with her. I pushed her away from me, and then I ran.'

Jordan folded his hands on the table. 'And somehow, in that charming exchange, you lost several drops of seminal fluid?'

'I never got undressed. I don't know whose semen they found, but it isn't mine.'

'Do you have any idea how unlikely that will seem to a jury? Especially once they hear the DNA scientist say it's your blood and your skin in that rape kit?'

'I don't care,' Jack said. 'It happens to be the truth.'

'Ah, right. The *truth*.' Jordan grabbed the papers, stuffed them into his folder, and stood up. 'For how long this time, Jack?' he said, and he strode from the conference room without glancing back.

The Honorable Althea Justice liked rare things. One-of-a-kind snuffboxes from Europe, Chinese silk, ink made from horse chestnuts. She lived in a glass home far more suited to the beach in L.A. than the woods of New England, drove a restored 1973 Pacer, and owned a puppy that had come thousands of miles from Belarus and was rumored to be one of thirty in existence in the world. She liked to stand out in a crowd, which was a good thing. As the only black female superior court judge, she really didn't go unnoticed.

The law had been a self-fulfilling prophecy for a little girl named Justice, and although no one in her family had been to college, the pattern of her life was as true to Althea as the lines that crossed the palm of her hand. It would have been remarkable for her to ascend to the bench as either a woman or a person of color – but the fact that she was both made her New Hampshire's answer to equal opportunity, and a bonafide wonder.

She was six-two in her stocking feet, which was the way she usually trekked through Carroll County Superior Court. Under all those black robes, who cared whether she was wearing shoes, and if anyone did, no one had the balls to bring it up to her. Attorneys who entered her courtroom did so knowing that they weren't going to be able to put one by her. A woman didn't get to where Althea had by falling for snow jobs.

Her new secretary was a young man who actually believed that kissing her ass was going to get him something . . . she didn't quite know what. A good position in the county attorney's office? A break, when it came his turn to try a case in front of her? He had a habit of running off at the mouth and citing little-known rulings that came from Bumfuck, Iowa, and other distant locales, as if Althea's life on the bench could only be better served by knowing such minutiae. The only task she'd assigned him so far was to walk her monster of a puppy on days when she was stuck in trial for hours, something for which he didn't really need a JD, but that he seemed to take as a windfall all the same.

It had been a rotten morning – her Belarussian ridgeback had peed in front of the kitchen sink, she'd been awake for over an hour and still hadn't had anything caffeinated to speak of, and to top it all off, she had gotten her period, which meant that smack in the middle of her schedule today she was going to be good for nothing but a hot water bottle and an OD of Midol.

'In ten seconds or less, Mark, and by all means time yourself: What have you got for me?' Althea asked, folding her bare feet beneath her.

'Black,' her assistant said, handing her coffee. 'Just the way you like it.' Then he blushed the shade of pomegranate. 'I didn't mean that to be a racial comment.'

Althea regarded him over the lip of the mug. 'It wasn't until you just said so.'

'I'm sorry.' Mark colored again. These white boys, with their face a whole palette.

Althea decided to take him off the hook. That way, she could always bait him again. 'Tell me what we have today.'

'Motions hearing in *State of New Hampshire v. Jack St. Bride*.'

She took the proffered file. 'The rape case?'

'Yes.' Mark took a deep breath. 'If you look in there, you'll see the research I've done, and some of my opinions.'

'Well, matter of fact, I do want to know if any of the counsel has been snooping around you, trying to size me up.'

Again, that blush. 'Well, Your Honor, there've been a few questions . . .'

'Prosecution or defense?'

Matt looked at his polished shoes. 'Both, ma'am.'

When Althea Justice smiled, which wasn't all that often, it transformed her face, like a valley being touched by the sun. She knew of this case; hell, with the reporters swarming on the steps of the courthouse like bees at a hive, it would be impossible not to know of it.

She thought of Matt Houlihan and Jordan McAfee, the counsel that would be standing in front of her a few hours from now, at the mercy of a big bad black bitch. 'Mark,' Althea said, grinning, 'this may turn out to be a fine day after all.'

An hour after the motions hearing in the St. Bride case, Jordan lay on his back in the woods, watching the sun leap from branch to branch like an iridescent squirrel. He could feel the moisture from the ground sinking into his skin, right through the shoulders of his dress shirt. The dirt smelled like dying things, but Jordan conceded that maybe his current state of mind was coloring his senses. He had a case that completely sucked, a dead end of a defense, and a client who wasn't willing to budge in any of the directions that would lead to a plea. Jack St. Bride *hadn't* had sex with Gillian Duncan in this very spot, in spite of the fact that his skin was under her nails and his blood was on her shirt. Maybe if Jordan stayed here long enough, the aliens that had apparently come down to rape Gillian would return to zap him with a death laser, so some other hapless attorney could be appointed to Jack's case.

'I had a feeling I'd find you here.'

Jordan sat up, squinting. 'Oh, it's you,' he said dully.

'You think Lancelot got that kind of reception?' Selena muttered, grunting as she tried to haul Jordan to his feet.

'You're my white knight?'

'Well, I'm trying to be. You're not exactly making it easy.'

She had wrapped herself around him to get him upright. Jordan could smell the soap she used – honey, and some kind of flower, mixed together and sitting cozy next to his own bar of Ivory. 'What are you saving me from?'

'Yourself,' Selena said. 'Despair. Root rot. Take your pick.' She regarded Jordan thoughtfully. 'I heard you had a lousy hearing.'

'Lousy?' Jordan laughed. 'I wouldn't say it was lousy. Downright abysmal. This judge has a chip on her shoulder the size of the whole goddamned courthouse. She ruled against my motion to suppress Jack's statement about not being with the girl that night. But she granted Houlihan's motion to admit Jack's prior conviction for sexual assault.'

'I heard you won one.'

'Yeah,' Jordan snorted. 'The rubber-stamp motion for a speedy trial, which I put in weeks ago. The one I wanted before I knew I'd be dealing with a client who changes his tune more often than a fucking jukebox.' He sighed. 'Oh, and did I happen to mention the DNA test came back?'

'And?'

'Jack's blood's all over the girl's shirt. His skin was under her nails. There was semen on her thigh, and although the results weren't quite as conclusive, it could be his, too.'

'Maybe it's *not* his.'

'Yeah, and maybe I'm Johnnie Fucking Cochrane.'

Selena smirked. 'Trust me, you don't have quite the same tan. Besides, Johnnie wouldn't lay down and let a prosecutor steamroll him.'

'Johnnie didn't sign Jack St. Bride as a client.'

Selena braced herself against the trunk of the dogwood. 'Can't win 'em all, Jordan.'

'Thanks for reminding me, because you know, that thought hadn't entered my consciousness for at least a half a second.'

Jordan skimmed his hands down the freckled bark of a tree. It reminded him of age spots, which reminded him that he was getting old, and what the hell did he have to show for it? And *that* reminded him that Jack St. Bride would turn fifty in prison, probably shouting with every breath that he hadn't committed a crime.

He turned on his investigator. 'What have you been doing?'

'What do you mean?'

'Other than eating my groceries and sucking up the air conditioning I'm paying for . . . what have you dug up about this case?'

'Nothing. Addie Peabody is still out of town, and she's our best hope to make Jack look good.'

'That's if she's still speaking to him,' Jordan pointed out. 'Being arrested in front of your girlfriend has an uncanny way of ruining a relationship. What else have you got?'

Selena sighed. 'Everywhere I turn, there's someone telling me what a good kid Gillian Duncan is. Smart, sweet, Daddy's little girl. Add that kind of credibility to the physical evidence . . . well, Jordan, there just isn't a lot I can offer here.' She reached down between her feet and pulled up the towhead of a dried dandelion. 'Here. Make a wish.'

'Just one?' Jordan said.

'Don't want to overload the magic, do you?'

He closed his eyes. 'I wish things were different.'

Selena held her breath until Jordan blew, scattering the seed pods over the wind. 'What do you mean?'

'I wish I could trade this job for whatever's behind door number one. I wish Jack St. Bride's blood wasn't on Gillian's shirt. I wish you and I could . . .'

His voice trailed off, and Selena stared at him. 'Could what?'

'Could find something to get our client acquitted.'

Selena dusted off her jeans. 'Nothing's gonna get done with us standing here. Let's go.' But Jordan didn't follow, and before she knew it, she was standing at the edge of the woods again. Frustrated, she tried to peer through the trees but couldn't make him out. 'You coming?' she called. 'I'm gonna be halfway home before you get out of the forest.'

In the clearing, Jordan turned at the sound of Selena's voice. *I'm gonna be halfway home before you get out of the forest.* 'Where are you?' he called.

'Waiting for *you!*'

Jordan hurried down the narrow trail that led toward the cemetery. He counted each footfall . . . thirty-three, thirty-four, thirty-five . . . and finally broke out of the thicker vegetation to find an annoyed Selena tapping her sneaker. 'Fifty-one,' Jordan announced.

'No, actually, I'm only thirty-eight. You're just giving me gray hair.' Selena turned her back on him. 'Can we just get going now?'

'No. Selena, where are we?'

She peered at Jordan. 'You hit your head on a branch back there?'

'This is where Saxton found Gillian. Where she'd caught up to her friends after the rape. Right?'

'Yeah. So?'

'I could hear you. When you called my name, I could hear you.'

Selena's mind picked up the ball Jordan had thrown. 'But

could you hear something other than a voice? Like two people wrestling?'

'I don't know. Wait here.' He ran back into the woods, then started kicking at the leaves. 'Can you hear that?'

Selena strained. Daytime sounds – birds, and trucks in the distance – were louder, but every now and then she got a slight sense of disturbance. 'Kind of,' she called back. 'Real faint, though.' Selena jogged to the clearing again. 'I'm guessing it's about fifty yards,' she said. 'You can hear a lot of things from fifty yards away.'

'Yes,' Jordan agreed, 'and you also can't get a lot done in the time it takes to walk it.' His hands went to the buttons of his trousers, and Selena took a step back. 'Don't flatter yourself; I'm testing something. Start walking slowly.'

Selena looked at him askance. 'What are you gonna do?'

'Simulate a rape.'

She looked down at his pants, then his hand. 'By yourself?'

'Simulate,' Jordan repeated. 'Not *stimulate.'*

Selena started to walk. She crept forward far more slowly than a girl would, especially one in a hurry to get home before her parents found her missing. She stopped once to shake a rock out of her sneaker and a second time to stare at a toad with black button eyes, and then finally reached the edge of the woods. 'I'm here.'

'Already?'

'If I went any slower, I would have grown moss.'

'Eighty-seven seconds,' Jordan said, approaching.

'Gillian said the rape took five minutes. Yet when she managed to catch up with her friends, they were only fifty yards away.'

'And if they'd been walking that slowly –'

' – then they would have heard a struggle,' Selena finished.

Jordan turned to her. 'Assuming,' he said, 'there was a struggle at all.'

June 2000
Salem Falls, New Hampshire

Delilah threw up after the lunch crush ended and before the supper crowd arrived. She sat at the small card table in the kitchen, a HandiWipes towelette wet down and plastered against her forehead. 'She's burning up, Roy,' said Darla.

'I'm fine. I just can't stand cooking clam chowder is all.'

Roy folded his arms across his chest. 'You've been making meatloaf.'

Delilah's runny red eyes focused on Roy, and she managed a tiny smile. 'Guess I'm sick, boss,' she said softly.

He squatted down so that he was at eye level. 'Now I'm worried. The Dee I know would never in a million years admit to it.'

Delilah rested her heavy head on her hands. 'Maybe in another million years, I'll feel good enough to argue that point.'

'One of those summer viruses,' Darla said. Looking at Roy, she added, 'I just hope she didn't give it to everyone who ate here this morning.'

Roy eyed her big frame uneasily. 'I could carry her up to my place . . .'

'No, her son's coming to take her home. I called him twenty minutes ago.' Darla blinked at him. 'So what are we gonna do?'

'Roy's gonna take over as my replacement, aren't you, Roy?' Delilah said. 'On account of otherwise, this diner's going to close . . . and that would kill Addie.'

'I can't do that,' he whispered. 'You know why.'

Delilah shrugged. 'Sometimes we don't have a choice about what life throws us. And right now, it's throwing you a spatula.'

At that moment, Delilah's son came into the kitchen. She let herself be lifted and supported by him, a lumberyard supervisor who was every inch as tall and forbidding as his mother. 'You all try to get along without me,' she said, and left.

Roy glanced at the flat black face of the grill, the steam rising like a song. He wouldn't be cooking, really. He'd just be finishing up what Delilah had started.

He inched toward the line where food was prepared. He could feel the ridges on the chopping block where knives had edged out their history the better part of the past twenty years. And he waited for his heart to stop, just like Margaret's had.

Roy, you daydreaming again or are you gonna cook me up Adam and Eve on a raft?

Just like that, he could hear his wife's voice again, teasing him about how long it could possibly take to fry two eggs and set them on a piece of toast. He could see her reaching up on tiptoe to put her ticket in the circular holder. He could feel the ache of the scar he'd gotten when she'd sneaked behind the line to kiss him and, lost in the moment, he'd pressed his hand flat on the open waffle iron.

'In the weeds,' he whispered, cook's lingo for being overburdened.

'Here.' Darla held out a white chef's coat so old it had moth holes in some places. 'Addie told me she'd been saving this for you.'

Roy took it slowly, then shrugged it on. To his surprise, it fit. He'd imagined that he'd grown a size or two, thick around his middle with stubbornness. Darla watched him button up, and she smiled a little. 'Don't you look smart,' she said softly.

She cleared her throat suddenly, as if she was wary of giving in to her emotions in front of someone else. 'What's the special tonight?' she asked briskly.

Roy curled his hand around the base of a wooden spoon, the gesture first tentative, then coming smoother, as if he were an old-time big leaguer lifting a bat once again. 'Anything,' he said with pride. 'You tell them I'll cook them whatever they want.'

Addie sat on a wicker chair across from Reverend Marsh and his daughter, and took a sip of her iced tea. 'Thank you,' she said. 'This is lovely.'

The reverend was a skinny stick of a man with an Adam's apple that jutted out like a burl. His daughter's hands were folded neatly in her lap; her eyes were fixed on a spot on the porch floor. Catherine Marsh no longer had long, silky dark tresses, an athletic body, and a winning smile. She was thinner, swimming in her oversize T-shirt and carpenter jeans, and her hair was cropped short. Addie stared at the girl as she traced a circle on the sweating side of her glass. *Did Jack do this to you?*

'I'm delighted you sought me out,' the reverend said. 'Sometimes I think today's papers are so frightened to explore religion they veer too far toward an atheist's position.'

After getting Catherine Marsh's name, Addie had looked her up in the local phone book. The Right Reverend Ellidor Marsh was listed in Goffeysboro, a tiny town thirty miles east of Loyal. Addie had called, knowing he would never invite her to his home to discuss the statutory rape of his daughter, and pretended to be a reporter on a nonsecular beat.

'I have something to confess,' she said now, setting her iced tea down.

The reverend smiled and tugged at his white collar. 'I get a lot of that,' he joked. 'But technically, I'll have to send you down the road to Father Ivey.'

'I'm not a reporter,' Addie blurted out.

Catherine Marsh's gaze lifted for the first time since she'd come, at her father's beckoning, to join them. 'I'm here because of Jack St. Bride,' Addie said.

What happened next was like an unexpected nor'easter: The Reverend Marsh's complacent demeanor was swept away only to be replaced with a cold fury so intense that it was easy to imagine him hurling damnation from a pulpit. 'Do not mention that man's name in my presence.'

'Reverend Marsh –'

'Do you know what it's like to realize that your daughter's been ruined by a man twice as old as she is? By a man whose moral compass is so defunct he can't see the wrong in seducing an innocent?'

'Daddy '

'No!' Ellidor thundered. 'I won't hear any of it, Catherine. I won't. And you, weak as any woman . . . weak as your own mother . . . believing that you *loved* him.'

'Reverend Marsh, I just wanted to know –'

'You want to know about Jack St. Bride? He's a calculating, depraved pervert who baited my daughter like a Pied Piper and used her own innocence against her to get her into his bed. He's a sinner of the worst kind – the sort of man who pulls angels out of heaven and drags them down for the fall. I hope he rots in Hell for what he did to my child.'

Catherine's features twisted in agony, or memory. Ellidor stood abruptly and hauled his daughter up against his side. 'Please leave,' he bit out, and he started inside.

Addie's head whirled. As condemnations went, this was fairly clear – Marsh truly believed his daughter had been wronged. And who knew a child better than her parent? It meant that the charge of sexual assault against a minor a year ago in Loyal had not been a misunderstanding. A horrible offense had occurred, and Jack had been at the root of it.

He had lied to her about Catherine Marsh. And, most likely, about Gillian Duncan.

Still, something made her call out at the last minute. 'Catherine!'

The girl turned, anchored by the reverend.

'Is that what happened?' Addie asked softly.

Catherine's glance slid to her father. She nodded, then let herself be swallowed up by his anger and buoyed into the house.

And that, more than anything, made Addie give up hope of Jack's innocence. After all, she had been like Catherine, years ago. She had survived a rape. And that was something no woman would ever consciously choose to claim as a memory – no, it was something that scarred you so deeply you couldn't forget.

Sitting up is so hard, when her head is this heavy. Heavy as the moon, dropped to the ground. Heavy with thoughts . . . things she should not be doing, things she can't quite remember now.

Someone comes to help her. A hand with hair on the back, sprinkled like pepper. Those hands, the pepper hands, reach for her, cup her breast as she tumbles down again. Her own hand, smooth and white, pushing at the ridge of his erection.

Blessed be.

Meg sat up in bed, wild-eyed, the covers falling away from her. The memories were like the ocean at the Cape, where they'd gone on vacation last summer. They kept running after her, and no matter what she did to try to keep them away, they managed to find her feet and suck her more firmly into the sand.

The hose sprayed wildly, soaking the girls who gathered barefoot around the Range Rover. Shrieks cut through the buzz of the summer air, falling flat into the puddles of soap on the driveway. Meg turned the nozzle away from Chelsea and Whitney and onto Gillian, who squealed and jumped out of the way.

'At this rate,' Charlie said, watching from the deck behind the Duncan house, 'your car won't be washed until October. I don't think they've managed to hit a sponge on anything but each other yet.'

Amos only smiled. 'I could care less about the Rover. Look at her.' Gillian turned, a smile on her face, her short hair sticking up in porcupine spikes. 'They make her act like the girl she used to be.'

'I know, Amos.' Charlie tried to say more, but there was a lump in his throat. How many times had he sat with his old friend after hours, drinking a beer, watching their daughters play? Who would have guessed that those children would grow up overnight? He set his bottle on the armrest of his Adirondack chair. 'How's she doing?'

Amos took a pull of his beer and grimaced. 'She goes to the appointments with Dr. Horowitz and sometimes it makes her cry, sometimes it makes her angry, sometimes it makes her just want to be alone. She still has nightmares.'

'Jesus.'

'Yeah.' Amos looked at his daughter. 'Every night.'

'It must be hard on you, too. Having to deal with this all by yourself.'

'No, I thank God that Sharon died before she had to see this happen. This would have killed her if the breast cancer hadn't. I mean, Christ, Charlie. I'm her father. I'm supposed to love her and watch over her. So how could I have let this happen?' Blowing softly over the lip of the bottle, he made it sing like an oboe. 'I would trade every cent I have,' Amos said quietly, 'for a chance to make her mine again.'

Gilly had grabbed the hose now and was launching an attack on her friends. She laughed, showering the others until they were soaked from head to toe. In that moment, she looked like any teenager.

Charlie rubbed his thumbnail along a hairline crack in the green paint of his chair. 'Do you ever wonder if there's some-one up there keeping count, Amos?' he asked softly. 'You know . . . if you wind up getting what's coming to you?'

Amos frowned. 'Gillian didn't deserve what happened to her.'

'No,' Charlie murmured, staring at him. 'Not Gilly.'

Selena figured it was like this: A girl who lied to her daddy about sneaking out of the house was probably hiding other things from him, too. And a girl whose daddy was the richest guy in town probably had been given a charge card billed to that same daddy sometime in the vicinity of her sixteenth birthday.

Hacking was illegal, but investigators knew how to bend laws to suit their needs. The first step, of course, was to make sure your uptight attorney was out for the night, and it didn't hurt to know his son had gone on a date, either. The second step was to mentally gather together everything you'd learned in years of investigative work . . . such as the fact that the average person's passwords were not nearly as complex as they ought to be. Selena guessed that Gillian's birthdate, in some permutation, was the key to her America Online account, and after three tries, she got it right. It was a little trickier to find her most recent online purchases – Selena abortively tried Amazon.com and Reel.com before finding a CD store with an account set up in Gilly's name. Breaking through the encryption in their secure ordering system took another ten minutes, and finally Selena had an American Express number.

She called the customer service line, and gave Amos Duncan's mother's maiden name when prompted – something she'd traced through public records.

'Yes, Gillian,' the representative said. 'What can I do for you today?'

'Well, there's a problem on my bill.' Selena pretended to be searching for a moment. 'On April twenty-fifth, for $25.60 at the Gap?'

Because Selena was spouting all this off the top of her head, it was no surprise when the representative didn't find the purchase. 'On April twenty-fifth?'

'Yes.'

'I see two charges listed for April twenty-fifth – one for $47.75 at the Wiccan Read and one for $10.70 at CVS. Nothing from the Gap. Are you sure you're looking at the right month's billing statement?'

Selena was furiously scribbling on the corner of Jordan's

newspaper. 'Oh, God, I feel like such a loser. This is my *MasterCard*,' she said, and giggled. 'Like, duh.'

'Is there anything else I can help you with?'

'Not today. Sorry about that,' Selena added, and hung up. CVS – not an extraordinary place to spend ten bucks. A nail polish, Kit Kat bar, and pack of gum probably cost that much. Or even, perhaps, a pack of condoms.

The Wiccan Read was a bigger mystery. 'Wiccan,' Selena said aloud, meandering into Thomas's room, where the big Webster's dictionary was kept for homework assistance. She scanned the *W*'s, but found nothing. *Wicked* was the closest, and although that might have described Gillian Duncan, it wasn't what Selena was looking for.

But she'd heard the word before; Selena would have bet on it. She logged onto the computer again, this time as herself, and settled into a search engine.

Wiccan, she typed.

After a moment, the first five hits of 153,995 came up.

Pagan and Wiccan Sites. The Wiccan and Faerie Grimoire of Francesca Celestia. How to Contact a Local Coven. Bright Blessings – the Awesomest Teen Wiccan Home Page.

And one that caught Selena's eye: *Why are we afraid of witches?*

Now Selena remembered where she'd heard the word. 'Why, Miss Gillian,' she murmured, clicking on the site to find a graphic of a cauldron, fathomless and bubbling black. 'What have you gotten yourself into?'

Thomas had his hand up Chelsea Abram's shirt and was thinking of British monarchs. *James I, Charles I, the Cromwells . . . Charles II, James II, William and Mary.* It was the most boring thing he could call to mind, thanks to a class in European history – God knew if he thought of the softness of Chelsea's skin or the scent that rose from it, he was going to come right then and there and have to suffer the humiliation of explaining the wet spot on the front of his pants.

She knew how to kiss. Boy, did she know. Her tongue curled

into his mouth, dancing and retreating until he could not believe that an hour before, he'd never tasted this ambrosia. Who would have guessed that Thomas would get to second base with a girl two years older than he was? Who would have guessed that this girl would have even agreed to go out on a *date?*

They were underneath the bleachers at the football field, a long-established makeout place for Salem Falls High. Because Thomas didn't even have a learner's permit, Chelsea had picked him up in her parents' car. They'd gone to a movie, and out for coffee after that – Thomas paying, as if that might make them both forget that she was older than he was. Now, they were stretched beneath a stadium bench, mapping each other's bodies with the slow and wondrous discovery that comes only the first time you touch someone. 'Thomas,' she breathed, 'like this.' Reaching up between her breasts, she unclasped her bra.

Oh, Jesus. Anne and George I and II and hell, all the Georges and William IV and Victoria . . .

Suddenly Chelsea drew back. Could a girl get shy when she was only half dressed? 'Do you . . . do you want to stop?' Thomas choked out, although he thought he might fling himself off the nearest cliff if she said yes.

'Do you?'

He couldn't see her eyes in the dark. Was she nervous . . . or did she think *he* was? 'Chels,' he said with absolute candor, 'I'd like to keep doing this for my next three lifetimes.'

Her smile caught the light of the moon. 'Only three?' she whispered, and her breasts spilled, soft as snow, into his hands.

Oh my God, Thomas thought. Chelsea tugged his shirt off and pressed against him, a line of fire licking their bodies where skin met skin. She bit his ear. 'Who are George and Elizabeth?'

'Good friends,' Thomas gasped, as she rolled him onto his back. A medallion that hung between her breasts swayed over his face. He reached for it.

'Leave it,' Chelsea said.

But it swung and clicked against his teeth, just when he was hoping to connect with something softer, pinker. Thomas held it up and squinted. 'Pretty,' he said. 'A Jewish star?'

'Those have six points. This has five,' Chelsea said. And then, 'Do you really want to talk about it?'

'No, I want to take it off.'

'I can't.'

'I'll hold it in my pocket. I swear I won't lose it.' He kissed the side of her neck and began to work the clasp.

'Thomas, stop. I promised to wear it all the time.'

'Promised who? Some ex?'

She didn't say anything, and Thomas stared at the little silver charm on her chest. He'd never seen one before – but maybe it was some funky religious symbol, a Hindu equivalent of the cross or something. Not that Chelsea looked particularly Indian.

Chelsea was watching him intently. 'Do you like me, Thomas?'

He could barely breathe . . . was this leading where he thought it was? He didn't think all the regents in the British Empire from the beginning of time would help him control his overloaded hormones if he actually started to have sex with Chelsea.

Nodding furiously, he swallowed hard.

'If I shared something with you, something I've never shared with anyone before, would you swear not to tell anybody?'

Holy cow. She was a virgin, too. Thomas felt all the blood in his body pool in his groin. 'Sure,' he croaked.

Chelsea lifted her hand and trailed it from her throat, over her breast, to the funny little necklace. 'I'm a Pagan,' she whispered, and kissed him.

The word echoed, fuzzy, in his mind. 'A Pagan?' Thomas repeated. 'Like those guys at Stonehenge?'

'Those are Druids. A Pagan believes in God . . . and the Goddess. And the pentagram . . . this star . . . shows the five elements we celebrate. Spirit, Air, Water, Fire, and Earth.' She stared soberly at Thomas, waiting for him to pass judgment. 'Weird, huh?'

'No,' he said quickly, although he wasn't sure he believed himself. 'So . . . you're just, like, really into nature?'

Chelsea nodded. 'Yeah, but that's not how a lot of people see it. When Gillian and Meg and Whit and I formed a coven, we knew we had to keep it to ourselves. We figured if people heard about it, they'd take it totally the wrong way.' Suddenly, she grinned. 'My God, Thomas, do you know how good it feels to tell someone this?' She wound her arms around his neck and kissed him deeply. 'Nine out of ten guys would be looking for my broomstick now, or expecting me to cast a love spell.'

Suddenly Thomas went still inside. 'You mean you're –'

'A Pagan, a witch, whatever you want to call it,' Chelsea said. 'All four of us are.'

His hands stopped roaming over Chelsea's back, and he suddenly realized that even if she ripped off her pants right now and climbed on him, he would be too distracted to do anything. For Christ's sake, there was a beautiful, half-naked girl next to him, and all he could think about was his father's case.

The crime scene was different in the still of the night. Owls called to each other from dark places in the sky, a symphony of crickets tuned their bows, and small creatures tangoed in the pine needles at Jordan's feet. He didn't really know why he'd come here. For inspiration, maybe? Certainly, he had a leg to stand on now for his defense . . . but it was shaky. The discrepancy in time and distance here didn't effectively exclude Jack as a rapist – it only suggested that Gillian Duncan was covering something up.

If Jordan were a betting man, he'd lay odds that Jack and Gillian had had sex and after the fact, she'd been mortified and had spun this story to explain away what had happened. But why wouldn't the other girls have heard the sounds of their passion? Why wouldn't Jack have told him, if that was the way it had gone down?

He said he hadn't touched Gillian. And there was also the strange fact that the other girls who had been there would have seen something – a look, a smile, a touch exchanged between Gillian and Jack that flirted with the possibility of sexual attraction. Yet not a single one of them had mentioned it. Were they protecting their friend? Or was it simply that – as Jack said – he'd never had sex with her?

Either Jack was a liar who had committed a brutal rape – a very fast and quiet one – or Gillian was a liar . . . and nothing had happened at all.

In the tree above Jordan's head, the great yellow eyes of an owl stared at him sagely. 'Whooo.'

'Wish I knew.' Jordan tilted his head to the sky. His eye caught a small flash of silver on a branch, a star that had fallen and gotten lodged in the crook of the tree. Curious, Jordan got to his feet and dusted off the seat of his jeans. He was just tall enough to reach the object when he stood on his tiptoes.

Damn. It was stuck.

Gritting his teeth, Jordan twisted his fingers more firmly around a loop and tugged.

He landed sprawled on the ground again, a thin strip of silver ribbon in his lap. 'What the –'

Ribbons, and little sachets. Weird shit.

Ribbons.

Jordan ran as quickly as he could down that fifty-yard path to his car and then drove straight to the Carroll County Jail.

'Think!' Jordan ordered.

Jack paced the confines of the small room. 'I told you,' he said. 'I remember the ribbons. They were wrapped around a tree. And the ends were loose. Fluttering, like.'

It sounded completely unbelievable. In fact, Jordan still would have scoffed at Jack's recollection if he didn't happen to have a piece of silver ribbon in his pocket. 'Like streamers at a high school dance?'

'Like a pole,' Jack clarified. 'A maypole.'

The only maypole Jordan had ever seen was a re-creation done by a touchy-feely granola-and-Birkenstock nursery school Thomas had gone to for exactly three weeks before his father had yanked him out. People in today's world didn't weave maypoles.

'The things hanging on the dogwood . . . were they ornaments of some kind?'

'Not Christmas tree balls, if that's what you mean. More like those little things that women stick in their lingerie drawers.'

'And Gillian Duncan was naked,' Jordan said.

Jack nodded. 'Two other girls had their shirts off, too, but got dressed when I came.'

Jordan bowed his head, utterly lost. 'Was it some kind of orgy?'

'With each other? They weren't . . . doing anything like that when I came.'

'What were they doing?'

Jack thought for a moment. 'Dancing. Around the fire. Like Native American warriors.'

'Ah, yes. Clearly, they were celebrating the kill of a buffalo.'

'A celebration,' Jack said slowly. 'That's what Gillian called it, too.'

It was after two in the morning when Jordan eased his way into the house, taking care not to wake anyone up. His mind was humming so strongly that it took him a moment to realize the lights were still on. When he stepped into the foyer, Thomas and Selena were waiting.

'You won't believe this,' Jordan began, grinning from the inside out.

'Dad,' Thomas interrupted, stealing his thunder. 'She's a witch.'

III

Now Jack did laugh and Jill did cry, but
her tears did soon abate;
Then Jill did say that they should play
At see-saw across the gate.

We are what we always were in Salem, but now the little crazy children are jangling the keys of the kingdom, and common vengeance writes the law!

– The Crucible

June 2000
Salem Falls, New Hampshire

Addie paid ten dollars for a copy of Jack's first conviction, but didn't know what she was going to do with it. Keep it in the fire-safe box where Chloe's birth and death certificates were? Burn it, in some kind of ritual? Bury it in the yard, with all her other dreams?

A night of tossing and turning had convinced her that Jack had spun lies as easily as a silkworm crafted threads, and the result was some-thing just as beautiful to behold. She couldn't blame him for telling her that he hadn't had a relationship with Catherine Marsh, or that he hadn't raped Gillian Duncan, or even that he loved Addie. A lie took two parties – the weaver of the tale and the sucker who so badly wanted to believe it.

The clerk of the Grafton County Superior Court handed Addie a receipt. 'Here you go,' he said. *'State of New Hampshire v. Jack St. Bride.'*

Addie thanked the man and looked at the court records.

'Jack St. Bride?' a voice said to her left.

The tall man wore a police uniform. He had salt-and-pepper hair, a nose that was too big for his face, and many laugh lines crinkling the corners of his eyes. 'Yes,' Addie answered.

'You know him?'

Her fist gripped the paper so tightly it bunched in her hand. 'I thought I did.'

Addie noticed there was something about Jack's name that brought a sad shadow to the man's eyes, just like it did to hers. 'I know,' he said finally. 'So did I.'

*　　*　　*

It was the first time Addie could recall sitting in a diner as a patron rather than as an owner. Jay Kavanaugh ordered an entire breakfast, but Addie wasn't hungry. She had to fight the overwhelming urge to stand up and get her own coffee from the burner.

'Doesn't surprise me,' Jay said, after hearing that Jack had again been charged with rape. 'Sexual perps tend to be repeaters. What does surprise me is that I fell for it the first time around.' Shaking his head, he added, 'I'm a cop, so I have this incredible sixth sense – like I can tell it's bullshit, pardon my French, from half a mile away. And I swear to God, I believed hook, line, and sinker that Jack was just some struggling prep school teacher – you know, an ordinary guy. Then it comes out that his family is rich as the Rockefellers and that in his spare time he wasn't doing lesson plans but seducing students.'

'The Rockefellers?' Addie said. 'Jack's broke.'

Jay glanced up. 'That's just something else he told you.' He shrugged. 'It's good to hear he's a career con artist. Makes me feel less like a moron.'

He continued talking as the waitress set down his plate. 'Jack was Mr. Spontaneous all the time – Go climb a mountain? Sure! Cover some teacher's class that period? No problem! – But every time I suggested we go out for a beer or to play a game of racquetball after his soccer practices, he turned me down. Couldn't go until late at night, he said. Told me he had a standing engagement at seven – and never, not once, did he back down from that. I figured it was some faculty meeting or something. 'Course, later on, the girl said that was when they met. Every night, seven P.M., in the locker room.'

It was both liberating and depressing to find this man, another casualty of Jack's. Yet no matter how grievously wronged Jay Kavanaugh felt, he had not let Jack slip beneath his defenses, into his heart, into his body. He had not heard Jack say *I love you*. He had not listened, wide-eyed, and believed it.

'Hey,' Jay said. 'You're a million miles away.'

'No, just thinking.'

'About Jack?'

Addie shook her head. 'About how much I don't like men.'

'Don't judge us all by Jack. Most of us are a lot stupider than he is and don't have nearly the finesse to carry off that kind of ruse.' Jay smiled gently. 'Hindsight's always twenty-twenty. And it doesn't hurt as much, after a while. I've had ten months to think on this. But I still remember sitting at my desk after I had to arrest him – my best friend! – and wondering how the hell this had slipped by me.'

Addie watched him spear the yolk of an egg. It ran across the plate, a yellow pool dammed by a wall of hash browns. 'How is the girl now?'

'She left Westonbrook. I hear that she's being home-schooled and that she doesn't keep in touch with friends who are still in Loyal.' He paused, then added quietly, 'I think she just wants to forget this ever happened.'

That was when Addie remembered Catherine Marsh had believed she loved Jack, too. 'She won't be able to,' Addie whispered.

In her hotel room, Addie packed up her suitcase again, with Rosie O'Donnell keeping her company on the TV. She folded her shirts and stacked them on top of her jeans. She tucked her boots into plastic bags so that they did not get anything else dirty.

'I swear, John,' Rosie was saying, 'I'm going to win. I've been practicing.' Addie looked up as the comedienne's face filled the screen. 'Kelsey Grammer and Joy Behar,' she said, 'do you know your potent potables?'

'What's a potable?' her bandleader asked.

'A drink,' Rosie said. 'If you were destined to be the celebrity *Jeopardy!* champion, you'd know that, as well as the largest lake in Africa and the fact that the queen in the Netherlands is second cousins to the Archduke Francis Ferdinand. I'm making that last one up, John, but see, only a celebrity *Jeopardy!* champion like myself would even *realize* this.'

Laughter from the audience. Addie felt her heart contract as she heard Jack's voice in her head. *They water down the questions for the celebrity tournament,* he'd told her. *Because otherwise, none of those stars would get a single one right.*

Jack would have. *Most of us are a lot stupider than he is,* Jay had said. 'Seven P.M. tonight, here on ABC,' Rosie announced. 'I'm telling you, John, this could be a whole new career for me.'

Addie remembered Jack telling her about prison, how his knowledge of trivia had saved him from being abused. She remembered unsuccessfully trying to distract him with her body during the show. *All that trivia in his head,* she used to think. *How can there be room for me?*

Suddenly, she began to tear through the papers on the table welcoming her as a guest to this hotel. There was a small guide to the Dartmouth– Sunapee region of New Hampshire, and a flyer from an outlet store, and a placard from a pizza place that would deliver until three in the morning. From underneath the mess of blankets and sheets on the bed, she unearthed the complimentary local newspaper. Scanning the pages, she finally found what she was looking for – the little grid of local television programming.

In Loyal, *Jeopardy!* was syndicated and aired on ABC. At 7 p.m.

Addie did not know nearly as much as Jack did about geography or presidents or even potent potables. She did not know if a discrepancy like this would have ever stood up in a court of law. But she did know that for one half hour a day, nothing would come between Jack and a television trivia show.

Not even Catherine Marsh.

The occult bookstore smelled like an apothecary, and rows of glass jars with small scripted labels held things that Selena really didn't want to consider. Books were jammed into the narrow shelves, with titles like *Anastasia's Grimoire* and *Transfiguration for Beginners* and *The Solitary Witch's Guide*. A cat with a bell around its neck stalked the countertop, and an opiate cloud of incense hung in the air.

Starshine glanced at the untouched cup of tea in Selena's hand. 'Go ahead. It won't turn you into a toad.'

She seemed to be a cross between an earth mother and a flower child, with stray braids dotting her silver hair and a ring on every toe. It made Selena nervous. She kept expecting to be zapped into nothingness, or for this woman to wiggle her nose.

She glanced around at the walls of the store. 'You get a lot of teenagers in here?'

'Too many,' Starshine said, and sighed. 'The spells attract most of the kids. They hear the word *witch,* and immediately think they'll be able to wave a wand and hurt the bullies in school or to make the star of the basketball team fall madly for them.'

'Something tells me they're not running home to tell Mom and Dad they're Wiccans.'

'No,' Starshine agreed, 'and it goes right back to the Inquisition, I'm afraid. Being a witch is not something that invites confidence, because too many people misunderstand what it means if you say that you are one. And unfortunately, I think teenagers are attracted to that part of Wicca – doing something, even something natural and innocent, behind their parents' backs.'

'Does Gillian Duncan come in here often?'

The older woman shrugged. 'Just recently, she came in looking for belladonna.'

'Belladonna? The poison?'

Starshine nodded. 'She wanted it for an obsolete recipe, once used for out-of-body experiences and psychic visions. Needless to say, I tried to redirect her focus.'

'How?'

The cat leaped into the woman's lap; she stroked its fur until its eyes slit shut. 'I told her to celebrate the upcoming sabbat instead.'

'Do you remember when that conversation occurred?'

'Right before Beltane,' Starshine said, then noticed Selena's blank look. 'The night of April thirtieth.'

'What if she found it somewhere else?' Jordan asked. He and Selena sat on a teak bench in his backyard, watching a blue jay fight a flock of finches at the bird feeder. They sat side by side, and Jordan could have told her exactly how many centimeters of space separated their bodies from shoulder to hip to thigh. Christ, the electricity between them was enough to keep the mosquitoes at bay.

Selena didn't seem to notice. Or if she did, she was doing a damn good job of hiding it. 'The belladonna?' she asked.

'Yeah. What if she made her recipe and passed it out the night of April thirtieth? Then Jack stumbles by, drunk, and Gillian hallucinates the assault.'

Selena frowned. 'It must have been some pretty good shit, then, to conjure up the semen on her thigh.'

'Okay,' Jordan conceded, 'that's a sticking point.'

'No pun intended?'

'I can't explain the semen. But that's not my job. All I have to do is make the jury think for a nanosecond that there might be another explanation for what happened that night, other than rape. And the victim's credibility is called into question if we prove that her recollections are drug-impaired.'

'Still, Jordan,' Selena argued, 'it's not like there are occult suppliers on Main Street. Belladonna's a poison. It isn't easy to come by.'

'She could have substituted another hallucinogenic drug.'

Selena snorted. 'From the local pharmacy?'

'From the high school dealer,' Jordan corrected, and then smiled slowly. 'Or from Daddy.'

It took three and a half hours for the Reverend Marsh to leave the house, three and a half hours that Addie spent sitting behind a small clot of hydrangea in the front yard. She waited until he had driven off in his Buick and then she knocked on the door.

'You lied,' Addie said, the minute Catherine Marsh opened it.

'I don't know what you're talking about.'

'You didn't have a relationship with Jack St. Bride. You never slept with him. I don't know why, Catherine, and I don't know how, exactly, but you somehow got this rumor started and managed to ruin his life.'

'He told me . . . he told me . . .'

'He didn't tell you anything he wouldn't have told any other student.'

Catherine started to protest but then crumbled. There was no other word for it – the edges of her mouth waffled in, her eyes drifted shut, and all her bravado collapsed. 'I didn't mean for this to happen,' she whispered. 'My father . . . he found birth control pills in my underwear drawer, and it made him crazy. Then he found my diary . . . and read that, too.' Catherine swallowed. 'It was only pretend. I mean, we all had crushes on Coach. When my boyfriend broke up with me . . . Coach took extra care to make sure I was okay, to let me cry on his shoulder. I pretended it was because he liked me, you know, *that* way, a little. So I wrote about him. I wrote about us.'

'Fiction,' Addie said, to clarify, and Catherine nodded miserably. 'And when your father went to the police? Did you ever think that maybe you ought to tell them?'

'I did. But they all thought I was just trying to keep him out of jail because I loved him.' She dashed a tear from her cheek. 'When I was lying, they hung on every word. And when I told the truth, no one listened.'

'Catherine –'

'I am so ashamed,' the girl whispered. 'I am so sorry I did this to him.'

Addie fought for control. 'Then help him now.'

* * *

'You're the last guy I expected to see,' Charlie said, holding the door open so that Jordan could walk inside.

'That's because I'm not here as an attorney,' Jordan answered. 'Just as a dad.'

Charlie invited Jordan to sit down on a floral couch with an afghan hanging over the back. 'That's right. I forget you have a kid.'

'Bad news, I guess.' Jordan grinned. 'We defense lawyers can procreate.'

That surprised a laugh out of Charlie. 'Your boy's in, what? His freshman year?'

'Yeah.' Jordan could feel himself sweating through the back of his short-sleeved polo shirt. He had absolutely no proof of what he was about to tell Charlie – this was a pure hunch, one that he hoped would prey on the detective's parental sensibilities and net Jordan a windfall. Short of this white lie, he didn't know how else to confirm his intuitions. 'Charlie, first things first. This is all off the record, all right?'

The detective nodded slowly.

'My son – Thomas – has been seeing Chelsea Abrams.'

'Oh?' Charlie said easily. 'She's a sweet kid.'

'Yeah. Well, he certainly thinks so, anyway.' They both laughed. 'This is a little awkward, Charlie,' Jordan said, exhaling heavily. 'Thomas came home with some information I thought I should pass along.'

At that, Charlie sat up, immediately alert.

'Chelsea said that the night the girls were in the woods, they were doing drugs.'

Charlie didn't move a muscle. 'My daughter doesn't . . . she wouldn't do that.'

'I didn't think so. And you have to know, given our circumstances right now, this was about the last thing I figured you'd want to hear from me. But as a father – well, hell, if someone knew that about Thomas, I'd want to be told.' He stood, wary of overstaying his welcome. 'It's probably a misunderstanding.'

'Probably.' Charlie led the way out of the house. He watched the lawyer walk down the slate path that led to the driveway. 'Jordan.'

For a moment, the two men simply stared at each other.

'Thank you,' Charlie said.

As laboratory technician, Arthur Quince had enough trouble trying to keep afloat at Duncan Pharmaceuticals without investigators coming along to foul up the rhythm of his day. Especially investigators who arrived with a light in their eyes, intent on linking your place of business to a crime. First the rape of his boss's daughter, and now a drug case right here in Salem Falls? What was this world coming to?

'I don't know if I'll be able to help you,' Arthur told Selena Damascus. 'On any given week, we might be making six drugs at a time.'

'Like which six?'

Jesus, the woman was like a dog with a bone. Arthur punched up records on his computer and pointed to the screen. 'Recently, we've been making fentanyl citrate, lidocaine hydrochloride, and phenobarbital sodium.'

'What about before that?'

He scrolled up to the previous three-week period, starting the week of April 24. 'Acyclovir, pemoline, risedronate, and atropine were in various stages of production.'

'Are any of those hallucinogens?'

'We're not in the habit of making drugs that are sold on the street.'

'I understand. That's why it's imperative that Duncan Pharmaceuticals be ruled out as the source of the substance we're investigating.' Selena lowered her voice. 'Look, Dr. Quince, I don't think you guys are responsible. But you find something like this in the halls of Salem Falls High . . . in the same town where there's a pharmaceutical company . . . well, to cover all of our own asses, if you'll excuse my language, we have to just make sure we're not talking about the same stuff.' She turned her attention to the screen again. 'How come that one has a star next to it?'

Arthur looked where she was pointing. 'Duncan Pharmaceuticals is introducing a new homeopathic line – prescription drugs derived from all-natural sources instead of chemical ones. The atropine was one of the drugs in that focus group.'

Selena hiked herself up on a stool beside him. 'Natural sources? Where does it come from?'

'The belladonna plant.'

'Belladonna?'

'That's right. You've probably heard of it. It's extremely poisonous.'

'Can you overdose on it?'

Immediately, Arthur bristled. 'Almost any drug on the market has adverse effects, Ms. Damascus.'

'What would some of these adverse effects be?'

'Confusion. Agitation.' Arthur sighed. 'Delirium.'

'Delirium? So it *is* a hallucinogen.'

At that moment, Amos Duncan entered the lab. Noticing Selena, he did a double take. He'd seen her around town, certainly, but because Selena had known better than to try to talk to Amos directly, there was no way he'd know she was there on Jordan's behalf. 'Arthur,' he boomed, walking toward them. 'I need to speak to you.'

'Ms. Damascus was just leaving,' Arthur hurried to explain. 'She's here gathering information for a drug case.'

In spite of what Arthur had thought, this information didn't make Amos the least bit nervous, as if he knew how tight a ship he ran. 'You work for Charlie Saxton? You've got my sympathy!' Amos said, but he was grinning. Selena grinned right back. If he wanted to mistakenly believe she was a local cop, she wasn't going to be the one to correct him.

No, he'd figure it out for himself when he saw her in the courtroom.

They wandered through the aisles of the music store, clicking their fingernails on CDs arranged neatly as teeth. Without any conscious effort, other eyes gravitated toward these girls, light to a black hole. And how couldn't you look? Such ripe beauty, bursting at the seams; such confidence, left behind them as sure as footprints.

Chelsea, Meg, and Whitney were oblivious to the power of their attraction. They shopped aimlessly, each of them as aware of their missing mate as a soldier with pain in a phantom limb.

Meg tripped and knocked over an entire display of CDs. 'Oh, gosh. Let me help,' she said in apology to the pimpled employee who came to clean up.

'Fucking cow,' he muttered.

Whitney turned, hands on her hips. 'What did you say?'

Reddening, the boy didn't look up.

'Listen here, you little toad,' Whitney whispered fiercely. 'With a snap of my fingers, I could make your dick curl up and rot.'

The kid snorted. 'Yeah, right.'

'Maybe I'm bluffing. And then again, maybe I'm a witch.' Whitney smiled sweetly. 'You wanna stick around and take that chance?'

The employee scurried into the back room. 'Whit,' Meg chided. 'I don't think you should have done that.'

'Why not?' She shrugged. 'He was pissing me off. And besides, I *could* do it, too, if I wanted.'

'You don't know that,' Chelsea said. 'And even if you could, you're not supposed to. Magick isn't about getting rid of everything blocking your path.'

'Says who? Healing's boring. So is all that crap about moon cycles. Now that we've figured out spells, we're supposed to just keep them all inside us?'

'It's safer that way.' Chelsea shrugged. 'Fewer people get hurt.'

Whitney laughed. 'That little asshole made fun of Meg. Just like Hailey McCourt.'

'She's better now,' Meg pointed out. 'And nicer.'

'She learned a lesson, thanks to us.' Whit stared in the

direction the boy had fled. 'The little weasel deserves to be humiliated.'

'And what about Jack St. Bride?'

The question, which fell from Chelsea's mouth like a burning match, devoured the air between them. 'Jesus,' Whitney managed finally. 'I don't think this is a public conversation, Chels.'

But now that it had burst from her, Chelsea couldn't stop. She held her hand up over her mouth, and still the words bled through. 'Don't you wonder, Whit? Don't you think about it all the time?'

'I do,' Meg murmured. 'I can't get it off my mind.'

Chelsea stared at Whitney. 'Gillian's not here now,' she said. 'She's never going to know what we talk about. And even if you won't admit it, Whit, you know that we shouldn't have –'

' – been discussing this,' Whitney said firmly. She surreptitiously slid a CD into her macrame purse and made her way out of the store, fully expecting her friends to follow her lead.

Charlie knew better. As a detective, the rules of evidence . . . and the methods of their collection . . . had been drilled into him for years. There had been recent cases where evidence was ruled inadmissible when taken without a teenager's consent from a room within his parents' house. Drug evidence.

'What are you doing?'

His wife's voice startled him out of his reverie, and he nearly stumbled out of Meg's closet. 'Just looking,' Charlie managed.

Barbara didn't bat an eyelash. 'For a corduroy skirt?'

He looked at the hanger clutched in his hands. 'For a shirt. One Meg borrowed.'

'Oh,' Barbara said. 'Try the dresser. Third drawer down.'

She left, and Charlie rested his head against the closet door. He didn't want Barbara to know what he was searching for. Didn't want to admit he was doubting his daughter.

He fingered a worn friendship bracelet tied around the knob of the door – striped red and blue and green, it was one Meg had made her first summer at sleep-away camp. She'd called home crying every hour of the first two days, insisting that keeping her there was a form of child abuse. But by the time Charlie and Barbara had driven up to Maine to get her, Meggie had settled in, and she sheepishly told them to go on home.

Kneeling, Charlie rummaged through nearly untouched sports paraphernalia – it'd taken him nearly a decade to learn that his little girl was never going to be a willing athlete – and shoes several sizes too small. There was a teddy bear with an eye missing and a poster Meg had made for a school project about the New Hampshire state bird, the purple finch. There was an old pink ballet bag and an assortment of dolls she had outgrown but couldn't bear to give away. Charlie smiled and reached for one, a naked baby with yellow hair and one stuck glass eye. A girl who sentimentally saved things like this wouldn't hide drugs from her father, would she?

He had seen enough teen drug cases in Salem Falls to know they followed a pattern: Either the child and the parents had a complete lack of communication between them or the child was resentful of the parents or the parents were too self-absorbed to really see what their child had turned into. None of that fit the bill for himself and Meg – they'd always been closer than most parents and kids. This was something McAfee had misunderstood. Maybe his kid had heard wrong. Maybe Chelsea, for whatever reason, had been lying.

Satisfied, Charlie went to stuff Meg's mess back into the closet in as disorganized a fashion as possible, lest she realize someone had been snooping through her things. In went the teddy bear, the hockey stick, the Rollerblades. He lifted the ballet bag and felt his hand close around something cylindrical and firm.

Ballet clothes, ballet shoes, ballet tights – everything in that bag ought to be soft.

Charlie unzipped the pink bag. Reaching inside, he pulled out a length of silver ribbon, long and silky. He removed a small stack of plastic cups and a thermos.

The cups and the thermos were empty, except for what looked like a residue of white powder. Cocaine? Charlie sniffed it, then touched his pinky finger to the powder and lifted it up to his tongue to taste.

It was probably nothing.

Weary, he ran a hand down his face and rubbed his tired eyes. He would get it tested anyway, just to put his mind at ease. He had a buddy at the state lab who could run a tox screen – and who owed him a favor.

That was what Charlie was thinking moments later when his pupils became so dilated he could not see.

As the wiper blades on Addie's car whispered rumors to each other, she drove aimlessly through the streets of Salem Falls. She needed to go home and unpack; she needed to get back to the diner as quickly as possible. But she found herself standing instead in the narrow plastic coffin of a phone booth, scanning the tattered white pages of the phone book for the street address of Jordan McAfee.

A few minutes later, a black woman opened the door of the house at the address she'd found. 'I-I'm sorry . . .' Addie stammered. 'I think I have the wrong address.' She headed into the driving rain, only to be called back.

'Addie Peabody, isn't it?' When Addie nodded, the woman smiled. 'My name's Selena, and no, I'm not the maid. Come on in and wait out the storm.'

It wasn't until she stepped inside that Addie remembered where she'd seen her before. 'You came to the diner,' she said out loud. 'You ordered hot water with lemon.'

'Damn, that's impressive!' Selena said, taking Addie's slicker. 'Jordan's due back soon. I know he'd like to talk to you. If you want, you're welcome to wait here with me.'

Addie sat down on an overstuffed couch in the living room. 'I'm here because of Jack St. Bride.'

'I see.'

'He didn't do it,' Addie said.

Selena sat down on the edge of the coffee table. 'Do you have an alibi for him?'

'No. It's just . . . I know he's innocent.' She sat forward, her hands twisted in her lap. 'I went to find out about his previous conviction, up in Loyal. And that girl . . . the one he supposedly seduced . . . she was lying. She never had a relationship with Jack.'

'Is she willing to testify to that?'

'No,' Addie whispered.

Selena's eyes softened. Addie's feelings were written all over her, clear as permanent marker on her pale skin. 'This may seem like I'm prying, Ms. –'

'Addie, please.'

'Addie. Why didn't you come to us two weeks ago?'

For a long time, Addie didn't answer. Then, she quietly explained, 'I needed to see for myself first if Jack was the man I made him out to be.'

Selena thought of the morning she'd told Jordan that she would not marry him. And of every single morning since then, when she'd second-guessed herself. 'I know you'd like to help, but without an alibi, there's not too much you can add to his case.'

'That's not why I came,' Addie said. 'I was hoping that *you* could help *me*.'

'Saxton here.'

'Hey, Charlie, it's me.'

Charlie froze. There was only one reason Albert Ozmander would have been calling, and it directly involved the thermos Charlie had seized from his daughter's room. Not that Oz knew where the thermos came from. As far as the toxicologist was concerned, this was just a routine workup on some evidence in an unnamed case.

He felt his foot tapping so nervously beneath his desk that he had to physically restrain himself with his own hand. 'Got a match for you,' Oz said, 'but it's a weird one. Don't ask me why the kids in your town aren't smoking pot or doing coke like the rest of the free world, Charlie, but this stuff tested positive for atropine sulfate.'

'Never heard of it.'

'Yeah, you have. It's a drug used to control digestive tract problems, among other things. You ever taken Lomotil?'

Once, God, yes, when he and Barbara had visited Mexico and got sick as dogs. Charlie squirmed just remembering it. 'Why would kids try to get off on an antidiarrheal?'

'Because if you take enough of it, it'll make you high. I'm sending the results right now.' The fax beeped on in the corner of Charlie's office; he watched the paper curl its way out and somersault into the wire bin beneath.

'Thanks, Oz,' Charlie said, and hung up the phone. He sat at his desk, hands covering his face. Meg, who had never lied to her father in her life; Meg, for whom he would tilt the world on its axis . . . Meg had somehow come to be in possession of this drug.

His heart sank so low that it changed his center of gravity, and Charlie had to fight his way upright so that he could reach the buttons of his phone. 'Matt,' he said, when the prosecutor answered, 'we have to talk.'

Jack dragged himself through the gray halls, trailing the officer who led him to the conference room where Jordan was waiting. The trial was only days away; no doubt his attorney had come with the prosecution's plea. Not that Jack was going to accept. He would stand up and hear a guilty verdict read twenty times by the jury, but he wasn't giving up his own freedom like an extra piece of gum he'd never miss. If they wanted him, they'd get him . . . kicking and screaming all the way to the appellate court.

'Save your breath,' he said to Jordan, as the CO opened the door. 'I'm not –' He stopped abruptly as he realized that Jordan was not the only one there. Sitting beside him, looking fragile and tired and so beautiful it made his stomach ache, was Addie.

Jordan stood up, sending ripples through Jack's shock. 'How did you –'

'Happy birthday,' Jordan said.

'It's not my birthday.'

'I know,' Jordan admitted, and he left the conference room.

Jack didn't know what to do. The last time he had seen Addie was during his arrest. He took a step toward her, his heart racing.

He had shamelessly used Addie during these weeks in jail, in solitary. She was the image his mind turned to for comfort. She was the reason he could survive in a cell – because presumably, one day, he would be able to get out and explain.

What if she had come to tell him she never wanted to speak to him again?

Addie turned away, and that stopped Jack in his tracks as effectively as any gate. 'Don't.' She closed her eyes and began to speak. 'I'm so sorry, Jack. That morning when Charlie showed up and started saying things, I shouldn't have heard him. I shouldn't have heard him, because I was supposed to be too busy listening to you.'

'Addie –'

'Let me finish. Please.' She looked down at her hands. 'I went to Loyal. I met Catherine. She . . . she's a very pretty girl.' Jack remained absolutely still. 'I'm ashamed that I even had to go there. I wish I could have just looked up at Charlie that morning and told him he had the wrong man. I wish I could turn back time and do it all over again . . . differently . . . except for one thing.' She looked up, smiling through her tears. 'A very wise man once told me that you can't look back – you just have to put the past behind you, and find something better in your future.'

And then he was in her arms, burying his face in the sweet fall of her hair and holding tight to the only anchor he had. His lips moved over her skin, her sorrow tightening his own throat. He swallowed, then whispered, 'Do you think I did it?'

Addie cupped his cheek. 'How can you know so much and not know the answer to that?'

Jack had been a hero in so many walks of life – academically, physically, socially. He knew what it was like to be the one other heads turned to follow, and he understood how far a fall it was from such a pedestal. But until this moment, when Addie handed over her trust like the keys to a golden city, Jack had never felt such honor.

'I wish you didn't have to see me here. Like this.'

'I'm not. I'm seeing you stretched out on a picnic blanket in my backyard with an entire feast you've cooked just for me.' Addie smiled at him. 'And I'm seeing me wearing . . . nope, I don't think I'm going to tell you.'

'That's cruel.'

'Guess you'll have to get out of here and see for yourself.'

He pulled Addie close again and held her until their hearts tuned together in perfect pitch. Then Jack spoke softly, so that his words were nothing more than a thought set on the shell of Addie's ear. 'About the past,' he whispered. 'I would do it all over. The conviction, the jail, the arrest – all of it – if that was the only way I'd get to meet you.'

Shadows chased across Addie's face in the spectral shapes of her rape, her daughter, her mother. 'Oh, Jack,' she said, her voice shaking. 'I love you, too.'

The last week of June 2000
Salem Falls, New Hampshire

You could fall asleep with your eyes open.

Meg knew this because sometimes, in school, she would be staring at a bug on the wall and suddenly class would be over. She didn't sleep well at night anymore, because of the Memory. If her mind chose to zone out in broad daylight, it was all right with her.

Meg tried to make sure there was always something to focus on, other than That Night. But she couldn't keep her father from talking about what he'd done for Matt Houlihan and who the witnesses were going to be at trial. She couldn't stop her friends from whispering about it. All of it was pulling at Meg, ripping her apart at the seams.

She ran into the house and past her mother. This was her obsession, a Lady Macbeth spot check she did every afternoon when she came home. She flung open her bedroom door, gasping for breath, and stuck her head inside the closet.

'Margaret Anne Saxton,' her mother said from the doorway.

Meg startled, smashing her head on the wooden frame of the closet.

'Honey, are you all right?' Meg's mother walked over and touched her forehead lightly, feeling for fever, or maybe insanity. 'You look like you're being chased by the hounds of hell.'

'No hounds,' Meg managed, with a weak smile. 'Only a heap of homework.'

'I'm worried about you. You don't look right.' She glanced at Meg's clothing. 'You're losing weight.'

'Jesus, Mom, you've been suggesting I go on a diet for years.'

'I never said that. I only felt that with a face as lovely as yours, you might want not to draw attention away from it.'

Meg rolled her eyes. 'I love you too, Ma,' she said dryly. 'Now can I please have some privacy? For once?'

The moment her mother closed the door, Meg dove into the closet. On her hands and knees, she tossed aside her dolls and shoes . . . but the ballet bag that had been there just yesterday afternoon was missing. 'Oh, shit,' she whispered, and then felt the hair on the back of her neck stand up.

Her father had quietly opened the door of her bedroom and now leaned against it, holding the pink sack. 'Looking for this?'

Meg hung her head. *Just shoot me,* she thought.

He came into the room, closed the door, and sat down on the floor across from her. 'You want to talk first, or should I?'

Suddenly, Meg felt herself dissolve. From the inside out, like those disgusting bacteria in sci-fi movies that leave people with Jell-O instead of organs. She felt her mind go blank.

'Meggie,' her father said, in a voice so quiet it made her ache, 'did you bring drugs to the woods that night?'

Meg shook her head, stunned. That thermos . . . the one Gillian had brought filled with iced tea . . . it had been full of *drugs?*

And her father believed that Meg was responsible.

Memories chased each other at the heels: the forest shimmying that night before her eyes; the white blanks still crowding out huge blocks of time in her mind; the four of them, hysterical and sobbing, when her father had found them. Suddenly, the dam burst. In her life, Meg had never cried like this, sobbing until she shook, until she couldn't make any sound at all, until her mother raced into the room in a panic. 'Charlie,' she heard her mother say, from a tunnel of distance. '*Do* something!'

Meg cried for Gillian, for the expression on her father's face, for what she was beginning to remember. She flung her arms wide and kicked at whoever came close to her.

In the end, a paramedic gave her a shot of Haldol. She

drifted back to earth like one of the flowers that had fallen from the dogwood that night. Her father's strong arms were wrapped tight around her, and his coffee breath fell onto her cheek. 'Meggie,' he said, his voice broken. 'Who?'

They were not speaking of the same thing, not at all, and in some small corner of her mind Meg knew this. But as her eyes drifted shut, as she fell headfirst into that night again, she murmured, 'It could have been me.'

It was the first time that Gillian had been in Matt Houlihan's office without her father sitting beside her. Granted, he was only a hundred feet away in the waiting room, maybe even had his ear pressed to the door, but the privacy was empowering. 'I hope you feel comfortable being here alone with me,' Houlihan said.

What a sensitive guy, Gillian thought. *Making sure the rape victim isn't threatened by a Big Bad Male and a small closed room.* She looked into her lap. 'I'm okay,' she said.

'The reason I asked to speak to you without your father present is because of some new evidence that I thought you might feel more comfortable discussing in private.'

Every cell in Gillian's body went on alert. She froze, waiting for him to speak again.

'Detective Saxton found a thermos and some cups in his daughter's room, Gillian. Meg said they belonged to you.'

Gillian was so relieved that *this* was the crucial evidence, she nearly laughed out loud. 'That's true.'

'Did the residue of drugs in the thermos and cups belong to you, too?'

Gillian blinked. 'What drugs?'

'Atropine. It's a prescription drug . . . that can also make you high.'

'I've never heard of it.'

'Well, according to Meg, you're the one who brought the drinks that night. Atropine and all.'

The bitch. 'Meg said that?' Gilly managed, her voice so tight she thought her vocal cords might snap like the strings of a rock guitar. 'I would never bring drugs. I would never *do* drugs.' She laughed, but it sounded forced. 'Mr. Houlihan, I've grown up around pharmaceuticals my whole life. My first memory is of my dad telling me to say no to drugs.' She looked toward the waiting room. 'Go ask him if you don't believe me.'

'If you didn't bring the atropine, who did?'

'I have no idea,' Gillian said. 'Probably Meg.'

'Meg's father is a policeman. Presumably, she's heard the same party line as you.'

'That's not my problem,' she snapped.

Houlihan sighed. 'I couldn't care less who's the dealer here, Gillian. That's not in the least important to my case. What I need to know is if you drank any of the tea that night.'

Before Gilly could answer, the telephone rang. The county attorney picked it up, spoke for a moment, and then turned, apologetic. 'I have to see someone before they go off to trial,' he explained. 'Will you excuse me?'

Two seconds later, Gillian was alone in the office.

Had she taken the drugs that night? Well, of course. But hearing that wasn't going to make Houlihan happy. Someone who took a hallucinogen wasn't a reliable eyewitness.

Then again, it had been nearly six weeks. No drug stayed in your system that long, especially one ingested in such a small volume. Houlihan could draw blood this instant and never know if Gillian was lying.

The ER had drawn blood.

The memory hit her; the doctor drawing vial after vial. Chewing on her bottom lip, Gillian stared at the folder on Houlihan's desk.

It took her less than a second to decide to open it. The front page gave the lab results from the rape kit. She skimmed the odd numbers and phrases until she came to the typing for victim, known sample. And all the drugs for which she had tested negative.

Atropine wasn't on the list . . . but it hadn't been flagged in her system, either.

She slid the folder back on the edge of the leather blotter just as Houlihan came in. 'I didn't drink anything,' Gilly said.

'You're absolutely certain?'

'Yes. Meg borrowed my thermos, but she brought iced tea. I *hate* iced tea.'

The lawyer studied her, then nodded, satisfied. He opened a drawer of his butt-ugly metal desk and began to unravel a silver ribbon. 'You have any idea what this is?'

'No,' she said, letting it slide through her fingers. 'Where did you find it?'

'With the thermos and cups.'

'Well,' Gillian shrugged. 'Then it must be Meg's, too.'

Addie came into the diner after the dinner rush to find Darla playing chess with her father in the kitchen. 'You're back,' Roy said.

An apron – her father was wearing an apron. Before she could get past this startling fact, Darla was in her face. 'I had to work double shifts, on account of Delilah getting sick, and don't think I'm not expecting time and a half.' Turning to Roy, she said, 'Check,' and then sashayed into the front room.

'Look at you,' Addie said, swallowing past the sadness in her throat.

'Yeah.' Her father laughed, twirling like a beauty queen. 'Go figure.'

'First time I up and leave, you go . . . you go . . .' That was as far as she got, and then the tears came. Exhausted, tired from putting on a brave face for Jack, she moved into her father's embrace, which had always been the softest spot in the world.

'Ah, Addie,' he said. 'I'm sorry about him.'

Addie drew back. 'He's innocent, Daddy.'

'Then why are you crying?'

'Because,' Addie said, 'I'm the only one who thinks so.'

Roy walked to the stove, then poured her a bowl of potato

leek soup. This he set down in front of his daughter with a spoon. 'Eat,' he ordered.

'I couldn't, even if I wanted to.'

He lifted the spoon to her mouth, made the soup trickle down the constriction of her throat. 'Isn't that fine?'

Addie nodded and lifted the spoon herself. Meanwhile, Roy moved around his kitchen, heaping potatoes and steamed carrots, breads and stuffings and gravies, all onto a tremendous platter. He piled it high with starches and placed it in front of Addie.

This time, she didn't even hesitate. She tucked into the meal with a hunger she had not even known she'd had, until her belly swelled. 'Better?' he asked.

Addie realized she no longer hurt inside. She imagined all these soft foods, rices and puddings and couscous, forming an extra barrier within. Her father had filled her, because he knew better than anyone that the best way to prevent a heartache was to cushion the coming blow.

'Relax,' Gillian said, looking at each of her friends. 'They don't know anything.'

They were sitting in a small garden behind the Duncan household, one hidden from public view by a thicket of roses. 'My dad is gonna kill me,' Chelsea said. 'If he finds out there were drugs there –'

'Why *were* there drugs there?' Whitney demanded. 'I'm a little curious, Gill, since you were the one responsible for bringing the refreshments.' The others looked at Gillian, too. 'I'm not saying I wouldn't have tried it . . . but I would have liked to have had the choice.'

'Whit, don't be such a priss. It was a pinch of stuff, so little that it wouldn't even affect you. God, you'd have gotten more of a buzz from a wine cooler.' Gillian stared intently at the others. 'Think hard. Do any of you remember getting high that night?'

'I was dancing around without a shirt on,' Whitney hissed.

'*Before* you drank a damn thing,' Gilly pointed out.

Meg's eyes were dark, striped with betrayal. 'My dad says it screws up the case.'

'Matt Houlihan doesn't think so,' Gillian said.

'Only because you told him that the drugs were mine. If a jury hears that you were stoned, they're not going to believe anything you say.'

'I wasn't stoned, Meg. No more than you were.'

'Then how come I have to be the fall guy?'

Gillian narrowed her eyes. 'Because if you don't, it's going to hurt all of us.'

'Says who?'

The other girls shrank back at Meg's response. You didn't cross Gilly. Everyone knew that.

'Look, Meg, this isn't about you or me; it's about sticking together so that our stories match. The minute that starts to fall apart, so does everything else.' Gillian swallowed, her throat working.

'You aren't the only one who can't forget that night. But the difference between us is that you don't *want* to.' Meg's hands closed into fists. 'You are so fucking full of it, Gillian. If I tell my father I never saw the thermos before, you think he'll assume we're witches? No, he'll believe exactly what I tell him . . . that you brought it so we could get high.'

Gillian went white. 'You wouldn't, Meg.'

'Why not?' Meg said, pushing her way out of the rose arbor. 'You did it to *me*.'

'That,' Matt sighed, 'is heaven. Do it again.'

In her stocking feet, Sydney Houlihan gingerly stepped on the small of her husband's back. He grunted, his face ground into the carpet. Beside them, in her baby seat, Molly clapped. 'I don't think this is the smartest thing for her to see,' Sydney said.

'What? Mommy walking all over Daddy? She's a little young for metaphors.' Matt grunted as Sydney hit a particularly sore spot. 'You know why I married you?'

'Because I was the only woman who agreed to this kinky stuff?'

'Because you weigh exactly the right amount.'

Sydney carefully stepped onto the carpet and sat down cross-legged. 'So what was it this time?'

'What was what?'

'Your back always gets pretzeled when you're stressed out about a case.'

Matt rolled over. 'Married you for your ESP, too.' He drew his knees up, stretching muscles along his spine. 'Gillian's friends were taking drugs the night of the rape.'

'And Gillian?'

'Said she wasn't.'

Sydney shrugged. 'So?'

'Well, no matter what, it's exculpatory. I have to turn it over to the defense.'

'It doesn't change the fact that she was raped, does it?'

'No,' Matt said slowly.

Sydney raised her brows. 'You think she's lying to you.'

'Ah, hell.' Matt got to his feet and started pacing. 'I don't know. She said it was her thermos but that Charlie's daughter brought the stuff. And that she didn't drink anything that night because she wasn't thirsty. I can probably get Meg to admit to procuring the drugs when I put her on the stand. But still . . . there were five cups there with residue in them – one for each of the girls and one for St. Bride. McAfee is going to be all over this.'

'Maybe it was poured for her but she didn't drink it.'

'Maybe.'

Sydney was quiet for a moment. 'Do you think she was lying about the rape, too?'

He shook his head. 'I've got too much evidence. The blood on her shirt, the scratches on his face, the semen.'

She wrapped her arms around Matt's waist. 'You never liked sharing your toys.'

'What's that supposed to mean?'

'You're growling because you have to turn over something that hurts your case.'

'But it doesn't,' Matt argued. 'Sure, it doesn't make Gillian look like an angel . . . but I can still get St. Bride convicted.'

Sydney leaned up and kissed his chin. 'Don't you feel better now?'

To his surprise, Matt realized he did. His back wasn't aching, and for the first time all day, he was itching to just get this case to trial already. 'That's the third reason I married you,' he said, and stamped a kiss on her mouth.

'Five cups don't mean squat, Jordan,' Selena argued.

'Reasonable doubt. All I have to do is plant the seed.'

'I don't care if you plant a whole frigging tree. You can't say that just because a cup was there that a kid drank out of it. Your car's in the garage. Does that mean I drive it?'

Thomas looked up from the kitchen table, where he was struggling through a trigonometry proof. 'Could you two take this somewhere else?'

But neither Jordan nor Selena paid him any attention. 'If I say that Gillian lied about taking drugs, it suggests that she lied about a number of things. Including this rape.'

'Jordan, listen to yourself! Matt Houlihan could drive a freight train through the holes in that argument.'

'You got anything better?' Jordan snapped. 'Because *I* don't. I have a client who says the victim came onto him, but he can't offer us any more details. I have proof that the victim is into some pretty strange shit, but discrediting her isn't going to acquit Jack. Which means, for God's sake, that if all I have to throw at Goliath is a fucking pebble, I'm going to wind up my arm as best I can.'

'For Christ's sake,' Thomas muttered. He started gathering his books and papers together, intent on moving to a quieter area. Like maybe a blasting zone.

Suddenly, all the fire went out of Jordan. He sank into a chair across from Thomas and rested his head in his hands. 'I'm sorry. I'm being an idiot.'

'No argument here,' Selena said.

'It's just that I only have four days, Selena, and then we're standing up in front of the judge. And everything you've turned up in the past week – well, God, it's fantastic. But I went into this assuming that I was trying a simple case – girl says guy raped her, guy has a previous conviction. Indictment, arraignment, trial. And suddenly, every time I turn around, there's something new – this witch stuff, and the drugs, and evidence that doesn't match up. This isn't the case I thought I had.' He pressed his thumb and forefinger deep into the sockets of his eyes. 'I want a year to prepare. Then the next second, I don't, because at the rate we're going we'll probably find out that Gillian's got connections to the Sicilian mob.'

'Nah. Although I did turn up something about her being a presidential intern.'

'Not funny,' Jordan muttered. 'I have no idea what to say happened that night.'

'Jack was beaten up badly hours before. You could say he was in too sorry a physical state to commit the crime.'

'But not so sorry a physical state that he couldn't manage to get to a bar and drink himself sick.' Jordan shook his head. 'I can defuse what the girl says, but I can't refute it. The only pieces of that night Jack can recall are laughable. Ribbons and bonfires and naked teenagers –'

'Naked?' Thomas squeaked. 'Chelsea was naked?'

'How am I supposed to get a jury to buy that? And then to vote for an acquittal?'

'That's why you need proof, Jordan,' Selena said gently. 'Reasonable doubt works most of the time . . . but like you said, the alternative you're proposing is so strange that it's still going to be hard to swallow. You need to hand the jury your own evidence, so that they know Gillian was playing witch in the forest that night. And a cup doesn't cut it.'

Thomas stacked his books and headed down the hall. 'See you,' he muttered. 'I'm sure you'll really miss me being in here.'

'I know,' Jordan sighed. 'But if she took the atropine, it was nearly two months ago. The half-life of the drug is about six hours. It's not like we can get a sample of her blood tonight and still find it swimming around in there.'

'We should have had her blood screened by a private lab right after Jack's arrest. What were we thinking?'

Jordan met her gaze. 'That she was telling the truth.'

Thomas's voice floated down the hall. 'You did have her screened,' he called out. 'In the ER.'

'Routine drug tests don't show atropine.'

'So . . . why couldn't you try it again with some fancy test? What did they do with the blood when they were done?'

'It went off to the state lab with the rest of the rape kit,' Jordan explained, and suddenly his jaw dropped. 'Holy shit, the rape kit. The known samples they used to type DNA came from blood that was taken that night.'

'And they save that stuff.' Selena was already out of her seat. 'How fast can you get the judge to sign off on a motion for independent testing?'

Jordan reached for the briefcase that held his laptop. 'Watch me,' he said.

Roman Chu had started Twin States Forensic Testing in a clean room partitioned off in his parents' garage. Having cultivated a reputation for getting things done in a fraction of the time it took the state lab to do them, he generated enough work to pay for his own building, and to hire ten employees who worked miracles for attorneys at the eleventh hour.

'I appreciate this,' Jordan said for the twentieth time.

After the judge had granted the motion, Selena had secured Gillian's blood sample from the state lab. The prep work had been done during DNA analysis: The blood had been spun down and separated from the cells, the serum frozen. All Roman had to do was run the mass spectrometry. Now, they both stared at the computer, waiting for the results. 'I want Cuban cigars,' Roman muttered. 'Not that crap from Florida you got me last year.'

'You got it.'

'And I'm still charging you for overtime.'

The screen blinked green, and suddenly a stream of numbers came up. Roman grabbed a reference text and compared it to what was on the computer, then whistled softly.

'Translate,' Jordan demanded.

Roman pointed a finger at the percentiles. 'The blood's got atropine in it.'

'You're certain?'

'Oh, yeah. The drug concentration's so high I'm surprised it didn't put her into a coma.'

Jordan crossed his arms. 'So what *do* you think the physical effect was?'

Roman laughed. 'Buddy,' he said, 'she was tripping.'

For the first time in nearly a decade, Addie took a lunch break during lunch hours. With Delilah and her father sharing the kitchen and Darla waiting tables, Addie had found herself wandering around useless. She would have gone to see Jack, but visiting hours were not until tomorrow – the night before the trial started. So instead, she went to see Chloe.

'This,' Addie said, 'was your favorite kind of day.' She set a small nosegay of Queen Anne's lace in front of Chloe's gravestone. 'Do you remember when we used to pretend it was summer, in the middle of January? With a beach blanket picnic, and the heat turned up, and you and me in our bathing suits in the bathtub.' She touched the granite slab. It was warm from the sun, nearly as warm as a child's skin. 'Is it summer all the time up there, Chlo?' she whispered.

What she wished, more than anything, was that she had a store of memories like those. Losing Chloe had been like reading a wonderful book only to realize that all the pages past a certain point were blank. Addie had been cheated out of watching her daughter get her first training bra, helping her choose a prom dress, seeing her eyes darken the first time she spoke of a boy she loved. She missed driving her to the high school, and getting ice cream cones and swapping halfway through to try the other flavor. She missed talking, and hearing an answer back.

'Miz Peabody?'

The sound of a girl's voice startled Addie so much she whirled around to find its source. Meg Saxton stood a few feet away, looking just as surprised as Addie.

'Meg . . . I didn't know you were here.'

There was a wall between them, invisible but thick. The last time Addie had spoken privately to Meg was at Chloe's funeral. Meg and Chloe had played together on the swing set in her yard. But here Meg was, all grown up, and Chloe was dead.

'How . . . have you been?' Addie asked politely.

'Fine,' Meg answered. Silence sprouted. 'Did you come to visit her?'

They both turned toward the gravestone, as if expecting Chloe to appear. 'I wish I'd known her,' Meg confessed. 'I mean, she was older than me, but I think . . . I think if things had been different, we could have been friends.'

'I think Chloe would have liked that,' Addie said softly. Tears filled the young girl's eyes, and she turned away, trying to hide. 'Meg? Are you all right?'

'No!' Meg cried, a sob hitching the word in half. 'Oh, *God*.'

Instinctively, Addie reached for her, and the contact was electric. Meg smelled of shampoo and cheap cosmetics and childhood, and Addie was overwhelmed by the shape and feel of a girl roughly the same age as Chloe. *So this is what it would have been like,* she thought, her eyes drifting closed.

Meg whispered so quietly that Addie didn't believe she had heard correctly. 'She's so lucky.'

'Who is?'

'Chloe.'

Addie's hands stilled. 'You don't mean that.'

'I do.' Meg wiped at her face with the bottom of her T-shirt. 'I wish I were dead.'

It hit Addie then, what Meg had been doing at the cemetery.

She had come back to the spot where the alleged assault had occurred. Jack hadn't done it – she knew this as surely as she knew that Chloe was buried close by – but something had rattled Meg that night, all the same.

Addie squeezed Meg's shoulders. 'I think we should go. This place has bad memories for both of us.'

Meg reluctantly glanced in the direction of the clearing. 'Ms. Peabody,' she whispered, miserable. 'I think . . . I think he touched me, too.'

'Touched . . . you?' Addie said, the words round, with no sound behind them.

'*Touched* me,' Meg repeated, mortified. 'You *know*.' And God help her, Addie did.

In the end, it came down to this: Being a mother was something that stayed with you, dormant, ready to flare at a single match-stroke of circumstance. And apparently it didn't matter if the child was one of your body or just one with a place in your heart – instinct was instinct.

Addie loved Jack. She believed him when he said he hadn't attacked Gillian Duncan. But she was a mother, and she knew what had to be done. So she took Meg to Charlie's office at the police station and closed the door behind them. She kept her expression blank. Then, holding Meg's hand tight for moral support, she listened as this girl – this friend of her daughter's – told Charlie what she'd told Addie minutes before.

Charlie knew the floor was stable, but he could feel it rocking beneath his feet. He cleared his throat for the hundredth time and swallowed, then turned on the tape recorder that sat between himself and his daughter.

Meggie was shivering, although she wore the blue uniform jacket that usually hung on the back of his office door. Her hands fell at elbow-length in the jacket, and it made him think of how he and Barb would dress her up when she was just a baby, crazy angel wings made out of real feathers and soft headbands with antennae, things like that that were immortalized in dusty photo albums.

Oh, Christ.

'Where, um, did he touch you?'

She couldn't look him in the eye, and that was fine, because Charlie couldn't look at her, either. 'Here. And here.'

'The victim,' Charlie said thickly, 'is indicating her left hip and breast.'

Every muscle in his body was rigid with tension. How was he going to tell Barbara about this? How was he ever going to finish? You could not be a detective when you wanted so badly to be simply a father.

'Charlie.' Houlihan's voice fell heavily. 'You don't have to do this.'

Charlie shook his head tightly. 'Meg, did Jack St. Bride expose himself to you?'

'No,' his daughter whispered.

'Did he touch you anywhere else? In any other way?'

'Did any part of his body come in contact with part of yours?' Matt asked quietly.

'Jesus Christ!' Charlie was out of his seat, punching the button on the tape recorder to shut it off. Why couldn't you rewind your own life? He paced to the far end of the room, Matt coming up beside him. 'My little girl,' Charlie choked. 'He did this to my little girl.'

'We'll get him,' Matt promised. 'We'll press charges for this, too.'

Nodding, Charlie started back to the table, only to be restrained by Matt. 'No,' the county attorney said. 'Let me.'

Molly lay curled like a fiddlehead against her flannel crib sheets, her thumb tucked in her mouth as she slept. Matt stared down at her and could easily imagine the kind of pain that Charlie was in right now. God, if someone ever did anything to his child, he couldn't be held accountable for his actions.

This latest drama was not what Matt needed the night before

the trial began. But Meg's accusations would be a different case, brought before a different judge on a different day . . . if there was enough evidence to try it. He would never have told Charlie, but part of Matt had to wonder how reliable Meg's tearful confession was. She had already been taking hallucinogenic drugs that night. . . . It was possible that this alleged assault was imagined.

And that was how it affected his current case – he could no longer risk Meg as a witness. If she testified to bringing the drugs and then confessed to being attacked, too, would the jury believe her? And if they didn't, would they still believe Gillian?

Matt couldn't say for sure whether Meg was going to help or hurt the case. He didn't need her to convict Jack St. Bride; therefore, he would simply omit her. He'd call Chelsea Abrams up for her eyewitness account, instead . . . and if her story didn't match quite as neatly with Whitney O'Neill's as Meg's had, it was still less of a gamble with the jury.

Matt touched his hand lightly to the sweet globe of his daughter's head. 'Good night,' he whispered, but for long minutes afterward, he made no move to leave her.

The moon slipped over the windowsill and beneath the covers, but Jordan and Selena didn't notice. Selena stared down at her arms, tangled with Jordan's just below her breasts. 'What are you thinking?'

'That I plead temporary insanity.'

'Ah.' Selena turned in his embrace. 'Feeling guilty?'

'No. I feel . . . I feel . . .'

She swatted at his hand. 'Yeah, I see what you feel.' Laughing, she darted out of the way. 'Get out of there.'

'That's not what you said ten minutes ago.'

'Maybe I'm pleading temporary insanity, too.'

They had fallen asleep sitting on the couch, watching reruns of *Perry Mason* on TVLand. Somehow, when they'd awakened, they'd been lying down in each other's arms, pressed together from chest to thigh. It was all the impetus they needed; a subliminal reminder that no matter how hard they tried, they weren't meant to be apart. From there, they'd been lucky to make it to the privacy of a bedroom.

'Hey, Selena?'

'Mmm?'

'Why didn't we do this a month ago?'

'Oh, take your pick: We were smarter then. We had better self-control.'

Jordan looked at her soberly. 'You really think that?'

For once, she had no smart answer. 'Actually,' Selena admitted, 'I don't.' She stared at him. 'How do you think this will all turn out?'

Jordan shook his head. 'I have no idea.'

Selena smiled against his chest. 'Are you talking about us, or the case?'

'Either one.' He sighed, choosing the easier route of conversation. 'All we've really been able to prove is that she's a witch.'

'A witch on drugs. I've thought about it,' Selena confessed. 'And I can explain away just about all the evidence, and clear Jack in my head. Except for that semen. That's not something you leave behind while you're just chatting it up with someone.'

'The semen's the most inconclusive evidence Houlihan's got. A jury will see that.'

'You hope.'

'I hope.'

'Jack could still be lying to you,' Selena pointed out.

'So could Gillian Duncan.'

They were quiet for a while, soaking up the heat and the memory of each other's bodies. 'Speaking of lies,' Selena whispered. 'I have to tell you something.'

Jordan came up on one elbow. 'What?'

'My car was ready two weeks ago.'

'I have to tell you something, too.' His teeth flashed in the darkness. 'Your car would have been ready *five* weeks ago, but I paid the mechanic to say the part was delayed.'

Selena came up on an elbow. 'You'd go to all that trouble to keep from losing your best investigator?'

Jordan leaned forward and kissed her lightly. 'No,' he said. 'I'd go to all that trouble to keep from losing you.'

They held hands across a cafeteria table, surrounded by men who had murdered others in fights and beaten their wives and burned houses to the ground with people still inside. A correctional officer stood guard. When Addie had first embraced Jack, the CO had tapped her on the shoulder and politely explained that sort of touching was not allowed.

Addie looked at the couple beside them. The man had a snake tattooed around his neck. His visitor was a woman with spiked green hair, an eyebrow ring, and a dog collar.

In fifteen hours, the trial would begin.

'Are you nervous?' she asked.

'No. I figure the sooner we get this over with, the sooner I'll be with you.'

Addie bent her head. 'That,' she said, 'will be wonderful.'

'I've been thinking about it, you know. We'll go to the Carribbean. June is the rainy season, but I figure we could both use a vacation. I want to be outside all day long. I want to *sleep* outside. Hell, maybe we won't even have to pay for a room.'

Addie choked on a laugh, one that rounded neatly into a little sob. She looked up at Jack and tried to smile.

'If you're that upset, sweetheart, I'll get us a hotel.' He spoke softly, stroking her palm with his thumb.

A deep, shuddering breath wracked Addie. 'What if –'

'Ah, Addie, don't.' Jack put his finger to her lips a moment before the guard frowned at the contact. 'Sometimes, when I think I'm going to lose it in here, I just imagine that I'm already out. I think about what we're going to do for the weekend, and whether the diner's going to be busy that day, and how all I want is for it to be nighttime so that I can sleep holding onto you. I think about us, six months from now. Six years from now. Until I can remember what it's like to have a normal life back.'

'A normal life,' Addie repeated, with longing.

'We can even practice,' Jack said earnestly. He cleared his throat. 'Hi, honey. What did you do today?'

Addie stared into his eyes, those beautiful ocean eyes. She thought of Meg. And then she imagined a beach as wide as the world, a froth of waves that raced over her feet and Jack's as they watched the sun seal another absolutely ordinary day. 'Nothing,' she said, smiling hard from the bottom of her heart. 'Nothing at all.'

1979
New York City

Jack and J. T. and Ralph hunkered down in the crawl space beneath the staircase that led up to the second floor of the St. Bride penthouse, a spot usually reserved for the vacuum but that worked equally as well as a clandestine spot for ten-year-old boys trading baseball cards and secrets. 'I'll give you Keith Hernandez for Luis Alvarado,' J. T. said.

'You think I'm a moron?' Ralph scowled. 'Hernandez is worth three White Sox.'

'I've got Bruce Sutter,' Jack said. 'I'll trade him for Hernandez.'

'Cool.'

The boys swapped cards, turning them over to read the stats, a faint bubble-gum smell enveloping the deal.

'I've got a Don Baylor,' J. T. said.

'California sucks this year.'

Ralph snickered. 'I wouldn't use a Baylor card to scrape dog shit off the street.'

'He's an MVP, you jerk.' But J. T. shuffled the card to the back of his shoebox all the same.

Suddenly, Ralph held up the crown jewel of baseball cards that summer, Willie Stargell from the Pittsburgh Pirates. 'I'm willing to trade. For the right price.'

Jack riffled through the heap of cards he'd collected. Ralph wouldn't take a Palmer or a Guidry, the two best players Jack had. There was only one other card he could even think of trading for equal value, although the player was just a really crappy outfielder for the Chicago White Sox who couldn't have hit a curveball if it were hanging dead still on a string in front of him. What made Jack's card the envy of every other young collector was the name on it.

'Holy shit,' J. T. breathed. 'Jack's got Rusty Kuntz.'

The three boys dissolved into fits of laughter. 'Man, you have *Kuntz,*' Ralph said.

'I need *Kuntz!*' J. T. cried, and then rolled on the floor, giggling so hard he couldn't catch his breath.

Ralph held out his hand for the card. 'Bet it's easy to give up Kuntz when you can get the real thing.'

'What's that supposed to mean?'

Ralph pursed his lips, kissing at the air. 'Oh, Jack,' he said in a falsetto. 'You are the awesomest boy in the whole school!'

J. T. snorted. 'Rachel Covington might as well take out a billboard at Yankee Stadium, she's so in love with you.'

'She is not,' Jack scowled. 'She's just a girl.' Okay, so she hung around him a lot since he'd gotten an older kid to stop spreading the rumor that she'd gotten her period when she was only eight years old. So what if she had big boobs stuffed into a training bra? All the girls were gonna, one day, and as far as Jack could see, they were an incredible nuisance, probably slapping you under the chin when you were trying to run for speed or distance.

'Jack and Rachel sitting in a tree . . .' Ralph sang out.

'Shut up!' Jack reached over and snatched his Kuntz card out of Ralph's hand.

'Hey!'

'I don't like Rachel Covington, okay?'

'Whatever,' Ralph muttered.

Suddenly the small door to the alcove opened. Corazon, the cook and housekeeper, frowned at them, fists planted on her thick hips. 'Out,' she ordered. 'I need to clean.'

The boys scrambled from their hiding place with their boxes of baseball cards, J. T. and Ralph elbowing each other as they walked down the hall. 'I don't have a girlfriend,' Jack yelled after them, squeezing Rusty Kuntz's card so hard it folded down the middle.

* * *

It turned out that Corazon wasn't just doing her routine sweep and vacuum of the penthouse. Jack's mother had called and told her to get ready for a guest. Jack sat on a kitchen stool, watching the Mexican woman slap at a lump of dough on the butcher block. He kept looking at it and wishing it was Ralph's face.

'You want some bread so badly,' Cora said, 'you might try the loaf that's already been cooked.'

'I don't want bread.'

'No? Then how come you stare like a starving man?'

Jack set his elbows on the counter. 'Just wishing I had something to beat up, too.'

Cora pushed the dough across the table. 'Be my guest.' She wiped her palms on her apron, leaving behind daffodil handprints. 'J. T. and Ralph left in some hurry today.'

Jack shrugged. 'They're losers.'

'Oh, *sí?* Just this morning you couldn't even sit through breakfast, waiting for them to show up.' She covered Jack's hands and molded the dough along with him, giving him a rhythm. 'You have a fight?'

'I don't like Rachel Covington. You know, I mean, I like her . . . I just don't *like* her. I don't *like* any girl.'

'They were teasing you about that?'

'All's I did was stick up for her because she was too scared to do it for herself.'

'Then it's no wonder she's fallen for you, *querido*.'

Jack leaned his cheek against his hand, heedless of the mark of flour he left behind. 'Cora, what makes girls like that? Why can't they just say thanks and get out of your hair?'

Corazon smiled at him. 'You know how your mother keeps her Christmas card list? How she sends to people who send her one, and that list gets longer and longer every year?'

'Yeah,' Jack muttered. 'I have to lick the damn stamps.'

'Watch your mouth,' Cora reprimanded. 'See, love's like that. Once you give it, even by accident, you're on that list forever.'

'What if I don't want to send Rachel a card back?'

The housekeeper laughed. 'You never know. Maybe she'll

keep them coming anyway. But maybe one day she'll go through that list and cross you off.'

'I don't want her to be in love with me,' Jack muttered. 'I'm gonna tell her to stop.'

'You can tell her, but that doesn't mean it's gonna change anything.'

Jack punched at the dough. 'Why not?'

'Because it's *her* heart,' she said, 'and she gets to choose where it goes.'

It was not unusual for Annalise St. Bride to come home with a mission in tow, one wearing spandex and high heels, who'd been stolen away from a pimp on Seventh Avenue. Often the woman would arrive at the penthouse sporting a split lip or a broken nose, gathering her shame as tightly around her as the cut-rate chenille coat she wore. She'd stay in the chrysalis of St. Bride House for a week or so, and then one day she would emerge from the guest room wearing Levi's and an oxford-cloth shirt, her hair pulled back in a ponytail away from her healing face, which was scrubbed free of makeup. Jack was always amazed at the transformation. They went in looking like old ladies; they came out as teenagers.

They were prostitutes. Jack wasn't supposed to know that, because he was only ten and his parents liked to pretend things like that didn't exist in New York City, along with muggings and rats in Central Park and a Democratic mayor. And he - wasn't allowed into their rooms. His mother went in and out like Florence Nightingale, carrying soup and clothing and books by women like Betty Friedan and Gloria Steinem, writers Jack's dad once described as chicks who wanted dicks. But even if Jack was supposed to pretend that the whore upstairs was no different than a visiting cousin, and even if his dad tended to simply look the other way when his mom went off on a tear like this, he knew the truth . . . and somehow it always left him feeling a little sick to his stomach.

* * *

Like always, once the penthouse was clean and the bread in the oven, an air of anticipation spread until it filled every corner. Jack sat on the stairs, idly leafing through his baseball cards but really just waiting to see who it was this time around.

At three-forty-five, his mother came home. And the woman she brought with her wasn't a woman at all.

For one thing, she was smaller than Jack. Her eyes were so large and black they dominated her face, and her tiny white slash of a mouth was the saddest thing Jack had ever seen. Her hands twitched at her sides, as if they desperately needed something to hold.

'This is Emma,' his mother said, and the girl turned and ran right back into the elevator.

That was the second thing that was different about this one: She didn't want to be here.

'Fine, then,' Annalise said. 'I'll go to jail.'

Joseph St. Bride sighed. 'Annie, I know it kills you to see this stuff. But you can't remove a child from her home without the permission of Child Protective Services.'

'Have you seen her? What did you expect me to do?' Her voice got so low that Jack had to work harder to eavesdrop from outside the library door. 'She's nine, Joseph. She's nine years old and her forty-year-old uncle is raping her.'

Jack knew about rape; it was hard to live with his mother, the queen of crusaders against violence against women, and not know about it. Rape had to do with sex, and sex was something too gross to even think about. He tried to picture Emma, the girl who'd been carried kicking and screaming upstairs, doing *that* with a grown-up. It made him gag.

'Go see for yourself,' his mother yelled, and all of a sudden they burst out of the library, so intent on their fight that, thankfully, they never noticed Jack sitting there at all.

He crept up the stairs after them and hovered outside Emma's room. They had locked her in. In all the years his mom had done this kind of thing, Jack couldn't remember a single woman getting locked in.

His father knocked softly. 'Hi, Emma,' he said gently. 'I'm Annalise's husband.'

Emma opened her mouth and began to scream. It echoed right through Jack's head and, he figured, probably broke some crystal downstairs. 'Just go outside,' Jack's mother ordered. 'She's obviously afraid of you.'

Joseph walked into the hall again, closing the door. Then he looked down at Jack. 'I'm sorry you had to hear that.'

From the spot where he was sitting, Jack shrugged. 'I'm sorry for Emma,' he answered.

Annalise went to court and got temporary custody of Emma. A month passed, and the girl began eating and looking healthier. But every night, she tried to run away.

Once, they found her under the stairs, where Jack and his friends liked to hide. Once, she was in the trash chute. Another time she made it all the way to the lobby before Corazon managed to catch up with her.

His mother said that it was because Joseph reminded Emma too much of what had happened. 'I'm not moving out of my own house,' Jack's father had thundered, and that started a fight between them that still flared like a brush fire every now and then.

Jack didn't say so, but he thought his mother ought to stop worrying what Emma was running away *from*. In his opinion, the big mystery was where she was heading.

He rigged up a burglar alarm. Jack stretched a length of nylon fishing line across the front of her door, and sure enough, he woke up to the sound of a soft thud against the carpet. He jumped out of bed to find Emma dressed and sprawled on the floor.

She looked up at him, evaluating whether she could take him down or whether he was someone she ought to be afraid of. 'It's okay,' Jack whispered. 'I'm not going to tell.'

He had not known until that moment that he was going to keep her secret, maybe even let her steal away, without sounding a siren. Emma's eyes narrowed. 'Bullshit.'

It sounded wrong on the mouth of a little girl, like a horde of flies swimming out of her lips the moment they opened. Jack held out a hand to help Emma up, but she rose without touching him. 'I'm getting out of here,' she said.

'Okay.'

'You can't stop me.'

Jack shrugged. 'I wasn't going to.' He crossed his arms, hoping he looked as cool as he thought he might.

Emma walked past him. God, if his mother found out what he was doing, he'd never hear the end of it. He watched the girl pad softly down the oriental runner on the staircase. 'Emma,' he whispered.

She turned.

'You like baseball?'

He had never in life wanted to spend any time with a girl, much less actually give something that could be construed as a gift, but he worked out a deal with Emma. Every night she didn't try to leave, he'd give her two of his baseball cards. She had no idea that Steve Renko and Chuck Rainey sucked, which meant that at least Jack wasn't losing any of his good stuff. They sat on the floor of his bedroom, and he taught her about batting averages and playing positions and the Cy Young Award.

She didn't speak much. When she did, it was weird. She talked about hearing the bed knock against the wall when his mother and father were doing it, which was totally repulsive. She said Corazon had forgotten what it was like to have a man in her bed. It was as if she wanted to shock Jack. But every time Emma got going, he just stared as if those flies were swarming from her lips again and didn't say a thing.

One night, he woke up to find Emma standing next to him. 'You overslept.'

He looked at the clock; it was two in the morning. 'Sorry,' Jack muttered, sitting up. Then he remembered that he didn't have anything else to give her. 'You've got half my baseball cards, Emma. I don't have any more.'

'Oh.' She looked very small in her nightgown and robe. The sash of the robe went around her waist twice. It was one of his; his mother had filched it from the closet.

Jack swung his legs over the side of the bed. 'So I guess if you're going to go, you'd just better go ahead.'

Emma looked down at the floor. She was a strange kid, always staring hard at the tiniest things. She knew how many freckles were on Jack's ear, and that the third stair riser had a crack in it that was shaped like a W. 'Maybe tomorrow night,' she said.

A week later, they lay side by side on his bed, not touching. Emma kept a buffer of a few inches between herself and everyone else she came in contact with; Jack had noticed that early on. 'Do you have a girlfriend?' Emma asked.

'No.'

'How come?'

Jack shrugged. 'I don't like girls.'

'You like me.'

Well, yeah. He did. He looked down at her. The question he'd wanted to ask forever swelled inside his stomach like a balloon. 'Where would you go?'

She didn't pretend to misunderstand him. 'Home. Where else?'

Of all the answers she could have given, that was the one Jack least expected. 'But . . . you can't,' he stammered. 'You just got away.'

Emma blinked at him. 'Your mother *took* me away. What makes you think I wanted to leave?'

Jack felt heat creeping up the neck of his pajama top. 'You weren't safe there. Your uncle –'

'Loves me,' Emma said fiercely. 'He loves me.'

Jack would have bet every single baseball card left in his possession that Emma didn't even know she was crying.

Jack found Corazon in the laundry room, separating colors from whites. 'You know,' she said, 'if I tell you another seven hundred times, maybe one of these days you might turn your clothes right side out when you put them in the hamper, eh?'

He hopped on top of the dryer, swinging his legs. 'Can I ask you something?'

'Sure.'

'How do you know if you love someone?'

Corazon looked up, her hands stilling for a minute. 'Well, that's quite a question,' she said. 'And usually it's something you figure out for yourself.'

'If you love someone, you want to take care of them, right?'

She smiled slyly. 'Someone's had a change of mind about Rachel Covington?'

'And if you love someone, you're not supposed to hurt them.'

'No,' Cora answered, 'but you usually do at some point, anyway.'

Well, that made the whole thing about as clear as mud. Jack thanked Cora and scrambled out of the laundry room, up the stairs. Emma's door was shut, as usual. But she'd managed to sneak out when no one was looking, because a stack of neatly banded baseball cards were set just inside the threshold of his own bedroom door.

That was how he knew she was planning to leave.

Eyelids, Jack thought, must weigh something like forty pounds each, or why would it be so hard to keep them up after midnight? He got down on the floor and did another fifty sit-ups, then paced around his room. He couldn't risk falling asleep, not yet. And his parents had only just gone to bed. He knew Emma would make sure they were sound asleep before she sneaked away.

At 1:20, Jack swallowed hard and walked to Emma's room. It was the first time he'd ever gone to her space instead of letting her come to his. And al-though he only had a vague impression of what must have happened between Emma and her uncle, he guessed it probably happened in her own bed.

Either this was going to work, Jack thought, or she was going to scream loud enough to bring down the whole building.

He turned the key in the lock she knew how to pick anyway and slipped inside on the slice of light from the hallway. One second Emma was facing the wall, and the next she was staring at him, her eyes huge in her face, her whole body going rigid.

'Shh,' Jack said. 'It's just me.'

That didn't seem to make it any better. Emma was dead silent, just as still.

'Can I sit down?'

She didn't answer, and with a slight pang in his stomach Jack realized that no one had ever asked for her permission. His weight tilted the mattress, and Emma rolled against his bent knee like a cylinder of wood. 'I wanted to show you something,' he whispered. 'I wanted to show you that someone who loves you doesn't always have to hurt you.' And taking a deep breath, he reached down and held her hand.

She froze. It was the first time they had ever touched, beyond accidental brushing when they passed baseball cards back and forth. She was waiting for him to do something else, something disgusting Jack didn't really want to picture in his head. But he just sat there, his fingers tangled with hers, until Emma's other hand came up to cover his, until she crawled into his arms like the child she'd forgotten how to be.

June 29, 2000
Carroll County Jail New Hampshire

Jack threaded his tie into a Windsor knot, pulled it tight, and tried his best not to think of a lynching. He smoothed the fabric down, never taking his eyes off the stranger in the mirror. Blue blazer, khaki pants, loafers, tie – this had become his trial uniform. And the man staring back at him was someone who understood that the legal system didn't work.

There was a sharp rap on the other side of the bathroom wall. 'Get moving,' a CO called out. 'You're gonna be late.'

Jack blinked twice, the man in the mirror blinked twice. He raised his hand to his forehead, where his hair was beginning to curl in the damp humidity of the shower room. He told himself it was time to go.

But Jack's feet didn't move. They might as well have been nailed to the cement floor. He grabbed the edge of the sink and tried to force one leg back but was literally paralyzed by the fear of what was yet to come.

The CO stuck his head into the bathroom. Humiliated, Jack met his eyes in the mirror, only to find that he could not force out a single word.

The guard wrapped his hand around Jack's upper arm gently and pulled until Jack fell into step beside him.

'I'm sorry,' Jack murmured.

The CO shrugged. 'You ain't the first one.'

'And don't forget to tell Darla the blue-plate special, when you decide,' Addie said.

Roy slipped his arm around his daughter's waist. 'We can

do fine without you.' He faced her, so proud of his girl in this pale peach suit, with low heels on her feet and her brown hair pulled back from her face with a simple gold clip. Christ, she looked like a professional businesswoman, not some two-bit waitress. 'You are beautiful,' Roy said quietly. 'Jack won't be able to take his eyes off you.'

'Jack won't be able to see me. I have to sit outside, sequestered, because I'm a witness.' Suddenly, Addie stripped off the fitted jacket of her suit. 'Who am I kidding?' she muttered, reaching behind the counter for her apron. 'I'm just going to drive myself crazy sitting there all day. At least here I'll be able to focus –'

' – on what's going on at court,' Roy said, interrupting. 'You have to go, Addie. There's something about you . . . like you're a lighthouse, and other people see the beam. Or an anchor, with the rest of us just hanging on to you for dear life. You ground us. And right now, I figure, Jack needs something to grab on to.' He held out her suit jacket, so that she could shrug it on. 'Go on, get down to that courthouse.'

'It's only six-thirty, Daddy. Court doesn't convene until nine.'

'Then drive slow.'

When he went back into the kitchen, Addie stood alone in the early light of the diner, watching the sun leapfrog over shadows on the linoleum floor. Maybe if she arrived early, she could find the entrance where the deputy sheriffs brought the inmates from the jail. Maybe she could be there when Jack was brought in, could catch his eye.

Then something beneath the counter stool where she liked to imagine Chloe sitting drew her attention. Shriveled and brittle, more brown than red – it took a moment for Addie to recognize it as the little bouquet she had once confiscated from Gillian Duncan, tucked into her apron and forgotten.

It was the craziest thing, but when she lifted the dead flowers to her nose, she could swear they were as fragrant as new blossoms.

* * *

Amos Duncan flattened his tie against his abdomen as he hurried downstairs to the kitchen. 'Gillian,' he called over his shoulder. 'We're going to be late!'

He headed toward the kitchen, intent on swilling at least one cup of coffee to settle his stomach before he began the grim hell of this trial. Houlihan would put Gillian on the stand first. The thought of his daughter sitting up there with a thousand eyes on her, television cameras rolling, and twelve men and women bearing witness – well, it was enough to make him want to kill someone. Jack St. Bride, in particular.

He would have given anything to take the stand in her stead, to make their life private again. But instead, all he would be able to do was watch, like everyone else, and see how it played out at the end.

The smell of coffee grew stronger as Amos entered the kitchen. Gillian sat at the kitchen table, dressed in the virginal white outfit Houlihan had hand-picked for her. She was shoveling cornflakes into her mouth behind a barricade of brightly colored cereal boxes.

Amos looked at her, nearly hidden from his view by the cartons. He fixed his coffee, black, the way he liked it. Then he slid into the chair across from his daughter.

There were three boxes blocking her from his view. He pushed the Life cereal box away. When he moved a second box, Lucky Charms, his daughter stopped chewing.

Finally, Amos shifted the cornflakes, so that he could see her unobstructed. Bright color stained her cheeks. 'Gilly,' he said softly, offering up a whole story in that one word.

Gillian reached for the Lucky Charms and set it up again, a wall. She took the cornflakes and the Life cereal and made barriers on either side of the first box. Then she lifted her spoon and began to eat in silence, as if her father were not there at all.

'Sydney!' Matt hollered at the top of his lungs, holding his squealing daughter at arm's length as she fought to hand him

the arrowroot biscuit she'd been gumming. 'Don't you do this to me, you little monster. This is my last clean suit.'

His wife rounded the corner, carrying a stack of clean laundry. 'Where's the fire?'

'Here,' Matt said, thrusting the baby into her free arm. 'And it's raging out of control. I can't have her mess me up, Syd. I'm on my way to court.'

Sydney brushed her lips over the baby's head. 'She just wants to give you her good luck charm, isn't that right, honey?'

'I'm not taking her cookie, dammit.'

His wife shrugged. 'Well, someone's going to be awfully sorry when the jury comes back with an acquittal.'

Matt gathered up his files and stuffed them into his briefcase. 'I'm just not a rabbit's foot kind of fellow.' He leaned down to kiss Sydney good-bye, then ran a light hand over the soft fuzz of his daughter's head.

Sydney followed him to the front door, bouncing the baby in her arms. 'Wave good-bye,' she told Molly. 'Daddy's going to go lock up the bad guys.'

Charlie took a deep breath and knocked on the bathroom door. A moment later, it opened, steam spilling into the hallway, his daughter's face hovering in the mist left in the wake of her shower. 'What?' she said belligerently. 'Did you come to strip-search me?'

She threw open the door and spread her arms, the towel she'd wrapped around her damp body riding low. He didn't know what to say to her. He didn't know who this girl was, because she no longer acted like his daughter. So he opted for the practical, the functional, as if pretending that the wall of mistrust between them was invisible would keep it from hurting every time he slammed up against it. 'Have you seen my badge?' Charlie asked. He needed it to complete his dress blues, before heading to court.

Meg turned away. 'You didn't leave it in here.'

Still, Charlie looked over her shoulder, at the edge of the sink, checking.

'What's the matter, Daddy?' she said. 'Oh, that's right. You don't believe me.'

'Meg . . .' He did believe her, and that was the problem. All he had to do was look at her and he saw her, again, sobbing at the station as she recounted a memory of being sexually assaulted. What Charlie wanted to do, more than anything, was turn back time. He wanted to go through Meg's closet and never find that thermos. He wanted to keep her under lock and key, so nothing bad would ever happen to her.

He had not broached the subject of the atropine with Meg. He could barely conduct a completely innocuous conversation with her, much less one charged with so much suspicion.

'Then again, maybe I've got your badge, Daddy,' Meg said, tears in her eyes. 'Maybe I hid it at the bottom of my closet.'

Charlie took a step forward. 'Meg, honey, listen to yourself.'

'Why? You don't.'

The sorrow broke over her, and she stood in her towel before him, crying so hard it made Charlie's chest ache. He grabbed for her, held her in his arms the way he had when she was small and had believed there were monsters hiding under her bed. *There are no monsters,* he'd told her back then, when what he really should have said was: *There are no monsters* there.

Suddenly, Meg went stiff in his arms. 'Don't touch me,' she said, drawing away. 'Don't touch me!' She pushed past him, running for the sanctuary of her bedroom.

As the door flew open in her wake, Charlie saw something glinting on the floor. His badge, which must have fallen behind the door when he was in the bathroom washing his hands. Charlie knelt and picked it up, fastened it, then looked in the mirror. There it was, shiny and silver, pinned to the requisite position on his chest – a shield that covered his heart but had not been able to protect it.

'Shit,' Jordan said. 'They beat us here.'

Selena squinted into the sun at the steps of the courthouse, thick with cameras and television reporters. 'Is there a back entrance?'

He cut the ignition. 'I have to run the gauntlet, you know that.' They got out of the car, Selena straightening her stockings and Jordan shrugging into his jacket. 'Ready?'

The reporters reminded Jordan of black flies, those horrible bugs that take over the Northeast for a few weeks every summer and fly heedless up your nose and into your ears and eyes as if they have every right to be there. Jordan pasted a smile on his face and began to hustle up the stone steps of the court, bowed in the middle from years of defendants trudging up in hope and down in victory or defeat. 'Mr. McAfee,' a female reporter called, making a beeline to his side. 'Do you think your client will be acquitted?'

'I most certainly do,' Jordan said smoothly.

'How will you account for the fact that he's been in jail for sexual assault before?' another voice shouted.

'Come on inside,' Jordan answered, grinning. 'And I'll show you.'

The press loved him. The press had always loved him. He was cocky and photogenic and had long ago mastered the art of the sound bite. He shouldered aside cameras and microphones, wondering how far behind he'd left Selena.

One step away from the top, a woman blocked his progress. She wore a blood-red turban and a T-shirt that read TAKE BACK THE NIGHT. 'Mr. McAfee,' she bellowed, 'are you aware that in the United States alone, 132,000 women reported a stranger rape last year – and that if you include the estimated number of women who don't report violence against them, there may be as many as 750,000 women who were raped?'

'Yes,' Jordan said, meeting her gaze. 'But not by my client.'

Jack sat in the rear of the small cell in the sheriff's office beneath the court, chewing on a thumbnail and staring at the floor between his shoes, completely oblivious to the fact that his attorney had arrived. 'Jack,' Jordan said quietly.

He was struck by how well Jack cleaned up. But then again, this was what Jack had been born to: preppy blazers and rep ties and loafers. Jordan offered a confident smile. 'You all set?'

'I suppose so.'

'I don't have to tell you what it's going to be like in there. You've done this drill before. A lot of shit's going to be said before it's over, and the most important thing you can do is keep your cool. The minute you blow up is the same minute the prosecutor proves that you're just one big violent act waiting to happen.'

'I won't blow up.'

'And remember, we get to go last,' Jordan said. 'That's the best thing about being a defense attorney.'

'And here I thought it was the truly fascinating people you got to fraternize with.'

A surprised laugh bubbled out of Jordan, but when he lifted his gaze, he found Jack staring at him, sober and intense. 'Did you know that the average sentence for a felon convicted of a violent offense is one hundred five months?'

Jordan snorted. 'Says who?'

'The Bureau of Justice Statistics. Over a million adults were convicted of felonies last year.'

'Maybe this year, the number will be 999,999.'

An uneasy silence settled over the men, punctuated by the cough of a prisoner two cells over. Jordan sighed. 'I have to mention something one last time, Jack. You still haven't given me much to work with here. But there are six men on that jury, and every single one of them has been in the situation where they're fooling around and then the woman's changed her mind at the last minute. As a defense against a rape allegation, it's an easy sell.' He leaned closer. 'Are you absolutely sure you don't want to go with consent?'

Jack's hands knotted together between his legs. 'Jordan, do me a favor?'

The attorney nodded, and Jack turned, his eyes cold. 'Don't ever ask me that again.'

★ ★ ★

Matt reached into his briefcase for his notes and found them glued together with the dried remains of a mashed arrowroot biscuit. Shaking his head, he began to carefully peel apart the pages of his yellow legal pad.

'Ooh,' winced Jordan McAfee, passing the prosecutor's table en route to his own. 'The last time I saw something like that was in law school, when a guy tossed his cookies in the briefcase of the judge he was clerking for.'

'Friend of yours, no doubt,' Matt said.

'Actually, I think he went on to become a DA.' Jordan hid a smile as one of Matt's papers ripped. 'Careful. You don't want to ruin your cheat sheet.'

'McAfee, I could try this case in my sleep and still win.'

'Guess that's your plan, then, since you're clearly dreaming.' He reached into his own briefcase and took out a pack of Kleenex, which he threw onto the prosecutor's table. 'Here,' Jordan said. 'A peace offering.'

Matt took a tissue to wipe the cookie residue off his legal briefs, then tossed the pack back to Jordan. 'Save the rest for consoling your client after the conviction.'

A side door opened as a deputy sheriff entered, escorting Jack to the seat beside Jordan's. He still wore his blazer and tie, but he was handcuffed. As the deputy released the cuffs, Jordan focused on his client, who was such a bundle of nervous energy that heat seemed to emanate from his body. 'Relax,' he mouthed silently.

That, Jordan realized, was nearly impossible. The gallery was full – media reps from states as far away as Connecticut were reporting on the trial, and there were a fair number of local townspeople who'd come to make sure that Salem Falls remained as morally pure as it had always been. Amos Duncan stared vehemently at Jack from his spot behind the prosecutor's table. There had to be close to 200 people in that wide audience, all with their attention riveted on the defendant . . . and not a single one in support of Jack.

'Jordan,' Jack whispered, a thread of panic wrapped around his words. 'I can feel it.'

'Feel what?'

'How much they hate me.'

Jordan remembered then that Jack had not ever suffered through an actual trial. His conviction had been a plea bargain – an uncomfortable hearing, but one not nearly as grueling as the one that was about to occur. The legal system sounded good on paper, but the truth was that as long as Jack sat beside a defense attorney, every person watching this trial would consider him guilty until proven innocent.

The six men and eight women who made up the jury and its alternates streamed solemnly in from a door on the side of the courtroom. Just before taking a seat, each one turned, scrutinizing Jack. Beneath the table, Jack's hands clenched on his knees.

'All rise!'

The Honorable Althea Justice billowed to a seat behind the bench. Her cool gray eyes surveyed the gallery: the cameras, the reporters with their cell phones, the tight rows of residents from Salem Falls. 'Ladies and gentlemen,' she said, 'I see we have a packed house today. So let's all start out on the right foot. At the first sign of any inappropriate behavior' – she glanced at a cameraman –'or any outbursts' – she glanced at Amos Duncan –'you will be escorted from my courtroom, and will remain outside it for the duration of the trial. If I hear a beeper or cell phone go off during any testimony, I will personally collect everyone's electronic devices and burn them in a pyre outside the court building. Finally, I'd like everyone to remember – including counsel – that this is a court of law, not a circus.' She slipped her half glasses down and peered over them. 'Mr. Houlihan,' the judge said, 'let's get rolling.'

'On the evening of April thirtieth, 2000, Amos Duncan kissed his daughter good-bye and went out for a quick run. She was seventeen years old, and although he worried about her every time he left her alone, he had chosen to live in Salem Falls because it was a safe place to raise his child. Amos Duncan certainly didn't expect that the next time he saw his daughter, she would be sobbing, hysterical. That her clothes would be ripped. That she'd have blood on her shirt, skin beneath her fingernails, semen on her thigh. That she'd be telling the police she had been raped in the woods outside Salem Falls, New Hampshire.'

Matt walked slowly toward the jury. 'The evidence that the state will present to you today will show that on April thirtieth, 2000, Gillian Duncan left her home at 8:45 p.m. She met up with her friends and went to a clearing in the woods behind the Salem Falls Cemetery. They made a small bonfire and enjoyed each other's company, teenagers having fun. And just as they were getting ready to leave shortly after midnight, this man came up to them.'

Matt jabbed his finger at Jack's face. 'This man, Jack St. Bride, approached the girls where they were sitting. He was unsteady on his feet. They could smell alcohol on his breath. He started speaking to them conversationally, even sat down with them to chat. When the girls made it clear they were on their way home, he stood up and left.

'Minutes later, Gillian and her friends departed on different trails. Worried about the safety of the smoldering ashes they'd left behind, Gillian decided to turn back and kick some dirt over the remains of their bonfire. At that moment, Jack St. Bride stepped into the clearing, pushed her to the ground, and brutally raped her.'

Matt faced the jury again. 'Ladies and gentlemen, my name is Matt Houlihan, and I'm an assistant county attorney for the state of New Hampshire. I met you all during jury selection, but I wanted to introduce myself again, because it's my job – as a representative of the state – to prove to you all the elements of this crime beyond a reasonable doubt. Jack St. Bride has been charged with committing aggravated felonious sexual assault against Gillian Duncan . . . but please, don't take *my* word for it.'

He smiled, his very best Opie Taylor grin, one that invited

the jury to believe that they were in excellent hands. 'Instead, I urge you to listen to Gillian Duncan, when she tells you what she suffered at the hands of Jack St. Bride. And to her girlfriends, who were also there that night. Listen to the detective who found Gillian after the attack, and who investigated the crime scene. Listen to an expert witness, who did DNA analysis on evidence collected from the scene. Listen to the doctor who examined Gillian Duncan after the assault.' Matt looked at each member of the jury. 'Listen carefully, ladies and gentlemen, because at the end of this case, I'm going to ask you to find Mr. St. Bride guilty . . . and on the basis of everything you've heard, you will.'

Jordan watched Matt return to his seat. The jury knew he was supposed to follow that opening act; most of the men and women in the box had their eyes turned expectantly on him. But he sat an extra moment longer, as if he, too, were considering Houlihan's words at face value. 'You know,' he said conversationally, 'if the only evidence you were going to hear was what Mr. Houlihan just laid out in his opening, then I'd agree with him a hundred percent. From everything he just said – heck, it sure does look like Jack St. Bride committed this crime. However, there are two sides to every story. And you're not just going to hear the state's version of what happened that night . . . you're going to hear Mr. St. Bride's version as well.'

He ran one hand lightly along the railing of the jury box. 'My name is Jordan McAfee, and I'm here to represent Jack St. Bride. And just like Mr. Houlihan, I want you to listen carefully . . . but I also want to remind you that things aren't always what they seem to be.' Suddenly, Jordan leaned forward, as if to pluck something from behind a juror's ear. The woman blushed as he stepped back, brandishing a shiny quarter.

'Objection,' Matt called out. 'Is this an opening argument or a David Copperfield show?'

'Yes, Mr. McAfee,' the judge warned. 'Did I not say something about turning this court into a circus?'

'I beg your pardon, Your Honor. I just wanted to prove a point.' Jordan grinned, holding up the coin. 'I think we all know I didn't just pull this out of juror number three's head. But it sure looked that way, didn't it? Like I said – things aren't always what they seem to be. Not even when you experience them firsthand.' Jordan flipped the quarter into the air – and after spinning, it appeared to simply vanish. 'It's certainly something to keep in mind when you listen to the prosecution's eyewitnesses.'

Matt sprang to his feet. 'Objection!'

'On what grounds, Mr. Houlihan?' asked the judge.

'Your Honor, the credibility of all the witnesses is in the hands of the jury. It's not for Mr. McAfee to determine whether testimony is credible or not . . . particularly during an opening statement.'

She arched a brow. 'Mr. Houlihan, can we just get *through* this opening statement?'

'I'd like a ruling for the record, Judge,' Matt said stiffly.

'Overruled.' She turned back to Jordan. 'Proceed.'

'Listen to everything,' Jordan advised the jury. 'But don't trust everything you hear. Picture what the witnesses tell you . . . but don't assume that's what actually happened. As Mr. Houlihan said, your job on this jury is crucial. Yet where the prosecutor would like you to act as a sponge, I want you to be a filter. I want you to ask yourself who was there. Ask yourself what they saw. And then ask yourself if you believe them.'

Rape victims, Matt thought, were the worst.

By the time larceny and assault cases made it to trial, victims put on the stand were angry about what had happened. In a murder case, of course, there was no victim left at all. No, it was only in a sexual assault case that someone who had been terrorized and was still, for the most part, traumatized, had to face her attacker from just a few feet away.

'That's him,' she replied in response to Matt's last question. She pointed with a trembling finger.

'Judge,' Matt said, 'may the record reflect that the witness has identified the defendant.' He stepped smoothly in front of her, again blocking her view of St. Bride. 'Gillian, what happened that night?'

Gillian bent her head, hiding her face. 'I told my father I was going to my house, but I wasn't, not really. We all lied, just to get out. Things had been so crazy . . . and our parents told us we couldn't . . . well, it was like a dare for us.'

'Where did you go?'

'To the forest behind the cemetery. There's a big dogwood there.' Gilly swallowed. 'We built a campfire, and we were just sitting around it telling jokes and trying . . . trying to act brave.'

'Who was with you?'

'Meg was. And Whitney and Chelsea.'

'What time was this?' Matt asked.

'Around eleven o'clock.'

'What happened next?'

'After midnight, we decided . . . that it was time to go home. We were putting out the fire when he showed up.'

'Who, Gillian?'

'Jack St. Bride,' she whispered.

'What was he wearing?'

'A yellow T-shirt. And jeans, and boots.'

'Did he say anything to you?'

'He smiled,' Gillian answered. 'He said hello.'

'Did you say anything in return?'

'We were all really scared. I mean, we all knew what everyone had been saying about him raping that other girl –'

'Objection,' Jordan said. 'Hearsay.'

'Sustained.' The judge glanced at the jury. 'You'll disregard that last statement.'

'You were scared,' Matt prompted.

'Yes . . . and all of a sudden he was right there with us, and looking a little wild. So, actually, none of us said anything. We were too terrified.'

'What happened next?'

Gillian seemed to draw into herself, remembering. 'He looked at the fire,' she said, 'and sat down. He asked us if we were roasting marshmallows. I remember thinking that . . . well, that it was an ordinary question. I expected someone who was supposed to be such a dangerous man to be . . . a little more dangerous.'

'Then what happened?'

'I told him we were just on our way home. He said that was too bad. Then he said good night and headed into the woods.'

'Do you remember which trail?' Matt asked, pointing to a map propped beside her.

Gillian touched a thin line arcing north, one that didn't lead back to the cemetery. 'This one.'

'Then what?'

'Well, as soon as he was gone we were all, like, *Can you believe it? Can you believe it was* him?' She hunched her shoulders. 'Then we left.'

'What path did you take?'

Gillian pointed to a trail that led to the northeast, tracing it to the far edge of the woods. 'I took this one,' she said softly. 'It's a shortcut for me. But the others were going toward the cemetery, because it was the quickest way back to their side of town.'

'Did you feel nervous about walking home alone?'

'No,' Gillian said. 'I mean, this guy who was supposed to be the Devil himself had left. What else was there to be afraid of, once he was gone?'

'What did you do next?'

Tears began to well in Gillian's eyes, and Matt's heart turned over. Christ, he didn't want to make her relive this. 'I hadn't gone more than a few seconds before I realized that I never checked the fire. I mean, we put it out and all, but it was still smoking a little. So I figured I'd go back and make sure it hadn't caught on again.' Her words stretched thin. 'When I got to the clearing, it was empty. I kicked dirt over the fire, and all of a sudden he . . . he grabbed me from behind. He must have been hiding . . . or . . . or following me,' she said.

'What happened next, Gillian?'

She made a low, horrible noise in the back of her throat. 'He pushed me down . . . and he put his hand over my mouth. He said if I made any noise, he'd kill me.' Turning her head away, Gillian shut her eyes. 'He pinned my hands up over my head and unbuttoned my jeans. He . . . he took a condom out of his pocket and told me I should put it on him.'

'Did he let your hands go?'

'Yes.' Tears ran freely down her face, into the collar of her dress. 'I pretended I was going to rip open the packet, and instead I scratched his cheek. I tried to get away. But he grabbed my wrists and pushed me back down and put the condom on himself.'

'And then?'

'And then . . . then . . .' She shrank back in the seat, her voice striped with pain. 'And then he raped me.'

Matt let that statement stand for a moment. 'How long did it last?'

'Forever,' Gillian murmured.

'Did he insert his penis into your vagina?'

'Yes.'

'Did he ejaculate?'

'I . . . I guess,' Gilly said. 'He stopped, anyway.'

'Was he saying anything while this was happening?' Matt asked.

'No.'

'Were you?'

'I was crying. I couldn't look at him.'

'Did you try to move at all?'

Gilly shook her head. 'He was holding me down. Tight. And every time I tried to roll away, he just shoved me harder into the ground.'

The jury was staring intently at Gillian. 'What happened after he was done?'

Her answer came softly, from a place deep inside her. 'He got up and zipped his pants,' Gilly said, wrapping her arms around herself. 'He told me if I talked to anyone, he'd come back for me.'

'What did you do?'

'I watched him go, and then counted to a hundred and started running.'

'Which direction did he leave in?'

'The path that went closest to my house,' Gillian said. 'So I ran in the other direction. Toward the cemetery. Where my friends had gone.'

'How long did it take you to catch up to the others?'

'I don't know. A few minutes, I guess.'

'What happened when you found your friends?' Matt asked.

'I couldn't stop crying. And my legs . . . they just collapsed. I felt so dirty, and I just couldn't get out what had happened.'

Matt walked toward the defense table. 'Had you ever seen Jack St. Bride before?'

'Yes.'

'When?'

She let her gaze slide over Jack, then fall to her lap like a stone. 'He worked in this diner in town. Every now and then, my friends and I went there.'

'Had you ever talked to him before?'

'Sometimes he'd come over to our table and start a conversation.'

Matt nodded. 'Did you ever indicate to him that you were interested in having a relationship with him?'

Gillian shook her head vehemently. 'No.'

'Is there any doubt in your mind, Gillian, that the defendant is the man who sexually assaulted you shortly after midnight on May first?'

The muscles in Gillian's jaw clenched. 'I can still feel his body on top of me. I smell him, sometimes, in empty rooms. And I wake up suffocating, sure that it's happening again.' Her eyes roamed the gallery until they clung tight to her father's. 'I don't have any doubts,' Gilly whispered. 'It was him.'

'Nothing further,' Matt said, and sat down.

The moment Jordan stood up, he could feel the tightrope beneath his feet. He needed to discredit Gillian carefully. Matt had spent a half hour here getting the whole courtroom to feel sorry for her; if Jordan was too harsh, the jury would turn against him rather than Gillian.

He gave her a moment to compose herself and approached her slowly, having learned from experience that even the most pitiful-looking stray puppies sometimes turned around and snapped. 'Ms. Duncan, when you were in the woods with your friends and Mr. St. Bride came up to you, did you feel scared around him?'

'Yes. I'd been told for weeks that I shouldn't be anywhere near him.'

'Yet you also said that the reason you went to the woods that night was to be brave. To defy your parents, who were making a "big deal" about staying away from Mr. St. Bride. So being close to him was the ultimate defiance, wasn't it?'

Gillian shook her head. 'I would never have done that.'

'Did you leave the minute he came up to you?'

'Yes.'

'By your own statement, though, Ms. Duncan, he asked you a question about roasting marshmallows and sat down with you all, isn't that true?'

A light glinted in Gillian's eyes. 'But then I told him we were all leaving, because it was the quickest way to get rid of him.'

'Get rid of him? Because you were still scared?'

She lifted her chin. 'Yes.'

'Yet you said that once he left, you weren't scared.'

'That's right.'

'You never thought Mr. St. Bride was going to attack you?'

Gilly shook her head. 'If I had, I would have stuck with my friends.'

'You never thought he would attack you, although everything you'd heard about him from your parents and friends indicated that he was waiting for the opportunity to assault young women?'

She was between a rock and a hard place – and knew it. Jordan waited patiently for her answer. 'N-no,' Gillian said.

'All right. You started to walk home and then turned around to make sure the fire was out?'

'Yes.'

'How far had you gone at that point?'

'Not far. Only a few seconds.'

'And Mr. St. Bride allegedly attacked you when you returned to the clearing?'

'That's right,' she said quietly.

'Had you seen him hiding there before you and your friends left?'

'No. He walked off down a path.'

'And how long after he left did you all depart?'

'A few minutes, maybe. Not long.'

Jordan nodded. 'If he expected you to be leaving the clearing, Ms. Duncan, then why would he have circled back to it to attack you? Why not lay in wait along one of the paths, where he had a better chance of intercepting you?'

Gillian stared at Jordan. 'I don't know.'

'If you hadn't decided to check on the ashes, you wouldn't even have come back to the clearing, isn't that right?'

'Yes.'

'Did Mr. St. Bride take off your clothes?'

'He pulled down my jeans and my underwear,' Gillian whispered.

'And your sweater? Did he take that off?'

'No.'

'Unbutton it?'

'No,' Gillian said.

'How about his own clothes?'

'His pants.'

'Did he pull down his pants before or after he pulled down yours?'

Tears filled her eyes, and she shook her head. 'Ms. Duncan,' the judge said kindly, 'I'm going to need you to answer the question.'

'I can't remember,' Gilly murmured.

'Did he pull down his pants before or after he asked you to put on the condom?'

'Before.'

'Was he still holding your hands over your head when he took off his jeans?'

'Yes.'

'How?'

'He kept one hand on my wrists,' Gillian said. 'He used the other one to pull down his pants.'

'So even though you were struggling against him, and he was using his lower body to pin you down and one hand to hold your wrists, he managed to unfasten his jeans and work them down over his hips?'

'Yes.'

'Tell me about how you scratched Mr. St. Bride that night.'

'It was after he threw me on the ground,' Gillian said. 'When he let go of my hands and told me to put on the condom, I went for his eyes, but I missed and got his cheek.'

'Which cheek?'

'His right.'

'Did you use one finger?'

'I used my whole hand.' Gillian made a claw. 'Like this.'

'Did you scratch him with four fingers?'

'I don't know. I just raked my hand down his face, trying to get away. Then he grabbed my hand and slammed me down really hard.'

'You said after Mr. St. Bride raped you, you counted to a hundred, then ran after your friends. Is that correct?'

'Yes.'

'How did you count?'

Gillian looked up, confused. 'What do you mean?'

'Well, how quickly? Was it one-two-three . . . or one-Mississippi, two-Mississippi . . .'

He shrugged. 'Maybe you could count to ten for us, today, like you did that night.'

She glanced at Matt Houlihan, who shrugged imperceptibly. 'One,' Gillian said slowly, 'two . . . three . . .'

When she reached ten, Jordan looked up from his watch and did some quick math. 'So you waited about eighty seconds before leaving the clearing?'

'I suppose.'

'Did you walk to your friends? Crawl? Tiptoe?'

'I ran. As fast as I could.'

'And it took several minutes to reach your friends?'

'Yes.'

'You're certain about that?'

Gillian nodded. 'It was about five minutes.'

Jordan pointed to the path on the oversize map that led toward the cemetery. 'This is the route you took?'

'Uh-huh.'

'Do you have any idea how long a distance this path is, Ms. Duncan?'

'No.'

'It's fifty-two yards. One hundred fifty-six feet,' Jordan said. 'Can you show me where, along this path, your friends were when you caught up with them?'

She pointed to the edge of the cemetery. 'Right here. Outside the woods.'

'And Detective Saxton found you, right at the spot where you stopped?'

'Yes.'

'While you and your friends were together in the woods, you had no alcohol and no drugs, is that true?'

'Yes.'

'Nothing to eat or drink for the entire hour you were there?'

'I had a snack. Cookies. That's it.'

'Did your friends have anything to drink that night?'

'Yes,' Gilly said. 'Iced tea.'

'Have you ever heard of the drug atropine?'

'Yes.'

'What do you know about it?'

'It's something my father's made in his lab,' Gillian said.

'Do you know how atropine is taken?'

'No.'

'Did you have any atropine that night in the woods?'

'No!' Gillian insisted.

'Are you aware that traces of atropine were found in the thermos containing the iced tea your friends had brought?'

'Yes. Mr. Houlihan told me.'

'Yet you are testifying under oath today that you didn't have any?'

'I didn't. I don't do drugs.'

Jordan approached the witness stand. 'Is it possible you could have been given some by accident?'

'I didn't drink the iced tea.'

'Could the drug have been slipped into something else you drank that night?'

'No,' Gillian said firmly. 'The only thing I had to drink was a soda, before I left my house. I didn't have any of that stuff, I swear it.'

Jordan turned away from her. 'You know, Ms. Duncan, you've told us all quite a lot about what happened that night . . . but you don't always tell the truth, do you?'

Gillian's brows drew together. 'Yes, I do.'

'Isn't it a fact that you have a long history of misrepresenting what really occurred? That shortly after your mother's death, you were taken to a psychiatrist because of repeated episodes of lying to your father?'

'I was nine,' Gillian said. 'And I was really confused at the time. I'm a totally different person now, and my father and I are really close. I tell him everything.'

'Everything?' Jordan repeated.

'Yes.'

'Then why didn't you tell him where you were really going that night?'

Gillian's cheeks colored brightly. 'I . . . I . . .'

'That's all right, Ms. Duncan,' Jordan said, sliding into place beside Jack. 'We already know the answer.'

As soon as Judge Justice called for a fifteen-minute recess, Jack turned to his attorney. 'I need to take a leak,' he said. He glanced nervously over his shoulder, where reporters were streaming out of the courtroom to call in information about Gillian's testimony to the papers.

Jordan called over the deputy. 'Can you take my client down to –'

'Nope,' the man said. 'It's backed up in the holding cell. Plumber's down there now.'

Jordan grimaced. He didn't want to take Jack out of the plastic bubble of the courtroom, where he would be a moving target for the media or anyone else who wanted a piece of him. But hell, a leak was a leak. 'Come on,' he muttered. 'I'll take you.'

The moment they stepped outside, cameras exploded like a meteor shower, blinding Jordan temporarily. 'No comment,' he said, dragging Jack toward the men's room and shoving him inside. 'Hey, guys, a little privacy?' he begged of the reporters, and held the door closed.

Jack stepped up to the urinal. 'How do you think it's going?'

'I think it's early,' Jordan said.

Suddenly, a toilet flushed, and the door to one of the stalls swung open. 'Mr. Duncan,' Jordan said, anxious to avoid an incident before it started.

But the man held up a hand. He stopped just inches away from Jack, who was furiously working to zip up his pants.

'They should have cut it off,' Duncan said, then walked out of the bathroom, leaving Jack to stare after him.

* * *

'Dr. Paulson, did you have occasion to treat a patient by the name of Gillian Duncan on May first?' Matt asked.

The ER doctor was comfortable on the stand. 'Yes, I did.'

'At what time?'

'Approximately one-thirty a.m.'

'Did you have any medical information about her when you approached her?'

'Yes. An ER nurse had taken a history and physical. She had a BP of one twenty over eighty, and a rapid heart rate. She was alert and oriented and in no acute distress, although she was frightened. She'd come in alleging a forcible vaginal sexual assault.'

'How did you examine Gillian?'

'First I had her undress over a sheet,' Dr. Paulson said. 'Then I did a basic general exam. Chest and cardiac exams were unremarkable. The abdomen was soft, nontender, and nondistended with normal bowel sounds. There was no rebound tenderness. Some significant bruising was present on the patient's right wrist; I took pictures of these.'

Matt asked permission to approach the witness, then handed Dr. Paulson the pictures. 'Do you recognize these?'

'Yes. They're the photographs I took of the patient.'

'Do they fairly and accurately represent the bruises on Gillian Duncan that night?'

'Yes, they do.'

'I'd like to move them in as State's Exhibits Two and Three,' Matt said. 'Doctor, what other examinations did you perform that night?'

'A pelvic exam. The external genitalia were unremarkable, and there were no visible signs of forced penetration. I used a colposcope, which is basically a large magnifying glass with a light on it, to see inside the vaginal canal.'

'What did you find?'

'The vaginal vault was unremarkable, without lesions or semen. The cervix was closed and without cervical motion tenderness. The uterus was small, anteflexed and anteverted, and nontender, and the adnexa were nonpalpable and nontender. The patient didn't report anal penetration, so the rectovaginal exam was deferred.' The doctor smiled at the jury. 'It's a lot of medical jargon, but basically, she looked normal on the inside.'

'Is it unusual to find no lesions or bruising or abnormalities inside a patient who has reported a violent sexual assault?'

'No,' the doctor said. 'Sometimes you get bruising; sometimes you don't. The vagina is made for sexual intercourse and, quite frankly, can withstand an awful lot. Often traumatic intercourse can occur without leaving behind any visible vaginal proof.'

'So how can you tell if someone's had intercourse?'

'Only by the presence of semen. However, its absence doesn't rule out intercourse, either. A condom could have been involved. A man might have had a vasectomy.'

'Did you examine any other area, Doctor?'

'Yes. I examined the patient's thighs and groin.'

'What did you find?'

'With an ultraviolet lamp, I detected the presence of what appeared to be semen.'

'What did you do?'

'I took a sterile swab from a sexual assault evidence recovery kit and swabbed the area.'

'What did you do with it?'

'I put the swab in the paper envelope included in the kit. I wrote my name and the date and the patient's name on it, then sealed it and put my initials over the seal.'

'Did you take any other physical evidence from Gillian that night?'

'Yes. I did a pubic hair combing and put the evidence in the kit. I clipped her fingernails and collected each one in a separate, sterile white paper envelope, which was also included in the kit. Finally, I drew blood from the patient for a known sample, marked it, and put it in the kit.'

'After you marked and sealed all these envelopes and swabs and vials, what did you do with the kit?'

'I handed it to Detective Saxton, who had brought the patient in.'

'Between the time you collected all of this evidence and the time you turned it over to the detective, did anyone else have access to it?'

'No.'

'Did you treat Gillian?'

'Yes. We gave her a heavy dose of antibiotics to protect against venereal disease, and a pill to prevent pregnancy.'

Matt crossed to stand in front of the jury. 'Dr. Paulson, when you first walked into the ER cubicle . . . when you first saw Gillian . . . what did she look like?'

For the first time during her testimony, the doctor's professional demeanor slipped. 'Very pale, and quiet. Lethargic. She was skittish, too, about having me touch her.'

'Is that behavior you've seen before in your line of work?'

'Unfortunately, it is,' Dr. Paulson admitted. 'In victims of sexual abuse and sexual assault.'

'If there's no semen in the vagina, Doctor, you can't tell from a pelvic exam if someone has recently had intercourse . . . right?'

Dr. Paulson regarded Jordan coolly. 'No, you can't.'

'And there wasn't any semen visible during Gillian's pelvic exam?'

'No, there wasn't.'

'Isn't it also true that you didn't find any bruising inside Gillian's vagina?'

'That's right.'

'You didn't find any bruising on her external genitalia?'

'No.'

'Did you find bruises on her face?'

'No.'

'Her neck?'

'No.'

'How about her upper arm, or her thighs?'

'No. Only on her right wrist, Mr. McAfee.'

Jordan crossed to the jury box. 'You found semen on Ms. Duncan's inner thigh?'

'Yes.'

'Did you know that this victim had reported to Detective Saxton that she was sexually active at the time this happened?'

'That wasn't part of my exam,' Dr. Paulson said.

'So you have no way of knowing if that semen you swabbed from Gillian Duncan's thigh had anything to do with this alleged assault or with some other man she had sexual relations with recently.'

'No.'

'Doctor, isn't it true that there is no physical evidence that conclusively supports Ms. Duncan's claim of being subjected to violent sexual intercourse that night? That all we really have is what Gillian said happened?'

'That's correct.'

'Do you have any way of knowing whether she was lying?'

Dr. Paulson shook her head. 'I don't.'

Whitney O'Neill was a nervous wreck. She kept chewing her fingernails, to the point where Jordan expected them to bleed at any moment. It was a small miracle, in fact, that she'd even made it through the direct examination. 'So ten seconds after you left the clearing with Meg and Chelsea, you called out to Gillian?' Jordan said, wanting clarification.

Whitney bit her lower lip. 'Yeah, but she didn't answer.'

'No one had suggested, prior to her departure, that she stay with you? Do some kind of buddy system?'

'No,' Whitney said.

'How much longer after you called out to her did Gillian come running up to you?'

'Um, maybe like another ten or fifteen minutes.'

Jordan walked up to the map Matt had brought. 'Do you know how far it is from the edge of the cemetery to the point where you and your friends lit the bonfire?'

'No.'

'Fifty-two yards, Ms. O'Neill. That's half the length of a football field.' Jordan took a few steps forward. 'Do you have any idea how incredibly slow you'd have to walk in order for it to take fifteen minutes to cover fifty yards of ground?'

'I, um, it may –'

'You could have been blindfolded, going backward in crab walk, and it would take you five minutes, at the most.'

'Objection,' Matt sighed. 'He's badgering my witness.'

'Have a care, Mr. McAfee,' said the judge.

'My apologies,' Jordan told the girl, but anyone could see he wasn't all that sorry.

'Maybe it didn't take fifteen minutes, exactly,' Whitney whispered.

'Are you telling me that you lied a minute ago? Under oath?'

Whitney blanched. 'No. I mean, it just felt like forever. Or about fifteen minutes.'

Jordan shrugged. 'You know what? Let's compromise. Let's say it took ten. Does that seem fair?'

The girl nodded vigorously.

'While it was taking you ten minutes to walk the fifty-two yards, your friend was supposedly within fifty-two yards of you, being assaulted. Given that extremely brief distance, don't you think you might have heard something going on?'

Whitney swallowed. 'I didn't. It was too far away.'

'You didn't hear your friend calling out?'

'No.'

'You didn't hear branches breaking? Or a scuffle?'

'No.'

Jordan stared at her for a moment. Then he asked for permission to approach the bench. 'Judge, I'd like a little leeway for a physical demonstration.'

Judge Justice narrowed her eyes. 'Mental browbeating isn't enough?'

'I'd like to make this particular point a little more realistic for the jury.'

'Your Honor,' Matt said, 'it's completely inappropriate for Mr. McAfee to re-create the scenario that night.'

The judge looked from one man to the other, then to the witness cowering on the stand. 'You know, Mr. Houlihan, I'm gonna allow this. Go ahead, Mr. McAfee.'

Jordan took a yardstick from Selena in the gallery. 'I'm just going to measure off fifty-two yards,' he explained. He paced his way down the aisle of the courtroom, through the double doors, and into the lobby. Conversation stopped as he continued past the banks of blue chairs and the office of the clerk of the court and a few vending machines. Finally, he rapped the yardstick on the floor and peered down the straight course, to where the witness sat. 'Ms. O'Neill,' he called, 'can you hear me?'

He saw her nod her head, saw her lips form the word yes.

Jordan strode back to the courtroom. 'Thank you,' he said. 'That's all.'

Whitney started to rise, intent on getting off the witness stand as quickly as possible. But before she could, Matt rose, furious. 'Redirect, Your Honor,' he barked. 'Ms. O'Neill, did you just hear Mr. McAfee call out to you from fifty-two yards away?'

'Um, yes.'

Matt pointed to the rear of the courtroom. 'If Mr. McAfee had been fifty-two yards away but pinned to the ground with someone else's hand over his mouth and fighting for his life against a rapist, do you think you would have been able to hear him call out?'

'N-no,' Whitney said.

Matt turned on his heel. 'Nothing further.'

At the breakfast table that morning, Thomas had asked if Jordan was going to cross-examine Chelsea Abrams. 'Don't know for sure,' he'd answered. 'It depends on what she says on direct.'

Thomas's shoulders had rounded so much his face had nearly

dipped into his cereal bowl. 'Just do me one favor,' Thomas had said. 'Try not to be a dick.'

That, in a nutshell, was why Jordan was going to blast Chelsea Abrams's testimony to pieces. Because the pretty girl looking up at him with a tiny smile was seeing him as Thomas's dad when she should have been considering him an adversary.

'Ms. Abrams,' Jordan said, standing up to do his cross, 'tell me again who was there that night in the woods.'

Confusion clouded Chelsea's eyes as she realized Jordan meant business. 'Meg, Whitney, Gilly, and me.'

'And Jack, my client?'

'Yeah.'

'And Jack left first.'

'Yes.'

'The rest of you, though, were standing together for a minute before you went home?'

'Yes.'

'So if anyone said something before you left, the four of you would have heard it?'

'Sure.'

'You testified that before you left, you asked Gillian whether she wanted you to walk her home.'

'Yes.'

'Where was Whitney standing when you asked this?'

'Right next to me.'

'After you and Whitney and Meg left, did anyone say anything?'

'No,' Chelsea said. 'We just walked down the path single file.'

He looked at the jurors, hoping to hell that every single one of them remembered that Whitney had said something different. 'Isn't it true that April thirtieth, the night you all met in the woods, was Beltane?'

He had to give her credit: Chelsea looked blankly at him. 'What?'

'Isn't Beltane a sabbat, according to the earth-based Wiccan religion?'

'I haven't got a clue.'

'Objection,' Matt said. 'The witness obviously can't answer this line of questioning.'

'Your Honor, if you'd just give me a moment –'

'So this time you can measure your way to Kentucky?' Matt said under his breath.

Jordan scowled. 'This goes toward my argument, Your Honor.'

'I'm giving you one more question, Mr. McAfee,' the judge warned.

'Isn't it true, Ms. Abrams, that you and your friends had gone to the clearing that night to celebrate Beltane, just as witches all over the world were doing at that time?'

At the prosecutor's table, Matt Houlihan was choking on something. Or maybe just trying to keep from laughing out loud. 'Objection!'

But before the judge could respond, Chelsea did. Her cheeks were bright with anger, and her expression was one only a teenager could manage, putting Jordan in a mental place she reserved for slugs and sewer refuse. 'I don't know *what* you're talking about, or what all this Bel-*whatever* stuff is. My friends and I went to chill. Period.'

'Mr. McAfee,' the judge said, 'you will move on. *Now.*'

The jury was looking at Jordan with nearly the same scorn as Chelsea. Okay, so maybe he'd pushed a little hard . . . and what he was driving at was, admittedly, nuts. He'd dismiss the witness. With luck, it would all work out in the end and Thomas would still be speaking to him.

Thomas.

Jordan silently winged an apology to his son. 'Ms. Abrams, do you wear jewelry?'

Again, that look. God, was it something they were teaching in public schools these days? 'No,' she said.

'No earrings?'

'Sometimes, I guess.'

'No bracelet or necklace or ring?'

'No.'

'Isn't it true that you're actually wearing a necklace right now?'

'Yes,' she said tightly.

'And isn't it true that you never take that necklace off your body?'

'Well, I –'

'Could you show it to us?'

Chelsea looked to the prosecutor for permission. Then she slowly tugged a long chain from the neckline of her blouse, to reveal the five-pointed star.

'What is that symbol, Ms. Abrams?'

'I don't know. I just think it's pretty.'

'Are you aware that a five-pointed star is called a pentagram?'

'No.'

'And that the pentagram is a symbol of pagan religions . . . the same groups that would have been celebrating Beltane the night of April thirtieth?'

Chelsea slipped the necklace beneath her collar again. 'It's just a necklace.'

'Of course . . . and you and your friends were just *chilling* that night.'

'Objection!'

'Withdrawn,' Jordan said. 'Nothing further.'

Later that day
Carroll County Courthouse

Oh, God, it hurt to see him here.

The moment Addie had been escorted into the courtroom as a witness, her eyes had zeroed in on Jack. Her heart hurt so badly she had to slide her hand inside her jacket, just to press down against the ache. When he smiled at her and nodded, as if to say she could get through this, Addie thought she was going to burst into tears.

Please, God, she prayed, as she was sworn in. *Just a small earthquake. A fire. Anything that will just stop this whole nightmare, right now, before I have to become a contributing party.*

At that moment, the doors of the courtroom burst open, and her father pushed his way inside. 'Dad!' He was carrying a huge basket, from which came the most delicious smell. Steam rose from beneath a blue checkerboard cloth that was tucked over the contents. He hurried down the aisle toward the bench and winked at his daughter. 'You knock 'em dead, honey,' Roy said. 'I gotta give these out while they're still hot.'

Setting the basket beside the court stenographer's machine, he opened up the napkin, filling the room with the aroma of freshly baked muffins. 'Here, Your Honor. You're the head honcho, so you get the first bite.'

By that time, Althea Justice had recovered her voice. 'Mr . . .'

'Peabody, at your service. You can call me Roy.'

'Mr. Peabody,' the judge said, 'you cannot come barging into the middle of a trial.'

'Oh, I'm not barging.' Roy began to place muffins on the

defense table, in front of the prosecutor, into the outstretched hands of the jury. 'Consider me the chuck wagon.'

'Be that as it may . . . is that *peanut butter?*'

'Good nose, ma'am. PB & J muffins. What makes mine different, though, is that the peanut butter is mixed right into the batter, instead of set in the center like the jelly. Comfort food, which I figured you all could use about now.' He hefted the basket and turned to the gallery. 'The rest are for you all,' Roy said. 'Except I wasn't counting on there being quite so many. So maybe you could all just share with your neighbor.'

'Your Honor,' Matt said, incensed, 'this man has no right to be here. He's a sequestered witness, for God's sake.'

Jordan swallowed a bite of the muffin. 'Ah, come on, Houlihan, don't get your knickers in a knot. He's just bringing us a treat.'

'He's blatantly trying to influence the jury,' Matt snapped. '*Look* at them.'

Every juror was either in the throes of peeling back the cupcake liner at the base of the muffin or stuffing a bite into his or her mouth. 'Mr. Peabody,' the judge said, her mouth full, 'I'm afraid I'm going to have to ask you to leave until you're called by the defense.'

'I understand, Your Honor.'

'You didn't happen to bring any milk, did you?' she asked.

Roy grinned. 'Next time. I promise.'

'There will not be a next time,' Matt thundered. 'I want the record to reflect that I object to this . . . this shenanigan McAfee's dreamed up.'

'Me?' Jordan cried. 'I didn't tell him to play Betty Crocker!'

'Mr. Houlihan, your objection will be so noted, after the court reporter has finished her snack,' the judge said. 'Now, really. This was nothing more than a lovely surprise, I'm sure. You go on and eat, and then we'll resume with your witness.'

'I will not eat that muffin,' Matt vowed.

The judge raised her brows. 'Well, Mr. Houlihan, it's a free country.'

Roy waved off thank-yous and exited.

'Your Honor,' Jordan said. 'Approach?'

The attorneys walked toward the bench. 'Yes, Mr. McAfee?' prompted the judge.

'If the county attorney isn't going to eat his, can I have it?'

Judge Justice shook her head. 'I'm afraid that isn't for me to say.'

'I hope you're enjoying this,' Matt snarled to Jordan. 'I hope you can sleep nights, knowing you've turned a rape trial into a farce.' He stalked back to his table and provocatively set his untouched muffin on the corner closest to the defense. 'The state calls Addie Peabody,' he said.

For over ten minutes, Addie had not let herself make eye contact with Jack. *You can get through this,* she told herself. *Just answer the questions*. 'You're not here today voluntarily, are you, Ms. Peabody?' Houlihan asked.

'No,' she admitted.

'You're still involved in a relationship with Jack St. Bride.'

'Yes.'

'Can you tell us what happened after you found him outside, unconscious?'

Addie twisted her hands in her lap. 'When he came to, I got him up to the bedroom. I cleaned him up with a washcloth, and we both fell asleep.'

'Did you get a good look at his face, Ms. Peabody?'

'Yes. His face had cuts all over it, and his eye was swelling shut.'

'Where was he scratched?'

'Over his eye, on his forehead.'

'Were there any scratches on his cheek?' the prosecutor asked.

'No.'

'How long did you sleep?'

'A couple of hours.'

'What woke you up?'

'I don't know. I think the fact that he wasn't sleeping beside me anymore.'

'What did you do?'

'I went to go look for him . . . and heard a noise coming from my daughter's room.'

'Was that unusual?'

Addie took a deep breath. 'Yes,' she said. 'My daughter died seven years ago.'

'Did you go in?'

Addie began to pull at a thread on the hem of her skirt. She thought of how life could happen that way – one slipped stitch, and suddenly the most solid binding could fall apart. 'He was boxing up her things,' she said softly. 'Stripping the bed.'

The county attorney nodded sympathetically. 'Did you argue?'

'Yes, for a few minutes.'

'Did the fight become physical?'

'No.'

'How did it end?'

She'd been sworn in and had known it would come to this moment – the point where her words might as well have been arrows, aimed right at Jack's heart. 'I told him I wanted him to leave.'

'Did he?'

'Yes.'

And if she hadn't forced him out, he wouldn't have been in the woods that night. He wouldn't have been anywhere near Gillian Duncan. It was what she'd wondered a thousand times . . . how could the blame have come to rest heavily on Jack, when she herself was so clearly at fault?

'What time was it when Mr. St. Bride left?'

'About nine forty-five.'

'When did you next see the defendant?'

'About one-thirty in the morning,' Addie whispered. 'At the diner.'

'Can you describe his physical appearance?'

Every word ripped into her. 'His cuts, they were bleeding again. He had a scratch on his cheek, and dirt on his clothes, and he reeked of liquor.'

'What did he say to you?'

Addie took a deep breath. 'That it had been a tough night.'

'Ms. Peabody,' Matt asked, 'was Mr. St. Bride with you between the hours of nine forty-five p.m. and one-thirty a.m.?'

She exhaled heavily but didn't reply.

'Ms. Peabody?'

The judge leaned toward her. 'You're going to have to give a response.'

She wanted to answer, but she wanted the answer to be the *right* one. She wanted to look the prosecutor in the eye and tell him that he had collared the wrong man, that the Jack she knew was not the person who had committed this horrible crime.

She wanted to save him, like he had saved her.

Lifting her face, Addie said, 'Yes, he was.'

The county attorney turned, shock written all over his face. 'I beg your pardon?'

'Yes,' Addie repeated, her voice stronger. 'He was with me that whole night.'

Houlihan narrowed his gaze. 'You're aware you're under oath, Ms. Peabody. Perjury is a criminal act.'

Her eyes were shining, damp. 'He was with me.'

'Really,' the prosecutor said. 'Where?'

Addie's hands stole over her heart, as if that might be enough to keep it from breaking. 'Right here.'

'When the police came to arrest Jack, what were you thinking?'

At Jordan's question, Addie looked up. 'I really didn't know what to think. It wasn't my finest hour.'

'What do you mean?'

'I was in shock. There had been rumors around town . . .'

'Rumors?'

'That Jack had done time in jail.'

'Did he ever tell you that he'd been convicted for sexual assault?'

'He told me that a girl had wrongly accused him of carrying on an intimate relationship. One of his students. And that he plea-bargained the case on the advice of his lawyer, because it was the way to serve the least time and put the whole thing behind him.'

Jordan frowned. 'But he specifically said he wasn't guilty?'

'Over and over,' Addie answered.

'And you believed him?'

'One hundred percent,' she vowed. 'But so many people in town were . . . well, they were like vultures, waiting to strike. And I guess I got so used to hearing people expect the worst of Jack that when the police came, at first, I . . . I did too.' She frowned. 'It wasn't until I sat down later and really thought, *This is Jack they took. Jack.* Then I knew that he couldn't ever have done what they said.'

'Ms. Peabody, you saw Jack being beaten up by five men that night?'

'Yes.'

'Was he fighting back?'

She shook her head. 'He passed out.'

'Did you call the police?' Jordan asked.

'No.'

'Why not?'

Addie looked at Matt Houlihan, then at the judge. She leaned toward the bench and whispered something to Althea Justice, who nodded.

'I didn't call the police,' Addie said, 'because I thought they might have been involved.'

When court adjourned for the day, Jordan handed his briefcase over the railing of the gallery to Selena. 'Try to get some rest,' he told Jack. A deputy cuffed him and led him silently through the tunnels that wound beneath the courthouse parking lot to the jail. Once they'd been buzzed inside, a guard took over Jack's transformation back to prisoner, leading him into the room near the jail entrance to strip. 'We'll take these right down to the dry cleaner and have 'em pressed,' the CO joked, folding Jack's trousers over his arm. Because Jack had left the premises, the guard waited until he was naked and then checked Jack's mouth, nostrils, ears, and anus for contraband.

This Jack St. Bride was a different man than the one who had come through the door two months ago in protective custody. His face was a blank wash of expression, like every other prisoner rotting in his cell. He shrugged out of his civilian clothes like a snake giving up its skin, as if he knew that it wouldn't fit him in this next stage of his life. Through the violation of the cavity search, Jack closed his eyes and did what he was told.

It didn't matter anymore, none of it. He'd seen the faces of the men and women on that jury – the way they'd cried along with Gillian Duncan, the slanted looks they knifed at him that they thought he surely could not feel. He'd watched his own attorney leave the courtroom, headed home to his own life – one that didn't factor in the innocence or guilt of Jack St. Bride and that wouldn't change, no matter what verdict was handed down.

Jack fell into step beside the guard and walked, docile as a fawn, toward his cell. *Get used to this,* he thought.

He might not yet have been sentenced, but it was only a matter of time.

'Oh my God,' Gillian said, sitting up on her bed the minute Meg opened the door of the bedroom. 'You have no idea how glad I am to see you.' The door cracked open a little wider, and Gillian saw her father standing behind her Meg. 'Daddy,' she said, startled.

His eyes were dark, hooded. 'I didn't know if you were up to a visit.'

'I am,' Gillian said quickly. 'Really.' She grabbed Meg's hand and yanked her inside, then waited for her father to close the door and leave them in privacy.

It was, Meg thought, as if their fight about the drugs in the thermos had never happened. Gillian fluttered around her like a gypsy moth, buzzing about the trial and the witnesses and who had said what. 'You have no idea how much I want to talk to Whit and Chelsea,' she chattered. 'But I'm sequestered, in case I need to be recalled by one of the lawyers later. Still, I heard that Whit was peeing in her pants. And that Thomas's father was a total prick to Chelsea.'

'That's his job,' Meg said, her mouth dry.

Gillian stepped in front of her. 'What's been said about me?'

'Nothing.'

'Oh, right. You haven't been on the stand yet. Do you think you'll be called tomorrow? It's not so bad, really. One of the jurors has the most disgusting mole on the side of her neck. I swear I couldn't stop looking at it the whole time –'

'I'm not testifying,' Meg mumbled.

'You're not?'

She shook her head. 'Mr. Houlihan, he changed his mind.'

Dumbfounded, Gilly stared at Meg. 'If this is something you're pulling because of that atropine . . .'

'Jesus, Gilly . . . does everything have to be about *you*?' Meg turned away, mortified. 'He touched me,' she confessed. 'He put his hands all over me, Gilly. I remembered.'

Beside her, Gillian stood like a stone sentry. 'He did not.' She raked angry eyes over Meg's disheveled form, her double chin, her dimpled arms. Her nostrils flared, once.

'Then why do I remember it?' Meg cried. 'Why can I feel his hands on my –'

'No!' Gillian slapped her so hard Meg's head snapped back and the red-pencil print of a hand stamped her cheek. Tears ran down Meg's face, and her nose was running, and she couldn't manage to hold onto a single thought. 'He did not touch you,' Gillian said. 'Do you understand?'

Meg nodded quickly.

'He touched *me*.' Gillian grabbed Meg's arm and squeezed it. 'Say it!'

'He touched you,' Meg sobbed.

'Good,' Gillian said, the fierce fire in her eyes banking. She reached for Meg, cradling her friend against her chest, wrapping her tight in her arms. She stroked Meg's cheek until the red print faded, then leaned down and pressed a kiss to her damp skin. 'That's right,' Gillian whispered. 'Don't forget.'

The jury was sluggish the next morning, something not helped by the first witness – a retired FBI soil analyst older than Methuselah who used far too many chemical terms to explain that the dirt found in the treads of Jack's boot was consistent with the known soil sample taken from the crime scene. By the time the prosecutor put his forensic scientist on the stand to explain DNA, Jordan almost felt sorry for him. Would the judge declare a mistrial if the entire jury went into a coma?

But Jordan had been counting on a typical DNA scientist – a brainy geek with a receding hairline and a technical vocabulary. What he got instead was Frankie Martine.

She easily could have moonlighted as a Playboy model, with her bee-stung lips and long blond hair and hourglass figure. Jordan glanced at the jury and wasn't surprised to find them all sitting up, listening. Hell, she could have recited a grocery list, and the six men in that box would have given her their undivided attention.

'You get half of your DNA from your mother, and half from your father,' Frankie said. 'You know how people say, "Oh, I've got my mom's nose . . . or my dad's chin.' In the same manner, we inherit thousands of genetic traits that mean nothing to anyone but us geeky forensic scientists.' She smiled at the jury. 'You with me?'

They all nodded. And the jury foreman, a bald man with a protruding belly, winked.

Surely he'd imagined that. Jordan did a double take as Frankie Martine continued, unfazed. 'For example, the average Joe doesn't know that he's CSF1P0 type twelve, thirteen . . . yet that's something that could come in handy if he's ever accused of a crime and the perp leaves behind DNA evidence of being CSF1P0 type ten, eleven.'

Jordan glanced at the jury box and nearly fell off his seat as the jury foreman winked again at the witness.

'Objection,' he said, standing up.

Matt Houlihan looked at him as if he were crazy, with good reason. Nothing Frankie Martine had said was objectionable.

'On what grounds, Mr. McAfee?'

He felt heat creeping up from his collar. 'Distraction, Your Honor.'

The judge frowned. 'Get up here, counsel.' Jordan and Matt approached the bench, hesitating at the scowl on the justice's face. 'You want to tell me what you're up to now?'

'Your Honor, I believe that the witness is distracting certain members of the jury,' Jordan said in a rush.

'Which members?'

The ones with Y chromosomes, Jordan thought. 'The foreman, in particular. I think Ms. Martine's physical attributes have, um, caught his eye.'

Matt Houlihan started to laugh. 'You have got to be kidding. The witness is a professional forensic scientist.'

'She's also quite . . . attractive.'

'What do you want me to do? Have her testify with a paper bag over her head?'

'The foreman keeps winking at her,' Jordan said. 'I have reason to believe that he's not concentrating on the task at hand.'

'Why does this happen in *my* court?' The judge sighed. 'I will not stand for you talking about the witness this way, Mr. McAfee. Even if you can't get your own mind out of the gutter, I have faith that the members of our jury can. Your objection is overruled.'

Jordan slunk back to his seat. The prosecutor approached his witness, shook his head, and continued. 'Ms. Martine, why is DNA used to profile evidence?'

'Let me put it in simple terms,' she said. 'You're driving to work and you're side-swiped by another vehicle. When you call to make a police report, they ask you to describe the car. The more information you give them, the more likely they'll be able to track down the exact car. So, if you tell the police only that the car was blue, well, it's not very helpful to their search, since there are blue trucks, blue cars, blue vans, of all makes and models. However, if you tell them that it was a blue Acura 1991 hatchback, with a sunroof and a SAY NO TO DRUGS bumper sticker, the easier it will be for them not only to find a car matching that description but also to determine that it was indeed the car that side-swiped you. The more characteristics you give, the smaller the pool of suspect cars becomes.

'Similarly, the more genetic characteristics I can give you about the evidence results in the more people I can eliminate. Therefore, when you do find a person who matches the profile, the less likely it is that someone else exists with the exact same criteria.'

'How complex is the analysis?'

'Very,' Frankie said. 'By its nature, it has to be extremely sensitive.'

'What precautions do you take to avoid contamination during your analysis of the evidence?' Matt asked.

'I work on only one piece of evidence at a time, label it immediately, and close it before I begin work on the next piece. I always work on the evidence before working on the known blood samples, and clean my scissors, forceps, and work surface between samples. I change my lab coats and gloves frequently and use as many disposable supplies as necessary, so there is no carry-over or contamination of DNA. Finally, I have designated samples during my analysis that contain no intentionally added DNA. If at any point in the procedure I detect DNA in these samples, I assume all the samples are contaminated, and I start over.'

The prosecutor turned around and slipped on a pair of plastic gloves. Then he held up a girl's blouse, spotted with blood. 'Ms. Martine,' he said, 'do you recognize this?'

'Yes. It's the blouse I was asked to test.'

Matt entered the clothing into evidence, and then asked Frankie to identify each swab and envelope and vial that had come from the rape kit. 'After testing all these items, what were your results?'

Frankie slipped a chart onto an overhead projector. This was the point at which a forensic scientist usually lost her audience. Unfortunately, Jordan thought, grimacing, that probably wasn't going to be the case here. The jury could see her legs, which – Jordan couldn't help but notice – were damn nice.

Item	CSF 1P0	TPOX	TH01	VWA	D16 S539	D7 S820	D13 S317	D5 S818
100	12, 12	8,11	6, 7	17, 17	12, 14	9, 12	9, 13	12, 12
200	12, 12	11,11	6, 7	15, 15	13, 13	8, 8	11, 11	10, 12
Shirt	12, 12	11,11	6, 7	15, 15	13, 13	8, 8	11, 11	10, 12
Nails	12, 12	11, (8)	6, 7	17, (15)	12, 14, (13)	9, 12, (8)	9, 13, (11)	12, (10)
Thigh	N/A	8, (11)	6, (7)	17, (15)	N/A	12, (8), (9)	13, (9), (11)	12, (10)

Appropriately, Frankie did a striptease of the chart, revealing each line only as she spoke about it. 'Line one hundred,' Frankie explained, 'is everything I can tell you about the victim's known blood sample. And each of those eight weird combinations of letters and numbers to the right is an area on the DNA chain. Think of it like that side-swiping car . . . the first column is the make of the car. The second column is the model. The third is the color . . . all the way up to the eighth column, the bumper sticker. At each location, the victim received one allele from her mother, and one from her father. For example, at the CSF1P0 location, Ms. Duncan inherited a type twelve from each of her parents.

'Line two hundred is the defendant's known blood sample. Each pair of numbers at those eight loci are alleles *he* inherited from *his* mother and father.' She pointed to the row beneath that. 'On the shirt Mr. Houlihan held up, I extracted DNA from the bloodstains. You'll see that at each location, the profile of the stains matches the profile of Mr. St. Bride.'

'How many other people might have a profile that matches the evidence?'

'It's not possible to DNA-type everyone in the world, so I apply a mathematical formula that helps me predict the answer to that question. According to my calculations, that profile is found only once in greater than six billion, which is the approximate population of the world.'

'Can you explain the next row to us?' Matt asked.

'I know that the DNA profile detected under Ms. Duncan's fingernails is consistent with a mixture, because at certain locations, there are three numbers – and a person inherits only two alleles. This isn't surprising. Ms. Duncan can't be eliminated as a possible cocontributor to the genetic material in this mixture, since I expect cells from her own hands were present. Of particular interest is whose DNA is mixed with hers. And based on the numbers in the profile of Mr. St. Bride – row two hundred – he cannot be eliminated as a cocontributor.'

'What would have eliminated him, Ms. Martine?'

'If a number came up at a location that was nowhere in his own genetic profile.'

'But that isn't the case in this particular mixture?'

'No,' Frankie said. 'It's two hundred forty million times more likely that the defendant is the cocontributor to that sample than a randomly chosen individual in the population.'

'And the thigh line?'

She frowned. 'That was a sample of semen, found on the thigh swab. Here, two locations I tested yielded inconclusive results.'

'What does that mean?'

'There wasn't enough DNA present to profile all eight loci,' Frankie said. 'In the remaining six, Mr. St. Bride could not be eliminated. It is seven hundred forty thousand times more likely that Mr. St. Bride is a cocontributor to the semen sample than another person chosen randomly from the population.'

'Thank you, Ms. Martine,' the prosecutor said.

And the jury foreman winked.

* * *

First, the cat died.

Now, it wasn't such a big thing, taken by itself. Magnolia had been suffering with diabetes for three years, and twelve was pretty old for a cat. It had happened, her mother said, while Chelsea was at court, testifying on behalf of poor Gillian.

That afternoon, her little brother had fallen off a jungle gym and broken his arm in three places.

'When it rains,' her father said, 'it pours.'

But they didn't know about the Law of Three; they didn't understand that all it took was one pebble to start an avalanche of dynamic proportion. What you did came back to you triple-fold – both the good . . . and the bad. Chelsea wasn't sure how much of that shit she believed, but she did know some things: She'd sworn an oath in a court of law and had gotten on the stand, and this was what had come of it. Her pet, her brother – by karmic proportions, she had one more devastation coming her way, to make up for what she'd done.

At dinner that night, she stared at her parents intently. Her mother had a mammogram scheduled the next day. Would it turn out to be cancer? Her father was planning on driving back to work that night . . . would he crash unexpectedly? Would she stop breathing, just like that, in her sleep? Would she wake up and find the Devil sitting beside her?

'Chelsea,' her mother said, 'you haven't touched your food.'

She couldn't stand not knowing what tragedy was coming. Pushing away from the table, she ran upstairs and locked her bedroom door behind her and rummaged through her drawers, finally finding what she'd so carefully buried.

Could you wipe out your misdeeds with good intentions, like an abacus working in reverse? Chelsea didn't know. But she tied the small bundle tight, with three knots. She stuffed it into a padded envelope that had come from an online CD store. She scrawled a new address across the front, added stamps, and ran out of her house with her parents' concerned questions trailing her like the string of a kite.

She ran until she reached the end of the block, where the big blue mailbox sat. Collection times, it said, were at 10 a.m. and 2 p.m. With shaking hands, Chelsea dropped the packet into the moaning mouth of the box. She did not think of Gillian. She did not think of anything that might change her mind. Instead, she focused on climbing the slippery slope of hope, which promised her that by noon tomorrow, her life might turn itself around.

'You analyzed the pubic hair combings in the rape kit, didn't you, Ms. Martine?' Jordan said, getting up from his seat.

'Yes.'

'What did you find?'

'No hairs with DNA foreign to the victim.'

Jordan raised his brows. 'Isn't it extremely difficult to violently rape someone without leaving behind a single pubic hair?'

'I see it all the time. We don't normally even test pubic hair when we have DNA, since hairs can be transferred in the most innocent of ways. For example, when you went into the bathroom during the last recess, Mr. McAfee, you probably came away with other people's pubic hair on your shoes, yet I'll assume that you weren't committing rape.'

She looked lovely, Jordan thought, even when she was reaming him. Abandoning that line of defense, he said, 'You testified that the blood found on the victim's shirt is a match for the defendant's, isn't that correct?'

'No. I testified that the locations I tested matched.'

'Whatever.' Jordan waved away the distinction. 'Can you tell whether the blood you tested came from a scratch on the defendant's cheek . . . or from a cut above his eye?'

'No.'

'Is it possible to tell from the blood on the shirt whether he was scratched by a human, or by a branch?'

'No,' Frankie said, then shrugged. 'However, DNA was found beneath the victim's fingernails, a mixture from which the defendant couldn't be excluded as a cocontributor.'

'Was the victim wearing nail polish?'

She smiled a little. 'As a matter of fact, she was. Candy-apple red. The nails were fairly long, too, which made for a very good sample of skin cells beneath.'

'Do you have to scratch someone to get his skin under your fingernails?'

'Not necessarily.'

'You can get his skin beneath your fingernails if you massage his scalp, right?'

'I suppose so.'

'Or if you gently rake your hand down his arm while you're flirting?'

The forensic scientist made a face that let him know what she thought of his alternative scenario. 'It's possible.'

'Let's examine some of the evidence,' Jordan said. 'The semen and the nail residue . . . those are both mixtures of DNA?'

'Yes.'

'Presumably, they're mixtures of the two known samples you have here – Ms. Duncan's and Mr. St. Bride's?'

'Possibly, yes.'

'Then how come the two lines aren't identical?'

'You're noticing the discrepancies in intensities – the numbers that are parenthesized versus the numbers that aren't. And those can come from a variety of sources,' Frankie explained. 'If we did the mixture of the DNA in the lab, it would be very precise – two drops of each cocontributor's blood. But a mixture that was handed to us to analyze may not be equally divided between the two contributors. Obviously, in the fingernail residue mixture I wasn't detecting as much DNA from the cocontributor as I was from the victim.'

'But if we're talking about semen, shouldn't there be a pretty good amount of DNA from the male?'

'Depends on how much sperm he has in it,' Frankie said. 'If he's a frequent ejaculator, he won't have much sperm. If he's a crack addict, he won't have much sperm. If he's an alcoholic or a diabetic, he won't have much sperm. Many factors are involved.'

'To your knowledge, Ms. Martine, is the defendant a frequent ejaculator?'

'I have no idea.'

'Do you know if he's a crack addict?'

'No.'

'Do you know if he's alcoholic or a diabetic?'

'Again, no.'

Jordan rocked back on his heels. 'So when you looked at those two different mixture profiles . . . it didn't bother you to see so many incongruities between them?'

She hesitated. 'An intensity difference isn't really an incongruity. Sometimes we'll see a number come up in parentheses that we didn't expect . . . but that can be due to many things – from the percentage of each contributor's DNA in the mixture, to whether or not the contributors are related. We don't exclude a suspect based on such an infinitesimal differentiation.'

'There's a big difference between being two hundred forty *million* times more likely than anyone else to be a cocontributor – such as in the fingernail sample – or being seven hundred forty *thousand* times more likely to be a cocontributor – like in the semen sample.'

'That's true.'

'What if you'd had results at the two locations that dropped out?'

'That's a big if, Mr. McAfee,' Frankie said. 'It's possible that your client might have been excluded. It's also possible that he might have been further *included*.'

'Isn't it true that certain labs test more than eight locations?' Jordan asked.

'Yes. The FBI lab does thirteen.'

'Isn't it possible that if you typed more systems, you might have excluded Jack as a suspect?'

'Yes.' She looked at the jury. 'If you narrow the search even further, to a 1991 blue Acura hatchback with a sunroof and bumper sticker . . . *and* a cracked windshield and dent on the fender and all-weather tires, the group of potential suspects shrinks even more.'

'Did the state ask you to perform this additional test?'

'Our state lab doesn't yet have that capability.'

'Ms. Martine, if you don't mind, may I add a line to your chart?' When she nodded, Jack walked up to the projector and set down a handwritten sheet, adding a new profile.

Item	CSF 1P0	TPOX	TH01	VWA	D16 S539	D7 S820	D13 S317	D5 S818
New	N/A	8, 8	6, 6	17, 15	N/A	8, 12	11, 13	10, 12

'Ms. Martine, is this sample different from the known sample you profiled of Jack St. Bride?'

'Yes.'

'So it would have come from a different person?'

'Theoretically,' Frankie said.

'Now, if you don't mind . . . could you estimate what we might see in a controlled mixture of line one hundred and the new sample . . . Gillian Duncan and a hypothetical suspect?'

Frankie picked up a marker and began to write on the bottom of her chart.

Item	CSF 1P0	TPOX	TH01	VWA	D16 S539	D7 S820	D13 S317	D5 S818
New	N/A	8, 8	6, 6	17, 15	N/A	8, 12	11, 13	10, 12
100	12, 12	8, 11	6, 7	17, 17	12, 14	9, 12	9, 13	12, 12
100 + New	N/A	8, (11)	6, (7)	17, (15)	N/A	12, (8), (9)	13, (9), (11)	12, (10)

'Ms. Martine,' Jordan asked, 'what does that line remind you of?'

'The semen profile.'

'So could the person who gave this hypothetical blood sample have been a contributor to the semen mixture?'

'Yes, this person would not be ruled out, either.'

'Then it's possible that there's someone *other* than Jack St. Bride walking around out there . . . someone with this particular DNA makeup, for example . . . who might be included as a suspect?'

Frankie met his eye. 'Anything's possible, Mr. McAfee, but my lab deals with concrete evidence. I didn't have this hypothetical blood sample, and I don't know this hypothetical suspect. But when you find him? You give me a call . . . and I'll run the tests.'

As Charlie tried to concentrate on the prosecutor's questions, his attention kept straying to Addie Peabody.

She sat behind the defense, almost in a direct line from Jack St. Bride, her eyes boring a hole into the back of the man's neck. Her hair was slipping out of a bun, and her suit – the only one she had, he'd bet – was wrinkled as a newborn's skin.

He didn't want to be there. He wanted to be home, unraveling the mystery that was his daughter. He wanted to grab Addie and shake her until all the truths Meg had confessed to her spilled onto the floor at Charlie's feet.

'What was her demeanor at that time?' Matt was asking, the words swimming to Charlie from a long tunnel.

Frightened. Withdrawn. Numb.

He had wanted to run home after Chelsea's testimony, to grab Meg and ask her if she, too, was a witch. But he had already accused her once, and look at where it had gotten him. What if he did it a second time? How much damage could be done before the bond between a father and his daughter was irretrievably broken?

Broken.

He didn't realize he'd spoken aloud until Matt asked another question. 'After you took her statement, what did you do?'

'I went to the station and typed up an affidavit for an arrest warrant,' Charlie said.

'Did you obtain this warrant?'

'Yes.'

'Where did you go to serve it?'

'Addie Peabody's house,' Charlie answered, and although he did not look her way, he could feel her straighten in her seat. 'I asked for Mr. St. Bride and told him he was under arrest for the aggravated felonious sexual assault of Gillian Duncan the previous evening.'

'What happened?'

'He said he was nowhere near her that night.'

'Did you ever go back to the clearing behind the cemetery?'

'Yes, the next morning.'

'What did you find?'

'The remnants of a bonfire,' Charlie said. 'Some spots where leaves were kicked around. A boot print.'

'Did you find a condom?'

'No.'

'A condom wrapper?'

'No.'

'Did you see Gillian again the next day?'

'Yeah,' Charlie murmured. 'I stopped in to check up on her.'

'How did she look?'

The way Meg does now, Charlie realized, and as he stared into the dark, empty eyes of Jack St. Bride, he could feel himself drowning.

Jordan stalked toward the witness before the prosecutor had even settled in his chair. 'The search you did at the cemetery wasn't the only search you did in conjunction with this case, was it?'

'No.'

'In fact, Detective, you searched your own daughter's room and found evidence that you believed was connected, correct?'

A memory flashed between them: Jordan sitting on the edge of Charlie's couch, as he awkwardly confessed his suspicions to the policeman. 'Yes.'

Jordan took an item from the prosecutor's table, one he'd requested to have brought along. 'Do you recognize this?'

'Yes. It's a ribbon I found.'

'Where?'

'In my daughter's closet.'

'What else did you find with this ribbon?' Jordan asked.

'Some plastic cups, and a thermos.'

'Was there a powdery residue in them?'

'Yes.'

'Which you had tested.'

Charlie nodded. 'Yes.'

'That powder was atropine, wasn't it?'

'That's what I was told,' he admitted.

'Do you know what atropine is?'

'A drug,' Charlie said.

'Isn't it true that atropine can occasionally produce side effects consistent with more traditional recreational drugs?'

'Yes.'

'So, in fact, Detective, the only evidence you found of a criminal act was in your own daughter's room, wasn't it? Because you didn't find anything at the cemetery that would indicate a sexual assault happened there, did you?'

'Not specifically.'

'Isn't it true that you asked Ms. Duncan to look at several condoms to see if she could pick out the one used that night?'

'Yes.'

'Yet she couldn't identify it, could she?'

'No . . . but I imagine she wasn't comparison-shopping at the time of the rape.'

The judge frowned at Charlie. 'Just answer the question, Detective.'

'When you found the girls that night, they were at the edge of the cemetery?'

'Yes.'

'How far was that from the spot where the bonfire had been lit?'

'The clearing is about fifty yards away,' Charlie said.

'How long did it take you to walk there?'

'I didn't time myself.'

Jordan walked toward Charlie. 'Longer than thirty seconds?'

'No.'

'Were there any obstacles in the way?'

'No.'

'No rocks you had to climb over? No ditches to fall into?'

'It's a flat, level path.'

By now, Jordan was almost face-to-face with the detective. 'After his arrest, my client told you he was innocent, didn't he?'

'Yes.' Charlie shrugged. 'So do most perps.'

'But unlike most perps, you didn't get a confession out of my client at the station. In fact, my client has steadily denied his involvement in this crime, isn't that true?'

'Objection!' Matt cried.

'Sustained.'

Jordan didn't blink. 'When you met Gillian Duncan at the edge of the cemetery, how did her clothing appear to you?'

'Dirty, covered in leaves. Her shirt, it was buttoned all wrong.' Charlie glanced at Jack. 'Like she'd had it ripped off her.'

'I have here the transcript of Ms. Duncan's testimony yesterday, Detective. Would you mind reading the section I've marked off?' Jordan handed Charlie a piece of paper.

' 'How about your sweater? Did he take that off?' ' Charlie read, and then gave Gillian's answer. 'No. 'Unbutton it?' No.'

'Thank you.' Jordan held up a photograph of Jack that had been placed on the evidence table. 'Did you take this photo of Mr. St. Bride?'

'Yes.'

'Is it a fair and accurate representation of how he looked when you arrested him?'

'Yes.'

'Take a look at the scratch on his face. Is that one scratch or five?'

'One.'

'Is that consistent with five fingers being raked across a face?'

Charlie suddenly remembered Gillian's hands twisting in her lap, how Amos had reached for one to hold. She'd had long fingernails, bright red, the same color polish his daughter had come home wearing that week after visiting Gilly at her house. 'I'm not sure,' Charlie murmured.

Jordan slapped the picture down. 'Nothing further.'

The incense cast a lavender cloud over Gilly's bedroom, and as she drew it in, she imagined that she was drifting with the smoke, dissolving, energy rising. Cinnamon sprinkled freckles over her mother's cheek, the worn photo tucked beneath a candle. 'I call upon the Earth, Air, Fire, Water,' she whispered. 'I call upon the Sun, Moon, and Stars.'

She did not know what was going on in the courtroom across town, and at this moment, she truly did not care. In fact, she was not thinking of her father, seated behind Matt Houlihan like the dragon who guarded Gilly's virtue. She was not thinking of Jack St. Bride. Sweet sage tickled the inside of her nose, and with all she had inside her, Gillian wished for her mother.

Just on the edge of the circle, she could see her, a translucent figure with a laugh that fell into the shell of Gilly's ear. And this time, something happened. Instead of the candle sputtering out and her mother simply disappearing, she looked Gillian in the eye and sang her name, a series of bells. 'You shouldn't,' her mother said, and the flame on the candle roared so bright it was blinding.

By the time Gillian realized the rug was on fire, her mother had gone. She batted at the flames but didn't manage to save the photograph. It was charred through, the only remaining fragment a piece of her mother's hand, now curled and scorched with heat.

Gillian threw herself down beside the ashes, breathing in the smoke and sobbing. She would not learn until much later that she had burned her hands putting out the flames, that each broken blister would scar in the shape of a heart.

* * *

Matt Houlihan was tired. He wanted to go home and have Molly fall asleep on his chest while Syd rubbed his feet. He wanted to drink himself into oblivion, so that when he was tottering at the edge of consciousness, he wouldn't have to see Gillian Duncan's face.

He was almost done.

That, more than anything else, drew Matt to his feet. He slipped a piece of paper from a manila envelope and offered it to McAfee, who'd known ever since the motions hearing that it was coming. 'Judge, the state has no more witnesses for its case in chief. However, at this time I'd like to offer a certified copy of the conviction of Jack St. Bride for sexual assault on a plea of guilty entered August 20, 1998, in Grafton County, New Hampshire. To wit, Mr. McBride admitted that he sexually assaulted a fifteen-year-old victim and received a sentence of eight months to serve in the Grafton County Correctional Facility.'

The jury gaped. They looked at Matt, they looked at the defendant, and they thought what any reasonable man or woman would think when presented with this evidence – if he's done it before, he most likely has done it again.

Matt placed the conviction on the clerk's desk, then looked directly at Jack St. Bride, hoping to hell the bastard was fully suffering the terror of being at someone else's mercy, someone who held all the cards. 'Your Honor,' Matt said. 'The state rests.'

1969
New York City

That morning, while drinking her imported Sumatran coffee, Annalise St. Bride had read a story in the *New York Times* about a woman whose baby had been born in a tree. The woman lived in Mozambique, a country suffering from a flood, and had climbed to safety when her hut washed away. The baby was healthy, male, and rescued by helicopter a day later.

Surely that was worse than what was happening now.

She had been on Astor Place shopping for the most darling christening outfit when her water broke. Two weeks early. The ambulance told her she couldn't get to Lenox Hill – the hospital where she'd planned to have her baby – because there was a parade blocking traffic one way, and a broken water main had locked up the conduit through Central Park. 'I am *not* going to St. Vincent's,' she insisted, as two paramedics hefted her into the back of the ambulance.

'Fine, lady,' one said. 'Then drop the kid right here.'

A band of pain started at her groin, then radiated out to every nerve of her skin. 'Do you know,' she gasped, 'who my husband is?'

But the paramedics had already set the ambulance screaming crosstown.

Through the tiny window over her feet, Annalise watched the city roll past, a palette of gray angles and swerving pedestrians. In minutes, they arrived at the last hospital in New York City she could possibly wish to be.

Drug addicts and homeless people were splashed along the sides of the building like decorative puddles; Annalise had even heard of patients who had died in the halls simply waiting to be cared for. It was a far cry from Lenox Hill, with its lushly appointed exclusive birthing suites meant to offer a couple the feel of being at home.

St. Vincent's? Being born in a tree was a better pedigree than *this.*

As the paramedics loaded the stretcher off the ambulance, she realized she had to fight in earnest. But the moment the wheels of the gurney slapped onto the pavement, she felt shock rocket through her. Her spine was shattering – she could feel the vertebrae at the base cracking, she was certain of it. In her womb, where she'd been carrying a baby, there was now a huge fist. It twisted like a puppeteer's, pulled so hard and so long that she writhed, at odds in her own body.

I am going to die, she thought.

When she opened her mouth, all she could say was, 'Get Joseph.'

She was admitted before the shifty-eyed drunks and the mothers with six sniffling children hanging like ornaments from their limbs. The curtained room smelled of alcohol and cleaning fluids, and Annalise's gaily wrapped package stuck out awkwardly, a Meissen vase in a Woolworth's living room. 'She's eight centimeters,' said the doctor, an Asian man with hair that stood straight, like a rooster's comb.

'I want to wait for my husband,' Annalise gritted out. The contractions were slicing her in half, like the magician's assistant.

'I don't think your baby's got the same idea,' a nurse murmured, coming up behind Annalise to brace her shoulders.

She and Joseph had toured the rooms at Lenox Hill, with their silk bedding and faux fireplaces. Just around the corner was their favorite Italian restaurant. Joseph had promised to bring her *penne alla diavolo,* the restaurant's specialty, the night she delivered.

Suddenly, there was a crash as a new patient was wheeled into the cubicle beside Annalise's. 'Maria Velasquez. Thirty-year-old female, primip, twenty-seven weeks' gestation,' the paramedic said. 'BP one thirty over seventy, heart rate one-oh-five sinus rhythm. Beaten up one side and down the other by her husband.'

Annalise stared at the curtain that separated her from this woman. The nurse behind her gently turned her face away. 'You concentrate on you,' she said.

'Are you having contractions?' The question came from the other side of the drape, the one Annalise was gazing at so fixedly she expected it to fly off its hangers at any moment in a feat of telekinesis.

'Sí, los tiene,' the woman moaned.

'Looks like she's bleeding. Could be a placenta previa. Call OB.'

Annalise licked dry lips. 'What's . . . what's the matter with the woman over there?'

Her doctor glanced up from a spot between her legs. 'I need you to push,' he said. 'Now, Annalise.'

She bore down with all her strength, squeezing her eyes so tight the room swam about her, and the words that filtered through the curtain came thin and quivering.

'No pueda!'

'It's coming . . . get me a gown and gloves, for Christ's sake.'

'BP's falling. She's ninety over palp.'

'Ah, damn. She's bleeding out.'

'Respire, Mrs. Velasquez. *No empuje.'*

'Primero salvo mi bebé! Por favor, salvo mi bebé!'

Annalise felt herself being opened from the inside, a seal yawning and widening. She had a sudden vision of Joseph pulling on a weekend turtleneck sweater, the wool stretching taut as his head slowly emerged to show his smile, his tousled hair.

'Here we go,' the doctor said.

* * *

'Ringer's lactate, wide open. Type and cross her. Where the hell is OB?'

'We've got to do this now. *Ahora,* Mrs. Velasquez. *Empuje.*'

'Pedi's here.'

'About time. Take the baby.'

'Él se llamo Joaquim!'

'Yes, Mrs. Velasquez. That's a lovely name.'

'One more push,' the nurse said to Annalise, 'and you're gonna have yourself a little one.'

'Suction the infant . . . I want him intubated and bagged with one hundred percent oxygen . . .'

'No quiera morir . . .'

'Pulse ox ninety-eight. Heart rate's one-fifty.'

A high whine of machinery. 'The mother's bleeding out.'

'Massage her uterus. Hard. Harder!'

'Hang pitocin, and two units of O neg on the rapid infuser. IV fluids wide.'

'Where the *hell* is OB? Put in a central line.'

Annalise grabbed the nurse's collar and pulled her close. 'I don't want to die.'

'You're not going to,' the woman said.

'One more push, Annalise. One good one.'

She clenched her teeth, pressed down, and suddenly her son came into the world.

'The baby's abdomen is filling with air.'

'You intubated the esophagus. Do it again.'

'Pulse ox sixty-three. Heart rate seventy.'

'Put in an umbilical line. Give him one cc of atropine, point three of epi, and three milliequivalents of bicarb.'

'Draw a blood gas.'

'She's coding!'

'He's in v-fib!'

* * *

Groggy, Annalise looked down at the healthy bundle in her arms and clutched him tightly.

On the other side of the curtain, two separate wars were being fought. One was to save the life of a woman who'd been beaten to near death by her husband. The other was to allow her child to have any kind of a life at all. From time to time, the curtain billowed in toward Annalise, the frenzy spilling into the limits of her own space.

She could identify two voices now, the doctor taking care of Mrs. Velasquez, and the doctor taking care of the woman's newborn.

'Starting chest compressions.'

'Charge the paddles to three hundred fifty watts . . . intubate her!'

Thump, thump, thump – the sound of electricity jolting to jump-start a body.

'Give her another one mil of epi.'

'Give him another point three of epi.'

Thump.

'Asystole.'

And a moment later, 'Asystole.'

Then the two doctors, speaking simultaneously. 'Call it.'

Annalise should have been moved up to OB but had been forgotten because of the crisis next door. Now, the voices that had swelled the curtain a half hour before were silent.

The clock on the wall ticked, an animal grinding its teeth. Very slowly, Annalise slipped off the delivery table, walked to the bassinet, and gathered her son into the crook of her arm. She was sore and sagging, but she had never felt so strong. She pulled back the corner of the drape that separated her from the body of Maria Velasquez.

The woman lay on her back, a tube rising out of her throat like a periscope. Her face and neck were jeweled with cuts and bruises. Annalise slipped down the blue sheet covering her chest, saw the belt of purple welts along the still-swollen abdomen.

Two hours ago, the worst thing in the world she could imagine was coming to a place like St. Vincent's to deliver a baby. She had cried because the labor room didn't have wallpaper, because the doctor who'd been the first person to touch her son had not been raised in a family that had come over on the *Mayflower.* She had believed that her child needed to start his life in a certain manner, so that he could grow up to be just like Annalise.

God help him.

Maria Velasquez lived in a city Annalise did not know, one where women were raped and beaten, then left to sink in their own sorrow. Annalise's friends worried about how to seat guests at dinner, how to turn down invitations politely; how to make sure the maid wasn't drinking on the job. If they ever noticed the others struggling to survive, they quickly turned away . . . because what you did not see, you did not have to account for.

Annalise, on the other hand, had heard this woman die.

The baby's body lay in a bassinet. He was the size of a half loaf of bread, his bones light as a bird's and stretched with thin skin. Juggling the weight of her own son, Annalise lifted Maria Velasquez's stillborn boy into her other arm.

What difference did it make if you were born in Lenox Hill, in St. Vincent's, in a tree? She glanced at Maria Velasquez's battered body and swallowed hard. What it came down to was simply that you had a chance to love and be loved.

She jumped when a nurse walked in. 'What do you think you're doing?'

'I . . . I just . . .' Annalise took a deep breath, and raised her chin. 'I just thought someone should hold him, once.'

The nurse, who had been ready to castigate her, stilled. Without saying a word, she nodded at Annalise and then stepped away, closing the curtain behind her.

* * *

The nurse who had been Annalise's labor coach came into her cubicle, accompanied by Joseph, who looked frantic and overwhelmed by his surroundings. She left them to their privacy, as Joseph approached Annalise and stared at the wonder of his son. The baby yawned and pushed a fist out of his blanket. 'Oh, Annie,' he whispered. 'I was too late.'

'No, you were just in time.'

'But you had to come here.' When Annalise didn't answer, Joseph shook his head, mesmerized. 'Isn't he something.'

'I think he just might be,' Annalise answered.

Her husband sat down beside her. 'We'll get you out of here right away,' he assured her. 'I already called Dr. Post at Lenox Hill, and he –'

'Actually, I'd like to stay at St. Vincent's,' she said, interrupting. 'Dr. Ho was quite good.'

Joseph opened his mouth to argue but took one look at the expression on his wife's face and nodded. He stroked the infant's head. 'Does he . . . have a name?'

Él se llamo Joaquim.

'I think,' Annalise said, 'I'd like to call him Jack.'

July 3, 2000
Carroll County Jail

Have you ever really held the hand of someone you love? Not just in passing, a loose link between you – but truly clasped, with the pulses of your wrists beating together and your fingers mapping the knuckles and nails like a cartographer learning a country by heart?

Addie reached for Jack as if she were drowning, their hands joined across the old table in the basement of the Carroll County Jail. She touched him with all the emotion she'd kept curtained inside her since her testimony. She touched him a thousand times, for every moment that she'd wanted to walk up to Jack at the defense table and lay a hand on his shoulder, press a kiss to his neck. She touched him and found that even something as innocent as the lacing of their fingers could raise all the hairs on the back of her neck and make her blood beat faster.

And she was so fascinated by the way they fit together – Jack's palm big enough to swallow hers whole – that Addie did not realize the man she was clutching was someone who desperately wanted to get away.

It was when he gently pried her fingers from his that Addie looked up. 'We have to talk,' Jack said softly.

Addie stared at his face. The stubborn jaw, the soft mouth, the fine golden stubble that covered his cheeks like glitter flung by a fairy – they were all still there. But his eyes – flat and blue-black – there was simply nothing behind them.

'I think it's going pretty well, don't you?' she said, smiling so hard her cheekbones hurt. She was lying, and they both knew it. Hanging over them like an impending storm was the unspoken memory of Matt Houlihan reading that former conviction. If that thundercloud had followed Jack and Addie home, every single one of the jurors was being dogged by it, too.

'Jack,' Addie said, rolling his name around her mouth like a butterscotch candy. 'If this is about my testimony – I'm so sorry. I never wanted to be subpoenaed.' She closed her eyes. 'I should have just lied for you when Charlie came that morning. That's it, isn't it? If I'd lied, you'd have an alibi. You'd be free now.'

'Addie,' Jack said, his voice painfully even. 'I'm not in love with you.'

You can be strapped to the most stable chair and still feel the world give way beneath you. Addie's hands clutched the edge of the table. Where was the man who had told her she was the bright light getting him through this misery? At what ordinary moment between yesterday and now had everything changed?

Sometimes, when I think I'm going to lose it in here, I just imagine that I'm already out.

Tears arrowed at the backs of her eyes, small, hot darts. 'But you said –'

'I say a lot of things,' Jack said, bitterly. 'But you heard the prosecutor. They're not always true.'

She turned her head toward the one window in the basement, a tiny square of dirty glass set nearly flush to the ceiling. She kept her eyes wide, so that she wouldn't cry in front of Jack. And maybe because of that, she had a clear vision of her father, years ago, after her mother had died. She'd found him one day in his living room, sober for once, surrounded by papers and mementos. He'd handed her a box of knickknacks. 'This is my will. And some . . . some stuff you ought to have. The first letter I ever wrote your mom, my medal from the Korean War.'

Addie had leafed through the box, her fingers going cold and stiff. These were the items you collected when someone died – as her father had done after they buried her mother, as Addie had only recently done with Chloe's things. You pulled the loose threads of their lives free, so that you could move on. Addie watched her father place his fancy gold watch into the box and understood: He was putting his affairs in order, so that she wouldn't have to.

'You're not dying,' Addie had told him, thrusting the box back into his hands.

Roy had sighed. 'But I might as well be.'

Now, Addie turned slowly toward Jack. He had no will to offer her, no medals, no memories. But he was giving her back her heart, so that when he left her life, there would be no strings attached.

'No,' she said firmly.

Jack blinked at her. 'I'm sorry?'

'You should be. Lying to me, like that. For God's sake, Jack, if you really wanted to end things between us, you should have used an excuse I might actually have believed. Like . . . you aren't good enough for me. Or that you didn't want me to suffer along with you. But to tell me you aren't in love with me . . . well, that's just something I don't buy.'

She leaned forward, her words aimed right at his heart. 'You love me. You do. And goddammit, I'm tired of having the people who love me leave before I'm ready for them to go. It is *not* going to happen again.' She stood up, anger and determination hanging from her shoulders like the mantle of a queen. Then she walked toward the door where a guard stood posted, leaving Jack to suffer the sucker punch of being abandoned.

'If you don't get to sleep,' Selena said, 'you're not going to be of any use tomorrow.'

Two in the morning, and they lay side by side in bed, staring at the ceiling. 'I know,' Jordan admitted.

'You're all knots.' She came up on an elbow. 'Although that seems impossible, after what we just did.'

'I can't help it. I keep hearing Houlihan reading the goddamn conviction.'

Selena thought for a moment. 'Then I'll make you think of something else.'

'Selena, I'm forty-two. You're gonna kill me.'

'Get your mind out of the gutter, McAfee.' She sat up cross-legged, drawing the sheet around her like a medicine man's shawl. 'So this guy gets sued because his mailman slips and breaks his pinky on a icy patch of his driveway. Two days later, the guy's wife sends a threatening letter, via her divorce attorney. He gets so fed up with lawyers that he goes to a bar to drink away his sorrows.'

'Now that,' Jordan interrupted, 'sounds promising.'

'Ten shots of tequila, and he's drunk as a skunk. He gets up on top of the bar and shouts at the top of his lungs, "All lawyers are assholes!" '

'Excellent. And this is supposed to relax me *why?*'

Selena ignored him. 'A man on the other end of the bar yells, "Hey! Watch your mouth." And the drunk guy sneers and says, "Oh? Are you a lawyer?" '

Jordan finished the joke. "No. I'm an asshole."

Selena looked crushed. 'You've heard it before.'

'Honey, I could have *written* it.' He sighed. 'I need to get a nice, relaxing job. Maybe there's an opening for an IRA operative.'

'You ought to try working for this lawyer I know,' Selena said.

Jordan smiled. 'You gonna sue me for sexual harrassment?'

'I don't know. Are you gonna sue me?'

'I can think of better things to do with you,' Jordan murmured, but when she expected him to reach for her, he simply turned away.

Selena leaned over him, her braids brushing his shoulder. 'Jordan?'

He caught her hand, wishing it could be just that easy to hold to the rest of her. 'Are you going to leave me again, Selena?'

'Are you going to smother me again, Jordan?'

'I asked you to marry me. I didn't realize that was a criminal act.'

'Jordan, you didn't want to marry me. You were still reeling after the Harte case. And I was the closest thing to grab onto.'

'Don't tell me what I wanted. I know what I wanted. You. I still do.'

'Why?'

'Because you're smart and you're gorgeous and you're the only woman I know of who would tell a defense attorney a really shitty lawyer joke at two a.m.' His grip on her wrist tightened. 'Because you make me believe that there are things worth fighting for.'

'Sleeping with me might make you a happier attorney, Jordan, but it doesn't make you work any harder for your clients.' She shook her head. 'You've always tangled up your work and your life. And you've made me do it, too.'

'Stay with me, Selena. I'm asking you now, so that you know it has nothing to do with the outcome of this case.'

'Maybe it should,' she said lightly, trying to joke her way out of this. 'Maybe we should ask the jury to decide, since you and I don't seem to be very good at it.'

'Juries hand down wrong decisions every day.'

She stared at him. 'Are they going to be wrong this time?'

Jordan didn't know if she was talking about the verdict for Jack St. Bride or for their own relationship. He lifted her hand and brushed his lips over her knuckles, a promise. 'Not if I have anything to say about it.'

By three o'clock in the morning, Gillian not only had counted 75,000 sheep but she'd moved onto other barnyard animals for diversity. Time passed exceedingly slow, each second melting. But then, she had reason to be anxious. In six hours, court would reconvene, and Jack St. Bride's attorney would have a chance to unravel all the work that the prosecutor had done.

She had tossed and turned so much that the covers were knotted. Sighing, she threw back the blanket and let the air cool her skin. At the sound of a footstep in the hall, she froze.

The light went on, and Gillian curled her hands into fists. The sound of running water, another creak. Very gently, very quietly, she reached down and drew up the quilt, a tight cocoon.

By the time her father opened her door, Gillian had turned to her side, pretending to be asleep. She felt the floor tremble as he crossed the room, sat on the edge of her bed. His hand fell like a prayer on her temple. 'My baby,' he whispered, the pain in his voice rocking her.

Gillian didn't move. She kept her breathing steady, even when a tear slid between her father's hand and her own cheek, as binding as glue.

Sad to say, the high point of Thomas's day was getting the mail. It wasn't even that he ever expected to get anything – well, the occasional solicitation for a credit card and some goddamned Boy Scouting magazine that he'd canceled when he was twelve but that had managed to follow him from address to address like a beleaguered ghost. But when you were fifteen and had to pick a daily peak experience from, oh, eating stale cereal for breakfast, reading assigned novels for next year's English class, and strolling out to get the mail, this won hands down.

Jordan McAfee, c/o Thomas McAfee.

The package was light and bulky and reminded him too much of a dead mouse that had been sent in the mail by the brother of a Mafia client of his father's who had been convicted. With trepidation, Thomas unsealed one end and shook a small notebook into his hands.

He frowned at it. A black-and-white composition book was no big deal. But this one was wrapped like a birthday gift in a glittery silver ribbon. On its front were the words *Book of Shadows.* Thomas untied the bow and let the notebook fall open. *How to Bring Money to You. Love Spell #35.* The entries were arranged like the insides of a cookbook – ingredients, followed by directions. They were lettered by hand, but the writing varied, as if many different contributors had worked on it. In the margins were small notes and funny faces, like the ones he made in his history binder when he was bored.

A longer entry: *Imbolc, 1999.* This one looked like a play written for four actors, with lines for each player. But the things they were saying, doing . . . it was like nothing he'd ever seen before. Brows drawing together, Thomas began to read.

'So you understand how important your answers are,' Jordan murmured, nervously regarding the woman at his side. With her wild silver hair and rope sandals, her silver bangles and swinging earrings, she seemed a little offbeat – more the kind of person you'd expect to find beside you at a Grateful Dead concert than telling you truths from the witness stand.

'Completely, Mr. McAfee,' Starshine said. She reached into her pocket and pulled out a small blue bag tied with purple thread. 'Would you give this to your client?'

'Jack? What is it?'

'A charm, of sorts. Just some bay laurel, High-John-the-Conqueror root, St.-John's-wort, and vervain. Oh, a little pine nut, tobacco, and mustard seed too, just in case. And of course, a picture of an open eye.'

'Of course,' Jordan repeated faintly.

'So that justice will look favorably on him.'

What to say to that? Jordan slipped the little bag into his breast pocket like a handkerchief, and Starshine ascended to the witness stand.

Immediately, she had the jury's attention. Starshine slipped her hand free of the long cowl of her sleeve and touched it to the Bible. 'I swear to tell the truth, the whole truth, and nothing but the truth, so help me God.' She smiled. 'And Goddess.' Then she turned to the judge. 'May I have just a moment?'

Judge Justice seemed beyond the power of speech. She waved the witness on.

Starshine reached into a hemp bag she'd carried up to the stand and withdrew a thermos, a green candle, a cup, a packet of sugar, and a spice bottle marked saffron.

'Here we go again,' Matt Houlihan muttered. Then, louder, 'Objection, Your Honor.'

'Sustained,' the judge said. 'Ma'am, I have to ask you what you're doing.'

But the woman was swaying slightly, her arms splayed and her eyes shut. 'Just raising energy, Your Honor,' Starshine said. 'I'm doing a safe-space spell.'

'I beg your pardon?'

'May I turn the chair? I need to be facing south.'

At the defense table, Jordan buried his face in his hands.

The judge deferred to the prosecutor, who let a smile creep across his face. 'Oh, by all means,' Matt said. 'If we need a safe-space spell, we need a safe-space spell.'

Starshine lit the candle, then poured some of the liquid from the thermos into its attached cup. 'It's just milk,' she said, then added the two packets. 'Mixed with a little saffron and sugar.' She lifted the cup to her mouth and inhaled deeply, her eyes drifting shut as she imagined a woman in black, a woman in red, and a woman in white all walking toward her. 'I have been with you from the beginning,' she said, and drank.

A calm settled over the courtroom. Even the people in the gallery could feel it, small susurrations of surprise swept through the rows. Starshine earthed the power in her mind, bound the spell, and released the circle. 'I think that takes care of it.'

Judge Justice turned to Jordan. 'Have fun, Mr. McAfee,' she said.

Jordan rose, shaking his head. On the one hand, having Starshine be a crackpot worked nicely with his defense, because Gillian was playing at Wicca, too. On the other hand, if the woman was too much of a nut, the jury would never believe anything she said. 'Do you know Gillian Duncan?' he began.

'Yes, I do. She comes into my shop quite often.' Starshine turned to the jury, suddenly a saleswoman. 'I run the Wiccan Read, an occult bookstore in Windham.'

'An occult bookstore? What's that?'

'We sell books and charms and herbs for people who follow earth-based religions.'

'When did Ms. Duncan last come into your shop?'

'On April twenty-fifth.'

'What was she looking for?' Jordan asked.

'Objection,' Matt called out. 'Hearsay.'

'Judge, this goes toward impeaching her credibility on what happened that night,' Jordan argued.

'Overruled, Mr. Houlihan. I definitely want to hear this one.'

Starshine continued. 'She wanted to ask me about witch's flying ointment.'

'Maybe we ought to back up for a moment,' Jordan said, feigning confusion. 'Witches?'

'Yes. That's just what followers of the Wiccan religion are called.'

'Can you tell us what Wiccans believe?'

'It's very simple, actually. First, do no harm, but follow your will. Second, that any witch is capable of raising energy, casting spells, performing magick, and communicating directly with the Goddess.'

'Objection, Your Honor,' Matt said. 'This is a rape trial, not an episode of *Bewitched*.'

Jordan turned. 'If I could just have a minute, Judge. I'm laying a little groundwork.'

The judge overruled the prosecutor. 'Are there many witches?' Jordan asked.

'Three to five million worldwide, but not too many come right out and tell you.' She glanced at the judge. 'Why, this lady herself could still be in the proverbial broom closet.'

'Don't count on it,' the judge said dryly.

'Old habits die hard, and discrimination is very real, although all witches really do is honor women and respect the environment. It's not unlikely for a witch to be blamed for things that go wrong in a town, or to be singled out as a Satanist.' She smiled. 'Why, in Salem Falls, you only have to look as far as the statue of Giles Corey on the green to remember the hysteria of 1692.'

'You said Ms. Duncan was asking about flying ointment. What's that?'

'Back in medieval times, witches used astral projection ointment to produce psychedelic effects. It contained elements like hashish and belladonna, which created the psychic tripping, if you will. Needless to say, we don't use it nowadays. Gillian came into my shop asking if I had a recipe for it.'

'What did you tell her?'

'That it was illegal. I suggested she should redirect her energy and celebrate Beltane instead.'

'Beltane? What's that?'

'The last of the three spring fertility festivals, a sabbat that marks the wedding of the God and the Goddess. In a word, Mr. McAfee,' she said, 'it's all about sex.'

'Is there a traditional way to celebrate Beltane?'

'Witches hang offerings of food and herbs to the God and Goddess in the branches of a tree. There's often a bonfire to leap over and toss away your inhibitions.'

'A bonfire?' Jordan repeated.

'Yes. And a maypole, and often there's handfasting, too –'

'Handfasting?'

'A trial marriage. You grab your intended's hand and jump the flames, and you're tied to each other for a year – a test period, if you will. And of course, after handfasting, there's always the Great Rite.' She laughed at Jordan's blank expression. 'Making love, Mr. McAfee, right out there in the fields of the earth.'

'Well,' Jordan said, coloring. 'That sounds festive.'

Starshine winked. 'Don't knock it till you've tried it.'

'Is Beltane celebrated on a certain date?'

'The same time every year,' Starshine said. 'At the stroke of midnight on April thirtieth, as the calendar rolls onto May first.'

It spoke volumes that the first person McAfee had put on the stand did absolutely no harm to Matt's case. It didn't matter to him if Gillian Duncan was a Pagan, a Buddhist, or a tribal shaman. Despite the hocus pocus and the candles and the safe space, nothing could take away from the fact that Gillian Duncan had been raped that night.

'Ms. Starshine,' Matt said. 'Do you have any way of knowing, other than by what she told you, that Gillian Duncan is a witch?'

'I'm not in her coven, if that's what you mean.'

'Were you in the clearing behind the cemetery on Beltane?'

'No. I was celebrating elsewhere.'

'In fact, you didn't see Gillian that night, did you?'

'No.'

'And you didn't see Mr. St. Bride that night, either?'

'I've never met the man,' Starshine said.

'So you have no way of knowing whether the defendant and Ms. Duncan were together on the night of April thirtieth?'

'No.'

Matt started to walk back to his seat but then turned. 'That safe-space spell you did when you got up here . . . is that something other witches would know?'

'In some form or another, a protection spell is fairly common, yes.'

'What does it protect you from?'

'Negative energy,' Starshine said.

'But if the defendant were to step up there right now and grab you –'

'Objection!' Jordan cried.

' – if he were to throw you onto the ground and pin you –'

'Sustained!'

' – could a protection spell keep a witch from being raped?'

'Mr. Houlihan!' The judge rapped the flat of her hand against the bench. 'You will stop *now!*'

'Withdrawn,' Matt said. 'Nothing further.'

Dr. Roman Chu was dressed like a skateboarder, with his hair on end and a black T-shirt that read SHREDDER. If Jordan hadn't known him personally, he would have assumed Roman was a kid plucked off the street and paid to play a part. But then the toxicologist was sworn in and began to speak, listing his credentials and his certification by three separate boards, as well as so many forensic testimonies under his belt that the prosecutor stipulated to his expertise. 'My job involves demonstrating evidence of drug intake by means of isolating, identifying, and quantifying toxic substances in biological materials,' Chu explained. 'Basically, I'm a very expensive bloodhound.'

'Can a forensic toxicologist tell if a drug is taken in a therapeutic dosage, or as an accidental or intentional overdose?' Jordan asked.

'Yes. We use modern analytical procedures like chromatography and spectometry to measure drugs, and then we identify the relationships between these drug levels and the clinical response to understand the pharmacological effect.' He smiled at the jury. 'We also go to graduate school and learn to use words that are never less than six syllables.'

He had them laughing, which was one of the reasons that Jordan loved to use Roman as an expert. 'Dr. Chu, did you analyze a sample from Gillian Duncan?'

'Yes, I did.'

'What were your results?'

'The blood sample I tested showed signs of the substance atropine.'

At the prosecutor's table, Matt went very still. The jury leaned forward, riveted by the proof that Gillian had lied.

'Atropine?' Jordan asked. 'What's that?'

'A drug used medicinally to relax the muscles of the intestine, to increase heart rate, to reduce secretions during anesthesia, and occasionally for treatment of asthma.'

'How long does the drug take to kick in?' Jordan asked.

'It's a very rapid onset, with peak plasma concentration within an hour, and the effects last between two and six hours.'

'For you to find atropine in a blood sample, how long ago would the person have to ingest it?'

'Within twenty-four hours of the specimen being drawn,' the toxicologist said.

'Was the level of atropine found in Ms. Duncan's blood consistent with a normal dosage?'

'The usual therapeutic dose is zero point one to one point

two milligrams. Her test showed a blood level of twenty-three nanograms per milliliter at about four hours after she drank it. With a drug half-life of three to four hours, that would correspond to a blood level of forty-six nanograms in the first hour. Working backward with the parameters of Ms. Duncan's weight, body fat, and approximate time of ingestion, that indicates a dose of ten milligrams of atropine . . . roughly ten to one hundred times the norm.'

'What does that mean?'

'Ms. Duncan had overdosed,' Chu said.

'Would that have impaired her functioning?'

'Oh, yeah. At a dose of just two milligrams, a person would have a rapid heart rate, palpitations, dryness of the mouth, dilated pupils, blurred vision. Up the dose to five milligrams and the person would also be feeling restless, having trouble speaking and swallowing, headaches, hot skin, reduced intestinal peristalsis. If you take ten milligrams of atropine, like Ms. Duncan, you'd feel all that, plus have a rapid, weak pulse; blurred vision; flushed skin; restlessness and excitement; trouble walking and talking; hallucinations; delirium and coma.'

'Are the effects lasting?'

'Nope. It's a short trip,' Chu said, grinning.

'But hallucinations are likely?'

'Yeah. In fact, recently in Holland four brands of Ecstasy were found to contain atropine, for that reason exactly.'

'Other people, then, have used atropine as a recreational hallucinogenic drug?'

Chu nodded. 'That's what I hear. In fact, those hallucinations are what usually tip a doctor off to the possibility of atropine poisoning . . . because atropine doesn't show up on a routine ER tox screen, and blows your short-term memory, which makes it very difficult to get an accurate sense of if or when the drug was taken.'

'Would you know if the things you hallucinated were real memories or not?'

Cho shrugged. 'You wouldn't be able to tell. Like all hallucinogens, from LSD to peyote, it creates altered perceptions.'

'Could someone in the throes of a hallucinogenic drug imagine a physical attack?'

'Objection,' Matt called out. 'This isn't the witness's area of expertise.'

'I'm going to allow it,' the judge said.

Chu grinned. 'Think of all those guys who scratched their skin off after tripping on angel dust, convinced they had bugs crawling all over. If you're using a psychedelic drug, what you believe to be true becomes true.'

'One final question,' Jordan said. 'Is atropine derived from any particular substance?'

'It comes from the liquid extract of a plant, which has a long and varied history of being used as a poison, an anesthetic, and to induce a trancelike state. Remember that sleeping draft Juliet drinks in the Shakespeare play? Same stuff.'

'What's the name of this plant, Dr. Chu?'

'Oh,' he said. 'That would be *Atropa belladonna*.'

Matt called for a fifteen-minute recess and left the courtroom fuming. He stalked upstairs, to the small conference room he'd secured to sequester the victim, on the chance that he needed to recall her after the defense finished its witness list. When he burst through the door, Gillian was bent over a table, doing a crossword puzzle.

'Don't you *ever* lie to me again.'

She dropped her pencil. 'W-what?'

He braced an arm on either side of her puzzle. 'You heard me,' Matt said angrily. 'You "had nothing to drink that night." '

'I don't know what you're talking about.'

'The atropine, Gillian. It was found in your blood.'

She looked positively stunned. 'But . . . but the test at the ER –'

'Wasn't conclusive,' Matt finished. 'A more refined test was done on your blood by the defense's toxicologist. And right now, that jury knows you lied about taking drugs – and is wondering what else you might have been lying about.'

Tears welled in her eyes. 'I didn't lie about being raped. I didn't. It was just that everyone already thinks I'm some kind of a slut, because this happened to me. I didn't want them thinking I was a drug addict, too. It was only that once. I swear.' Raising a ravaged face to Matt, she asked, 'Is he going to get off now? Because I was so stupid?'

Matt felt the fight draining out of him, but he wasn't going to give her false hope. 'I don't know, Gillian.'

'He won't be acquitted.'

At the sound of a third voice, both Matt and Gillian turned. Amos Duncan stood in the doorway, stiff and uncomfortable. 'Mr. Houlihan wouldn't let that happen.' Gillian's father walked closer, until he stood with his hand on his daughter's shoulder. 'This may be a setback, but it's not a devastation. Isn't that right, Mr. Houlihan?'

Matt thought of the twelve jurors and what they'd just heard. 'You're preaching to the choir,' he said, and stormed out of the room.

'Isn't it true, Doctor, that hallucinogens produce a wide range of effects?' Matt asked.

Chu laughed. 'That's what I hear, but I may have to plead the fifth if you want me to get more specific.'

'It's possible that one person might have a great trip on a drug and another person could . . . as you said . . . scratch his skin off?'

'Yes. It depends on dosage, potency, personality of the user, and the environment in which the drug is taken.'

'So if you take this drug, you're not even guaranteed to have hallucinations?'

'Not necessarily.'

'Did you see Gillian Duncan in the early hours of May first?'

'No,' Chu said. 'I've never met her.'

'Then you don't know what her personality is like.'

'No.'

'You don't know the environment she was in at the time.'

'No.'

'You don't even know the potency of this particular drug, do you?'

'No.'

'Did you see her after she was brought to the ER to be examined because of a sexual assault?'

'No.'

'So you don't know if she was having hallucinations, do you?'

'No.'

Matt advanced on the witness. 'You said that the drug stays in the bloodstream only a few hours, is that correct?'

Chu nodded. 'Yes.'

'And when was the sample you examined drawn?'

'At approximately two a.m.,' the toxicologist said.

'Ms. Duncan arrived at the woods with her friends at approximately eleven p.m. that night. Do you have any way of knowing whether Ms. Duncan took the drug before she went to the woods that night?'

'No . . . but based on the levels in her blood at one-thirty a.m., if that was the case, she'd be dead now.'

'Still, given that two- to six-hour time frame, the drug could have been taken after the rape, isn't that right?'

'I guess so.'

'And that would affect your calculation of the dosage amount, right?'

'Yes.'

Matt nodded. 'You don't know who provided the atropine that evening, do you?'

'No.'

'Isn't it possible that Mr. St. Bride arrived in the woods and suggested they take it?'

'It's possible.'

Matt crossed to the jury box. 'Can you smell atropine, if it's placed in a drink?'

'Usually not.'

'Can you taste it?' he asked.

'No.'

'So if Mr. St. Bride handed Ms. Duncan an open soda can with this drug already mixed into the beverage, she might drink it and not even know she was ingesting an illegal substance?'

'I suppose.'

Matt nodded thoughtfully. 'Dr. Chu, have you ever heard of Rohypnol?'

'Yes.'

'Can you explain what it is, for those of us who don't know?'

'It's called the date-rape drug,' Chu explained. 'In recent years, there have been cases where men slip the substance into a woman's drink, render her unconscious, and then proceed to sexually assault her.'

'Why is Rohypnol so frighteningly effective?'

'Because it's odorless, tasteless. The victim usually doesn't even realize she's ingested it, until it's too late. And it doesn't show up on a routine hospital tox screen.'

'Aren't every single one of those properties something that could be said about atropine?'

'As a matter of fact,' Chu said. 'Yes.'

Fighting the Haldol she'd been prescribed was a losing battle. The moment her eyes closed, Meg was back there: *The woods were swimming, as if they'd all been dunked underwater, and bright pink flashes of light kept spinning at her like creatures from a video game. Meg's head felt light as a balloon, and every time she opened her mouth, the stupidest sounds came out . . . not words or her voice at all.*

'Come, come,' Gilly was saying, waving them over to congratulate the happy couple. Whitney staggered over, but Chelsea was too busy plucking the stars from thin air. 'Meggie, you, too,' Gilly ordered, and Meg's own traitor legs carried her there.

Matt Houlihan had blown a cannon right through the best argument Jack's lawyer had offered so far. Addie couldn't get past that, and as a result, her hand was shaking so badly by the time the coffee poured out of the little vending machine in the basement of the courthouse that she spilled it all over her skirt and the floor. 'Oh,' she cried, bending down to clean up the mess before she realized she didn't even have a napkin.

'I've got it.'

A pair of spit-polished black boots stepped into her field of vision. Then Wes Courtemanche knelt and began to mop up the spill with his own handkerchief.

Addie's cheeks burned. She had no reason to be embarrassed, but there it was, all the same. 'Thank you,' she said stiffly, taking the handkerchief from his hand to finish.

'Addie,' he said, and touched the back of her wrist.

It took her a few seconds to get the courage to look up. 'I'm sorry,' Wes murmured. 'I didn't know it would all come to this. And . . . well, I never meant to drag you into it.'

'You didn't, Wes. I did that all by myself.' Flustered, she fisted the handkerchief into a ball. 'I'll wash this and get it back to you.'

'No.' He plucked it from her hand. 'Time was, I would have died twice over to hear you offer just that, but the truth is, Addie, you were never meant to do my wash.'

Addie took in his earnest eyes, his strong body, his steadfast loyalty. 'Wes, you're going to find a woman one day who can't wait to mix her whites with yours.' Biting her lip, she added, 'I'm sorry it wasn't me.'

Wes shook his head, then slipped her a smile edged in regret. 'Not as sorry as I am,' he said, and gently helped her to her feet.

Jack stood at the window of the small conference room. 'You ever hear of a guy named Boris Yetzemeloff?' he asked Jordan.

'No.'

'Guy who raped eighteen women in the forties, in Mexico. He was convicted, sentenced to a life term. Twenty years into it, he had a heart attack and was pronounced dead for twenty minutes before paramedics resuscitated him.' Jack turned to face his attorney.

'They let him go after that. Said he'd served his life sentence.'

Jordan pinched the bridge of his nose. 'The only decent piece of trivia I know is that it's against the law to cross the state boundaries of Iowa with a duck on your head.'

Jack didn't crack a smile. 'Good to know.'

'So what are you trying to tell me, Jack?' Jordan asked. 'That you've got yourself tried and hung already, before you even get on the stand?'

'Can you honestly tell me that my testimony is going to make a difference?' Jack answered softly. 'It's not even a testimony, for God's sake. It's a big gaping blank.'

'I explained to you what Dr. Chu said. If you drank any of the tea that night, your memory of the evening might never come back.'

Annoyed, Jack kicked a chair out of the way. 'I want it all here,' he said, holding out his hands. 'Right at my fingertips. I want to remember what happened, Jordan, if only so that when I'm rotting away in prison I can pull it out every now and then and remind myself that I was innocent.'

'You've got a gut feeling, Jack,' Jordan sighed. 'That's going to have to be enough.'

The men fell silent, tangled in their own thoughts. Overhead, a fluorescent bulb hummed like an insect. Then Jack sat down across from his lawyer. 'Can I ask you something?'

'Sure.'

'Do you believe I'm innocent?'

Jordan let his eyes slide away from Jack. 'It has no bearing on my role as your attorney, you know, if I –'

'I asked you a question. Not as attorney and client. As one man to another.' Jack stared directly at Jordan. 'Please.'

Jordan knew what Jack needed; knew that it was his responsibility as an attorney to keep his key witness calm, no matter how slender a testimony he had to offer. 'Of course I believe you,' he said. 'So does Selena. And Addie.' Jordan forced a smile. 'See, you have all kinds of disciples.'

Just none of them, he thought, *on the jury.*

Dr. Flora Dubonnet had the face of a sparrow, the body of a stork, and the voice of Minnie Mouse on helium. It was all Jordan could do to keep from wincing every time she answered one of his questions, and he kept sending murderous looks toward Selena, who'd found this pediatric forensic shrink on the Internet . . . *clearly* not over the phone.

'Did you review some documents in this case?' Jordan asked.

The answer was a high-pitched squeal.

Jordan watched the jury cringe. Fingernails on a chalkboard, that's what it was.

'Doctor,' Judge Justice said, 'I'm very sorry, but I'm going to have to ask you to speak up.' She hesitated, then added, '*Very* sorry.'

'I said yes,' Dr. Dubonnet repeated.

'What did you review?' Jordan asked.

'The psychiatric records of Gillian Duncan, from the year she was nine years old.'

'In your expert opinion, what do they reveal?'

She turned to the gallery and chirped, 'The girl showed tendencies of being a pathological liar.'

Somehow, in that voice, it didn't pack quite the same punch. 'Can you give some specific examples that led you to this diagnosis?'

'Yes. Collateral sources contradicted her accounts on a number of occasions, and sometimes her statements were completely implausible. For example, she flatly denied shoplifting although she was found holding the items in her hand. She was mutilating herself, cutting up her arms, and refuting this even when the evidence was presented to a doctor. On another occasion, she ostracized a neighborhood girl by spreading rumors, then denied it, although numerous fingers were pointed at her as the originator.'

'Why would a child do these things, Doctor?' Jordan asked.

'In Ms. Duncan's case, it probably had to do with getting noticed. Her mother's death was an event that generated pity and attention for Gillian, and in her mind, the best way to continue that focus on herself was to keep creating fiascoes of some sort.'

'In your opinion, Doctor, when a child is diagnosed as a pathological liar, what happens by the time he or she grows up?'

'Objection, Your Honor,' Matt said. 'This expert's projection on children in general has absolutely no bearing on what did happen with Gillian Duncan.'

'Overruled,' the judge murmured.

'The rule of thumb in psychiatry,' Dr. Dubonnet replied, 'is that boys who lie have conduct disorders and become sociopaths . . . whereas girls who lie have personality disorders and become manipulative in interpersonal ways.'

'Thank you,' Jordan said. 'Nothing further.'

Matt stood immediately. 'Doctor, you've never talked to Gillian Duncan, have you?'

'No.'

'All you've done is read records that took place almost half her lifetime ago?'

'Yes.'

'Your *rule of thumb* . . . you can't really say that every boy or girl follows this path, can you? You're just making a broad assumption about what often happens?'

'That's correct.'

'And you have no way of knowing if that's what happened to Gillian, do you?'

'No.'

'Isn't it true that Gillian had just lost her mother at age nine?'

'So I understand.'

'And that was the reason she began therapy, correct? Not because she had been lying compulsively.'

'Yes.'

'You said that the reason you believed Gillian was a pathological liar was because as a kid, she started some rumors about a younger woman and then denied them?'

'Among other things.'

Matt smiled. 'Forgive me, Doctor, but when I was a kid, we just called that being a girl.'

'Objection!'

'Withdrawn,' Matt said. 'Isn't it true, though, that this is what girls do all the time? Boys punch each other; girls start rumors?'

'Objection,' Jordan called again. 'I want to know when Mr. Houlihan got his clinical psychology degree.'

'Withdrawn. Doctor, you also mentioned a shoplifting incident that Ms. Duncan denied?'

'That's right.'

Matt turned and stared directly into Jack's eyes. 'Well, isn't it fairly common for a person who commits a crime to deny that he's done it?'

'Ah . . . oftentimes . . .'

'Isn't it fairly common for a person who commits a crime to deny that he's done it, even when there's physical evidence linking him to the crime?'

'I – I suppose so.'

'So it isn't all that unusual, is it, Doctor, to lie to get out of trouble?'

'No.'

'Does that make someone a pathological liar?'

Dr. Dubonnet sighed. 'Not necessarily.'

Matt glanced at the witness. 'Nothing further.'

He smelled like sweat and blood. His smile was sweet, too, and Meg would have bet he had no idea what he'd just gotten into. Dutifully, she pressed her lips to his cheek and almost immediately lost her balance. She fell into his lap, heard his grunt as her full body hit. 'You okay?' he asked, only trying to help her up, his hands sliding awkwardly over her chest and wide bottom before he got the leverage to do it.

What you want and what you get are two very different countries; sometimes imagination builds a bridge before you have the chance to realize it won't hold weight. He hadn't been fondling her;

he'd been breaking her fall. But oh, had Meg wished otherwise.

And in that moment she realized that she hadn't been the only one.

This time, Roy brought sandwiches. Roast beef piled high on a crusty roll, tuna salad on wheat, even veggie pitas for the meatless crowd. The judge and the jury and even Jack gratefully dug into this treat, but Matt sat with his back stiff, his untouched turkey sub resting on the corner of the prosecution's table.

'It's the chives,' Roy confessed to the clerk, who'd asked a question about the ingredients in the chicken salad. 'You don't expect them, which is why they come right back and bite you.'

Head leaning against his hand, Matt drawled, 'Your Honor, does this witness have anything to contribute to the defense's case besides a large dose of cholesterol?'

'Getting around to it,' Roy muttered, taking his seat. He straightened his tie, cleared his throat, and scowled at Matt. 'Skinny folk always have an attitude.'

With his roast beef sub in one hand and his notes in the other, Jordan stood. 'Can you state your name and address for the record?'

'Roy J. Peabody. I live above the Do-Or-Diner, in Salem Falls.'

'Where were you the afternoon of April thirtieth, Mr. Peabody?'

'Working,' Roy said.

'Do you know who Gillian Duncan is?'

'Ayuh.'

'Did you see her that day?'

'Ayuh.'

Jordan took another bite of his sandwich. 'Where?' he asked, then swallowed.

'She came into the diner 'bout three-thirty.'

'Was Jack working at that time?'

'Sure was.'

'Did you ever see the two of them together?' Jordan asked.

'Ayuh.'

'Can you tell me about that?'

Roy shrugged. 'She came in and ordered a milk shake. Then she changed her mind, said she wasn't hungry, and walked out. I saw her go 'round back, to where Jack was putting the trash into the Dumpster.'

'You saw this?'

'My cash register sits next to a window,' Roy said.

'What exactly did you see?'

'She must have said something to him, because he looked up after a minute and they started talking.'

For taciturn Roy, that pretty much said it all, too. Jordan hid a smile. 'How long did they talk?'

'Had to have been ten minutes, because I changed the cash drawer then. Takes some time to count up all those bills and coins.'

'Thank you, Roy.' Jordan lifted the sandwich. 'For everything.'

As soon as Matt stood up for his cross-examination, Roy turned to the judge. 'Can I ask *him* a question?'

She seemed surprised, but nodded. 'All right, Mr. Peabody.'

'What the heck was wrong with my muffin?' Roy barked.

'Excuse me?'

'You didn't eat it, did you? Just like you didn't eat my sandwich today.'

'It wasn't a personal affront, Mr. Peabody. I was making a statement,' Matt said.

''Bout what? That my food isn't good enough for you?'

'If you take muffins from a witness, you're more likely to believe him.'

Roy blinked, confounded.

'Let's just say I'm on a gluten-free diet,' Matt said with a sigh. 'Do you mind if I ask *you* a few things now?'

'Go on ahead. I took the whole afternoon off for you.'

Matt rolled his eyes. 'Mr. Peabody, were you inside when you saw Gillian leave?'

'That's what I said.'

'And Gillian went around the back of the diner?'

'Yes.'

'Was your window open?'

'No, Addie says it's a waste of the air-conditioning.'

'So you didn't hear who called whom over, then?'

'No. But I sure noticed she was pissed off when she left.'

Matt looked at the judge. 'I'd like to move to strike that statement.'

'I wouldn't,' Judge Justice said. 'Mr. Peabody, what led you to believe she was angry?'

'Her nose was so high in the air I thought she'd trip on the sidewalk. She was walking a mile a minute. Huffing, like she was fit to tie Jack.'

Jordan grinned from ear to ear. If he won this trial, he'd eat lunch at the Do-Or-Diner every day of his life from now on. And he'd tip Roy, as well as his waitress.

'Do you know, Mr. Peabody, why she was angry?'

'Can't say.'

'Well, for example, what if he'd made an improper advance toward her? Wouldn't that have upset her?'

Roy slanted a look at Jack. 'I suppose.'

'Or if he touched her inappropriately? Might that account for a rapid retreat?'

The old man hesitated, then said, 'Maybe.'

Matt walked back to the county attorney's table and picked up his sandwich. He took a huge bite, chewed and swallowed. 'Thank you, Mr. Peabody,' he said, smiling. 'It's not every day a defense witness caters to the prosecution, too.'

Meg knew better than to cast a spell that tried to control another person. If a spell was going to work, it meant that energy and power poured through you into someone else – so a connection had been made between the two of you. Which meant if you sent harm out, eventually you'd be the recipient of it, too.

Hexing, though, wasn't the same as using magick to destroy. After all, when they'd cast a spell for old Stuart Hollings, they were trying to get rid of his tumor. A growing cancer had to be dissipated. And a person who repeatedly threatened the safety of others had to be stopped. That was why Meg had to do a binding spell.

It was the first time she'd ever cast a circle by herself. Meg knelt between the shrubs in her backyard, praying her mother wouldn't come home early from work. A black candle burned in front of her, and an ashtray she'd dug up from the attic held a stick of incense.

She was supposed to have a poppet, a wax or cloth doll made to represent the person she wanted to stop from doing harm. But Meg had never been crafty and so had no idea how to go about making a representation of someone. In the end, she'd rummaged through her closet, into the bin of old Barbie and Ken dolls she'd had as a kid. Naked, the doll was obscene, the hair matted. Meg sprinkled it with salt water and whispered the words she'd copied from a grimoire at the Wiccan Read. 'Blessed be, you creature made . . . uh, in China . . . and changed by life. You are not plastic, but flesh and blood. You are between the worlds, in all the worlds, so mote it be.'

She held the doll in her hands and imagined a silver net falling out of the sky. Then she took a length of red ribbon from the pocket of her shorts and wrapped it tight around the doll's hands, mouth, and groin. Finally, Meg took all the energy that trembled through her nerves, feeding her fear, and she directed it into the doll, until the thin figure jumped out of her palms and fell onto the ground before her. 'By Air and Earth, by Water and Fire, so be you bound, as I desire.'

Meg would not be hurt again. She would not let anyone else be hurt again, either. Lies were only as strong as the suckers who believed them; and figuring that out late, Meg knew, was better than never figuring it out at all. Opening the circle, she took a spade from her mother's gardening set and buried the doll beneath the roots of a hydrangea bush. On top of this, she set the heaviest rock she had been able to drag over. And when the poppet meant to represent Gillian Duncan was safely underground, Meg patted the mound with satisfaction.

In the middle of Matt's cross of Roy Peabody, the bailiff walked up to Jordan and handed him a note. 'You've got to be kidding,' he muttered, balling it up in his hand. He waited until the prosecutor had finished and then asked to approach the bench.

'Your Honor, could we take a ten-minute recess?' he asked.

'You've had plenty of time to confer with your client,' Matt began.

'I'm not going to talk to my client. If it makes you happy, you sit here and baby-sit him.' Jordan turned to the judge. 'This is a personal matter, ma'am.'

She nodded and granted Jordan the time. He hurried back to the defense table, motioned to Selena, and strode out of the courtroom.

Thomas was waiting for him there. 'This'd better be good,' Jordan said.

'I think it is.' He held out his hand, presenting a notebook. 'This came in the mail for you.'

Jordan stared daggers at his son. 'And you felt the profound need to bring it to me in the *middle* of a trial?'

'Book of Shadows,' Selena read, taking it from Thomas. 'I saw these at the Wiccan Read, when I was there.'

'If Starshine felt the need to send a gift, I could have used a good-luck charm.'

'I don't think Starshine sent it, Jordan,' Selena said quietly, pulling the silver ribbon that Thomas had used as a bookmark out in a long spool.

Jordan fingered the ribbon. Then he took the book from Thomas's hand and flipped through it, skimming. The last page with writing on it held his attention for a long time.

It was little-known fact, but witnesses were allowed to use anything – anything at all – to refresh their recollection.

Engrossed, Jordan did not take his eyes from the final entry. He touched the page with reverence. 'Where did it come from?'

Thomas thought for a moment before he answered. 'A good witch,' he said.

Sitting on the witness stand, Jack looked warily at the enemy.

His lawyer.

At first, Jordan had not wanted Jack to testify, believing that he usually did a better job of speaking for his clients. But his defense so far consisted of a witch, a pair of toxicologists, a shrink, and Roy – it sounded more like the punch line to a joke than a legal rebuttal. Jack was well spoken, clean-cut, educated – even if he had nothing to counter Gillian Duncan's story, he would look good sitting on the stand.

It was no small measure of irony that the last person in the world Jack would ever trust was the only one who could help him now. As he sat on the stand and watched Jordan's antics – his hand motions, his calculated frowns at the jury – Jack thought, *They are all alike. Liars, the lot of them.* And just as he'd been screwed once before by a lawyer, Jack believed he'd be screwed again.

Don't act defensive or angry or they'll think you capable of violence, Jordan had said moments ago. *Just follow my lead. This is what I do for a living.* But that was impossible for Jack to do. It was as if Jordan stood at the bottom of a cliff urging Jack to jump, trusting the promise he'd catch him . . . yet Jack was still beaten and bruised from his last fall.

Jordan leaned close, so that only Jack could see his anger. 'Pay attention, dammit,' he hissed. 'I can't do this without you.' Then a pleasant expression whitewashed his features, and he said, 'What happened next?'

He was back there for a moment, their laughter sparkling over his head like stars, close enough to catch. 'I was on the edge of a clearing in the woods,' Jack said slowly, 'and when I looked up, there were a group of girls standing there. Naked.'

That single word stilled the court. 'Wait a second.' Jordan shook his head. 'You're telling us you stumbled upon a bunch of naked girls?'

'I know. That's exactly what I thought, too. That I'd had so much to drink I was hallucinating.'

'I can imagine. What else do you remember?'

Jack shook his head. 'It looked . . . well, like nothing I'd ever seen. There were candles. And ribbons, hanging from the trees.'

Jordan crossed to the evidence table and lifted one. 'Ribbons like these?'

'Yes. But longer.'

'Can you recall anything else?'

Jack closed his eyes, struggling. 'Only bits and pieces. Like I'll close my eyes and see the bonfire. Or I'll wake up in the morning and there's a sweetness on my tongue, a taste I can place from that night.' He shook his head, frustrated. 'But there's so much of it that's just empty space, and the things that do come to me make no sense.'

Jordan began to walk toward his client. 'Do you remember any particular items laying around that night?'

'Objection,' Matt called lazily. 'If the witness is drawing a blank, Mr. McAfee isn't allowed to fill in the picture with his own crayon.'

'Sustained.'

Undeterred, Jordan caught Jack's eye. 'Is it annoying to be unable to remember what happened that night?'

'You have no idea.' Jack reached deep for the words. 'I know I didn't do what they say. I just know it. But I can't see it clearly.'

'What do you think it would take to jog your memory?'

'I don't know,' Jack admitted. 'God knows I've tried everything.'

'Me, I have to hold some souvenir in my hands, and boom, I'm back there.' Jordan grinned. 'I have a foul ball I caught during game seven of the 1986 American League championships, the one when Henderson hit a three-run blast off Donnie Moore of the California Angels. Every time I pick it up, I think of the Sox pulling ahead from behind and making it into the World Series.'

'Once again, Your Honor, objection. As much as I love getting Mr. McAfee's life history, it's beside the point.'

'But Judge, it's not. I'd like to enter into evidence this notebook and let the witness use it to refresh his recollection.' Reaching behind the defense table, Jordan took the black-and-white composition book from Selena, then brought it toward the evidence table.

'Approach!' Matt yelled, coming to his feet.

'All right, Mr. McAfee, what's up your sleeve now?' Judge Justice asked.

'Your Honor, the rules of evidence say I can refresh my witness's memory with any document at my disposal. This is a *book of shadows* – a witches' log, if you will, that documents the Pagan ritual that took place the night of the alleged crime.'

Judge Justice turned it over in her hands, flipping through it, then handed it to Matt to examine. 'This is inappropriate, Your Honor,' Matt insisted. 'The witness didn't write a single page of this book . . . he has no original knowledge of what's in it. His memory isn't going to be *refreshed* by reading it – it's going to be created new.' He narrowed his eyes at Jordan. 'Mr. McAfee is finding a way to put words into his client's mouth.'

'Even if the witness was not a party to its creation, Mr. Houlihan, the defense is welcome to use this item to spark a memory.' The judge turned to Jordan. 'I myself saved a souvenir cup from the 1975 World Series, game six, when Carlton Fisk's fly stayed inside the foul line by inches, and as long as I have that godawful plastic mug, I'll never forget the magic of that moment. Objection overruled.'

As soon as Jordan handed the composition notebook to his client, Jack's hand began to shake. 'That night,' he murmured. 'She was writing in this, under the dogwood tree.'

'And then?'

'She stood up,' Jack said slowly. 'She stood up, and she said my name.'

A more sober man would have turned and walked away, but Jack could not hold that thought in his mind. It was too full with other things – ribbons hanging where they did not belong; a knife set perpendicular to a white candle; the scent of cinnamon; the simple fact that she was asking for him. 'You're just in time,' Gillian said. 'We've been waiting for you.'

Clearly, he was asleep and this was a dream. A bad dream. The car following him, his run-in with Wes, and now, these half-dressed girls. Yes, it all made sense now. This was a trick of the mind. He felt safer now, knowing it was not real.

When Gillian took Jack's hand, his entire body jerked. 'Oh,' she said soothingly, running her fingers through his hair. 'Poor Jack.' She touched the cuts on his brow and cheek, then lifted her discarded shirt and dabbed at the blood.

Her beautiful breasts were an inch from his mouth, and they looked as real as anything he'd ever seen. From the far corners of his mind, Jack began to struggle. 'I can't . . . I need to . . .'

'Stay here.'

Gillian finished for him. She smiled at her friends. 'What's the one thing we haven't done tonight?'

The short, plump girl's mouth rounded. 'You wouldn't, Gilly.'

Jack could suddenly see the scene as if from a great height. This girl, his hand in hers, the ribbons fluttering behind them. You cannot be here, he warned himself, because . . . but he could not finish the sentence. He willed his feet to move, but he was too drunk. Get away, he thought, and did not realize he'd spoken aloud until Gillian turned to him. 'Don't you like us?'

'I have to go,' he said, his voice breaking.

'But you'll help me first, won't you? I need a man for this.'

Jack made himself a deal: He would reach something up high or open a pickle jar and then he'd be on his way. But to his surprise, Gillian laced his fingers with hers and tugged him toward the fire. She began to run, until he had no choice but to do what she did, to leap it.

They fell to the ground. Gillian's face was flushed. 'Now you're tied to me, for a year.'

Jack didn't understand, but then he didn't understand much of anything. The forest was spinning around him. He watched the girls pour drinks from a thermos, pass out biscuits. 'For you,' Gillian said, and maybe he would have even drunk it if one of the other girls hadn't lost her balance and fallen on top of him.

'Steady.' He looked at her – Meg, that was her name, and she was related to a detective in town – but in that moment, she might well have been Catherine Marsh. That was how pure the need was in her eyes. Jack's heart began to pound, and he turned to the other girl, the taller one, and to Gillian – and they all looked that way. They all wore that expression. That want, that incredible one-sided want that had nearly ruined him before.

Jack staggered upright and crashed through the woods, finding the path he had come in on. He stumbled forward for nearly a minute, and then Gillian came running up from behind. She was near tears, her hair wild around her face. 'The fire – we can't get it out. We're going to burn the whole forest down. Please,' she begged. 'You have to come.'

He followed her to the clearing, where there was no fire . . . and no one else. Before he could ask her what was going on, she threw her arms around his neck and pressed her mouth to his. He choked on the whole of her; he backed up along the edge of the glowing fire, unsure which was the greater danger. Gillian writhed against him, aiming to slip under his skin. And then she took his hand and brought it up to her breast, holding his gaze the whole time, so that he knew this was an offering.

'No,' Jack whispered. 'No.' He put his hands on Gillian's forearms and set her away, fireflies sparking around their bodies. 'I said no,' he answered more firmly. No. The pine needles quivered, the stars slipped from their perches, history looped back on itself. This was not Gillian Duncan; this was Catherine Marsh. And Jack was being given the chance to defend himself, in a way he never had last year. 'You get away from me,' he said, his chest heaving, 'and you stay away.'

But Gillian Duncan, who had always gotten what she wanted and then some, grabbed at him. 'I cast a spell,' she insisted. 'You came to me.'

'You *came to* me,' *Jack corrected. 'And I'm leaving.' With a shove, he sent Gillian sprawling, and he ran down the path so far and so fast that for the first time in months, he managed to outstrip his past.*

'Jack,' Jordan asked. 'Did you rape Gillian Duncan on the night of April thirtieth?'

'No.'

'How did your skin get under her fingernails?'

'She was trying to keep me there, when I kept trying to get away. Her hands kept grabbing at me. And when she . . . kissed me, she had her fingers raking into my scalp.'

'How did you get the scratch on your face?'

'From a branch, when I was running. I had it before I ever saw her that night.'

'How did your blood get on her clothes?'

'She used her shirt to dab at my cheek.'

Jordan crossed his arms. 'Do you have any idea how difficult it's going to be for these twelve people to believe your story?'

'Yes.' His eyes swept the jury members, compelling them to listen. 'I could lie to you and tell you a version of that night that's easier to digest . . . like that we were getting intimate and then she changed her mind at the last minute . . . but that isn't what happened. The truth is just like I told it. The truth is I didn't rape her.'

'Then why would Gillian make up a story like this?'

'I don't know. I don't really know her at all, in spite of what she's said. But if I were seventeen and I was discovered in the woods doing something I didn't want my father to know about . . . I guess I'd spin a different story, too. And if I were really smart, I'd dream up a tale that would ruin the credibility of the person who'd intruded . . . so that no one would believe him, even if he told the truth.'

Jack met his attorney's eyes. *That,* Jordan communicated silently, *is the best we can do.* 'Your witness,' he said, and offered Jack up for sacrifice.

It was all Matt could do to not laugh out loud. That had to have been the absolute worst defense he'd ever heard in his life, and he truly believed he could get up and speak Swahili and still manage to win this case. 'Ribbons, candles, naked girls . . . are you sure, Mr. St. Bride, that you didn't leave out any pink elephants?'

'I'm sure I would have had no trouble remembering those,' Jack answered dryly.

'But you yourself say it's hard to believe.'

'Just being honest.'

'Honest.' Matt snorted, to let Jack know what he thought of that assessment. 'You testified that you were very drunk. How can you be sure this recollection is accurate?'

'I just know it is, Mr. Houlihan.'

'Isn't it possible that in your . . . drunken stupor . . . you raped Ms. Duncan and then blacked it out of your mind?'

'If I was drunk enough to suffer a blackout,' Jack countered, 'surely I was too drunk to be physically capable of sexual intercourse.'

Matt turned, surprised by the gauntlet the defendant had thrown. 'So your theory of why Gillian Duncan became hysterical, sobbing, claimed you raped her, went to the hospital to undergo an invasive physical exam and have a sexual assault kit done, reported the rape to the police, and now has come to tell a panel of strangers the intimate details of how you sexually assaulted her . . . is because she was scared of her *father?*'

'I don't know. I'm just telling you what happened.'

'All right,' Matt said. 'You've given us your explanation for why your skin was found beneath Ms. Duncan's fingernails . . . because she was grabbing at you to get you to stay, correct?'

'Yes.'

'Ms. Duncan didn't give you the scratch on your cheek – the injury was sustained in the woods, on a branch?'

'Yes.'

'Your blood was on her clothes because she was trying to clean up that scratch by dabbing it with her shirt?'

'Yes.'

Matt frowned. 'Then what's your explanation for why semen matching yours was found on her thigh?'

'Objection!' Jordan leaped up, furious. 'Approach!'

The judge waved the attorneys closer. 'The semen wasn't a match,' Jordan said angrily. 'The state's expert even deemed the results inconclusive.'

Matt scowled. 'She said this defendant was seven hundred forty thousand times more likely to have been the donor of the semen than anyone else. Those are still pretty damn good odds.'

'However,' the judge said, 'it's too prejudicial. The jury has the information about the semen; they can do with it what they will. I'm sorry, Mr. Houlihan, but I'm not going to allow you to pursue that line of questioning.' She turned to the jury as the lawyers returned to their corners. 'You'll disregard that last question,' Judge Justice instructed, although Matt's words still hung in the air, as sharp and as precarious as a guillotine's blade.

'Mr. St. Bride,' Matt said, 'you find yourself in the woods with a quartet of teenage girls who are not only perhaps interested in having sex . . . but are *naked* . . . yet you don't turn around and run as fast as humanly possible away from there?'

'I said I needed to get away, over and over.'

'Actually, you said you jumped over a fire hand in hand with one of them. And that you looked around closely enough to see there were things hanging from the trees.'

'I also said that Gillian Duncan was the one who came on to *me,*' Jack said, trying very hard to keep his voice from rising.

'Was anyone else around when she attacked you?'

'No.'

'Where were the other girls?'

'I don't know.'

'How convenient. Was she still naked?'

Jack shook his head. 'She had gotten dressed.'

'And then she proceeded to throw herself at you?'

'Yes.'

Matt crossed his arms. 'This five-foot-four, one-hundred-ten-pound girl forcibly held you there?'

'I got away as quickly as I could. I said no, shoved her off me, and ran. Period.'

'So . . . this is the second time in a space of two years that a teenage girl has falsely accused you of sexual assault?'

'That's correct.' Heat climbed the ladder of Jack's neck.

Matt raised his brows. 'Aren't you asking the jury to believe you're the unluckiest man on the face of this earth?'

Jack took a deep breath. 'I'm asking the jury to believe me.'

'Believe you,' Matt repeated. '*Believe* you. Huh. Mr. St. Bride, you heard the expert who testified that soil from your boots matches the soil in the clearing of the woods?'

'Yes, I did.'

'And you heard the DNA expert who showed that your blood was on Ms. Duncan's clothing and your skin was underneath her fingernails?'

'Yes.'

'You heard Ms. Duncan testify that you were with her that night?'

'Yes.'

'And you heard Ms. Abrams and Ms. O'Neill corroborate that?'

'Yes, I did.'

'You've seen numerous amounts of evidence that place you at the crime scene, isn't that right?'

'Yes.'

Matt tilted his head, questioning. 'Then how come when the police came to arrest you, the very first thing you did was lie about being there?'

Jack's mouth opened and closed, no words rising to the surface. 'I – I don't know,' he finally managed to say. 'It was an instinctive re-sponse.'

'Lying is an instinctive response for you?'

'That's not what I meant –'

'But,' Matt argued, 'it's what you said. Did you or did you not already lie once about your whereabouts that night?'

'Yes, I did,' Jack murmured.

The prosecutor turned and pinned him with his gaze. 'Then why should the jury believe you *now?*'

'He's good,' Selena mused. 'He's really, really good.'

Jordan slammed the car door and stalked up the walk toward his house. 'If you're such a huge fan, then why don't you go sleep with Matt Houlihan tonight?'

The defense had rested and court had been dismissed. Closing arguments would begin the next morning, which meant Jordan had approximately seventeen hours to conjure sheer brilliance. Burning against his heart was the little packet Starshine had given him for Jack's defense. He was going to sleep with it under his goddamn pillow; at this point, he'd take any help he could get.

He knew and the prosecutor knew – and even the jury knew – that Jordan had not conducted a defense of his client – he'd simply tried to make Gillian out to be something other than the little princess she made herself out to be. But a witch could be raped. A drug user could be raped. And if Jordan had been sitting on that jury, he would not have been inclined to believe anything Jack St. Bride had to say.

At the door, he tried to jam his key into the lock and couldn't manage to get it to fit. 'Goddamn,' he said, wedging it in again. *'Goddammit!'*

A second attempt, and the key stuck fast. With a mighty wrench, Jordan managed to pull it free of the hole, then swore and hurled his entire key chain into the bushes off the porch. He stared after it, his whole body shaking.

'Jordan,' Selena said, touching his arm.

He burrowed into her embrace, pressed his face against her neck, and silently apologized to Jack St. Bride.

Addie volunteered to close up the diner. 'Come upstairs,' Roy urged through the door of the ladies' room, as she changed. 'We'll have iced tea, watch a little TV.'

Zipping up her uniform, Addie came out of the restroom. 'Dad, I need to do this. I *want* to do this.' What she really wanted, actually, was to hit something until her bones broke. Scouring floors, scrubbing counters, wiping the grill – these were better uses of her time.

She pushed past her father into the kitchen. It always seemed like a ghost town after hours, bathed in shades of gray and haunted by the scents of the foods it had harbored. Addie picked up the wire brush that hung on the side of the stove and began to scrape down the grill with brusque, mechanical movements.

'I'll help you, then,' her father said, rolling up his sleeves.

'Dad.' She met his eyes. 'Right now, I just want to be alone.'

'Ah, Addie.' Roy moved forward, hugging her tightly, until the wire brush dropped from her hand and her sob curled into his chest like a kitten's mewing.

'I'm not going to be able to say good-bye,' Addie whispered. 'Visiting hours aren't until next Wednesday. And by then . . . by then, he could be in the prison in Concord.'

'Then you'll go visit in Concord. I'll drive you every day after work, if I have to.'

Addie offered him a weak smile. 'On what, Dad? The lawn mower?' She squeezed his hand. 'Maybe I will come up for iced tea, all right? Just give me a while to sort things out in my head.'

She felt her father's eyes on her as she took a jug of bleach from a shelf and began to wash down the dishwashing table and stainless sinks. Her mother used to say that a little bleach could go a long way toward making the shabbiest circumstances shine.

Her mother had not been in love with Jack St. Bride.

Once Roy went upstairs, Addie attacked the kitchen. She rubbed down the sneeze guard of the cold table and wiped clean its cool innards. She scraped burned patches from the base of the oven. She scrubbed and washed until her knuckles bled within her rubber gloves, and she had to wrap her hands in a damp dishcloth, just to ease the pain.

She was working with such a frenzy, she never heard the front door of the diner open. 'I hope you're paying yourself well,' Charlie said.

Addie jumped a foot, slamming her head against the base of the warming table. 'Oh!'

'Jeez, Addie, are you all right?' Charlie rushed forward to help her, but the moment he was within the range of being able to touch, they both froze. Addie backed off, her hand to her forehead.

'Fine. That was just stupid of me.' She hugged her arms to her chest. 'Is this about Jack?'

Charlie shook his head. 'Is there . . . could we sit down for a second?'

Nodding slowly, Addie followed him into the front room of the diner. They slid across from each other in a booth. The barrier of a table between them helped, and being away from the bleach fumes cleared her head. But Charlie showed no signs of speaking. 'How is Meg?' Addie asked after a moment.

'All right. Thanks for asking.' Charlie tapped his fingertips on the table. 'After all that's been said in that courtroom, I don't know what's going to come of her, really.'

'Take it one day at a time.' Addie looked at the clock. Swallowed.

'Addie,' Charlie said, 'I owe you an apology.'

Her eyes reluctantly met his. 'Why?'

'I've been listening to the testimony. And I've been helping the prosecution for weeks. And it's made me . . . it's made it all come back clearer than ever. God, I'm doing a shitty job of this . . .' Charlie rubbed his hand over his face. 'I thought I'd live in Miami, get a job on the force, and just forget Salem Falls. Then Chief Rudlow invited me back north, and I told myself enough time had passed to just wipe away the memory. After nearly a decade, I assumed that if I didn't think about it, no one else would, either.' He hunched over the table, as if drawing strength from within. 'But you've thought about, every day, haven't you?'

Addie closed her eyes, then nodded.

'I knew what was coming that afternoon under the bleachers, when Amos called you over. I was drunk, sure, but I knew what I was doing. And for reasons I can't even stand to think of, I went along with it . . . and then followed the others, when they acted like it hadn't happened at all.' Charlie lowered his gaze. 'Damn, Addie, how do you tell someone you're sorry you ruined their life?'

It took Addie a long time to speak. 'You didn't ruin my life, Charlie. You raped me. There's a difference: One, I couldn't keep from happening . . . but the other, I could. I *did.*' She thought of Chloe, of Jack. 'The more you get past pain, the more it goes from coal to diamond.'

Charlie's eyes were red-rimmed, stricken. 'I'm not going to ask you to forgive me, and I know I can't ask you to forget. But I want you to know, for whatever it's worth, that I don't forgive myself . . . and I'll never forget, either.'

'Thank you,' Addie whispered, 'for that.'

She heard the door jingle closed behind him and she sat at the booth with her legs completely limp, waiting for her heart to stop beating triple-time. After all these years, who would have expected validation? After all these years, who would have expected that simply hearing the words made her feel like starting over?

She was jolted out of her reverie by the sound of the door opening again. Charlie must have forgotten something. But before she could turn around, Addie heard the voice of a young woman, the thud of a suitcase being dropped on the floor. 'They said I'd find you here.'

And suddenly Addie was face to face with Catherine Marsh.

July 5, 2000
Carroll County Courthouse

The air in the courtroom was thick the next morning, so heavy with anticipation it beaded on the foreheads of the reporters and misted the lenses of the camera crews. Judge Justice strode to the bench with the air of a magistrate whose mind is already turned toward her next case. 'I believe we're starting the day with closing arguments,' she said. 'Mr. McAfee, are you ready to begin?'

Jordan stood. 'Actually, Your Honor, I need to reopen my case.'

A moment later, he and Houlihan were standing at the bench. 'I have another witness,' Jordan explained. 'An unexpected one, whose testimony is crucial to the defense.'

'Perhaps you'd like to tell me why you didn't know about her before?' the judge asked. 'Does the state know this witness and what they're going to testify to?'

'No, I don't,' Matt said, irritated. 'The defense already rested. You didn't see me dancing a parade of new witnesses in front of the court after the prosecution finished.'

'Judge,' Jordan explained, 'it's the victim from my client's previous conviction. She's recanting.'

'Which is totally irrelevant. It's too late,' Matt insisted.

The judge stared at each lawyer in turn, then addressed the jury. 'Ladies and gentlemen, you may recall that yesterday the defense rested. However, the court is going to allow Mr. McAfee to reopen his case to call one final witness.'

Jordan smoothed down his tie and glanced toward the rear of the courtroom. 'The defense calls Catherine Marsh.'

She was small and shaken, and Jordan had his doubts about whether she would even make it to the stand without assistance. But at the steps, Catherine rallied, repeating the words to swear herself in in a true, ringing voice.

'How old are you, Ms. Marsh?'

'I'm sixteen.'

Jordan glanced at his client. 'Do you know Jack St. Bride?'

It was the first chance Catherine had to see her former teacher. She met Jack's eyes, and a story hung between them, one torn into a spotty snowflake pattern by contrition. 'Yes, I do,' she murmured.

'How?'

Catherine took a deep breath. 'I'm the one he was convicted of sexually assaulting last year.'

A gasp rolled through the courtroom like a tide. 'Why are you here today, Ms. Marsh?'

'Because.' Catherine looked at her knotted hands. 'I let it happen the first time, and I'm not going to be responsible for letting it happen a second time.'

'What do you mean?'

'Jack St. Bride never sexually assaulted me. He never touched me inappropriately. He never did anything wrong at all. He was the best teacher I ever had and . . . and maybe I thought of him that way and wished he would be attracted to me . . . but it never happened.'

'Why did you let him get convicted, then?' Jordan asked.

A single tear rolled down Catherine's cheek as she took a deep breath. 'Coach believed in me and was kind to me. When I had a boyfriend and wanted to have sex for the first time, Coach took me to a clinic to get birth control pills. He didn't want to, but he did it, because it was so important to me. And when the same guy broke up with me, all I could think was that I wished he'd been more like Coach – more mature, more into me, more . . . Jack.' She looked at the jury. 'I started to write about him . . . about us . . . in my diary. I made it up, the way I wanted it to be. And when my father found my birth control pills and read my diary – God, for a moment, I just wanted it to be true. I wanted to believe what my father believed . . . that I was someone Coach was attracted to, instead of just the other way around.

'By the time I tried to take back what I'd said, it was so big and so ugly, I couldn't swallow it down. I was a little girl playing with dolls who turned out to have real feelings and real lives that could get ruined.' She looked into her lap. 'My father and the prosecutor and the judge – they all thought I was protecting a man I loved.' Catherine turned, addressing the jury. 'The last time I told the truth in court, nobody believed me. I need you all to believe me now.'

'Thank you, Ms. Marsh,' Jordan said. 'Your witness.'

Matt leaned forward in his chair, elbows resting on knees, hands clasped. 'All right,' he said slowly, getting to his feet. 'Where were you on the night of April thirtieth?'

'In Goffeysboro,' Catherine said.

'You weren't in the clearing behind the cemetery here in Salem Falls, were you?'

'No.'

'So you don't know whether something happened to Gillian Duncan that night?'

'No.'

'In fact,' Matt accused, 'all you know is that a year ago, you made a terrible mistake.'

'Yes.'

'And a year ago, you were so in love with this man you didn't want him to get hurt, correct?'

'Yes,' Catherine murmured.

He softened quite suddenly, his face rounding into a friendly smile. 'You wish things with Coach St. Bride had ended differently, don't you, Ms. Marsh?'

'Like you can't imagine.'

'Even now, you don't want to see him get hurt, do you?'

Borne along on his questions, Catherine shook her head vehemently. 'Of course not. That's why I came today.'

'What a surprise,' Matt said. 'Nothing further.'

Jordan watched Catherine leave the witness stand. 'Once again, Your Honor,' he said, 'the defense rests.'

* * *

'This,' Jordan said to the jury, 'is going to be hard.'

He walked to the box, where they sat in anticipation of his closing argument. 'When you hear a young girl like Gillian Duncan say she was raped, you want to believe her. You don't want to find out that she's making things up, or that there are inconsistencies in her story. You want to think a girl like that would come in and tell you what really happened . . . but the fact is, you can't just assume that what Gillian Duncan said is the truth.

'Gillian Duncan had specifically been told by her father not to go out at night. That there was a dangerous man running loose. So what did she do? She tried to see what she could get away with. She just didn't realize that it was going to get away from her . . . and that's why we're here today.'

Jordan set his hands on the railing, leaning into the jury box. 'The judge has instructed you, and will instruct you again, that you need to listen to all of the evidence . . . not just Gillian's testimony. And the evidence in this case shows there are too many inconsistencies for you to find Jack St. Bride guilty of aggravated felonious sexual assault.'

Jordan began to tick off a list on his fingers. 'Gillian told you that she was going to the woods to hang out with her friends, but in reality she went into an occult bookstore and spoke to the proprietor about celebrating Beltane. Jack told you he saw ribbons and candles and an altar . . . something strange and difficult to believe, to be sure. Yet silver ribbons were found later at the scene of the crime, and in Meg Saxton's bedroom closet.'

Ticking off another point, Jordan continued. 'Gillian said that her friends left, and that she headed home in the other direction. But she'd arrived in the company of friends specifically because she believed that Jack St. Bride was dangerous. After meeting him face to face, why would she leave by herself and run the risk of meeting up with him?'

Then Jordan gestured down the central aisle. 'And Gillian said that after the rape, she counted to one hundred and ran as fast as she could to catch up to her friends. Ladies and gentlemen, the distance she had to go from that clearing to where her friends were is approximately half a football field in length. It takes a high school linebacker about six seconds to cover that distance. Now, Gillian isn't a high school linebacker . . . but according to her testimony, it took her five minutes to travel that path. Five minutes, plus the length of time it took her to count to a hundred. Does it seem likely that a young girl who was scared, hysterical, and running as fast as possible would move that slowly? Does it seem likely that from only half a football field away, her friends would never have heard her struggles?'

Jordan walked to the evidence table and held up the picture of Jack's scraped cheek. 'You heard evidence that Mr. St. Bride's DNA was found beneath Gillian's fingernails. We don't contest that . . . but he told you she was grabbing his arm in an effort to keep him there. He said the lone scratch on his cheek came from a branch . . . consistent with a single twig raking the skin, rather than five long red fingernails.

'You also heard that these girls were taking drugs that night. What kind of drugs? The kind that don't show up in a tox screen at the hospital. The kind that Gillian didn't mention to the police when she made her statement. The kind that obliterate your short-term memory of an event and cause hallucinations.'

Jordan shook his head. 'It doesn't add up. And the reason it doesn't is either because Gillian doesn't remember it clearly or because she doesn't want *us* to. Afraid of her father's reaction to discovering her drug use and her commitment to witchcraft, Gillian Duncan pointed a finger in blame at the man who stumbled unexpectedly on her secrets. She told a lie about Jack St. Bride before he had a chance to tell the truth about *her*.

'The only crime Jack St. Bride committed was being in the wrong place at the wrong time. It happened once before with a girl this age – a gross miscarriage of justice. Jack came to Salem Falls, expecting to turn over a new leaf . . . but was seen as a stain on the community. People waited for him to make a mistake that might lead to his exile . . . and Gillian's accusation became just the match to start a conflagration.

'There's been a witch hunt here in Salem Falls,' Jordan said, turning toward his client. 'But the victim, all along, has been Jack St. Bride.'

Matt smiled at the jury. 'We've heard about witches,' he said. 'We've heard about Beltane. The only element that's been missing in this court is the Devil . . . unless, of course, you happen to include Jack St. Bride.

'What matters at this trial isn't whether Gillian is a witch, or whether she crawled to her friends on her belly, or even whether she was experimenting with an illegal substance. What this comes down to is evidence – hard facts that prove Jack St. Bride committed rape. Evidence like the defendant's DNA, found beneath Gillian Duncan's fingernails. Evidence like his blood, found on her shirt. Let Mr. McAfee explain that away, if he'd like. But he can't account for that drop of semen on Gillian's thigh. It's not something you tend to leave behind without having intimate contact. According to the expert who testified, the chance of randomly selecting an unrelated individual other than the defendant whose DNA matches the crime scene DNA at the locations tested is one in seven hundred forty thousand. That's a big number, ladies and gentlemen. Realistically, where did this semen come from, if not Mr. St. Bride?'

Matt turned toward the jury. 'Evidence,' he repeated. 'You heard Gillian Duncan speak of the most brutal and intimate event of her life, although it clearly pained her to do so in front of strangers, with cameras in her face and a judge hanging on her words. You heard her describe the gathering of evidence for a sexual assault kit – one of the most invasive exams a young girl can undergo. And you heard the testimonies of two girls, a police detective, and an ER doctor, who all agree that Gillian was hysterical when she was found.'

Matt raised his brows. 'On the other hand, nothing in Mr. St. Bride's testimony matches anything else you've heard from eyewitnesses that night. He's got a convenient explanation for the bruises and the scratch on his face. He's got a convenient explanation for why he was at the bar drinking. He's got a convenient explanation for why he was in the woods. But he doesn't have any proof, ladies and gentlemen. All he has is his story . . . which, to use Mr. McAfee's terms, doesn't add up.' Matt stared hard at the jury. 'Jack St. Bride has more incentive than anybody in this entire courtroom to lie to you, because he has more at stake. Having been in jail before, he knows he doesn't want to go back.'

The prosecutor started back. 'The defendant chose to go out and get drunk. Is that what impaired his judgment enough to rape a girl? Maybe. Is his violent nature what caused him to rape a girl? Maybe. It doesn't matter. What matters is that he did it. And that the state has proved he did it, beyond a reasonable doubt.

'Mr. McAfee has offered you a lot of mumbo jumbo about Gillian's actions and behavior . . . because he can't offer you the truth.' Matt leaned over the counsel table, his finger two inches from Jack's face. 'But the truth is that this man went into the woods on April thirtieth, 2000. This man jumped Gillian Duncan and ripped her clothes off and forced her to have sex with him. This man,' Matt said, 'is the one I'm asking you to convict today.'

Jack was brought back to the sheriff's holding cell pending the jury's verdict. The deputy who was on the front desk was an older man with a white handlebar mustache and a tendency to whistle 'Smoke Gets in Your Eyes.' He nodded as Jack passed, en route to a six-by-six space that was beginning to feel frighteningly comfortable.

Jack stripped off his jacket and tie and lay down on the metal bunk, pressing his fists against his eyes. How big a difference could Catherine Marsh make? Jordan said it would depend on whether the jury wanted to hang its hat on her testimony, although to Jack, one young girl with a case of puppy love seemed an awfully meager reason for acquittal.

Once the jury handed back a conviction, he would be taken directly to the state penitentiary in Concord. If he were sentenced for the maximum term, he would be fifty-one years old when he was released. His hair would have gone gray, his stomach soft, his skin lined. He would have age spots on the backs of his hands, markers for all the empty years gone by.

He would miss the feel of snow on his face. And the taste of Irish whiskey. He would miss the pattern of his mother's china and the luxurious width of a double bed and the thin orange line where dawn bled into day.

He would miss Addie.

In the distance, Jack could hear the muted conversation of the deputy in the front office. Maybe Jordan had come to tell him the verdict was in. Or maybe some other prisoner had been brought here, to purgatory, to wait.

The thick-soled shoes of the deputy squeaked on the linoleum, stopping in front of Jack's cell. 'I'm going to take a whiz,' he announced.

'Good for you.'

'I'm telling you this,' the deputy said slowly, 'because I have no control over who comes through that door when I'm gone, if you understand what I'm saying.'

Jack didn't. 'Believe me, if some nut comes in here and shoots me in cold blood, I'd probably thank him for it.'

The deputy laughed, already halfway down the corridor. Jack lay back down, covering his eyes with his forearm.

'Jack.'

It wasn't real – it couldn't be. Addie stood on the other side of the bars, close enough to touch.

Without a word, Jack lunged forward, sticking his arms through the slatted steel and working them around her as best as he could. Her face came up to the cold metal, her nose and mouth jutting forward enough to meet his. She was pushing so hard to get closer that Jack could see red lines forming on her cheekbones and jaw, a cell of their own making.

His hands cupped her face, tilted her forehead against his. 'I didn't think I would get to see you,' he confessed.

'I traded the deputy a chocolate cream pie,' Addie said. 'For five minutes.'

Bringing his lips up, he kissed her brow. 'What would he have done for a whole meal?' Jack held her back when she would have burrowed closer, tracing his hands over the delicate bones in her face and the bridge of her nose, lighting slight as a butterfly on her eyelids and trailing her lips like a whisper, over and over.

'W-what are you doing?'

He stroked her brows, her widow's peak. 'Taking you with me,' Jack said.

In that moment, an incredible peace fell inside him. He would not be like the other prisoners in the state pen. He would never be like them, because he'd been exposed to something truly beautiful, and it had gotten into his system. For the rest of his life, he would carry it around, hot as a secret under his skin, and just as jealously guarded.

'I will never forget you, Addie Peabody,' Jack said softly, covering her mouth once more.

He tasted of grief. She swallowed his sorrow like a seed, and breathed hope to the center of him. 'You won't have to,' Addie promised. 'I'll be here waiting.'

The sound of the deputy hurrying down the hall made Addie step back, although her hands still rested loosely in Jack's. 'Sorry to break this up,' the man said, 'but you have to go.'

'I understand,' Addie said, her throat closing like a bud.

'Not you, ma'am.' The deputy turned to Jack. 'Verdict's in already.'

Some of the jury looked at him; some didn't. 'It's normal,' Jordan assured him. 'It doesn't mean a thing.'

'Mr. Foreman,' Judge Justice said, 'have you reached a verdict?'

The cameras buzzed behind Jack's shoulder, and he concentrated very hard on making the muscles of his legs work. If he were being recorded for posterity, he wanted to be sure he could stand on his own two feet.

'We have, Your Honor,' the foreman said.

'Will the defendant please rise?'

Jordan locked his arm through Jack's, to draw him to his feet. Weak-kneed, Jack managed to remain upright and breathing.

'Mr. Foreman, how do you find the defendant on the charge of aggravated felonious sexual assault?'

Jack glanced at the jury, still poker-faced. The foreman looked at the paper he held in his hands. A thousand years later, he read, 'Not guilty.'

The cry of outrage from Amos Duncan was drowned out by the immediate whoop of delight behind Jack, as Selena Damascus hopped the barricade and threw herself into Jordan's arms. And then Addie was in his own, and Jordan was shaking his hand, telling him he'd known it would turn out this way all along.

The world revolved, a haze of glances and jurors and camera lenses. 'The defendant is free to go,' the judge called over the melee, and that one word fixed in Jack's consciousness and bloomed, obliterating all the noise and joy and surprise of the moment. *Free*. Free to go home. Free to shout out his innocence in the middle of the town green. Free to pick up the yarn of his life and see how it would knit together.

A liberated man, Jack turned around with a grin on his face – and found himself staring at the people of Salem Falls, who now had even more reason to hate him.

Amos Duncan wanted to take the prosecutor apart, piece by piece. 'You said he'd be locked up for years,' the man growled. 'And now I have to see him on the streets of the town where my daughter and I live?'

Matt couldn't possibly feel any worse than Duncan wanted him to feel. Losing cases was always a disappointment . . . losing one that seemed to be open and shut was downright devastating.

'What can I say?' Matt answered humbly. 'Amos, Gillian – I'm so sorry.' He began to gather his notes and papers, stuffing them haphazardly into his briefcase.

'I hope you carry this with you, Houlihan,' Duncan spat. 'I hope you can't sleep at night, knowing he's out there.'

In counterpoint to her blustering father, Gillian's voice was quiet and firm. 'You said it was a sure thing.'

Matt glanced at her. He looked at Amos Duncan, too. Then he thought of McAfee's closing, of the atropine in Gillian's blood sample, of Catherine Marsh testifying that she'd been afraid of her father. 'Nothing's a sure thing,' he muttered, and he walked up the aisle of the courtroom, heading home.

The champagne bottle popped, shooting its cork into the ceiling of Jordan's porch. Foam sprayed and ran down the sides, soaking Selena's toes and the wooden slats beneath her feet. 'To justice!' she cried, pouring some into Dixie cups.

'May she continue to be conveniently blind,' Jordan said, toasting.

Thomas grinned, lifting his own glass. 'And deaf and dumb, when you need it.'

They drank, giddy with the sheer delight of winning. 'I knew I wanted to get back into trying cases again,' Jordan said, and behind his back, Thomas and Selena rolled their eyes. 'Of course, I couldn't have done it without the two of you.'

'If you're feeling so charitable, then you can explain to Chelsea why I'm not a complete jerk.'

'Ah, that's easy,' Selena said. 'Just tell her you take after your mother.'

'Thomas.' Jordan slung his arm around his son's shoulders. 'We'll have her over to dinner, and I'll show her my enchanting side.' He smothered a laugh. 'No pun intended.'

Selena poured herself a second glass of champagne. 'She could bring along something to drink . . . or something to slip into the drink.'

'Very funny,' Thomas muttered.

Jordan, on the other hand, grinned at her. 'Maybe I'll get some atropine myself, stir it into your hot water, and tell you that we tied the knot.'

'Maybe you wouldn't have to drug me for that,' Selena said lightly, but her words fell flat.

There was a thick beat of silence. 'Do you –' Jordan asked, staring hard at her.

Selena's smile started slow, then unrolled like a banner. 'Yeah. I do.'

When they fell onto the porch swing in a tangle of arms and legs and joy, Thomas discreetly slipped into the house. He walked down the hall into his father's bedroom, sat on the bed, and unzipped the linings of each of the two pillows. It took some rummaging, but he managed to find them – the small herbal charms Chelsea had given him weeks before. Red cloth, filled with sweet-smelling flowers and a penny, then tied with blue ribbon in seven knots. 'You can't force someone to love someone else,' Chelsea had warned, when he asked her to make these. 'All a spell can do is open a person's eyes to what's out there.'

Thomas had shrugged. 'I think that's all they need.'

As his father and Selena embraced outside, Thomas slipped the charms back into their pillows. And then, toasting himself, he drank down the rest of his champagne.

Charlie knocked on the door of his daughter's bedroom. 'Hi,' he said, sticking his head in the door. 'Can I come in?'

'Since when do you ask?' Meg shot back. She didn't look at him.

This angry girl, huddled on her bed, looked nothing like the child who'd once followed him around with a tinfoil badge pinned to her dress, so that she could be just like her father. Betrayal sat between them, a monster of enormous proportions. 'I guess you heard that Jack St. Bride got acquitted.'

Meg nodded. 'Gillian's a mess about it.'

The detective sighed. 'Understandable, I guess.' He took a deep breath. 'We can still press charges, if you want.'

His daughter shook her head, her cheeks flaming. 'No,' she murmured.

'Meggie?'

'I knew,' she blurted out. 'I knew that Gillian was doing all this just to hurt Jack. At first I didn't care, because of the things . . . the things I remembered. But now I know they weren't real.' Meg's round, sweet face was turned to his, waiting for him to make it all better, the way he used to do when she'd fallen down and scraped her knee. A Band-Aid, and a kiss. If only that was what it took once they grew up. 'Gilly lied . . . and she told us to lie . . . and we did it, because we were all so afraid of what would happen if we didn't. Maybe we were a little curious, too, to see if we could pull it off.'

'Pull *what* off?'

Meg picked at a cuticle. 'Punishing him. Ruining his life. Making him leave Salem Falls. Gillian just wanted to get him back – not for what he did to her, but for what he *wouldn't* do.'

She had known about Gillian lying? And hadn't told him? 'Why didn't you come to me, Meg?'

'Would you really have listened, Daddy? People hear only what they want to hear.'

He was the last person qualified to lecture his daughter on falsehoods and moral responsibility. Addie Peabody's name flashed through his mind like a stroke of lightning, and he touched his daughter's hand. 'Maybe we'll go talk to someone,' Charlie said. 'Someone who can sort things like this out, who does it for a living.'

'Like a psychiatrist?'

Charlie nodded. 'If you want.'

Meg suddenly seemed very, very young. 'You'd go with me?' she whispered.

Charlie held out his arms, and his daughter crawled right where she belonged. He rubbed her spine, buried his face in her hair. 'Anywhere,' he vowed, 'and back again.'

For a horrible moment, Addie thought she had lost him. She moved through the house, wondering if she'd imagined his acquittal, calling his name and getting no answer.

Finally, she discovered Jack sitting out on Chloe's wooden playset. In her bare feet, she padded out across the lawn to settle on a swing beside him. 'Want a push?' she asked.

Jack smiled softly. 'No thanks. I'll jump when I'm ready.'

He untangled his fist from the chain and laced his fingers with

Addie's. They sat in summertime silence, bordered by the songs of crickets, watching the hot wind jump like a monkey through the fingers of the trees. 'How does it feel?' Addie asked quietly.

Jack brought his fist to his chest. 'Like the whole world has settled right here.'

She smiled. 'That's because you're home.'

'Addie,' he said, 'the thing is, I'm not. I can't stay here.'

'Of course you can.'

'I meant that I can't stay in Salem Falls, Addie. Nobody wants me here.'

'I do,' she said, going very still.

'Yes.' Jack reached for her hand, and kissed it. 'That's why I'm going to leave. God, you saw what happened today, after we left the court- house. The mother who pulled her kid away from me on the street. The guy at the diner who walked out as soon as he saw I was there. I can't live like that . . . and neither can you. How are you going to run a local business when people start ostracizing you, too?'

Maybe it was the heat breaking as the night rolled into Salem Falls, maybe it was the memory of her daughter playing in this very spot, maybe it was just a soul that had suffered too much to give up without a healthy fight – but at that moment, Addie made a decision. She stood, planting her feet on either side of Jack, to keep him where she wanted him. 'I already told you,' Addie said, her eyes blazing, 'you don't get to leave me behind.'

'But Addie, I'm a drifter. You have a place where you belong.'

'Yes. With you.' She kissed him, her faith a brand.

By the time Addie lifted her head, Jack was smiling. 'What diner?' he murmured, and yanked her onto his lap.

'My father can run it. He needs that. And I have . . . oh, about forty-two weeks of vacation time accrued.'

They swung lazily as the sun set, licking a fire up the slate path and charging the stars in the night sky. Jack imagined taking Addie to Greece, to Portugal, to the Loire Valley. He envisioned her by the Trevi Fountain, in the Canadian Rockies, on the top of the Empire State Building. 'We'll visit my mother,' he said, the thought forming in his mind like a crystal. 'I think she'd like to meet you.'

'She lives in New York?'

Jack nodded. It was as good as place as any, he thought, to find a happy ending.

Shortly after midnight, Amos Duncan awakened. He lay in bed, gathering his sixth sense around him like an extra blanket, certain that something wasn't right.

Shrugging into his robe, he padded down the hall to Gillian's bedroom. The door was wide open, the covers on her bed thrown back.

He found her in the kitchen, sitting at the table in the dark. A glass of milk sat in front of her, untouched. Her head rested heavily on the heel of her hand; her eyes were focused on something only she could see.

'Gilly,' he whispered, so he wouldn't startle her.

She came out of her trance, blinking, surprised to find him there. 'Oh,' she said, flustered. 'I was . . . I just couldn't sleep.'

Amos nodded, his hands in the pockets of his robe. 'I know. I understand. But Gillian . . . maybe it's better this way.' She turned her face to his, so like her mother's in this half-light. 'Maybe we should just get on with our lives. Try to put this past us. Make things the way they used to be.'

When Gillian glanced away, Amos touched her jaw. 'You know I'm only looking out for you, Gilly,' he murmured, smiling tenderly. 'Who loves you most?'

'You do,' Gillian whispered.

Amos held out his hand, and she placed hers in it. Then he pulled her into an embrace, an old, old dance. Gillian closed her eyes, years past tears. Her mind was already a million miles away by the time her father's mouth settled over hers, sealing their deal once again.

Salem Falls

JODI PICOULT

A Readers Club Guide

A CONVERSATION WITH JODI PICOULT

Q: What was your initial inspiration for this book? Are you a fan of witch folklore and legend?

A: I wanted to write an update of *The Crucible*, because so many of the themes in Arthur Miller's play are still so timely: the concept of a town excluding someone they don't believe to be fit; the way lies spread so much faster than truth; the very idea that truth is a subjective quantity, at the mercy of many influences. When I was mulling this idea over for a book, I knew I'd have to come up with a modern-day witch hunt – and my thoughts went straight to a rape trial, since that's usually a he-said/she-said scenario, with a jury deciding whose story is more believable. Other than a trip to Salem, Massachusetts, when I was little, I didn't really know very much about witches – historical or modern. After doing a little research, though, I decided that after all those alleged witches had suffered in Salem, they deserved to be the ones pointing the finger this time around – and thus I created my coven of teenage girls.

Q: You seem to be well versed in modern witchcraft and the basic tenets of the religion. Do you have friends who are Wiccan, or was this solely the product of research?

A: Although there is a large population of Wiccans close to where I live, I didn't personally know anyone who followed the religion. So – as I do with all things I don't know but want to write about – I set out to do a little research. I found some Wiccans and interviewed them; I read extensively; I studied Books of Shadows (there was one very funny incident in my son's first-grade class at Halloween, where I brought in a frothing dry-ice punch for a snack and happily volunteered to try my hand at casting a spell . . . but that's a whole different story). I learned that the fastest-growing group of Wiccans are teenagers – if you think about it, it makes sense: many teens are attracted to the religion because they think it's about spells that might net them popularity or love or power (it's not), and as an added boon, being a witch is something to hide from your parents. To this end, I found some Wiccan websites and chat rooms, and posed as a teen interested in Wicca to see what I might be able to learn . . . and in Gillian's case, learn incorrectly. Since the publication of *Salem Falls* in hardcover, I have received fan letters from practicing Wiccans, who praise me for treating their religion sensitively and accurately; and I'm very proud of this endorsement.

Q: You deal with rape very carefully in this novel, and from many different angles. Were there inherent challenges working with this issue, as it is often a touchy subject for readers and writers alike?

A: My biggest fear when I was writing *Salem Falls* was that I would somehow not convey equally the horror of being raped and that of being wrongly accused as a rapist. The last thing I wanted to do was trivialize the trauma of rape by suggesting that the majority of women fabricated their claims; likewise, I didn't want to hold convicted rapists up as role models simply because a very small fraction of them are innocent. To this end, I created the character of Addie to balance the character of Jack – I wanted readers to be invested in both of their stories, and to understand that they were *both* violated by someone of the opposite sex. The truth is, for every Jack St Bride, there is an Amos Duncan; for every Addie Peabody, there is a Gillian. When I wrote about Jack's prior conviction, I wanted readers to understand that rape trials are such a crapshoot that a defense attorney might indeed recommend to his wrongfully accused client that he simply plea-bargain for a misdemeanor rather than risk a felony conviction by a jury. I also wanted to explore the way victims in a rape trial are often victimized even more – which is why thousands of rapes go unreported every year. There is no easy way to talk about rape, because every case is different. But for this very reason, I wanted my novel to address the challenges it poses both legally and emotionally – in the hopes that it would get readers talking.

Q: Was there a particular concept that you wanted readers to come away with after having read this novel?

A: Yes. That a lie can outpace the truth every time, even though the difference between them is paper-thin. And that you never really know anyone as well as you think you do.

Q: The experience of parents – especially mothers – seem to dominate your novels. How has having children strengthened your ability as a writer and your understanding and compassion for the characters in your books?

A: Technically, being a mother has made me more skilled at writing on the fly – that is, being interrupted to be asked a question about a spelling test, or to exult over an art project, or to attend a teacher's conference, and then pick right up where I left off. But most of all, being a mother allows me to be surprised on a daily basis. You'd think that, having spent every single moment of a child's life with him or her, you'd know them inside out. And yet, every day, my kids amaze me or confound me or astound me. The flip side of this is that I have discovered parts of myself that I never knew existed before I had children: patience, ferocity, pride. This theme of constant rediscovery – especially when you naïvely believe you know it all – is something I explore in *Salem Falls*, as well as many of my other books.

Q: In many of your books, love works as a kind of saving grace – sometimes the only one. Do you think love conquers all?

A: Don't laugh, but sometimes when I write about love I think of a flying squirrel. There's got to be a moment when that baby squirrel looks from the end of one branch to the tree six feet away and thinks twice about making a leap. Falling in love is no different; it's the moment that we close our eyes and throw away everything that seems reasonable and hope to God there's someone or something waiting to catch us on the other side. Either we're lucky . . . or we wind up bruised and battered on the ground. Jack and Addie are two characters who have crashed. In *Salem Falls*, the challenge was to create a relationship between people who have lost everything once by getting close to someone. How can you make someone who has been burned stick his hand back in a fire?

I guess I'm an optimist, because I believe that love has the same kind of selective amnesia that childbirth does (you completely forget how much it hurt the last time around until you're in the delivery room again). So to me, it's conceivable that people like Jack and Addie, who have every reason in the world to be hermits, might try for a connection just one more time. If love *doesn't* conquer all, it certainly has the ability to heal us until we are willing to close our eyes and jump once again, for good.

Q: Are any of the characters in your novels autobiographical? Do you base any of them on people that you have personally known, or do you craft them completely from your imagination?

A: I never 'write' people I know into a book, because my characters spring fully formed and to endow them with the personality of someone who already exists would cheat both parties. However, I often give characteristics or features or even dialogue from my friends and family to my fictional characters, when it fits. If you're my friend or kid or husband, anything you say or do is fair game. For example, in *Salem Falls*, Wes tries to seduce Addie – 'How do you like your eggs in the morning?' – and she gives a pretty funny answer: 'Unfertilized.' That nugget came from a Sunday night dinner at our house. We were discussing the world's worst pickup lines, and my friend Aidan offered that one – and well, it just seemed too hilarious not to use in a novel.

Q: Tell us a little bit about your writing process. Do you map out the entire plot before you begin writing, or do things develop as you go along? How do you combat writer's block?

A: I often know what's going to happen in a book before I start it – especially one like *Salem Falls*, where there's a big surprise at the end. I have to leave clues throughout the book so that when you read that last page, you can go back and say to yourself, 'Oh, of COURSE!' However, in the process of writing a book, every single time, I surprise myself in some way. In *Salem Falls*, it was the history between Addie and Charlie – I truly didn't know about that until I began to type their final conversation in the book.

I usually start with a germ of an idea (like rewriting *The*

Crucible). Then I push the envelope, until I feel like I have a story I can work with – and then I figure out how much I don't know. That's the point when I do research, either by meeting with experts and learning first-hand, or reading or combing the Internet. When I feel that I can write my characters with authority, I decide who will narrate the story. And I don't let myself start writing until I have a killer first line.

It usually takes me nine months to write a novel, from start to finish of first draft. Sometimes I spend more time doing research; sometimes I spend more time writing. It depends on the book. However, I work steadily – and I don't believe in writer's block. I spent too many years carving writing time out of my children's nap schedule to believe that one needs to be inspired to get work done. Certainly, there are some days my writing flows better than others, but even if I'm particularly unmotivated, I sit myself down and work . . . because the next day, no matter how bad it is, I'll have something to edit.

READING GROUP GUIDE FOR
SALEM FALLS

1) Throughout the novel, the author uses quotes from Arthur Miller's *The Crucible* and from the story of Jack and Jill. How do these quotes increase your understanding of the story as a whole? In what ways do these seemingly disparate sources work in terms of the subject matter?

2) After pretending to be sick from school, Gillian explains to her friends, 'I am not faking; I'm method-acting.' Method acting is often described as a tool for telling the truth of a character under imaginary circumstances. How might this definition help us better understand Gillian's actions and her motivations in this novel? What is the truth in her life that needs to be shared?

3) The tension between truth and fiction is a major theme here. Similarly, the concept of believing in lies so strongly that they become truth also powers this narrative. To what extent do you think Gillian and the other girls actually believe their own lies? Does this change for any of them by the end?

4) Throughout history, witches have been the victims of persecution. Recently, witchcraft and pagan religions have gotten a lot of attention both in the media and in popular culture. What drives our fascination with witches and witchcraft? Why do you think some people seem to find it so threatening?

5) In the same vein, what is so attractive about witchcraft to the girls of Salem Falls, either in the stereotypical sense or in the realistic sense? Or to any girls, for that matter?

6) Do you know any people who practice Wicca? If so, how authentic is the author's presentation of the religion? To what extent is this book about spirituality/religion, and its abuse?

7) In *Salem Falls*, much is made of the individual characters' point of view. People seem to see what they need to see in order to keep their world in order. In what way are characters in this novel affected, either positively or negatively, by the lenses through which they see the world?

8) What is the significance of Jack's role as a history teacher? How about his vast knowledge of trivia?

9) By the end of the story, the majority of the residents of Salem Falls prove themselves to be rather suspicious, closed-minded people, yet somehow Addie is not this way. This is interesting in light of the personal tragedies she has endured through her life – many of which would make most people distrustful or bitter. What is it about her personality or her experiences that allows her to take Jack in off the street?

10) Delilah tells Jack early in the novel, 'I think that all of us have our ghosts.' Although she may be literally addressing Addie's situation, how does this concept apply to the other characters in *Salem Falls*? Which ones, if any, successfully exorcise their ghosts?

11) Who do you consider to be the strongest character in this story? Discuss the different ways strength manifests itself

in this novel and the various degrees to which the characters maintain their strength – or fail to.

12) How much does setting affect this novel? How similar is the world of *Salem Falls* to the world of *The Crucible* and *The Scarlet Letter*, books from which the author clearly draws?

13) At one point, as he is watching his students walk to the locker room, Jack thinks to himself, 'Beauty is truth, and truth, beauty.' Do you agree with this? What do you think the novel suggests?

14) Do you believe that Jack, in light of all his experiences, should be totally free from blame? Are there instances when his judgment seems to be off, or is he truly the unluckiest man in the world?

15) Jack's mother forgives the prostitute that her late husband was seeing, so much so that she invites her to live with her, yet she immediately turns on her own son when he is accused of rape. How can one account for this shift in her character? Is it a shift? Were you surprised that she did not ask for his side of the story, or do you think there is some sort of solidarity among women that transcends familial ties?

16) Picoult tells the story of Jack's life backward, to the moment of his birth. How do these flashbacks affect the present-day story, and why do you think she chose to do this?

17) Should a verbal accusation of rape be enough to set the judicial wheels turning? Explain, using the examples of both Catherine Marsh and Addie Peabody.

18) Compare the father/daughter relationships of Addie and Roy, Gillian and Amos, Charlie and Meg, Matt Houlihan and Molly, and Catherine and Reverend Marsh. How does the bond formed between parent and child influence each of their actions?

If you enjoyed Salem Falls *read on for the first chapter of Jodi Picoult's most recent novel,* Vanishing Acts, *also available from Hodder . . .*

JODI PICOULT

Vanishing Acts

Prologue

I was six years old the first time I disappeared.

My father was working on a magic act for the annual Christmas show at the senior center, and his assistant, the receptionist who had a real gold tooth and false eyelashes as thick as spiders, got the flu. I was fully prepared to beg my father to be part of the act, but he asked, as if *I* were the one who would be doing *him* a favor.

Like I said, I was six, and I still believed that my father truly could pull coins out of my ear and find a bouquet of flowers in the folds of Mrs. Kleban's chenille housecoat and make Mr. van Looen's false teeth disappear. He did these little tricks all the time for the elderly folks who came to play bingo or do chair aerobics or watch old black-and-white movies with soundtracks that crackled like flame. I knew some parts of the act were fake – his fiddlehead mustache, for example, and the quarter with two heads – but I was one hundred percent sure that his magic wand had the ability to transport me into some limbo zone, until he saw fit to call me back.

On the night of the Christmas show, the residents of three different assisted-living communities in our town braved the cold and the snow to be bused to the senior center. They sat in a semicircle watching my father while I waited backstage. When he announced me – *the Amazing Cordelia!* – I stepped out wearing the sequined leotard I usually kept in my dress-up bin.

I learned a lot that night. For example, that part of being the magician's assistant means coming face-to-face with illusion. That invisibility is really just knotting your body in a certain way and letting the black curtain fall over you. That people don't vanish into thin air; that when you can't find someone, it's because you've been misdirected to look elsewhere.

I

I think it is a matter of love: the more you love a memory, the stronger and stranger it is.

– Vladimir Nabokov

Delia

You can't exist in this world without leaving a piece of yourself behind. There are concrete paths, like credit card receipts and appointment calendars and promises you've made to others. There are microscopic clues, like fingerprints, that stay invisible unless you know how to look for them. But even in the absence of any of this, there's scent. We live in a cloud that moves with us as we check e-mail and jog and carpool. The whole time, we shed skin cells – forty thousand per minute – that rise on currents up our legs and under our chins.

Today, I'm running behind Greta, who picks up the pace just as we hit the twisted growth at the base of the mountain. I'm soaked to the thighs with muck and slush, although it doesn't seem to be bothering my bloodhound any. The awful conditions that make it so hard to navigate are the same conditions that have preserved this trail.

The officer from the Carroll, New Hampshire, Police Department who is supposed to be accompanying me has fallen behind. He takes one look at the terrain Greta is bulldozing and shakes his head. 'Forget it,' he says. 'There's no way a four-year-old would have made it through this mess.'

The truth is, he's probably right. At this time of the afternoon, as the ground cools down under a setting sun, air currents run downslope, which means that although the girl probably walked through flatter area some distance away, Greta is picking up the scent trail where it's drifted. 'Greta disagrees,' I say.

In my line of work, I can't afford not to trust my partner. Fifty percent of a dog's nose is devoted to the sense of smell, compared to only one square inch of mine. So if Greta says that Holly Gardiner wandered out of the playground at Sticks & Stones Day Care and climbed to the top of Mount Deception, I'm going to hike right up there to find her.

Greta yanks on the end of the fifteen-foot leash and hustles at a clip for a few hundred feet. A beautiful bloodhound, she has a black widow's peak, a brown velvet coat, and the gawky body of the girl who watches the dancers from the bleachers. She circles a smooth, bald rock twice; then glances up at me, the folds of her long face deepening. Scent will pool, like the ripples when a stone's thrown into a pond. This is where the child stopped to rest.

'Find her,' I order. Greta casts around to pick up the scent again, and then starts to run. I sprint after the dog, wincing as a branch snaps back against my face and opens a cut over my left eye. We tear through a snarl of vines and burst onto a narrow footpath that opens up into a clearing.

The little girl is sitting on the wet ground, shivering, arms lashed tight over her knees. Just like always, for a moment her face is Sophie's, and I have to keep myself from grabbing her and scaring her half to death. Greta bounds over and jumps up, which is how she knows to identify the person whose scent she took from a fleece hat at the day-care center and followed six miles to this spot.

The girl blinks up at us, slowly pecking her way through a shell of fear. 'I bet you're Holly,' I say, crouching beside her. I shrug off my jacket, ripe with body heat, and settle it over her clothespin shoulders. 'My name is Delia.' I whistle, and the dog comes trotting close. 'This is Greta.'

I slip off the harness she wears while she's working. Greta wags her tail so hard that it makes her body a metronome. As the little girl reaches up to pat the dog, I do a quick visual assessment. 'Are you hurt?'

She shakes her head and glances at the cut over my eye. '*You* are.'

Just then the Carroll police officer bursts into the clearing, panting. 'I'll be damned,' he wheezes. 'You actually found her.'

I always do. But it isn't my track record that keeps me in this business. It's not the adrenaline rush; it's not even the potential happy ending. It's because, when you get down to it, I'm the one who's lost.

I watch the reunion between mother and daughter from a distance – how Holly melts into her mother's arms, how relief binds them like a seam. Even if she'd been a different race or dressed like a gypsy, I would have been able to pick this woman out of a crowd: She is the one who seems unraveled, half of a whole.

I can't imagine anything more terrifying than losing Sophie. When you're pregnant, you can think of nothing but having your own body to yourself again; yet after giving birth you realize that the biggest part of you is now somehow external, subject to all sorts of dangers and disappearance, so you spend the rest of your life trying to figure out how to keep her close enough for comfort. That's the strange thing about being a mother: Until you have a baby, you don't even realize how much you were missing one.

It doesn't matter if the subject Greta and I are searching for is old, young, male, or female – to someone, that missing person is what Sophie is to me.

Part of my tight connection to Sophie, I know, is pure overcompensation. My mother died when I was three. When I was Sophie's age, I'd hear my father say things like 'I lost my wife in a car accident,' and it made no sense to me: If he knew where she was, why didn't he just go find her? It took me a lifetime to realize things don't get lost if they don't have value – you don't miss what you don't care about – but I was too young to have stored up a cache of memories of my mother. For a long time, all I had of her was a smell – a mixture of vanilla and apples could bring her back as if she were standing a foot away – and then this disappeared, too. Not even Greta can find someone without that initial clue.

From where she is sitting beside me, Greta nuzzles my forehead, reminding me that I'm bleeding. I wonder if I'll need stitches, if this will launch my father into another tirade about why I should have become something relatively safer, like a bounty hunter or the leader of a bomb squad.

Someone hands me a gauze pad, which I press against the cut above my eye. When I glance up I see it's Fitz, my best friend, who happens to be a reporter for the paper with the largest circulation in our state. 'What does the other guy look like?' he asks.

'I got attacked by a tree.'

'No kidding? I always heard their bark is worse than their bite.'

Fitzwilliam MacMurray grew up in one of the houses beside mine; Eric Talcott lived in the other. My father used to call us Siamese triplets. I have a long history with both of them that includes drying slugs on the pavement with Morton's salt, dropping water balloons off the elementary school roof, and kidnapping the gym teacher's cat. As kids, we were a triumverate; as adults, we are still remarkably close. In fact, Fitz will be pulling double duty at my wedding – as Eric's best man, and as my man-of-honor.

From this angle, Fitz is enormous. He's six-four, with a shock of red hair that makes him look like he's on fire. 'I need a quote from you,' he says.

I always knew Fitz would wind up writing; although I figured he'd be a poet or a storyteller. He would play with language the way other children played with stones and twigs, building structures for the rest of us to decorate with our imagination. 'Make something up,' I suggest.

He laughs. 'Hey, I work for the *New Hampshire Gazette,* not the *New York Times.*'

'Excuse me . . . ?'

We both turn at the sound of a woman's voice. Holly Gardiner's mother is staring at me, her expression so full of words that, for a moment, she can't choose the right one. 'Thank you,' she says finally. 'Thank you so much.'

'Thank Greta,' I reply. 'She did all the work.'

The woman is on the verge of tears, the weight of the moment falling as heavy and sudden as rain. She grabs my hand and squeezes, a pulse of understanding between mothers, before she heads back to the rescue workers who are taking care of Holly.

There were times I missed my mother desperately while I was growing up – when all the other kids at school had two parents at the Holiday Concert, when I got my period and had to sit down on the lip of the bathtub with my father to read the directions on the Tampax box, when I first kissed Eric and felt like I might burst out of my skin.

Now.

Fitz slings his arm over my shoulders. 'It's not like you missed out,' he says gently. 'Your dad was better than most parents put together.'

'I know,' I reply, but I watch Holly Gardiner and her mother walk all the way back to their car, hand in hand, like two jewels on a delicate strand that might at any moment be broken.

That night Greta and I are the lead story on the evening news. In rural New Hampshire, we don't get broadcasts of gang wars and murders and serial rapists; instead, we get barns that burn down and ribbon-cuttings at local hospitals and local heroes like me.

My father and I stand in the kitchen, getting dinner ready. 'What's wrong with Sophie?' I ask, frowning as I peer into the living room, where she lays puddled on the carpet.

'She's tired,' my father says.

She takes an occasional nap after I pick her up from kindergarten, but today, when I was on a search, my father had to bring her back to the senior center with him until closing time. Still, there's more to it. When I came home, she wasn't at the door waiting to tell me all the important things: who swung the highest at recess, which book Mrs. Easley read to them, whether snack was carrots and cheese cubes for the third day in a row.

'Did you take her temperature?' I ask.

'Is it missing?' He grins at me when I roll my eyes. 'She'll be her old self by dessert,' he predicts. 'Kids bounce back fast.'

At nearly sixty, my father is good-looking – ageless, almost, with his salt-and-pepper hair and runner's build. Although there were any number of women who would have thrown themselves at a man like Andrew Hopkins, he only dated sporadically, and he never remarried. He used to say that life was all about a boy finding the perfect girl; he was lucky enough to have been handed his in a labor and delivery room.

He moves to the stove, adding half-and-half to the crushed tomatoes – a homemade recipe trick one of the seniors taught him that turned out to be surprisingly good, unlike their tips for helping Sophie avoid croup (tie a black cord around her neck) or curing an earache (put olive oil and pepper on a cotton ball and stuff into the ear). 'When's Eric getting here?' he asks. 'I can't keep this cooking much longer.'

He was supposed to arrive a half hour ago, but there's been no phone call to say he's running late, and he isn't answering his cell. I don't know where he is, but there are plenty of places I am imagining him: Murphy's Bar on Main Street, Callahan's on North Park, off the road in a ditch somewhere.

Sophie comes into the kitchen. 'Hey,' I say, my anxiety about Eric disappearing in the wide sunny wake of our daughter. 'Want to help?' I hold up the green beans; she likes the crisp sound they make when they snap.

She shrugs and sits down with her back against the refrigerator.

'How was school today?' I prompt.

Her small face darkens like the thunderstorms we get in July, sudden and fierce before they pass. Then, just as quickly, she looks up at me. 'Jennica has warts,' Sophie announces.

'That's too bad,' I reply, trying to remember which one Jennica is – the classmate with the platinum braids, or the one whose father owns the gourmet coffee shop in town.

'I want warts.'

'No, you don't.' Headlights flash past the window, but don't turn into our driveway. I focus on Sophie, trying to remember if warts are contagious or if that's an old wives' tale.

'But they're green,' Sophie whines. 'And really soft and on the tag it says the name.'

Warts, apparently, is the hot new Beanie Baby. 'Maybe for your birthday.'

'I bet you'll forget *that,* too,' Sophie accuses, and she runs out of the kitchen and upstairs.

All of a sudden I can see the red circle on my calendar – the parent-child tea in her kindergarten class started at one o'clock, when I was halfway up a mountain searching for Holly Gardiner.

When I was a kid and there was a mother-daughter event in my elementary school, I wouldn't tell my father about it. Instead, I'd fake sick, staying home for the day so that I didn't have to watch everyone else's mother come through the door and know that my own was never going to arrive.

I find Sophie lying on her bed. 'Baby,' I say. 'I'm really sorry.'

She looks up at me. 'When you're with *them,*' she asks, a slice through the heart, 'do you ever think about *me?*'

In response I pick her up and settle her on my lap. 'I think about you even when I'm sleeping,' I say.

It is hard to believe now, with this small body dovetailing against mine, but when I found out I was pregnant I considered not keeping the baby. I wasn't married, and Eric was having enough trouble without tossing in any added responsibility. In the end, though, I couldn't go through with it. I wanted to be the kind of mother who couldn't be separated from a child without putting up a fierce fight. I like to believe my own mother had been that way.

Parenting Sophie – with and without Eric, depending on the year – has been much harder than I ever expected. Whatever I do right I chalk up to my father's example. Whatever I do wrong I blame squarely on fate.

The door to the bedroom opens, and Eric walks in. For that

half second, before all the memories crowd in, he takes my breath away. Sophie has my dark hair and freckles, but thankfully, that's about all. She's got Eric's lean build and his high cheekbones, his easy smile and his unsettling eyes – the feverish blue of a glacier. 'Sorry I'm late.' He drops a kiss on the crown of my head and I breathe in, trying to smell the telltale alcohol on his breath. He hoists Sophie into his arms.

I can't make out the sourness of whiskey, or the grainy yeast of beer, but that means nothing. Even in high school, Eric knew a hundred ways to remove the red flags of alcohol consumption. 'Where were you?' I ask.

'Meeting a friend in the Amazon.' He pulls a Beanie Baby frog out of his back pocket.

Sophie squeals and grabs it, hugs Eric so tight I think she might cut off his circulation. 'She double-teamed us,' I say, shaking my head. 'She's a con artist.'

'Just hedging her bets.' He puts Sophie down on the floor, and she immediately runs downstairs to show her grandfather.

I go into his arms, hooking my thumbs into the back pockets of his jeans. Under my ear, his heart keeps time for me. *I'm sorry I doubted you.* 'Do I get a toad, too?' I ask.

'You already had one. You kissed him, and got me instead. Remember?' To illustrate, he trails his lips from the tiny divot at the base of my neck – a sledding scar from when I was two – all the way up to my mouth. I taste coffee and hope and, thank God, nothing else.

We stand in our daughter's room for a few minutes like that, even after the kiss is finished, just leaning against each other in between the quiet places. I have always loved him. Warts and all.

When we were little, Eric and Fitz and I invented a language. I've forgotten most of it, with the exception of a few words: *valyango,* which meant pirate; *palapala,* which meant rain; and *ruskifer,* which had no translation to English but described the dimpled bottom of a woven basket, all the reeds coming together to form one joint spot, and that we sometimes used to explain our friendship. This was back in the days before playtime had all the contractual scheduling of an arranged marriage, and most mornings, one of us would show up at the house of another and we'd swing by to pick up the third.

In the winter, we would build snow forts with complicated burrows and tunnels, complete with three sculpted thrones where we'd sit and suck on icicles until we could no longer feel our fingers and toes. In the spring, we ate sugar-on-snow that Fitz's dad made us when he boiled down his own maple syrup, the three of us dueling with forks to get the sweetest, longest strands. In the fall, we would climb the fence into the back acreage of McNab's Orchards and eat Macouns and Cortlands and Jonathans whose skin was as warm as our own. In the summer, we wrote secret predictions about our futures by the faint light of trapped fireflies, and hid them in the hollow knot of an old maple tree – a time capsule, for when we grew up.

We had our roles: Fitz was the dreamer; I was the practical tactician; Eric was the front man, the one who could charm adults or other kids with equal ease. Eric always knew exactly what to say when you dropped your hot lunch tray by accident and the whole cafeteria was staring at you, or when the teacher called on you and you'd been writing up your Christmas list. Being part of his entourage was like the sun coming through a plate-glass window: golden, something to lift your face toward.

It was when we came home the summer after freshman year in college that things began to change. We were all chafing under our parents' rules and roofs, but Eric rubbed himself raw, lightening up only when we three would go out at night. Eric would always suggest a bar, and he knew the ones that didn't card minors. Afterward, when Fitz was gone, Eric and I would spread an old quilt on the far shore of the town lake and undress each other, swatting away mosquitoes from the pieces of each other we'd laid claim to. But every time I kissed him, there was liquor on his breath, and I've always hated the smell of alcohol. It's a weird quirk, but no stranger than those people who can't stand the scent of gas, I suppose, and have to hold their breath while they fill up their cars. At any rate, I'd kiss Eric and inhale that fermenting, bitter smell and roll away from him. He'd call me a prude, and I started to think maybe I was one – that was easier than admitting what was really driving us apart.

Sometimes we find ourselves walking through our lives blindfolded, and we try to deny that we're the ones who securely tied the knot. It was this way for Fitz and me, the decade after high school. If Eric told us that he had a beer only every now and then, we believed him. If his hands shook when he was sober, we turned away. If I mentioned his drinking, it became my problem, not his. And yet, in spite of all this, I still couldn't end our relationship. All of my memories were laced with him; to extract them would mean losing the flavor of my childhood.

The day I found out I was pregnant, Eric drove his car off the road, through a flimsy guard rail, and into a local farmer's cornfield. When he called to tell me what had happened – blaming it on a woodchuck that ran across the road – I hung up the phone and drove to Fitz's apartment. *I think we have a problem,* I said to him, as if it was the three of us, which, in reality, it was.

Fitz had listened to me speak a truth we'd taken great pains never to utter out loud, plus a newer, magnificent, frightening one. *I can't do this alone,* I told him.

He had looked at my belly, still flat. *You aren't.*

There was no denying Eric's magnetism, but that afternoon I realized that, united, Fitz and I were a force to be reckoned with as well. And when I left his apartment armed with the knowledge of what I was going to have to say to Eric, I remembered what I had written down during that backlit summer when I was trying to guess the rest of my life. I'd been embarrassed setting the words to paper, had folded it three times so Fitz and Eric wouldn't see. Me – a tomboy who spent hours in the company of boys pretending to be a swashbuckling privateer, or an archaeologist searching for relics, a girl who had been the damsel in distress only once, and even then had rescued herself – I had written only a single wild wish. *One day,* I'd written, *I will be a mother.*

As one of Wexton's three attorneys, Eric does real estate transfers and wills and the occasional divorce, but he's done a little trial work, too – representing defendants charged with DUI and petty thefts. He usually wins, which is no surprise to me. After all, more than once I have been a jury of one, and I've always managed to be persuaded.

Case in point: my wedding. I was perfectly happy to sign a marriage certificate at the courthouse. But then Eric suggested that a big party wasn't such a bad idea, and before I knew what had happened, I was buried in a pile of brochures for reception venues, and band tapes, and price lists from florists.

I'm sitting on the living room floor after dinner, swatches of fabric covering my legs like a patchwork quilt. 'Who cares whether the napkins are blue or teal?' I complain. 'Isn't teal really just blue on steroids, anyway?'

I hand him a stack of photo albums; we are supposed to find ten of Eric and ten of me as an introductory montage to the wedding video. He cracks the first one open, and there's a picture of Eric and Fitz and me rolled fat as sausages in our snowsuits, peeking out from the entrance of a homemade igloo. I'm between the two boys; it's like that in most of the photos.

'Look at my hair,' Eric laughs. 'I look like Dorothy Hamill.'

'No, *I* look like Dorothy Hamill. You look like a portobello mushroom.'

In the next two albums I pick up, I am older. There are fewer pictures of us as a trio, and more of Eric and me, with Fitz sprinkled in. Our senior prom picture: Eric and I, and then Fitz in his own snapshot with a girl whose name I can't recall.

One night when we were fifteen we told our parents we were going on a school-sponsored overnight and instead climbed to the top of Dartmouth's Baker Library bell tower to watch a meteor shower. We drank peach schnapps stolen from Eric's parents' liquor cabinet and watched the stars play tag with the moon. Fitz fell asleep holding the bottle and Eric and I waited for the cursive of comets. *Did you see that one?* Eric asked. When I couldn't find the falling star, he took my hand and guided my finger. And then he just kept holding on.

By the time we climbed down at 4:30 A.M., I had had my first kiss, and it wasn't the three of us anymore.

Just then my father comes into the room. 'I'm headed upstairs to watch Leno,' he says. 'Lock up, okay?'

I glance up. 'Where are my baby pictures?'

'In the albums.'

'No . . . these only go back to when I'm four or five.' I sit up. 'It would be nice to have your wedding picture, too, for the video.'

I have the only photo of my mother that is on display in this house. She is on the cusp of smiling, and you cannot look at it without wondering who made her happy just then, and how.

My father looks down at the ground, and shakes his head a little. 'Well, I knew it was going to happen sometime. Come on, then.'

Eric and I follow him to his bedroom and sit down on the double bed, on the side where he doesn't sleep. From the closet, my father takes down a tin with a Pepsi-Cola logo stamped onto the front. He dumps the contents onto the covers between Eric and me – dozens of photographs of my mother, draped in peasant skirts and gauze blouses, her black hair hanging down her back like a river. A wedding portrait: my mother in a belled white dress; my father trussed in his tuxedo, looking like he might bolt at any second. Photos of me, wrapped tight as a croissant, awkwardly balanced in my mother's arms. And one of my mother and father on an ugly green couch with me between them, a bridge made of dimpled flesh, of blended blood.

It is like visiting another planet when you only have one roll of film to record it, like coming to a banquet after a hunger strike – there is so much here that I have to consciously keep myself from racing through, before it all disappears. My face gets hot, as if I've been slapped. 'Why were you *hiding* these?'

He takes one photograph out of my hand and stares at it long enough for me to believe he has completely forgotten that Eric and I are in the room. 'I tried keeping a few of the pictures out,' my father explains, 'but you kept asking when she was coming home. And I'd pass them, and stop, and lose ten minutes or a half hour or a half day. I didn't hide them because I didn't want to look at them, Delia. I hid them because that was *all* I wanted to do.' He puts the wedding picture back in the tin and scatters the rest on top. 'You can have them,' my father tells me. 'You can have them all.'

He leaves us sitting in the near dark in his bedroom. Eric touches the photograph on the top as if it is as delicate as milk-weed. 'That,' he says quietly. 'That's what I want with you.'

It's the ones I don't find that stay with me. The teenage boy who jumped off the Fairlee-Orford train bridge into the Connecticut River one frigid March; the mother from North Conway who vanished with a pot still boiling on the stove and a toddler in the playpen; the baby snatched out of a car in the Strafford post office parking lot while her sitter was inside dropping off a large package. Sometimes they stand behind me while I'm brushing my teeth; sometimes they're the last thing I see before I go to sleep; sometimes, like now, they leave me restless in the middle of the night.

There is a thick fog tonight, but Greta and I have trained enough in this patch of land to know our way by heart. I sit down on a mossy log while Greta sniffs around the periphery. Above me, something dangles from a branch, full and round and yellow.

I am little, and he has just finished planting a lemon tree in our backyard. I am dancing around it. I want to make lemonade, but there isn't any fruit because the tree is just a baby. How long will it take to grow one? *I ask.* A while, *he tells me. I sit myself down in front of it to watch.* I'll wait. *He comes over and takes my hand.* Come on, *grilla, he says.* If we're going to sit here that long, we'd better get something to eat.

There are some dreams that get stuck between your teeth when you sleep, so that when you open your mouth to yawn awake they fly right out of you. But this feels too real. This feels like it has actually happened.

I've lived in New Hampshire my whole life. No citrus tree could bear a climate like ours, where we have not only White Christmases but also White Halloweens. I pull down the yellow ball: a crumbling sphere made of birdseed and suet.

What does *grilla* mean?

I am still thinking about this the next morning after taking Sophie to school, and spend an extra ten minutes walking around, from the painting easel to the blocks to the bubble station, to make up for my shoddy behavior yesterday. I've planned on doing a training run with Greta that morning, but I'm sidetracked by the sight of my father's wallet on the floor of my Expedition. He'd taken it out a few nights ago to fill the tank with gas; the least I can do is swing by the senior center to give it back.

I pull into the parking lot and open the back hatch. 'Stay,' I tell Greta, who whumps her tail twice. She has to share her seat with emergency rescue equipment, a large cooler of water, and several different harnesses and leashes.

Suddenly I feel a prickle on my wrist; something has crawled onto my arm. My heart kicks itself into overdrive and my throat pinches tight, as it always does at the thought of a spider or a tick or any other creepy-crawly thing. I manage to strip away my jacket, sweat cooling on my body as I wonder how close the spider has landed near my boots.

It's a groundless phobia. I have climbed out on mountain ledges in pursuit of missing people; I have faced down criminals with guns; but put me in the room with the tiniest arachnid and I just may pass out.

The whole way into the senior center, I take deep breaths. I find my father standing on the sidelines, watching Yoga Tuesday happen in the function room. 'Hey,' he whispers, so as not to disturb the seniors doing sun salutations. 'What are you doing here?'

I fish his wallet out of my pocket. 'Thought you might be missing this.'

'So that's where it went,' he says. 'There are so many perks to having a daughter who does search and rescue.'

'I found it the old-fashioned way,' I tell him. 'By accident.'

He starts moving down the hall. 'Well, I knew it would turn up eventually,' he says. 'Everything always does. You have time for a cup of coffee?'

'Not really,' I say, but I follow him to the little kitchenette anyway and let him pour me a mug, then trail him into his office. When I was a little girl, he'd bring me here and keep me entertained while he was on the phone by doing sleight-of-hand with binder clips and handkerchiefs. I pick up a paperweight on his desk. It is a rock painted to look like a ladybug, a gift I made for him when I was about Sophie's age. 'You could probably get rid of this, you know.'

'But it's my favorite.' He takes it out of my hand, puts it back in the center of his desk.

'Dad?' I ask. 'Did we ever plant a lemon tree?'

'A *what?*' Before I can repeat my question he squints at me, then frowns and summons me closer. 'Hang on. You've got something sticking out of . . . no, lower . . . let me.' I lean forward, and he cups his hand around the back of my neck. *'The Amazing Cordelia,'* he says, just like when we did our magic act. Then, from behind my ear, he pulls a strand of pearls.

'They were hers,' my father says, and he guides me to the mirror that hangs on the back of his office door. I have a vague recollection of the wedding photo from last night. He fastens the clasp behind me, so that we are both looking in the mirror, seeing someone who isn't there.

* * *

The offices of the *New Hampshire Gazette* are in Manchester, but Fitz does most of his work from the office he's fixed up in the second bedroom of his apartment in Wexton. He lives over a pizza place, and the smell of marinara sauce comes through the forced-hot-air ducts. Greta's toenails click up the linoleum stairs, and she sits down outside his apartment, in front of a life-size cardboard cutout of Chewbacca. Hanging on a hook on the back is his key; I use it to let myself inside.

I navigate through the ocean of clothes he's left discarded on the floor and the stacks of books that seem to reproduce like rabbits. Fitz is sitting in front of his computer. 'Hey,' I say. 'You promised to lay a trail for us.'

The dog bounds into the office and nearly climbs up onto Fitz's lap. He rubs her hard behind the ears, and she snuggles closer to him, knocking several photos off his desk.

I bend down to pick them up. One is of a man with a hole in the middle of his head, in which he has stuck a lit candle. The second picture is of a grinning boy with double pupils dancing in each of his eyes. I hand the snapshots back to Fitz. 'Relatives?'

'The *Gazette*'s paying me to do an article on the Strange But True.' He holds up the picture of the man with the votive in his skull. 'This amazingly resourceful fellow apparently used to give tours around town at night. And I got to read a whole 1911 medical treatise from a doctor who had an eleven-year-old patient with a molar growing out of the bottom of his foot.'

'Oh, come on,' I say. 'Everyone's got something that's strange about them. Like the way Eric can fold his tongue into a clover, and that disgusting thing you do with your eyes.'

'You mean this?' he says, but I turn away before I have to watch. 'Or how you go ballistic if there's a spider web within a mile of you?'

I turn to him, thinking. 'Have I always been afraid of spiders?'

'For as long as I've known you,' Fitz says. 'Maybe you were Miss Muffet in a former life.'

'What if I were?' I say.

'I was *kidding*, Dee. Just because someone's got a fear of heights doesn't mean she died in a fall a hundred years ago.'

Before I know it, I am telling Fitz about the lemon tree. I explain how it felt as if the heat was laying a crown on my head, how the tree had been planted in soil as red as blood. How I could read the letters *ABC* on the bottoms of my shoes.

Fitz listens carefully, his arms folded across his chest, with the same studious consideration he exhibited when I was ten and confessed that I'd seen the ghost of an Indian sitting cross-legged at the foot of my bed. 'Well,' he says finally. 'It's not like you said you were wearing a hoop skirt, or shooting a musket. Maybe you're just remembering something from *this* life, something you've forgotten. There's all kind of research out there on recovered memory. I can do a little digging for you and see what I come up with.'

'I thought recovered memories were traumatic. What's traumatic about citrus fruit?'

'Lachanophobia,' he says. 'That's the fear of vegetables. It stands to reason that there's one for the rest of the food pyramid, too.'

'How much did your parents shell out for that Ivy League education?'

Fitz grins, reaching for Greta's leash. 'All right, where do you want me to lay your trail?'

He knows the routine. He will take off his sweatshirt and leave it at the bottom of the stairs, so that Greta has a scent article. Then he'll strike off for three miles or five or ten, winding through streets and back roads and woods. I'll give him a fifteen-minute head start, and then Greta and I will get to work. 'You pick,' I reply, confident that wherever he goes, we will find him.

Once, when Greta and I were searching for a runaway, we found his corpse instead. A dead body stops smelling like a live one immediately, and as we got closer, Greta knew something wasn't right. The boy was hanging from the limb of a massive oak. I dropped to my knees, unable to breathe, wondering how much earlier I might have had to arrive to make a difference. I was so shaken that it took me a while to notice Greta's reaction: She turned in a circle, whining; then lay down with her paws over her nose. It was the first time she'd discovered something she really didn't want to find, and she didn't know what to do once she'd found it.

Fitz leads us on a circuitous trail, from the pizza place through the heart of Wexton's Main Street, behind the gas station, across a narrow stream, and down a steep incline to the edge of a natural water slide. By the time we reach him, we've walked six miles, and I'm soaked up to the knees. Greta finds him crouching behind a copse of trees whose damp leaves glitter like coins. He grabs the stuffed moose Greta likes to play catch with – a reward for making her find – and throws it for her to retrieve. 'Who's smart?' he croons. 'Who's a smart girl?'

I drive him back home, and then head to Sophie's school to pick her up. While I wait for the dismissal bell to ring, I take off the strand of pearls. There are fifty-two beads, one for each of the years my mother would have been on earth if she were still alive. I start to feed them through my fingers like the hem of a rosary, starting with prayers – that Eric and I will be happy, that Sophie will grow up safe, that Fitz will find someone to spend his life with, that my father will stay healthy. When I run out, I begin to attach memories instead, one for each pearl. There is that day she brought me to the petting zoo, a recollection I've built entirely around the photo in the album I saw several nights ago. The faintest picture of her dancing barefoot in the kitchen. The feel of her hands on my scalp as she massaged in baby shampoo.

There's a flash, too, of her crying on a bed.

I don't want that to be the last thing I see, so I rearrange the memories as if they are a deck of cards, and leave off with her dancing. I imagine each memory as the grain of sand that the pearl grew around: a hard, protective shell to keep it from drifting away.

* * *

It is Sophie who decides to teach the dog how to play board games. She's found reruns of *Mr. Ed* on television, and thinks Greta is smarter than any horse. To my surprise, though, Greta takes to the challenge. When we're playing and it's Sophie's turn, the bloodhound steps on the domed plastic of the Trouble game to jiggle the dice.

I laugh out loud, amazed. 'Dad,' I yell upstairs, where my father is folding the wash. 'Come see this.'

The telephone rings and the answering machine picks up, filling the room with Fitz's voice. 'Hey, Delia, are you there? I have to talk to you.'

I jump up and reach for the phone, but Sophie gets there more quickly and punches the disconnect button. 'You *promised,*' she says, but already her attention has moved past me to something over my shoulder.

I follow her gaze toward the red and blue lights outside. Three police cars have cordoned off the driveway; two officers are heading for the front door. Several neighbors stand on their porches, watching.

Everything inside me goes to stone. If I open that door I will hear something that I am not willing to hear – that Eric has been arrested for drunk driving, that he's been in an accident. Or something worse.

When the doorbell rings, I sit very still with my arms crossed over my chest. I do this to keep from flying apart. The bell rings again, and I hear Sophie turning the knob. 'Is your mom home, honey?' one of the policemen asks.

The officer is someone I've worked with; Greta and I helped him find a robbery suspect who ran from the scene of a crime. 'Delia,' he greets.

My voice is as hollow as the belly of a cave. 'Rob. Did something happen?'

He hesitates. 'Actually, we need to see your dad.'

Immediately, relief swims through me. If they want my father, this isn't about Eric. 'I'll get him,' I offer, but when I turn around he's already standing there.

He is holding a pair of my socks, which he folds over very neatly and hands to me. 'Gentlemen,' he says. 'What can I do for you?'

'Andrew Hopkins?' the second officer says. 'We have a warrant for your arrest as a fugitive from justice, in conjunction with the kidnapping of Bethany Matthews.'

Rob has his handcuffs out. 'You have the wrong person,' I say, incredulous. 'My father didn't kidnap anyone.'

'You have the right to remain silent,' Rob recites. 'Anything you say can and will be used against you in a court of law. You have the right to speak to an attorney, and to have an attorney present during any questioning—'

'Call Eric,' my father says. 'He'll know what to do.'

The policemen begin to push him through the doorway. I have a hundred questions: *Why are you doing this to him? How could you be so mistaken?* But the one that comes out, even as my throat is closing tight as a sealed drum, surprises me. 'Who is Bethany Matthews?'

My father does not take his gaze off me. 'You were,' he says.

Once you've read one, you'll want to read them all . . .

Plain Truth

£6.99 Paperback
OUT NOW

My Sister's Keeper

£6.99 Paperback
OUT NOW

Vanishing Acts

£12.99 Hardback
OUT NOW

The Pact

£6.99 Paperback
OUT NOW

Perfect Match

£12.99 Hardback
Publishing September 2005

Keeping Faith

£12.99 Hardback
Publishing January 2006

Tenth Circle

£12.99 Hardback
Publishing April 2006

JODI PICOULT

PLAIN TRUTH

‘A suspenseful, richly layered drama, Picoult’s novel never loses its grip’ *People*

A shocking murder shatters the picturesque calm of Pennsylvania’s Amish country – and tests the heart and soul of the lawyer who steps in to defend the young woman at the centre of the storm . . .

The discovery of a dead infant in an Amish barn shakes Lancaster County to its core. But the police investigation leads to a more shocking disclosure: circumstantial evidence suggests that eighteen-year-old Katie Fisher, an unmarried Amish woman believed to be the newborn’s mother, took the child’s life. When Ellie Hathaway, a disillusioned big-city attorney, comes to Paradise, Pennsylvania, to defend Katie, two cultures collide – and, for the first time in her high-profile career, Ellie faces a system of justice very different from her own. Delving deep inside the world of those who live ‘plain’, Ellie must find a way to reach Katie on her terms. And as she unravels a tangled murder case, Ellie also looks deep within – to confront her own fears and desires when a man from her past comes back into her life.

Moving seamlessly from psychological drama to courtroom suspense, *Plain Truth* is a fascinating portrait of Amish life – and a moving exploration of the bonds of love, friendship, and the heart’s most complex choices.

HODDER

JODI PICOULT

MY SISTER'S KEEPER

'This astounding novel is beautifully and thoughtfully written, and focuses on difficult moral choices' *Good Housekeeping*

'In my first memory, I am three years old, and I am trying to kill my sister. Sometimes, the recollection is so clear I can remember the itch of the pillowcase under my hand, the sharp point of her nose pressing into my palm . . .'

Anna is not sick, but she might as well be. By age thirteen, she has undergone countless surgeries, transfusions, and injections to help her sister, Kate, fight leukaemia. Anna was born for this purpose, her parents tell her, which is why they love her even more.

But now she can't help but wonder what her life would be like it if weren't tied to her sister's . . . and so she makes a decision that for most would be too difficult to bear, and sues her parents for the rights to her own body.

'This beautifully crafted novel will grab readers with its stunning topic' *People*

HODDER

JODI PICOULT

KEEPING FAITH

Somewhere between belief and doubt lies faith.

For the second time, Mariah White catches her husband with another woman, and Faith, their seven-year-old daughter, witnesses every painful minute. In the aftermath of a sudden divorce, Mariah struggles with depression and Faith begins to confide in an imaginary friend.

At first, Mariah dismisses these exchanges as a child's imagination. But when Faith starts reciting passages from the Bible, develops stigmata, and begins to perform miraculous healings, Mariah wonders if her daughter might indeed be seeing God. As word spreads and controversy heightens, Mariah and Faith are besieged by believers and disbelievers alike, caught in a media circus that threatens what little stability they have left.

Is Faith a prophet or a troubled little girl? Is Mariah a good mother facing an impossible crisis – or a charlatan using her daughter to reclaim the attention her husband withheld?

'Addictively readable, raising valid questions about religion without getting maudlin. For a novel, that in itself is a miracle'
Entertainment Weekly

HODDER

JODI PICOULT

THE PACT

'Engrossing . . . Picoult has a remarkable ability to make us share her characters' feelings of confusion and horror . . . *The Pact* is compelling reading' *People*

The Hartes and the Golds have lived next door to each other for eighteen years. They have shared everything from family picnics to chicken pox – so it's no surprise that in high school Chris and Emily's friendship blossoms into something more.

When the midnight calls come in from the hospital, no one is prepared: Emily is dead at seventeen from a gunshot wound to the head, inflicted by Chris as part of an apparent suicide pact. He tells police the next bullet was meant for himself. A local detective has her doubts. And the Hartes and Golds must face every parent's worst nightmare and question: do we ever really know our children at all?

'The novelist displays an almost uncanny ability to enter the skins of her troubled young protagonists' *New York Times*

HODDER

JODI PICOULT

PERFECT MATCH

What happens when you do all the right things for all the wrong reasons? As an assistant district attorney, Nina Frost prosecutes the sort of crimes that tear families apart.

But when Nina and her husband discover that their five-year-old son Nathaniel has been sexually abused, it is her own family that is devastated. The world Nina inhabits now seems different from the one she lived in yesterday; the lines between family and professional life are erased; and answers to questions she thought she knew are no longer easy to find.

Overcome by anger and desperate for vengeance, Nina ignites a battle that may cause her to lose the very thing she's fighting for.

'Picoult's novel . . . reminds us how easy it is to jump to conclusions and to do all the wrong things for all the right reasons' *Glamour*

HODDER